ASHES IN VENICE

A Vengeance Thriller

GOJAN NIKOLICH

Black Rose Writing | Texas

ISBN: 978-1-68433-891-7
PUBLISHED BY BLACK ROSE WRITING
www.blackrosewriting.com

Printed in the United States of America
Suggested Retail Price (SRP) $20.95

Ashes in Venice is printed in Calluna

*As a planet-friendly publisher, Black Rose Writing does its best to eliminate unnecessary waste to reduce paper usage and energy costs, while never compromising the reading experience. As a result, the final word count vs. page count may not meet common expectations.

PRAISE FOR

ASHES IN VENICE

A Vengeance Thriller

For Srećko and Erika

ASHES IN VENICE

A Vengeance Thriller

"When you're crazy, every dream comes true."
—*Detective Sergeant Frank Savic*

"And the smoke of their torment will rise for ever and ever.
There will be no rest day or night for those
who worship the beast and its image,
or for anyone who receives the mark of its name."
—*Revelation 14:9-11*

– 1 –

Shirtless in the heat at night, Jasper Colt peeled his naked back from the filthy vinyl chair next to the open window. He had watched and waited for hours, though he had all the time in the world. The ticking clock, the rising and setting of suns, meant nothing to him. Time does not fly. Time only dies.

He opened the refrigerator in the kitchenette at the Starbright Motor Lodge and breathed the icy air as if standing before a door on a winter night. He took his beer and drank and studied the lump of something furred and rotting on a wire shelf crowded with nameless leftovers. The sharp reek filled the room. How these people lived, he thought. How these people lived.

He sat and checked his wristwatch and continued reading his book: a story of witches in stone castles and cold blowy nights on a dark and rocky Scottish seashore with its mad and murderous king plotting a foul and delicious revenge.

"Nobody writes like that, anymore," he said softly, surprised at how muted his voice sounded in the small hot room with the bathroom sink dripping behind him in the dark.

Footsteps shuffled down the hallway where a man and woman continued to scream at each other. *These people, how they live.*

Just suppose, Colt thought as he looked up from the book: what if Shakespeare had a cousin, a crazy cousin named Fritz, and this misfit Fritz lived a parallel and equally ripe and genius life, yet would remain unrecognized while his famous and immortal kin would be remembered forever. How unfair would that be? And what if he — Jasper Colt, literary sleuth, uncovered this injustice, finally bringing forth the story of a playwright whose lost works were as worthy as those of cousin Billy.

He smiled, the argument in the hallway growing more violent, so he laughed loudly and said: "That would be something."

Colt continued his reverie. It was something to take his mind off the other things.

He'd laughed so loudly that he worried if the unpleasant ape at the front desk, the motel manager who he had despised immediately, would hear him. Because of the way they look and sound — their eyes, their smell, sometimes people tell you who they really are. This was one of Colt's skills: deciphering people, noticing the smallest details. How they paced their words and held their arms, how they scratched the side of their face or ran one hand through their hair. That little vein pulsing on someone's throat. A nervous tic here and there. Each movement revealed a riddle that told a tale.

He took a pull on the beer as he stepped to the window and studied the street. Through palm branches that rattled dryly outside, the downtown casino buildings glowed in the distance beneath a starless sky. A block away, piles of trash and twisted blankets, tarps and small tents were arranged in a row against a chain-link fence where hunched shapes sat homeless in the glow of a tiny camp stove.

Colt watched a Las Vegas police patrol car drive by as expected, red tail lights brightening as it slowed and turned toward the district substation, where he knew they were changing the evening patrol shift.

A city bus passed, leaving behind a cloud of diesel stink that pierced the after-smell of tangled bougainvillea that grew outside the open motel window, beneath which sat the noisy air conditioner that Colt had unplugged.

In the empty street a cat yowled and a dog bark answered it, and from a room down the hall a woman began to bawl loudly, her cries followed by a sharp slap and then silence.

He could not let go of the thought of this newly contrived novelty of Shakespeare's second cousin, Fritz. How painful it would be to suffer such obscurity.

Colt was in the cheapest motel in the cheapest part of town. The blinking sign outside was broken. There was a shuttered laundromat next door, a cement box with barred windows and a door covered with plywood, where broken conduit and bent rebar poked from slabs of torn concrete. And from a patch of heaving asphalt a shrub had somehow sprouted against impossible odds, green with new life beneath the blue glow of the sputtering neon sign.

Colt returned to his book. And then the man he had been waiting for finally emerged from the building across the street, a wrecked and nameless warehouse, and he fumbled in his pocket for his keys as he walked to a parked car.

Colt set aside the book and opened his physician's bag. He withdrew a zippered leather surgical kit. He took out the serrated Adson forceps and the Iris scissors and lay those on the kitchen counter top. He took the 18-gauge needles and loaded the two syringes that lay on the disposable fenestrated drape and he walked calmly outside. He would not need the drape but it was a habit to put it aside and Jasper Colt was a man comforted by his orderly habits.

The man was bare-chested beneath greasy denim coveralls. He carried a coffee cup that he put on top of the car as he struggled with the lock. He shouted a garbled profanity when Colt came without a sound and easily pulled him down. The cup fell and bounced into the street and the man hardly felt the stab of the needle in his shoulder, where the numbers Colt knew were tattooed inside the snarling mouth of a brightly colored dog.

The man was bald with a fuzzy scalp that spread like a cap to the tops of each ear. But there was enough long wispy blond hair on the back of his head and Colt grasped it, slamming the man face-down on the street. He flicked away the spent syringe and watched it skitter against the curb.

Colt pressed his palm down against the man's face. He spoke in the reassuring way you might use to comfort a disruptive child, and he said sweetly:

"Now hush."

There was an angry burst of cursing and scrabbling feet as the man struggled but Colt bounced his knee sharply against the man's back.

"Hush, I said."

The man smelled of cigarettes and whiskey and a sour, crotchy sweat odor lifted from the dirty coveralls.

Colt wrapped the noosed wire around his throat.

The man choked and tried to speak. "If you want money. I got some money."

He brought his hand toward his back pocket and Colt easily peeled it away as he tugged on the wire noose.

"Try that again and your head comes off, so work with me."

The man gasped, his fingers trembling as he tried to reach for the wire at his throat.

"There's money in my wallet."

Colt yanked him by the hair and told him to stand.

Inside the motel room, he took something shiny from the black bag and pointed with it at the sofa. He pulled on a pair of surgical nitrile gloves.

"Sit."

And the man sat, his eyes darting toward where another row of instruments lay neatly spaced apart on the small coffee table: cardio clamps, tissue forceps, the hemo grips and chest spreaders arranged like tools for some strange and implausible home repair project.

Colt touched the scalpel blade to the man's cheek as if marking it for future exploration.

"My wallet," the man said in a raspy voice. "Just take it. Go on."

"You must have wax in your ears. You're not listening."

Colt twisted the blade tip. He gave the wire a tug.

He poked the bleeding ear with a gloved finger, inquisitively, as if he was giving an anatomy lesson. "Now...there's the triangular fossa, and there's the anti helix."

Colt pressed his finger deep into the ear. "Most of the blood is actually right...there, but I didn't want to get too messy. Even in this shit bucket, I don't want to make a mess."

Colt smiled and brought his arm to the side in a grand operatic gesture, as if inviting someone for a quick tour of the miserable motel room.

"Go ahead, please," Colt said as he quickly tightened a plastic cable tie around the man's crossed wrists. "Nobody here cares if you scream."

They got so snotted up, these people. Always drooling and spitting, which was why he wore the gloves and took off his shirt whenever possible. There was too much body fluid in this business. Farts and grunts and sudden squirts and all sorts of mysterious exhalations, and this asshole was performing as expected.

4

He nicked the man's scalp with the blade and watched the bead of dark blood race down along his cheek. Somewhere deep behind the frontal cortex of his brain lay a small chunk of shapeless gray jelly as big as a thumb, where Colt knew the man was experiencing a confusing mix of uncontrollable fear and anger.

It was adrenaline time.

"You can't spell, did you know that? Your fourth grade teacher would be so proud, you stupid shit." Colt said. He pointed to one of the many tattoos on the man's arm.

Colt looked at his wristwatch; six minutes since the first injection.

The man rolled clumsily from the sofa and made a goat sound and tried to crawl away, his shoes shaving tufts from the dirty shag rug. Colt, holding the wire taught, stepped on the man's head.

The man tried again to reach for his pocket. "There's money in my wallet. For godfuckingsake, take it."

"Look," Colt said. "You wet yourself."

He jerked the wire. There came a soft, popping sound and the blood leaked freely, soaking the man's coveralls and dribbling down his arm to where the tattoo of a naked woman riding a motorcycle proclaimed, *Keep Smilleing.*

Colt held up the photograph.

"Are you paying attention, or should we clean that ear again? Please don't shit in your pants. Sweet almighty Jesus, you people always manage to take a dump at the worst possible moment."

He held up the gleaming scalpel to the light and the man opened his eyes wide and stared as Colt drew a circle in the air with the blade.

"Don't speak, just look carefully at what I'm showing you in this photograph," Colt said. "I once removed a man's lips because he wouldn't shut up. He kept talking nonsense and not listening to me. We're getting very close to that situation here. Do you understand? One simple circular incision, and there goes the old levator labii. You could be lipless. On top of everything else that's about to happen, do you want that?"

Colt studied the ceiling and shook loose the wire coil like he was paying out a fishing line.

He lifted the man and pushed him against the wall. He picked him up from behind with one arm so he would stand on the sofa and tossed the loose length of wire up to the hooks he had already screwed into the ceiling.

The man tried to turn his head for a look. "Shit."

"Wonderful word, *shit*," Colt said. "There's jack shit, and oh shit and bullshit. Did you recognize the person in the picture, shithead?"

A nod.

"No shit, Sherlock," Colt said, and he took the scalpel and cut both coverall straps and watched the trouser legs fall and slide to the man's ankles. His polka dot boxer shorts were soaking wet.

"Did you know that Shakespeare never once used the word shit in any of his plays? He wrote hundreds of colorful insults without requiring that word."

Something creamy and pink flowed from the man's nose as he gulped and tried to catch his breath. His tongue poked from between his teeth. He tried to twist his hands around and reach for the wire, but when he raised his arm the noose only tightened. Spit came to his lip corners and the man opened his mouth to scream but nothing came out except that bleating goat sound, the blood from the wire now showing where a tiny, delicate necklace hung from the man's neck.

Colt briefly lost his temper. He'd told himself he would not, but he did.

"You useless sonofabitch," he growled and tore away the little necklace and put it in his pocket. "How can you wear such a thing?"

Colt took a deep breath and studied the man's feet and glanced at the row of instruments on the table.

"A timeless and wonderful word, shit," he said. "You can simultaneously shoot the shit and lift a shitload of something while precisely describing it as a piece of shit. Such a magical language we have, don't you agree?"

Colt pinched the man's arm, the wiggling gesture almost playful. As if he were getting ready to tickle someone.

"You couldn't feel that, could you? In a short time you'll be much more relaxed. I've heard it described as feeling like that pleasant instant before sleep comes, a brief sensation of falling. However, when the pain returns I want it to come suddenly and without a chance of you fainting. But I must warn you. You have never experienced such blinding and unrelenting pain in your entire life. Never."

6

Colt again held up the photograph from the office of the Clark County coroner. The man began to cry.

"You're sentimental? What a sweetheart. I'll tell the mother...that you wept, that you showed some measure of humanity," Colt said.

Gasping, the man stared at Colt. "You're fucking crazy."

"Am I?" Colt said. "You know, the words we say carry weight. We're accountable for our words, almost as much as we must answer for what we do."

He strapped the rope beneath the man's arms and looped the knotted end over the ceiling hooks and tightened everything up until the man was standing balanced on the balls of his feet. Colt stepped away.

"I don't want you hanging yourself by accident, but if you try to scream too loud that wire will only get tighter, but not enough for you to choke. It will only hurt. I'd like you to enjoy the show for as long as possible, but it will be your choice."

Colt glanced at his instruments and checked the time.

"Speaking of entertainment, did you know Tolstoy thought Shakespeare was a trivial hack? I disagree, of course. He only wrote about kings and queens as if they were ordinary people. There's nothing so enjoyable as an ordinary person being allowed to sit in judgment of the gods."

The man wheezed and managed to speak: "What are you talking about? What's going on? This is crazy."

The portable oscillating surgical bone saw lay on the sofa and Colt stepped over and disconnected it from where it had been charging, the short-circuited wall socket cover now dark with soot. He held the tool in front of the man's face and pressed the power button.

"This won't hurt a bit..."

When he was finished, Colt turned on the bathroom light. He rinsed his arms, dried off with a towel and cleaned himself with an alcohol wipe. He stoppered the sink and plugged the overflow drain with the towel and twisted open both faucets. He took another swig of the beer before stepping back and wetting the tip of the bottle with the man's saliva. He placed the open bottle in the refrigerator. He stood and allowed the deliciously cold air to wash across his heavily muscled arms and bare chest.

Outside, newspapers somersaulted down the empty street. The palm trees rustled and night insects sawed from within the flowering bush that somehow managed to cling to life outside the motel window.

Colt whistled softly and walked to where he had tossed the spent syringe. He kicked it through the curbside sewer grate. He didn't want someone innocent to get hurt. He stepped to the parked car and with a tweezer removed the toothpick he had already jammed into the door lock, replacing it with another he'd carried from the motel.

The police car, as expected, cruised slowly past the motel on its way to the station as Colt stepped into the shadows of the dark alley, peeling off his surgical gloves as he walked and tossing them into a trash dumpster, the black leather bag swinging from his hand as if he were some frontier physician heading to his next house call.

He walked slowly, in no hurry, without fear in this dangerous neighborhood and again looked at his wristwatch. He was pleased with how quickly he had worked.

Time does not fly, he thought. Time only dies.

– 2 –

Detective Sergeant Frank Savic grew up in a happy household that said the word *shit* in three languages.

He knew his shit in all of its colorful etymological diversity. Had he ever dropped the f-bomb in front of his Italian mother she would have quickly broken his jaw. Saying shit, however, was as harmless as uttering the word crap or shucks or gee whiz, as long as the neighbors didn't hear you. It was only a word.

As a verb, from his mother: "Go cut the grass again. It looks shitty."

And a noun, from his Serbian father: "She's right. It's bullshit. Do it again."

When his father took him to the Saturday night fights at Chicago's old Marigold Arena, a place where such language was set free and traveled at will, he always thought the names the wrestlers had were the ones they were born with: Dick the Bruiser, Big Moose Cholek, Gorgeous George, Killer Kowalski, Pepper Gomez, Yukon Eric, Seaman Art Thomas, El Califa, Bobo Brazil and Gorilla Monsoon.

Birth announcement: "Mr. and Mrs. Monsoon wish to announce the birth of their adorable baby boy...*Gorilla.*"

He was 10 years old and his favorite wrestler was Edouard Carpentier, a Canadian fighter born in France with the Polish name of Édouard Ignacz Weiczorkiewicz who had shapeless cauliflower ears that looked like smashed wax.

The Marigold, a former 1920s cabaret that once hosted a burlesque troupe of dancing girls called the "Myriad of Mythical Maids," was a gloomy dark cavern with a cement floor that smelled like beer and sweat and cigar smoke. The metal folding chairs were sticky. Savic could see why his mother didn't want him going there. It was absolutely enchanting, a place where his father cursed twice as much and more creatively than he did at home, allowing little Frankie Savic to expand his own growing vocabulary even more.

The 1,800-seat arena with its swinging ceiling saucer lights, a few blocks from Wrigley Field, where if the walls could truly speak they would be censored and washed with soap, closed in 1964 and was replaced by a church.

His mother was certain that watching these wrestlers would forever corrupt his heart and soul and turn him, like Al Capone and Frank Nitty, into a street gangster bound for Cook County Jail. But Frank saw only nuanced poetry and graceful ballet when 265 lb. Bruno Sammartino did a flying leg scissors around the giant neck of the 600 lb. Haystacks Calhoun.

Enhanced by the noise and the drinking and the shouted palette of colorful oaths that filled the dark and stinking arena, he floated like stardust.

Like the unencumbered swearing that went on among his immigrant neighbors at The Marigold, his parents would gather all three household tongues into a single United Nations of Profanity, inventing new international word combinations that would make a linguist dizzy. Growing up, Savic assumed everybody spoke this infinitely flexible Balkanized paisano English.

Approaching Ellis Island in 1951 aboard a cargo ship packed with other refugees who were fleeing the pulverized cities of WWII Europe, it was told that his father gazed up in astonishment at the looming Manhattan skyline and told his wife, "Shit, will you look at that!" His mother had told him how those thousands of New York lights reaching into the sky made it seem as if the entire city was on fire, and she was afraid to board the government ferry that would take them ashore.

"I was scared as shit," she said.

His maternal grandmother, then in her 80s, turned to Savic one day while standing in the kitchen of her tiny apartment near the Chicago Stockyards and pointed at a cake that had failed to properly rise in the oven. Lifting her hands, her arms wobbling, she said in her musical Lombardy dialect: "Oh, my...now doesn't that look like shit."

Used as a vague noun, as an exclamation of surprise or something that denotes trouble or displeasure, "shit" had always been for Frank Savic the vulgar Olympic gymnastic star of language elasticity.

You can foretell the future by declaring that shit is about to hit the fan. What fan? And where was the first fan at which some unknown, cussing person hurled said shit? It was a mystery that likely had its roots in proto-indo-European speech before it was used by preliterate Germanic tribes when they cursed the invading Romans. From there it migrated to old English and was transmuted as splendid verbal goulash directly into the welcoming mouth of Frank Savic. What a timeless and wonderful word.

Savic was daydreaming about all of this -- the long and proud heritage of shit, the stale sweat and beer smell of gladiators drawing blood at a long-gone wrestling arena -- just as Captain Paul Monaghan informed him that he had said the word shit 17 times during that morning's staff meeting in a stuffy, over-chilled office at the south substation of the Las Vegas Metropolitan Police Department.

Savic hated meetings. He hated taking notes and he hated to pretend that he was paying attention.

"Did you really have to talk like that when my boss was here?" Monaghan said.

"I didn't notice," Savic said. "I mean I didn't notice I said it that many times. It just comes out, you know."

"Well, the chief noticed and he mentioned it to me and now I have to worry about that on top of everything else around here. Really, Frank? You said shit every time you opened your mouth during a fifteen-minute meeting. How's that possible? I mean, seventeen times? Sometimes it's like you got that disease..."

"Tourette's? You think I have Tourette's. That's a weird thing to say, Paul. You counted?"

"No...he counted. The Commissioner counted. He made little check marks on his legal pad. I watched him do it. I thought he was doodling, just like you like to doodle at these things. But he was making marks right there next to your name. Jesus, Frank, he wrote your name in giant letters with a Sharpie. You were a English major in college. Can't you find another word to use?"

"Are they going to fire me? Are they going to fire you?"

"No," Monaghan said. "You said you were retiring next month, remember?"

"Okay, good," Savic said. "Then I don't give a shit."

– 3 –

During an important trial, the judge often asked the janitor Paul Bartoni to clean the linoleum hallway in the old courthouse like it was a hospital instead of just another busted government building on the bad side of town. Judge Carpenter was a sonofabitch that way, but he was also fair and polite, so Bartoni guessed that's the way it had to be if you spent all day dealing with the scumbags who paraded through this place every day.

The judge called him *boss* like that was his nickname, which it wasn't, but Bartoni figured it was only a friendly ataboy for him being the courthouse maintenance supervisor all these years. Bartoni and three other janitors on the crew kept the place ship-shape without complaint or any surprises, which was the way the judge liked things.

It had been that way between the two of them for the past twenty-five years: same cranky sourpuss judge, the same ancient courthouse, and all three now only a few weeks shy of retirement, whether they liked it or not. Maybe Bartoni would buy the judge a bottle; a thank you for being such a decent fart all these years, though he didn't know if the old man really drank. It would be an awful waste of a good bottle if he didn't.

Today the courthouse was buttoned up tight, and the place was humming. Like in something was about to happen humming. The delivery bay doors were locked, and the judge told Bartoni he should latch the basement windows so those crazy newspaper monkeys and TV people wouldn't try to sneak in to get their pictures.

This was the day they were sentencing the guy who'd killed all those people, mostly young folks they said, and since the courthouse didn't have a secure sallyport for delivering prisoners, they'd be bringing the killer directly from the alley through the employee cafeteria door. The media with their cameras and the gawkers were already bunched up outside the main courthouse entrance, where newsroom satellite trucks lined the street, but old judge Carpenter had fooled all of them.

After the hallway floor got mopped, dried and shined up so you could eat off of it, the judge came out from his chambers dressed in his black robe and inspected things and gave Bartoni a somber nod. He told one of the Sheriff's deputies to see if the clerk and bailiff were ready to open the big oak double doors that lead into the main courtroom.

"And make sure they put four deputies on that man," the judge said. "I don't want anybody acting stupid like last time, understand? And full restraints, too."

Bartoni watched the two unmarked county jail transport vans park by the small loading ramp next to the cafeteria door. He'd witnessed a lot of famous cases at the courthouse, but Bartoni knew that today was the end of the judge's very last trial and maybe he was just being sentimental and wanted everything perfect. Bartoni was happy because it was probably the final time he'd be mopping that long damn hallway.

Sergeant Frank Savic, the detective from North Metro, stood outside on the sidewalk and watched while the prisoner stepped from one of the vans. Bartoni unlocked the cafeteria door and watched Savic push aside his jacket and rest one hand on his pistol holster when they quickly brought the prisoner inside. He was a very big man, the killer. The longer you looked at him, the bigger and uglier he got. You couldn't take your eyes off of him.

Bartoni nodded at Savic, who he'd heard was also retiring soon from the police department. It seemed everything and everybody, the courthouse included, was being put out to pasture.

There was an audible hum of muffled voices, a rising murmur like when a good hitter steps up to home plate at a ballpark, when the sheriff's deputies finally led the killer into the courtroom, his shackled feet and hands rattling as he shuffled across the wooden floor and squeezed his enormous bulk behind a table stacked with paper folders and binders. He could barely fit his legs under the table. His attorneys looked up from their computer screens as their client crossed his cuffed arms across his broad lap and leaned back leisurely, like he had all the time in the world, the blue tattooed tail of a serpent appearing briefly from behind the collar of his orange prison jumpsuit.

He had long, pubic chin whiskers on a fleshy scrotum face and with his large and feminine pale blue eyes he squinted out across the courtroom and smiled as if pleased with the crowd's reaction. Those eyes were what got you, Bartoni thought. They were too big and pretty for that catastrophe of a face with the big, blinking camel eyelashes that made it look like he was wearing makeup.

Bartoni watched all this from the hallway door where he stood leaning on his mop as four deputies positioned themselves like sentinels in front of the judge's high bench.

The killer grinned and shrugged when judge Carpenter squinted sternly over his reading glasses, told the prisoner to stand up straight, and began to explain that day's legal proceedings, which included a statement by the mother of one of the killer's many victims.

Bartoni now watched a woman walk slowly to the front of the courtroom.

Felicia Mendez gripped the wooden podium with both hands and looked up at the judge, who now tapped something into his computer while the killer made a noisy show of getting to his feet. Someone sneezed and a door creaked open and closed softly, the shuffling of shoes and whispers as a late-comer entered the courtroom. A phone rang in someone's pocket; a familiar child's lullaby, the tune so heartbreaking and ironically cruel at this moment that Felicia briefly felt that she could not breath.

She had decided not to look directly at the killer while she spoke and the judge had allowed her to turn the speaker's podium so it would face away from the public defender's table. It would be too much to look at the monster. She already felt like throwing up.

Felicia was striking, a petite and delicate beauty with flowing dark hair that today was gathered sensibly into a low, braided bun from which she nervously brushed away a loose curl with her hand. She smiled politely toward Judge Carpenter and with both hands reached down and smoothed her skirt, suddenly fearing that what she had worn on this day might not be appropriate for such a terrible and somber occasion. She became conscious of her long, brightly painted fingernails and wondered if she might have also worn too much makeup.

She touched the pendant at her neck, squeezed it briefly and slid her purse onto the podium compartment shelf. The hand bag matched her black shoes; shiny faux French-heeled pumps, the kind you find in a shopping mall bargain store next to the aisle selling $19.99 wrist watches. It was Felicia's best pair.

She pulled a tissue from the box they'd placed for her on the podium and smoothed it flat. She excused herself and blew her nose and kept her eyes closed. She took another deep breath.

Felicia worried again that the skirt might be too short and that her brightly colored fingernails would invite attention. Nobody had given her advice about what to wear. She felt uncomfortable and exposed, a sense of vulnerable nakedness welling up inside as she realized that every eye in the crowded room was now staring at her. Pitying her.

And him. He would be looking, too. With those awful and frightening eyes.

But Felicia Mendez knew she had only one job today and she was determined to do it well.

She allowed herself to glance quickly toward where the killer stood, his undefined and fleeting peripheral shape so large and exaggerated that it seemed to dominate everything, the two attorneys at his side diminished and small, like cartoon elves sitting next to a giant. Behind him in the packed courtroom sat the policeman, Savic, who had arrested the killer of her thirteen-year-old son. The detective smiled and nodded his encouragement, as if he had been waiting for her to turn around. This made her feel better. This made her feel like she was not alone.

Felicia forced herself to look directly at the killer. Now he was smiling at her, rubbing together his meaty hands, lifting one arm to scratch his shaved head. Look at the monster, she thought. How his legs can't fit under the table.

During the trial she had sat in the public gallery, close enough to study the pleated folds of fat on the back of his head. She remembered the massive shoulders and the way he would reach and massage those oddly misshapen ears. He was always scratching, grinding his hips impatiently against the chair like he had somewhere to go. As if the trial might be interrupting his busy schedule.

During the trial she had looked at that hangy thing on his ear. A small round hangy thing like a pea inside a fleshy pod, a deformity that caught her eye immediately and so she kept studying it whenever he reached and scratched his ear. Scratched that strange hangy thing on his ear that was bluish, like the blue and white skin of a fish; like there was no blood there, and so it must have been itchy all the time. When he swallowed it would move up and down, the hangy guppy-shaped thing, and the turning of his head would be enough to make it swing. That hangy pea pod oblong thing, swinging back and forth. Pale blue and fishy white. Of all the things in the courtroom during the painful hours of the long trial, she only remembered looking at that hangy thing.

It seemed crazy at the time, wondering if her boy might have seen it, too. It would be just like him. He always noticed details; such a smart and lovely child. Too sensitive and tender for this harsh world. Her baby. It was sad, that he might have noticed the hangy pea pod thing just before he was killed. Somehow, she felt closer to her baby boy knowing that maybe he had seen the hangy thing, too. She and her son had been alike in that way, aware of the smallest detail that wasn't really worth noticing. Of course her beautiful boy must have seen the hangy thing.

But today she could not see it from where she stood waiting to say whatever she wanted to the man who had murdered her son.

Felicia caught a movement from the corner of her eye; the glassy snow globe lens of a ceiling camera turning and scanning the room. She heard the judge's voice explaining to those in the courtroom about certain legal technicalities and the importance of the statement Felicia would be allowed to make that day. No outbursts in the courtroom, he warned. She could say whatever she wanted.

The small district court chamber was paneled with polished blond wood suited for a mid-century family rec room. Fake cathedral windows showed empty white sky and distant desert mountains that made Felicia feel numb and insignificant, swallowed by the world.

She turned and looked at Savic again. The policeman nodded. He was the only person she was happy to see.

He was wearing the brown suit today. She liked the brown, unfashionable suit. You look good in brown, she thought. You got a haircut. For me, you got a haircut. I bet your wife never noticed.

That morning she had been careful to wear the good blue skirt and the new light gray blouse with the linen jacket, the pumps...and the pendant her son Jimmy had given her on his last Christmas on earth.

Felicia felt weightless, as if she could at any moment blow away. Look strong, she thought. You have a lifetime in which to cry.

The killer, William Parker Jardine, smirked and whispered to his attorney, his thick freckled neck confined tightly inside the jumpsuit collar. As if anxious for the proceedings to begin, he leaned and drummed the table impatiently with his fingers and then stopped and frowned with mock surprise when the judge once again glared at him.

Tattooed in blue ink on top of that right hand, and also on his arm, were the numbers: 14-9-11.

Felicia remembered the evidence photos shown by the prosecuting district attorney during the trial, enlarged to poster-size and mounted on easels for everyone to see. In them Jardine stood naked, his back turned to the camera, his posed torso a canvas of writhing snakes, crossed black swords centered above his buttocks. Grotesque cartoon hands cupped a woman's ridiculously large water balloon breasts. A dagger floating above a lightning bolt on his right shoulder, all of it suspended within a crimson border surrounding the initials WPJ. Flames licked up the back of his hairy arms.

In another photo Jardine stood proudly facing the camera, his crotch cupped in one hand with improbable modesty, more flames tattooed across his chest. That was the first time she had noticed those unusually large, feminine eyes on that leering, piggish face.

The medical examiner's report, read aloud during the trial in a slow, droning monotone voice by the prosecutor, said that Jimmy's back had been crushed in two places; the fifth and seventh vertebrae. She'd begged Savic to let her see each of the forensic charts and Coroner's photos; the bolt cutters that Jardine had used on her boy; the poster sized pictures of the blood-spattered walls of the room where her son had died. She needed to see and carefully study everything, as if ignoring such disgusting images would be an insult to Jimmy's memory.

Jardine had also made a video, played for the court on a large TV screen, in which her son turned screaming at the camera as if rescue might possibly lie behind the lens. In the soundless and blurred clip the child cried for his mother, mouthing *mommy-mommy* in a pitifully mute scream until the recording briefly showed Jardine's smile before it dissolved into a burst of flashing light.

His silent screams haunted her: *Mommy, mommy.*

The courtroom walls were wrapped in a faded mural that showed frontier pioneers marching behind their wagons. Girls in bonnets, smiling boys in floppy hats and suspenders romped alongside. The painted mountains were snowcapped and Felicia wished she was there now in the cold, instead of in this hot and airless room where the ceiling camera now pointed at her.

Jardine stifled a yawn. He groaned and lifted one leg and stretched it beneath the table as he forced a loud cough, an explosive phlegmy cackle that again annoyed Judge Carpenter, who glared at the killer's public defenders as he shook his wrists from his black robe and motioned for Felicia to begin speaking.

Here it was, she thought. Stay strong for Jimmy.

"Mrs. Mendez?"

One of the public defenders whispered into Jardine's ear.

The judge said again: "Please, Mrs. Mendez?"

Mommy, mommy.

Felicia nervously began to read from a sheet of paper that had been folded and unfolded many times. Her rehearsed speech. She dabbed one eye, smudging her makeup.

She leaned across the podium and adjusted the microphone stem as she turned toward the killer.

"You," she said, hesitating. "You took my little boy. You..."

Her voice, inexplicably stronger, belonged to someone else as she screamed at the killer.

"You...dirty...fuck! You dirty filthy monster fuck!"

Jardine, though his attorneys looked concerned, seemed amused at this, smiling with heartless mockery at Felicia as if he had just been praised for some great and noble deed. He turned and looked around the courtroom.

"Face this way, Mr. Jardine," the judge said. "Don't make me tell you again."

Felicia tried to swallow but her throat was dry, so terribly dry that she thought her tongue might stick to her teeth.

"I think every day how my Jimmy suffered because of you...."

The snowy mural mountains on the wall looked inviting and cool. She knew they were not real. Today nothing was real.

"This is bullshit," she finally said in a deeper voice that seemed surprisingly calm and self-assured. "So bullshitty and stupid."

She crumpled up the sheet of paper and tossed it to the floor. She slid her hand into the purse hidden out of sight in the little podium cubby, glancing briefly up at the judge before stepping back as if she had decided to return to her seat. Instead, Felicia Mendez slowly reached down and carefully removed her shoes.

At first William Parker Jardine dodged away from the knife almost playfully, stumbling on his shackles and bumping into his attorney, who reached up and tried to stop the sudden momentum of his client's heavy bulk. A Sheriff's deputy leaped forward and tried to grab Felicia's arm. Now shoeless, she easily squirmed away and lurched deftly again toward the killer, dodging another pair of reaching hands. The razor sharp bamboo kitchen paring knife half hidden in her palm was very tiny and when Felicia raised her arm, nearly everyone in the courtroom assumed the grieving mother was merely pointing an accusing finger at the killer. The alarmed judge stood and pounded his desk and called for order. Out in the hallway, Paul Bartoni the janitor hopped aside as more deputies rushed past him into the courtroom.

Felicia swung her arm in a wide and aimless arc, catching Jardine squarely in the center of one cheek. He seemed genuinely surprised and touched the bleeding wound and looked down at his hand. The blade had opened a deep, squirting cut that raced across the killer's face like a crooked smile. Felicia raked her arm sideways once more and felt the knife scrape against his teeth, Jardine's severed lip spurting blood that splattered onto Felicia's new blouse with such force that the spray lifted in a mist onto the lens of the camera that was filming everything.

A gob of shapeless spit burst from Jardine's mouth, sailing across the room and landing with an audible splat on the prosecutor's desk, from which the lawyer recoiled and sidestepped like he was avoiding a flying mortar. The District Attorney shouted "Jesus shit!" and fell sideways into an assistant, who then stumbled forward across the two-wheeled cart stacked with William Parker Jardine's case files.

Jardine tipped back his head and roared. He raised his chained hands to his bleeding mouth. Two more deputies tried to hold him, but the killer easily dragged both men across the courtroom until another officer rushed up from behind with a flying tackle that sent the whole bunch to the floor. They finally pulled Jardine away, a broken chair leg tangled in his shackles, the floor smeared with blood.

Felicia Mendez calmly dropped the little knife that she'd easily hidden at the bottom of her purse in a makeup pouch they'd failed to inspect at the courthouse entrance, her bowed arm slowly lifting high in the air as if she'd just phrased a graceful ballet pirouette. As if she'd completed a successful dance in a drama that had been rehearsed many times. Such a delicate gesture, so beautiful.

She looked out across the room with its tipped tables and scattered papers and glanced up and smiled at the bloodied lens of the ceiling camera. She brushed aside her undone hair and calmly wiped away her smudged makeup with a fingertip. The long strawberry trail of blood on the floor led to the open hallway door from which came more loud shouting as they continued to wrestle with a very angry William Parker Jardine, who was screaming with a peculiar lisp about the little bitch who had sneaked a candy ass knife through the goddamn courthouse metal detector.

And then Detective Sergeant Frank Savic came and covered Felicia's torn and bloody blouse with his brown jacket and wrapped his arms around her. He smelled like aftershave.

She heard her little boy's voice crying, *mommy, mommy...*

Paul Bartoni started walking back toward the janitorial closet, figuring he'd need his wheeled mop bucket again so he could clean the hallway. He was sure Judge Carpenter would want the hallway clean.

– 4 –

Oren Carver took another sniff, but this did not smell like ink. He had an important big job in blue ink running that morning, but this wasn't it.

Reflex Blue right out of the can has a certain odor. Offset printing spot colors were manufactured these days with a vegetable base and you can tell when somebody is mixing up a batch when a big press has been running hot and fast for a long time.

Whatever this was, it was not ink.

He walked to the back of the shop and checked the lunchroom where the staff of Four Palms Printing and Graphics, Inc. sometimes forgot to put their food back into the refrigerator, but everything looked clean and tidy. The floor was swept, the microwave wiped off and the fridge was cleaned and closed according to the instructions that were pinned to the wall next to the employee time clock.

Carver poured himself the first cup of coffee of the day and walked to the office and turned on his computer. He checked both restrooms to see if something was plugged up, then headed to the bindery, where print jobs were sorted, folded, cut and boxed before being shipped or delivered to customers. The smell got stronger.

He called out for his pressman, Carlo Cavilleri, who had been scheduled to begin his shift at 5 a.m. so he could finish a rush job for one of Four Palms' largest customers. Carver now heard the high-pitched beeping sound of an equipment malfunction alarm — the familiar warning signal that indicated a jam on the shop's brand new Ammendingen Turbomatic paper cutter.

"What the hell!" Carver shouted when he saw Carlo laying on his back across the wide steel cutter table with his arms stretched out like he was making a snow angel. At first, it seemed as if the pressman was trying to adjust something beneath the cutter's long guillotine blade, but Carver quickly realized that Carlo's head was actually clamped beneath the 36-inch-long knife. His reaching arms were flung backwards, his shoulder twisted to one side like he had tried to squirm out of the way of the plunging blade.

The machine's red warning light continued to blink frantically as Carver stepped away and covered his mouth with one hand.

He squatted on the cement floor, where Carlo's severed head now stared back at him from where it had rolled beneath a table stacked with that month's Town of Four Palms Crier community newsletter. The waxy goblin face lay cheek-down in a pool of blood.

Carver stood and banged his head against the edge of the cutting machine as he stumbled backwards into another pool of gummy blood. He ran to his office, where he fumbled with the phone before he could finally dial 911.

When he arrived at the shop nearly ten minutes later, Four Palms Police Chief Harry Nesmith took out his giant, foot-long combination tactical flashlight and stun gun and aimed it beneath the cutter table. The light beam, designed to temporarily blind someone within a range of two meters, illuminated the details in a harsh and surgically bright light: tufts of hair, the splashed blood everywhere, some of it covering a smoking electrical coil beneath the machine, and tiny pieces of bone stuck to a rubber table caster.

"The hell?" Nesmith said. "We got us a first class mess here."

Oren told Nesmith he'd seen enough and would rather not get closer.

"That's the way I found him. I didn't touch a thing," he said. "I just turned off the buzzer and went back and called. I think I'm getting sick."

"You just get a grip, Oren," Nesmith said. "Let me try to sort things out. You didn't do anything wrong. Go someplace and sit."

The police chief squatted and looked up at where Carlo's bent legs hung from the edge of the cutter table.

"What buzzer?" Nesmith said.

"It's when the machine jams. I figured something was wrong when I came in and heard the buzzer. Carlo likes to load too much paper and if you do that, the thing goes off."

"Never seen a rig like this before," Nesmith said. "That's some blade."

"Yes, sir," Oren said. "I came in and there he was. Just like you see him. I didn't touch a thing, no sir. Just hit the button for the buzzer."

"So you said."

Nesmith took his phone and snapped a few pictures. He paced back and forth in front of the machine, studying it. He shined the flashlight on Carlo's legs.

"Look, he pooped," Carver said, pointing to where a perfectly round turd was starting to emerge from the cuff of Carlo's pants. Like it was peeking out, trying to sneak away.

Nesmith took a small notebook from his shirt pocket and started writing. "You suppose he just slipped and fell? Maybe leaned too far and fell, something like that?"

Oren spoke through the paper towel he was holding over his mouth. He walked across the room and started cranking open a long row of shop windows.

"Fell backwards like that? No way," Oren said. "The operator has to push both of those red buttons under the table at once or it won't work," he said. "No way you can fall like that by accident. You'd have to jump up on the table, spin around and just about squeeze yourself under the blade and then reach over with both hands. You'd have to have monkey arms. Carlo wasn't that tall. You can see he's just a little guy. No way he fell."

"Was," Nesmith said.

"Yeah. Was."

Nesmith nodded. "Like you'd fire one of those ballistic missiles? Use the two buttons, like in the movies. So nobody could make a mistake and, you know, start a war with Russia?"

"Right. You hit both buttons with two hands at the exact —and I mean at the exact same time, and that's the only way the blade can fall. No other way to do it. No sir."

"How much does a rig like that cost?" Nesmith said.

"Twenty-two."

"Hundred?"

"Thousand," Oren said.

Nesmith whistled and squinted at the ceiling. He stooped under the table again, searching with the fancy flashlight.

"Wonder where his hands went?"

"I didn't notice that," Carver said.

"Well, I don't see them," Nesmith said, writing in his notebook. "I see his head down there. No hands, though."

Carver pushed away a few tables and stools and boxes of paper stock. He crouched down and watched Nesmith use the flashlight again.

"You're right," Carver said. "I don't see no hands at all."

With the bright flashlight beam the police chief followed the path of two long pneumatic rubber hoses that snaked along the floor beneath the cutter toward a vacuum pump and the tightened vertical chain gear that drove the heavy blade. He squeezed forward and duck-walked and looked at the nests of paper dust that hung in clumps beneath the steel table. He saw more crusty blood spray covering the clamped cutter blade that was now jammed in the down position.

Both men inspected the cement floor like they were searching for misplaced car keys.

"Suicide?" Nesmith said.

"Wouldn't do it this way, would you?"

"I suppose," Nesmith said. "How much paper can that thing cut?"

"A thousand sheets of twenty-pound bond. Goes through it like butter. You're looking at a full ton of downward pressure."

Nesmith whistled again. "Twenty-two thousand bucks, you say?"

"I got a ten year loan," Oren said. "Not sure how this gets covered under the warranty."

After a few phone calls by Nesmith, during which he seemed to be having trouble getting somebody to respond to an actual homicide over at the county building twenty-five miles away, investigators from the coroner's office finally arrived. They processed the crime scene and put Carlo's head in a Styrofoam ice cooler. Nesmith helped lift the body off the cutter table, and when they were about to put the corpse into a zippered rubber bag the shy turd clinging to Carlo's pants came loose, fell to the floor and rolled away with supernatural speed that made both Oren and Nesmith look at each other in wonder, as if that morning's spookiness had somehow just risen to a higher level.

One of the investigators dropped the turd into a labeled plastic baggie and put that inside the cooler next to Carlo's head.

"I wouldn't touch anything, Oren," Nesmith said.

"The mayor wants those newsletters," Carver said as he watched them wheel the body away. "How am I supposed to cut them?"

"Nobody reads it," Nesmith said. "I'm happy you have the town's business, Oren…but nobody reads that thing. The Mayor's wife, she writes it and she can't write worth a damn."

The police chief squatted and looked under another table stacked with a notepad job waiting to be cut. Something shiny was down there. He picked up the broken gold necklace and held it up toward the fluorescent ceiling light.

"I don't remember him ever wearing that," Oren said. "I don't let my people wear jewelry back here. Too dangerous with this machinery. I don't even like them wearing long sleeve shirts. It's too easy to get caught in a press roller. My worker comp insurance rates are already sky high."

Oren walked to the cutter and looked closely at where the machine's beveled eight-inch-wide blade had been nicked.

Nesmith examined the necklace."You ever allow children back here?"

Carver shook his head. "Absolutely not."

Nesmith walked over to a wall dispenser and pulled out a paper towel and wrapped it around the necklace.

"Strange, he'd be wearing something like this," he said and held up the wrapped chain. "It's a kid's necklace, something cheap you'd buy in one of those dollar stores. There's a little angel on the chain."

Nesmith leaned up against the paper cutter, took off his cap and wiped his forehead with his sleeve. He put the flashlight back in its leather belt pouch and sighed deeply.

" Woke up this morning and thought it was just another day at the office. Did my drive around town, dropped some legal notices off at the newspaper. I was thinking about lunch, maybe heading to that new barbecue place out on the highway, when you called me. Never figured I'd be looking at some headless son of a bitch and trying to figure out who stole his hands."

Nesmith pointed at the cutter. "Twenty-two grand, you say?"

– 5 –

Detective Sergeant Frank Savic's Harley-Davidson backfired just short of the Moapa exit, so he reached past his knee and twisted a troublesome chrome valve until the stalling engine gave a throaty belch and finally settled down.

Painted against the cloudless sky were the desert mountains, a faint red smudge on the horizon that he'd been thinking about all week. No special reason; he'd never seen much of what lay north of the city, but some random travel show on TV convinced him that he needed to go there to clear his head. He had not had a day off since the Jardine trial began. An aimless ride on his motorcycle was just what he needed to freshen up his cluttered head.

He liked the desert, even when he glimpsed a piece of it through the office window at the North Metro Substation. The lack of green comforted him, as if trees and grass would cheapen the scenery. The desert, dead and waterless, made him feel at once out of place and at ease. Today was not a good day to see people. He had a lot of problems to think about.

Savic goosed the temperamental bike into the next truck stop, a cement and neon oasis with two convenience stores, a 10-bay washing complex, a laundry and shower facility plus a dental and chiropractor's office, outdoor movie theater and a workout room from which a lady trucker in yoga pants now emerged carrying her gym bag.

He parked outside the store, where he purchased cheese nachos with jalapeños on a paper plate and a wrinkled bratwurst that had likely been broiling on metal rollers since Christmas. He took his meal outside to the curb, where he sat in the shade next to the parked Harley and watched a forty-foot motorhome attempt to negotiate a turn around one of sixteen diesel pump islands.

The RV, decorated with a decal wrap of a blowing American flag, was hauling a pair of matching scooters on a trailer. When the driver clipped a trash can while attempting to maneuver around the fuel island, he tried to back up and nearly rammed a parked two-seat BMW with Arizona plates, from which a lovely woman emerged and waved her arms at the enormous rig like she was hazing a herd of cows.

Savic stopped chewing. She wore a tight, sleeveless tee shirt that came straight from a spray paint can. No bra. Delicate white sandals on long, tanned legs. She was gliding, not walking, displaying an ignorance of gravity in the way a trotting colt is unaware of its own effortless gait and beauty. She moved with the bouncy stride of a runway model, tossing back her hair as she glanced with disinterest at Savic, who sat holding his nacho, a middle-aged oaf ogling the wonders of the female form that now stood before him like a vision.

He did a quick calculation: she was only 40 percent dressed, maybe 38.7, tops. Most everyone on a beach is 12.6 percent dressed. A praying nun comes in at about 92.4.

I'm invisible, he thought. Transparent. A dork of indeterminate age and physical condition, dropped from the sky like a paper scrap, not worth anyone's attention. He smiled and nodded and immediately knew it was the wrong thing to do.

As if she'd noticed a movement from a great distance away, Miss Young & Achingly Lovely answered Savic's nod with a vacant stare. Her blond hair lifted in the hot breeze. She glanced at her phone and with her other hand touched the back of her slender neck and this lifted her clingy shirt to reveal a bellybutton ring that shined in the sun. Savic smelled her flowery perfume as she strolled past. With brief interest, she studied the parked motorcycle. Savic, who wore a red polka dot bandanna to cover his half-bald head, smiled through his cheddar cheese teeth, but the girl only sneered and lowered her gaze as if harboring some private joke before she hopped the curb and disappeared into the truck stop store. Everything on her had bounced when she hopped the curb, and that was what left Savic entranced long after she went into the store. He stared at the spot where she had walked.

Another motorcycle rolled up and parked alongside Savic's Harley. The man dismounted, took off his helmet and pointed with his chin.

"Hey, fat boy," he said.

Savic chewed and chased his mouthful with a gulp of coffee. He looked over his shoulder, hoping the comment had been meant for someone else.

"Your bike," the man said, pointing. "Spankin' new Fat Boy Softail. Very nice. Love the side pocket saddlebags. About five hundreds bucks more than I'd want to spend."

Savic crushed the empty nacho plate, tossed it underhand into a trash basket and picked his tooth with one pinky. He turned and squinted at the visitor, hardly in the mood for a conversation, his thoughts still lingering on the girl. His long-gone vigor, his aching back, the annoyingly tight fit of his leather vest on a gut that refused to stop growing; he ruminated on these sad topics in three quick seconds.

Yes, he thought. She was dressed at 38.7 percent, tops.

The stranger, a near-geezer dressed in ill-fitted leathers, had a white pony tail. He was skinny, with one of those horizontal guts that jutted out from his assless torso like he'd swallowed a watermelon. He wore heavily-buckled post apocalyptic riding boots and he shook one leg as he dismounted and leaned the bike onto its old fashion kick stand. He motioned at it proudly.

"Old flathead," he said. "Nineteen-sixty-four. Put it together from parts myself. Except for the Sportster front end, she's pretty much pure."

Savic admired the machine. Maybe he could just grumble a polite comment and be done with it. Instead, he said: "Old school twin pistons. Nice."

The heavily chromed motorcycle had worn saddlebags with vintage stitching. The brass seat brads spelled out somebody's initials. Braided leather streamers hung from modest, standard ape bars with one of the mounted controls fastened with black electrical tape.

"Never been good with engines myself," Savic said. "Bleeding brakes is about my limit. I'm impressed with your machine. I just got my bike a few months ago. Had an old banged up Norton before that, so I'm no expert, believe me. Still getting used to this beast."

"This rascal drove me crazy for two years," the ponytailed man said, jerking his chin at his own bike. "She's an evil ball buster, that's for sure.

Kick start ignition. A heat shield that boils your nuts off in summer. It's strictly a highway bike. Your baby, now that's got to be rubber mounted, am I right?"

"I've never been one for a lot of fanny time," Savic said and nodded. "I'm strictly a Sunday rider. Just something that lets me relax."

"Put in three hundred miles today myself," the man said and slapped the side of his shin as he loosened one of his Mad Max boot buckles. "I need to wake up this damn leg."

"That seat can't be comfy," Savic said.

The man winked and now massaged his leg slowly with both hands. "Brother, we don't ride for the comfort do we?"

He wore a tasseled leather vest with an Indian thunderbird stitched across the back. Bad boy cycle club patches that were probably fake ran across both front pockets. If they were larger and more prominent, Savic knew, the owner of that jacket might get into deep shit if he walked into the wrong biker bar at the wrong time, where certain logo fonts and designs were deemed proprietary art in some gang circles. Gangs in these parts, Savic knew from experience, took their graphic arts very seriously.

The man stretched his leg again and tapped his boot heel against the asphalt as if it might somehow repair his knee problem. The top of his left boot toe had a deep shifter crease. He pulled off fingerless road gloves and slapped them on the candy-red fuel tank and opened and closed his hands like he was shaking out the cold.

"Old bitch looks sexy, but she vibrates something awful," he said, which Savic thought would make a dandy movie trailer tagline for a biker porn film.

An older couple in matching white shorts stepped from the huge motorhome that had finally negotiated the fuel pump. A varnished wooden plaque above the RV's door said: "The Nelsons. Home is Where We Park It." The two seniors, their flip-flopped feet striding in tandem, walked hand-in-hand toward the convenience store. They embraced and nuzzled on the sidewalk like teenagers, the man opening the door, his hand lingering on his wife's hip.

Savic thought about the plans he and Maria once had. They'd chosen their own rig, big enough for the two of them, but that cross-country travel fantasy was put on hold when she got sick. They'd talked about spending a month in Italy, where her people were from, where they had met while he was stationed at Aviano air base; maybe rent a B&B outside Verona, close to the train station so they could make day trips into the Veneto. Now she required notes taped to the wall to identify the furniture in her room at the nursing home. Window. Door. Light switch. Bathroom.

The truck stop goddess with the belly ring and impossibly long legs that seemed to tread on air, emerged from the store. Both men stopped talking and regarded her studiously, as if examining some rarity of nature they would never witness again. As if watching the arrival of a generational comet or solar eclipse. Something that should be observed with protective eyeglasses.

She was carrying an enormous cup of coffee—some iced, sugar-free, vanilla latte with soy milk, and texting furiously on her phone with her other hand, smiling at the screen, those perfect teeth incandescent against her face. She carried a magazine tucked under her arm and leaned slowly into the BMW's passenger door and tossed it onto the back seat.

Savic thought: the way that flimsy shirt was hiked up across her tummy, she was now 32.3 percent dressed, if not less.

"My goodness," ponytail man said and took a deep breath like he'd just witnessed the best sunset of his life.

"Go on, tell me there is no God."

"We're pitiful," Savic said.

"Yes, sir. Damn straight, we are."

They watched her drive away and kept looking in that direction long after the car turned onto the interstate frontage road and headed south toward the city.

The two men looked down at their feet and observed a moment of silence.

Savic had been wondering that week how much the new Harley would fetch. The house, nearly paid off, might net him a couple hundred thousand in the bloated Las Vegas market, enough to cover four years of Maria's care. He already owed the nursing home most of his yearly salary, and he was months behind on the payments. The thought of Maria being kicked out of the home because he didn't have enough money sickened him. The way it worked, their common net worth would have to dwindle to near zero before the government would pick up the tab. Even then, she'd have to move into some crackerjack place on the other side of town.

Then there was the load he'd pissed away at the Venetian Hotel casino in a desperate stab at catching up on his Blackjack debt. The gambling disaster haunted him and it didn't take much to be reminded of the outrageous number blinking inside his head like a neon theater marquee: $18,000 and change, all of it on credit cards that had since been canceled.

Savic's fellow girl ogler walked over and sat down on the curb. After a brief one-sided discussion about the glorious merits of shaved twin cams and adjustable air shocks on certain Japanese crotch rockets, the man took out a breath mint tin and withdrew a rolled cigarette that didn't look like a Marlboro. He offered it to Savic.

"No thanks."

"I don't mean for you to smoke it here. It's a gift from a road brother," the man said. "Got it in Denver. Good, clean commercial stuff. No twigs and sticks. Got some cookies, too, if you want. Hey man, there's no cops around."

Savic smiled. "You never know."

"About the cops. Or the twigs?"

"Both," Savic said.

Savic stood, bowing his sore back. He finished his coffee. An electric sciatica jolt tingled up the side of his leg. He'd jacked up his back in court yesterday during that stunt by Felicia Mendez, but he was grateful that the Jardine trial had finally come to an end. The investigation had sucked the life out of him. After they cleaned the place up, the judge insisted that everyone, including the bleeding and heavily bandaged prisoner, return to the courtroom so he could deliver his expected sentencing.

Savic felt like perfect shit, the truck stop bratwurst coming to life in his gut as it battled the caffeine-soaked nacho cheese. He agonized again about his senseless casino gambling adventure. Before he loaded up the credit cards, he'd already emptied their vacation fund, money that Maria had saved from her nursing job at the hospital.

Window. Door. Light switch. Bathroom. That's what the little notes at the nursing home said.

Savic struggled with his helmet, wondering if it was actually possible to gain weight in your head.

He thought about calling Felicia, who was in custody at the county jail. The assault charge would probably get dismissed and Savic wanted to set the record straight about any involvement between the two of them. She had the wrong idea, though he had to admit that he'd probably given her some foolish and misleading signals. He was just trying to be kind and comforting. He should have known better. He'd already decided to avoid her now that the Jardine case was in the can. He didn't look forward to the conversation he admitted he had to have with her. As everyone now knew, Felicia Mendez had a temper.

Savic tried to stretch the cramp from his back. His head felt too tight inside the helmet.

His Harley friend lit his stubby and held his breath and flashed a stupid, cross-eyed grin.

"Somebody might smell that," Savic said.

The man pinched out his smoke and examined it drowsily and put it back into the tin. He motioned across the street toward the Comfort Inn.

"Maybe I better just spend the night," he said. "Did four hundred miles yesterday. A few times a year I get to pretend I'm somebody else. The wife, she's glad to get me out of the house for a while. I might be pressing things if I stay on the road today."

He again offered the open tin in his outstretched palm like it was a plate of party appetizers.

"You sure? I've got plenty."

Savic shrugged and lifted his leg over the seat. He twisted the ignition and touched the carburetor stem. The bike immediately backfired and stalled.

"Like I said, cops could be around," Savic said, watching as white smoke drifted from beneath the Harley's seat cushion.

"I can smell a badge a mile away," the man said.

Savic cranked the ignition and the bike died and sputtered to life again.

"Mine did the same thing," the man said, shouting while Savic throttled the engine. "Took it to a shop and they changed the ground wire and put in a new speed sensor. That seemed to help. Now I only get trouble after high RPMs and high temps. Never seems to be an issue in cool weather, but I guess around here that's not an option."

Savic shrugged and pretended he couldn't hear. He waved and throttled the bike toward the highway ramp. He decided not to bother with interstate traffic and turned instead onto the two-lane frontage road that would take him through the gentle desert hills. There was a small cafe he knew where it would be cool and mostly empty. He'd decided to head back home. Sorting out his life was not in the cards today. He had work to do and he wanted to see his wife.

Miles up the road, traffic had bunched into a crawl that stretched ahead in a curving line of red tail lights. Beyond the jammed vehicles scraps of blowing black smoke lifted into the cloudless sky. Two semi trucks were nosed into each other and a small crowd stood gawking at something out of view next to the frontage road. One semi stood jackknifed, its trailer tipped and twisted off the skid plate. The other sat with its crushed hood ablaze, the driver standing close by and holding a towel to his head. No police or ambulance had arrived, so Savic wobbled the Harley along the loose gravel road shoulder until he came to where a vehicle sat with its smashed hood and front axle resting atop a collapsed guard rail, the driver's shape slumped forward against the blown-out windshield.

Smoke began to rise from beneath the wreck, and when Savic finally rolled up someone from the road began shouting and pointing down at the car. A siren wailed from the direction of the interstate, where Savic knew the ambulance was probably racing back to the Moapa exit in order to head south again on the frontage road. It would take too long for it to reach the wreck.

The woman sat folded forward and face-down against the dashboard, her legs lost in the tangled mess of broken metal and plastic beneath the steering wheel. Savic stumbled to where he could kneel and look into the vehicle. The engine was still running and he smelled leaking fuel and saw that the dry bunchgrass beneath the car's ruptured gas tank was already wet, the fuel pooling under his boots.

Savic twisted sideways and tried to squeeze himself past the crumpled door panel and across the car seat. He reached blindly, following the steering post with his hand until he finally found the keys, pushed the shifter with his forearm and pulled them away.

His hand and the keys came to rest in her soft lap and when he tried to unlatch the seat belt he saw the white sandal laying on the floor of the car.

35

He tried to squeeze closer and lift the collapsed wreckage from her trapped legs, but he could not. He lay there for a moment trying to think of what to do next. The radiator hissed loudly and he heard the crackle of the burning grass beneath the car and tried to lift his soaked boots off the ground so they would not catch fire.

He braced himself and once more tried to push up against the dashboard with both hands, the loose and broken windshield glass collapsing, but it was too much. He rammed his shoulder against what was left of the steering column, trying not to touch what he could see of the woman's trembling and bleeding knees. The smell of the smoke grew stronger and when he finally felt the dashboard move slightly he tried to twist it away from her legs, but he could not. She screamed and arched her back against the seat and lay still, shivering and taking short, frantic breaths.

It was the girl from the truck stop.

Now she snapped back her shoulders and squirmed violently, crying out before she again sat perfectly still with her eyes open wide as she studied the ceiling. She glanced over briefly at Savic, but turned away calmly as if his presence was unimportant and of no consequence to her situation. As if it didn't matter at all if anyone was there.

She took more quick, shallow baby breaths, her eyes darting from side to side as if taking stock of her awful predicament and she started shivering again, her shoulders slamming convulsively back against the seat.

"Don't move, dear," Savic said, but the woman only rolled her eyes and looked straight ahead through the spidered windshield that was covered with blood that looked like it had been splashed there from a cup. Savic could not see where her legs went. The steering wheel had snapped away and a pool of fresh blood had gathered below the accelerator pedal where her perfectly white sandal lay.

"Don't move," Savic said again. "I can hear the ambulance. You'll be okay. Just hold on."

She closed her eyes and reached slowly for the dashboard. A police siren wailed from the highway and her long hair fell across her face as she looked down and searched again for where her legs should have been. Sand blew against the car and the hot gust lifted her hair. Savic smelled her perfume.

She began to cough blood through her broken front teeth, gulping in small and measured breaths. Her little tee shirt was nearly torn away, so Savic peeled off his leather vest and tried to cover her up. Her eyes flickered open and closed. She looked so frail. Her cell phone rang from somewhere inside the car; a bouncy rap tune that repeated itself insistently. Her jaw popped as she tried to open her mouth. She cried out softly, a long and bird-like keening, and slapped her hand up and down against the seat as if tallying the consequence of some regretful decision.

Again, the hot desert wind blew into the car and she rocked forward and abruptly stopped breathing as if the two events were inextricably related, a part of some grand tableau that could not occur without the other. She looked like a drowsy child going to sleep, fragile and so young, as she peacefully closed her eyes.

He gently held her warm hand and stayed until the EMT came and reached through the window and touched his shoulder. He had seen death before and this should not have been different, yet it certainly was. It was not the same and he could not explain it. In such a circumstance, he could not explain it at all.

Savic stepped away and showed his badge to a trooper and went and sat on his motorcycle to watch while they lifted her onto a gurney. The underside of the car finally caught fire, the flames curling up with surprising speed through the open window, and someone came and sprayed everything with foam. Through the smoke Savic watched as the paramedic fitted what was left of the woman's legs with a white bubble sleeve. He pressed the oxygen cup to her expressionless face while his partner did chest compressions until they exchanged looks and both nodded and stopped what they were doing. They covered her. The hand he had held moments ago, the wrist hung with sparkling jewelry chains and little colored charms, hung free and from beneath the shrouded gurney her blond hair swung against the draped gray sheet as they rolled her away.

Savic sat for a long time next to his bike, looking at what was left of the BMW, its bright yellow paint the only color against the rising brown dust that stretched to the horizon. Nothing out there but flinty bare rocks and sand, a broken wasteland.

After the traffic jam cleared and while he was driving nearly alone on the highway Savic felt his phone vibrate in his front shirt pocket. He pulled over and saw the text from Captain Monaghan at the station, along with five waiting voicemail messages from Felicia Mendez.

– 6 –

Captain Paul Monaghan was wearing his starched powder blue shirt with the stitched epaulets and pinstripes that made him look like a drum major in a marching band. His red necktie was knotted perfectly, trousers razor-creased as if he'd just stepped into a classroom at UNLV, where he taught occasionally as a visiting lecturer on Law Enforcement Investigation Protocols.

He and Frank Savic had been rookies together, graduating from the twenty-four-week course at the Southern Desert Regional Police Academy as number one and thirty-sixth in their class, respectively. Monaghan, teased over the years by Savic for his academic credentials — a B.A. in criminal justice and an M.A. in metaphysics, had quickly made his captain's bars before he turned thirty-five. Savic, with a legendary knack for annoying the brass and arriving late for meetings, had taken his sweet time to climb the career ladder, waiting nearly two decades before he could pin on his blue and gold sergeant's badge. He'd always been a late bloomer, but he was also a good detective.

When Savic walked into the office the next morning he was wearing his old denim biker's vest, the U.S. Air Force logo stitched across the back in faded thread, his black sneakers a substitute for the boots that had been stained by the woman's blood and soaked in gasoline at the car accident scene. His Arizona Diamondbacks baseball cap was turned backwards and he was wearing shades when Monaghan handed him black coffee in a paper cup and pointed to the case folders stacked on the captain's conference room table.

"How's Maria?" Monaghan said.

"I got tied up yesterday so they let me stay past visiting hours. But we had time together, yeah," Savic said. "It's the same. Good days and bad days. I just hope she knows I'm there. I think she does. I don't know why I call it a rehab place. It's a home. An old people's home. Somehow it doesn't make sense her being in a place like that when she's not old."

Monaghan began to arrange the case files he had prepared for their meeting.

"My wife stopped by last week," he said. "She said it seems nice enough, that home. Her and Maria talked."

"They're packed to the gills," Savic said. "I was lucky to get her in. But it's a soap opera. Never thought geezers could get in so much trouble. Last week they caught one of the guys –– Robles, is his name, selling black market Viagra pills in the cafeteria. I guess it's a thing. He had something worked out with Jamal the shuttle bus driver, whose wife works for a urologist. Robles' nickname is Mister Blue and he's been peddling his boner pills at fifty bucks a shot for the past two months. Had zip lock baggies hidden under his bed. I see something new every time I go there."

Savic flipped through one of the folders. He held up an eight-by-ten photo labeled with the District Attorney's logo and waited for Monaghan to finish scribbling something on an iPad with a stylus.

"I guess you could call it poetic justice," Monaghan finally said, holding up the screen that showed another picture of Carlo Cavilleri, this one sent to him that morning by the coroner's office in Nye County.

"Parole officer said he'd been working there for about six months. It's a podunk place out by the Cali border. He'd been on the street for almost a year on an apprentice work-release program they started when he was doing his time at the old Silverheel prison."

"That town is a sandbox," Savic said, swiping slowly through the series of forensic pics that showed Cavilleri in various positions of deathly repose.

"It's the closest town to the prison. Back in the day they called it Devil's Island. Pretty lax as far as security, because it's so old. If you did manage to escape there was nowhere to go. The closest road is miles away, if you made it that far through the desert."

"There's a plan to fix the place up," Monaghan said. "Some mega-million project the governor is all hot about. His PR people are all over it.

I don't see it, though. They can hardly hire anybody from NDOC to work out there anymore. I think they just let Cavilleri loose because they don't have any room."

"That's smart," Savic said. "Springing a killer like him."

Savic turned the iPad upside down, then sideways, then upside down again as the photo readjusted itself.

"Looks like he's doing the limbo dance."

Monaghan smiled at the photo, "Yeah, and he didn't quite make it under the broomstick."

Savic opened another folder bursting with stapled documents and envelopes gathered together with rubber bands and paperclips, remembering his phone call to the mother of the teenage girl Carlo Cavilleri had murdered nearly a decade ago, explaining to her without success how a minor legal technicality, tampered evidence and a botched autopsy had resulted in a prison sentence of only eight years, the same as a felony DUI.

The woman, her breathing getting more labored while the translator on the three-way phone call tried to explain why the killer of her daughter had received the same jail time as a repeat offending drunk, finally erupted with a shrieking scream and cursed Savic, Clark County, the State of Nevada and the entire United States judicial system. Before she hung up she called Savic's own birth unfortunate and one of God's great failures and offered his long-dead mother her condolences for spawning such a shameful human being. In Spanish, the condemnations sounded lyrical.

Savic leafed through the familiar and wordy Nevada Bureau of Investigations report and peeled away the blue security sticker that had sealed the envelope for all these years. He glanced at the sloppily printed and inadequate evidence inventory that had been introduced at the trial by the public defender, a move that was shot down as inadmissible by the judge. Clipped to the sheet were a few old ink jet prints of Cavilleri's many tattoos, each labeled and referenced to its known gang affiliation.

"I forgot that he hung around with Billy Jardine for a while," Savic said and held up the photo of Cavilleri's right hand with its line of blue numerals.

"They were roomies at the county jail years ago until Jardine did that stunt with the laundry truck and hit the road. Funny how these idiots turn into Bible scholars once they get locked up. They just love to quote chapter and verse of whatever bullshit they happen to have spinning around in their heads at the moment."

"Not the brightest hour for the sheriff," Monaghan said. "Having his big profile prisoner escape in a pile of underwear. If I remember, they just spent six months trying to extradite Jardine from out east, and then he gets loose. Didn't bode well for the Sheriff's re-election, if I remember."

Savic held up the pair of enlarged thumbprints labeled with a faded time and date stamp.

"What's this, Cap?" Savic said. "I thought they found the body in Four Palms? It says the prints were processed by the Carson City PD. Why would we ship the body four hundred miles just to get prints?"

Monaghan smirked almost gleefully as if he'd been waiting for Savic to ask that exact question.

"We didn't," he said and grinned. "Nye County sent a team to Four Palms and that's where they did the preliminary. In fact, the corpse is still there on ice. Since his parole is handled out of Las Vegas they weren't sure about the jurisdiction. I think it's actually a budget thing with the Nye coroner, but there it is."

"But these prints..." Savic said.

"Stay with me, Frank," Monaghan said and began to loosen his tie. "The victim's hands got shipped UPS to Carson City. Our boy's paws were packed in a sports cooler, very neatly I might add. Actually, it shipped from one of those mailbox places here in town, so whoever mailed them drove all the way back here to the city from Four Palms just to send the victim's hands six hours back in the same direction to Carson City. Paid in cash. UPS clerk remembers zip and the shop's cameras were out of whack that day after a power failure, which seems iffy to me and not a coincidence. It's all we have for now. The return address is another mailbox service with a bogus location. Is your head spinning yet?"

"Actually, my head's been twirling for a few days now," Savic said and dropped the case file on the table.

He handed Monaghan an envelope from the Police Benevolent Association.

"Look, Paul...while I'm here, they said you need to sign my retirement request so I can give the union some dates. I thought this would be easy, but why am I surprised? Nothing with the union is ever easy."

Monaghan took the envelope but didn't open it.

"Frank, I've been meaning to talk to you about that," he said. "The retirement. I know this has been in the can for a while and that you already delayed things until the Jardine trial got settled, but nobody here knows the Cavilleri case like you. That was your baby. I'd have to spend a week getting somebody up to speed and you already know the background. You're the only one who can handle this. Give me another thirty days, okay?"

Savic leaned back in the fancy high-back leather conference chair, one of six that encircled the table.

"Jesus, Paul..." Savic said.

"...and Joseph and Mary," Monaghan added. "Oh, it's only a month. I know you can tidy this up. You're the only one that can. I'm short staffed here, and all I got on the payroll is first year detectives. I'll have the commissioner ask the union to take some short cuts with your pension schedule so you won't really lose much time. I need you, Frank. I really do. I know you just got the Jardine case out of your hair, so I understand what I'm asking. Especially with Maria, it's been a rough time for you."

Savic stared out the window. There was a smoky haze today from a controlled burn the Bureau of Land Management was doing out in the valley. The top of the Venetian Resort was barely visible and most of the taller casinos along Las Vegas Boulevard appeared as pale silhouettes. He looked at the calendar hanging on the wall behind Monaghan's desk and ticked off the weeks before the next payment was due for Maria's stay at the home.

He rolled his chair forward and leaned across the table. "Look, if you can talk to somebody and push my vested date up a few months with the union, it bumps my pension package into a better category. It's only a few bucks, but if I'm on the clock here for thirty more days I'd appreciate the favor."

"Done," Monaghan said and stood and slapped Savic on the shoulder as he handed him the rest of the Cavilleri file. "There's a personnel budget meeting at the Mayor's office today and I'm sure the union rep will be there. I'll bring it up. In fact, I wouldn't mind getting involved in this case, if you want the company. I need to get out of this place for a while. I'm tired of seeing the same ten people here every day."

Somebody's scanner echoed in the police station garage as Savic walked downstairs to the parked Harley. Two officers on their radios chattered back and forth about a smash and grab over on Pecos that was turning into a foot chase through the neighborhood. In his younger days he half enjoyed calls like that: sprinting through alleys and crawling over fences, chasing some bad guy. The kids played videos games like that today.

Two flying bats chased a ball of circling moths beneath the garage lights, their wings like softly fluttering fabric in the dark ceiling shadows. Other bats hung upside down in unlit corners of the garage like little umbrellas. A simple way to live, he thought: hunting and flying, hunting and flying and doing it all over again every day with not much else to worry about. He envied them.

The two-hour drive took him through the Amargosa Desert, where the white lunar landscape formed by hydraulic mining a century ago stretched alongside the road like little sugar hills. The two-lane route, which Savic had taken a few times for an interrogation at the old territorial correctional facility at Silverheel, was as straight as a pencil, the distant baked mountains hinting at where the dry plain broadened into the horizon over Death Valley.

The town of Four Palms had a single traffic light and a tidy municipal park with a baseball field surrounded by artificially watered date palms where a dog was kicking up dust as it chased a tennis ball in the scorching heat.

The dog's owner sat on a bench in the shade of one of the trees, drinking from a plastic jug while he watched Savic park his backfiring motorcycle. Savic nodded and the man raised his water bottle and held out his other hand to retrieve the fetched ball from the panting dog, which looked like it was ready to drop dead from heatstroke.

There were two liquor stores and a main street cafe. Construction equipment — backhoes, loaders and dump trucks, were parked in an open field. A large billboard that Savic could not read announced some coming building project. A tiny brick bank structure with fake Greek columns sat alone next to an abandoned Ben Franklin shop with "1910" engraved in stone above the shuttered doorway. A colorfully painted work crew trailer served as the town's tiny library. A few locked retail shops, their smeared windows showing For Lease signs, told the rest of the story.

A large new municipal building stood at the end of Main Street. A fountain sprayed water in front of the Town Hall, where two new four-wheel police SUVs sat parked next to a shaded courtyard. The empty, rocky desert stretched beyond the town limits, dwarf sand dunes disappearing into the horizon.

The Four Palms Police Department was located next to Town Hall. Except for the parked squad cars and a lone county utility worker being hoisted up a power pole in a cherry picker, there wasn't another soul in sight. The guy and the dog in the park had vanished. The place was dead and dry and hot.

A surprisingly large human wearing a holstered 9mm Glock on a sagging black duty belt introduced himself from the front steps. The man's standard khaki ensemble was topped with a straw cattleman's Stetson that looked too small and tight for his head.

He held out his giant hand: "Harry Nesmith. Your office said to expect you."

"Frank," Savic said.

The police chief of Four Palms immediately began an impromptu monologue.

"You know, I did twenty years with the Denver PD. Spent most of that on Colfax Avenue, which back then wasn't a garden spot of humanity. When I saw they needed somebody in this town, well...me and the wife figured what a nice way to put a quiet ending on my career. I had enough with chasing pimps and thieves. Figured I'd hang around a few years here and retire with a couple of nice state pensions. Now here I am getting ready to talk about some dead sonofabitch who got his head chopped off. Right here in my little town."

Nesmith glanced at the bulge of Savic's non-standard .45 showing from beneath the denim vest. His badge was clipped crookedly to his belt.

"A bit out of uniform today, aren't you sergeant?"

"It was supposed to be my day off," Savic said and peeled off his bandanna, revealing a two-toned forehead.

"I was actually ready to meet with the police union today to take care of my retirement paperwork. I guess it's like you being tired of chasing crooks. I need a change, too."

"I understand you were involved with our dead fellow at one time," Nesmith said. "Your captain filled me in on the phone."

"Arrested him some years ago," Savic said, noticing the embossed cactus pattern on the police chief's tooled cowboy boots. "Lost track of the case. Until today. Sometimes these people don't give you a rest, even after they get locked up."

They walked across the courtyard and through a heavy metal security door. Savic heard a basketball pounding somewhere on an indoor court. He passed empty cells and a day room with a giant TV where two men in jailhouse jumpsuits were playing Foosball. Another prisoner sat hunched over a laptop computer. The police facility seemed abundantly outsized for such a small community.

"Nice digs," Savic said.

"Highway money," Nesmith said. "The state bought land from the town for the new interchange last year. There's something else in the works they won't talk about. Feds kicked in more money on top of that in matching funds. A budget windfall for us, you might say. We actually lease space here to the county. It sort of dropped in our lap, don't ask me how. That big project over at the old Silverheel facility, even though it's down the road a way, has something to do with it. They need a place for the employees to live and this is the only town within decent driving distance. Some of the corrections folks who work there now live in a trailer park near the prison, but that's not a good arrangement at all for anybody who has a family. Got a county bond issue coming up for new schools, a swimming pool, and we just finished building a new medical clinic. Guess you might call us a bedroom community now. I'm not looking forward to it, but we've got to hire police staff like you wouldn't believe. Teachers, too. Just brought on two doctors. One of them is a surgeon and he'll be contracted by the state to service the prison. This town hasn't had a real doc for seventy-five years. So much for my idea of being a police chief in a sleepy little town."

They were buzzed into a freshly painted hallway that led down metal stairs into a basement. Savic could smell the wet paint. The AC hummed loudly and when they entered another room the temperature suddenly dropped twenty degrees.

"County coroner figured he'd do his job right here. We've got more space than he does over in Tonopah and they'll be turning this into a real autopsy room, anyway. From what I hear, the new prison expansion also means they'll be sending some inmates here soon for medical treatment. I'm not excited about those people being driven around town, no sir. Too much can go wrong, but it's not up to me to decide. This is all the Governor's pet project, yes sir. Every time he talks about it on TV he's smiling like he just scored a lottery ticket."

What was left of Carlo Cavilleri lay on a stainless steel examination table mounted on a tilting pneumatic pedestal that could be adjusted by a foot pedal. There was a deep sink basin at one end with three high faucets, the tallest leading to an overhead spray nozzle that now dangled from a rubber hose a few inches above Carlo's bushy crotch.

Savic had seen his fill of the various versions of the dead, who often looked like they were moving when they certainly were not, unless you stared at them for a while. And then they seemed to move. They almost always looked uncomfortable, even in death. They were twisted and jacked this way and that, slumped or folded up, but almost never straight. A person who was laying there straight and comfortable, well, that would make Savic concerned. The dead always looked heavy, like they were ready to sink into whatever they were laying on. Even when they were small, the dead looked heavy. A bed, the floor, the dirt or in the grass. They always looked heavier than they really were. Occasionally, they wore an expression of beatific calm, but that was rare. Usually it was a look of embarrassment or concern or anger. Or surprise, which was understandable. They never looked sad or unhappy, just mostly pissed off. Death, Savic always thought, is the second most important thing that ever happens to a person.

The loud AC fan blasted arctic air into the windowless room and Savic zipped his vest and the police chief rubbed his bare arms as he bent to read the body tag that was fastened to Cavilleri's toe with a wire grocery twisty.

"Funny thing," Nesmith said. "Fella' delivered those same tags from the print shop just last week. We'd been using these flimsy paper things, so I thought I'd upgrade. Ironic, don't you think?"

"So you knew him?" Savic said.

"Everybody here knows everybody," Nesmith said. "I knew he was on parole, if that's what you're asking. Was informed as soon as he came to town. He never caused any trouble, and I looked at the summary file the DA sent and he's been a good boy since he got out of prison. The print shop took him on, kind of a second chance thing. I guess everybody can use a second chance. Your boss said he'd done some real bad stuff."

Savic put on his reading glasses and stooped over the torso. He lifted the stained white muslin bag that covered the raw stub of Cavilleri's severed neck.

"Bad wouldn't exactly be my first word choice," he said. "You got kids?"

The chief nodded. "Three. All grown."

"Well, our headless horseman here made sure somebody's child never did grow up."

The neck had been cut cleanly, one vertebrae sliced perfectly at the horizontal so that Savic could make out tiny nerve filaments constricted into woolly bunches within the core of the spine itself. Bits of marrow had leaked out and clung dried like wood glue to the steel table. There wasn't a mark on Cavilleri's face. His forearms, except for the tattoos, showed no cuts or scratches. The actual autopsy would answer most questions, but Savic couldn't see any obvious sign of a struggle prior to death.

He took out his pad and made a note of the radiating bruise on Cavilleri's shoulder. He had remained alive long enough to develop a rash from the apparent injection. There was a puncture wound there and then the faded pink smear of dried blood that ran up the side of the neck next to a shallow circular cut.

"I didn't see details in his parole file," Nesmith said. "The murder and all that. Heard he only did under ten years. And you said he was a killer?"

Savic lifted the lid to the stainless steel box freezer that now contained Cavilleri's head.

Without looking up, Savic said: "You wouldn't do to a lab rat what this scummy shit did to that girl. The court and the prosecutor both screwed up big time and didn't do their jobs, and they came up against a rookie public defender who actually did his job quite well. We eventually locked him up for a prior armed felony that the DA had shoved aside so he could go ahead with the murder charge. If it wasn't for that he would have walked free. It's a long story, but basically it was an embarrassing circus of lazy government lawyer work and some very timely luck for our boy here."

Like a piece of statuary, Cavilleri's frozen head stared back from the ice, a frieze on a marble temple column, eyes closed and puffy like those of an allergy sufferer, the skin darkened into a bad tan. Clots of blood filled his nostrils and his lips were pressed into a look of consternation, like he was disappointed in something.

"I don't get why the hands got shipped," Nesmith said. "Why bother with something like that?"

Savic closed the freezer lid. "I'm sure we're both not surprised anymore about what people will do. I remember a guy out of Henderson years ago who mailed his ex-wife something special for Christmas. He was a high roller at the Freemont and got the sloppy end of a nasty divorce. Had low level connections with the mob, the old Tony Acardo crowd out of Chicago, and he found out his wife was playing around with a blackjack dealer and it didn't have anything to do with cards."

Nesmith took the bait. "What did he send his wife?"

"Her boyfriend's dick," Savic said. "Wrapped up in a holiday cheese sampler basket. Had a bow on it, sticking up between the Gouda and the provolone cheese and a package of fancy crackers that were shaped like hearts."

Nesmith half smiled and shook his head and handed Savic a three-ring binder. "I was asked to give you a copy of my report. Said they'd send you the computer file. However that stuff works. It's all there, as much as I know. I'd rather not get involved, anyway. I got enough to do around here. So this guy shipped somebody an actual dick, or are you shittin' me?"

"Yep. Pecker in a basket," Savic said.

"Around here, somebody kicks his dog and it makes the newspaper. I like things that way," Nesmith said. "That's why I left Denver. Got tired of that nonsense."

The room smelled like vinegar. Cavilleri's headless and handless torso looked like a vandalized museum sculpture.

"The report has everything," Nesmith said. "Some kind of fancy commercial paper cutter is what did it. He was forcibly jammed into the machine. The head and hands don't seem to have been cut simultaneously, which seems impossible to do, if you ask me. It happened early in the morning, probably around five or so. The owner of the print shop discovered the body when he came in at eight. And then those damn hands showed up at your place. End of story. Oh, and he shit his pants something awful before he died, which tells me the poor sonofabitch might have had enough time to know what was coming. It's all in the report."

Savic wanted to tell the chief of police of Four Turds, Nevada that his annoying insights into criminology were a bore.

Instead, he politely said: "Thank you, chief Nesmith. You've been extremely helpful. We look forward to receiving the full autopsy."

Nesmith started to cover the corpse with a sheet when Savic stopped him. He asked the police chief for his flashlight and studied closely where he'd noticed a metallic glint on what was left of Cavilleri's neck. The blood had congealed around a knob of bone where a short length of shiny wire was now embedded. He lifted away the piece of metal with his pocket knife and held it to the light.

"Just a question, chief," Savic said. "But did you happen to find a neck chain anywhere?"

Nesmith nodded. "I did. It's in the report."

"Your people might want to look again at the chain," Savic said and lay the metal chip on the table.

Nesmith said. "I'm sure they will. You telling me how to do my job?"

"A colleague sharing a professional observation, is all."

Nesmith turned and headed for the door "It was a kid's necklace. That thing around his neck. Creepy, if you ask me, an adult wearing a child's necklace."

"Well, we have a few ideas about that," Savic said. "Thanks for your help. I can find my way out."

"Suit yourself," Nesmith said.

"I usually do," Savic said.

Outside, Nesmith called out to Savic.

"That fella's pecker. How'd they get it to stand up straight in the basket? Seems it might be a hard thing to do, make a dead penis stand upright like that. I'm no doctor, but that doesn't sound right. You pulling my leg, sergeant?"

Savic had to think. "I'm also no dick expert, but I suppose you'd blow air into it."

Nesmith shook his head and smiled as he flapped a dismissive goodbye with one hand and watched Savic noisily throttle the backfiring Harley down Main Street.

Savic drove a different route home past the stretch of highway where the young woman had her accident. A flayed car tire sat next to the guard rail along the frontage road, the stripe of burned rubber on the asphalt but little else to show that someone's short and promising life had ended there.

– 7 –

Mr. Gompers from Room 67 was having a conversation with the hallway wall. He was starting to slide to the floor when Jamal the shuttle bus driver ran over and hoisted him up into his wheelchair.

Mrs. Kraus from 112 was already parked in the front lobby, smiling at nothing in particular, when Frank Savic arrived and signed the visitors' book at the reception desk. She wheeled herself over and gave Savic a sly smile, tugged at his sleeve and asked the same question she asked every morning.

"Young man," she said. "Can you show me the way out of here? I'd like to go home now."

"Why, good morning," Savic said. He kneeled and took the old lady's hand like he was about to give it a gentlemanly kiss. "Now why would you want to do such a silly thing?"

"I really don't know."

"That's what I thought. There's nothing good out there, you know. It's nice and cool in here. It's busy and dusty and hot outside. All that traffic. You're safe here."

"Really?"

"It's much better in here. There's nothing interesting out there."

"Okay," she said and smiled. "You're always so helpful."

On the way to Maria's room he stopped by the accounting office. Mrs. Gardener's desk was empty, a fish tank bubbling noisily behind her chair, a cup of coffee sitting next to her computer. He stepped away, happy that he could avoid another conversation about his miserable finances.

In the cafeteria Savic looked at the menu: Danish rolls, blueberry muffins and the Quinoa breakfast bowl again. He would order the meatloaf dish and sweet potatoes for lunch for Maria. He wasn't sure what *dish* meant. Maybe it was a surprise. Whenever they didn't know the details of a meal somebody would write "dish" on the chalkboard. Hamburger dish. Sausage and beans dish. Most things to eat here were pureed and mashed and mixed with something else. Dinner usually looked like six shades of beige, so when they tossed in broccoli or a salad, the unexpected burst of green seemed startling. The meals were odorless. There was only the feeling of a smell, like electrically charged air after a rain storm. Except for the soup smell. The place always smelled like soup.

Maria sat by the window with both hands folded in her lap, watching the birds in the trees in the small garden outside the Wind Mountain Memory Care Center.

She looked around the room and then at her husband as if she suddenly realized where she was.

"Ospedale?"

"That's right, honey. You're sort of in the hospital." Savic gave her a lingering kiss on the cheek.

"You've been sick, remember?"

They called the patients "residents" and the dusty windows in Maria's room were hung with curtains decorated with dancing blue elephants. The rattling air conditioner vent beneath the window blew up against the curtains, billowing them back and forth, animating the elephants, and that was what Maria was staring at after she turned to her husband, again confounded by his presence.

She blushed and looked at the checkered linoleum floor.

"She keeps telling me they won't let her wash her hair," Savic said, turning to the nurse who was replacing a box of tissues on the nightstand next to Maria's bed.

He took his wife's hand, but she turned away and looked out the window.

"I'll tell the office," the nurse said.

This was Nurse Fahey, the skinny one. She dressed in Full Nurse Mode; the only thing missing was the white starchy hat that looked like a paper envelope. Everything else was official and properly nursey: white shoes,

53

white stockings, white cloth waist belt around her white uniform. The very white and spongy shoes. Nurse Fahey ran the place.

Wind Mountain was the best Savic could afford. It's cheapness – the fake plastic chandeliers, the lumpy linoleum, the way the hallway baseboards were stained and cracked with dents from a thousand wheelchair collisions, made him feel guilty and pissy about Maria's situation.

"I told the office," Savic said. "She doesn't talk much about anything lately, but she does talk about wanting to wash her hair. It seems to be important to her. She was always fussy about her hair."

"Then I'm sure they'll take care of it."

"I've told them three times," Savic said.

The home was a former elementary school. Boxy, identically sized classrooms had been partitioned into sleeping quarters and the gym was now a cafeteria, the painted basketball court foul line stripes still showing on the varnished wood floor. The buffet table sat on the freethrow line. The lingering soup broth smell made things feel damp. At this time in the morning there was a humming noise in the hallway as the residents began to emerge from their rooms. Mostly it was the people in wheelchairs who spent much of the day parked at odd angles throughout the building like stalled bumper car drivers at an amusement park.

"This morning she thought Doctor Belmont was her cousin," nurse Fahey said, smiling. "And she got plenty mad about something you did to her new Buick."

"We haven't had the Buick for fifteen years," Savic said.

Maria grinned. She watched the little birds outside lift from a tree and squawk past the window.

"We've been very understaffed, mister Savic," nurse Fahey said. "Your wife has been with us for how long now?"

"Brought her on Mother's Day."

"You have children?"

"No," Savic said. "But it felt shitty bringing her in on Mother's Day."

"Ospedale?" Maria said again.

"Yes, honey...this is one of the nurses I'm talking to right now," Savic said. "She's very nice and she's the boss here. She'll take care of you when I can't come and visit."

"Un Ospedale? Non sono malato."

"You got sick. So we had to bring you here. So you wouldn't get sicker."

She pulled away and squinted. "Lei sono il dottore?"

"Oh, boy. Now she thinks I'm the doctor," Savic said.

He smoothed a wrinkle on Maria's robe. She smiled at the window. The birds had returned.

"After the MRI last week they told me it might have been a small stroke."

"Her chart shows a heart condition, too," nurse Fahey said.

"The doc said the early onset could have made it worse. Kind of aggravated things."

"That's possible," the nurse said. "The heart condition, I mean."

She scribbled on the clip board fastened to the foot of the bed and wrapped a blood pressure cuff around Maria's arm.

"She seems to be coming down with something, maybe a cold. The doctor doesn't want her sick right now. Her resistance is quite low. If it turns respiratory, it could be a big problem. We've had something going around with our other patients. It's not even flu season yet."

"Bella," Maria said. She pushed her finger against the window glass and followed the path of one bird's flight toward another tree. She made a great show of sighing as if she couldn't get the air out of her lungs fast enough.

"Maybe I should let her take a nap," Savic said. "They told me at the front desk that she had a rough night."

"You can sit with her until she does. I think it calms her when you're here. You know, she doesn't like to take a walk anywhere unless you're with her. I've tried to see if she wants to use the wheelchair, but she doesn't like that at all. Will you be having breakfast with us today?"

"Not this morning. I'll be coming back tonight, like usual."

"I know you will," the nurse said. "She's lucky to have a visitor every night. Not everyone here has someone. When did she start speaking that way? In Italian. Mr. Bascone in 106 sometimes talks to her. She gets frustrated when she thinks I don't understand what she's telling me."

"Off and on, about a month ago," Savic said. "I haven't talked the lingo for years, but all of a sudden she starts with the old country stuff. Out of the blue, just like that. She'll go in and out, a little English mixed up with

Italian. She speaks four languages besides English, you know. She used to be a nurse. Over at St. Boniface, in radiology. She worked in the MRI room."

Savic smiled at his wife. "We met in Italy when I was in the Air Force. I was taking a class, one of those training things Uncle Sam makes you do overseas so you don't get bored. It was at a university about an hour outside of Aviano Air Base. She was a translator for the government. My mother was Italian, so we could talk. We got married before I shipped home. That's the story. And now she won't speak English half the time."

"Actually, it's not uncommon. I've seen the old people, the immigrants, they start remembering things in the language of their childhood and it seems to comfort them. Makes things predictable and safe."

Nurse Fahey patted Savic on the shoulder before she left the room. "As long as you understand her, that's what matters."

Maria cocked her head as if trying to place her husband's face. He touched her cheek and her eyes followed his hand.

She bent close, smelling the gasoline odor from the car accident.

"Puzzi di benzina," she said, smiling, and then continued in Italian, "My husband likes to work on his cars, you know."

He remembered the last time she'd given him the same suspicious look. He had returned from the DA's office and a meeting with Felicia Mendez about her scheduled victim's impact statement during Jardine's sentencing appearance. The lawyers had stepped outside for a conference, leaving Savic and Felicia sitting alone on the small office sofa. It would have been unusual to have a law enforcement officer at such a meeting, especially someone involved with the case, but Felicia had insisted that Savic be present. Savic had butted heads with the DA over the years, but in this case the prosecutor consented, if only as a reluctant thank you to the detective for delivering to him such a politically fruitful case. It was Savic who had made the arrest; who had tracked Jardine cross-country during a year-long investigation that now made it possible to put the infamous killer behind bars for the rest of his life.

They chatted about soaring Vegas apartment rents, the casino where Felicia worked as a gaming hostess, and the fact that William Parker Jardine would certainly die in prison with no chance of parole. Felicia had agreed with the prosecutor that requesting a death sentence would prolong the trial and give Jardine the publicity he craved. Also, once on Nevada's death row, there was almost no chance that an inmate would be executed. There had been nearly two hundred death sentences in the past thirty years and half had been overturned by the courts. Only a dozen cases resulted in an execution and in all but one instance the inmate himself had volunteered to be put to death. Everyone agreed there was no chance Jardine would do that.

While they were talking, Felicia leaned and gave Savic what seemed to be a casual kiss on the cheek and thanked him again for his support. Nothing flirty about it, Savic thought at the time. It seemed innocent, and so he lightly tapped her knee and squeezed her hand in what he thought was a harmless gesture of friendship.

She was dressed nicely that day: a sleek black dress and high heels, a thin scarf wrapped across her slender shoulders. Her heavy perfume — something that wouldn't be out of place at the casino where she worked, enveloped both of them on the cramped sofa in the DA's office. An alarm bell rang in Savic's head when another of Felicia's innocent pecks on the cheek turned into a long, lingering wet kiss that included her hand fluttering along his arm and her little ass bumping up against his hip. He tried to squirm away, but she clung to his arm and brought her hand to his cheek and pulled him close. She gave him a long, smoldering stare and stroked his face and smiled.

"Listen, Felicia..." he began. "Sorry..."

"I'm not," she said. "We both shouldn't be, you know that."

"We have to talk about this. I think you have the wrong idea."

They both stood abruptly when the attorneys returned and quickly started talking about the legal details of the case. The DA made a clumsy show of not noticing as Felicia, smirking, smoothed down the hem of her skirt. Savic cleared his throat and pretended to look at a notebook he'd quickly pulled from his jacket pocket. He hoped the other attorneys in the room were oblivious to what was going on, but then realized they certainly were not.

Instead of shutting things down immediately, he drove Felicia home and dropped her at the curb in front of the apartment building on Delroyo Avenue. She asked him up for coffee and Savic politely declined. It had been his best chance to straighten things out, but he didn't have the spine to do it. Just didn't have the nuts to tell her that he wasn't dumb or interested enough to take things up a notch.

When he told Paul Monaghan about this, the captain teased him all that day, telling Savic that he should know better than to get close to someone whose emotions had been run ragged.

"You're a sucker, Frank. A sentimental softy," Monaghan said. "If you think she'll drop this, you're just dumb. That little firecracker attacked a three-hundred pound psycho with a paring knife. What makes you think she'll give up on you? You're doomed."

"I think she knows I'm not interested."

"You're blind, Frank," Monaghan said. "The longer you don't bring this to a head, the worse it's gonna' get. Put your big boy pants on and make it go away before she starts picking out the Bahamas honeymoon package."

When he visited Maria later that night she smelled the perfume immediately and cringed away.

"Mi chiamo, Frank," Savic said. "I'm Frank. I'm your husband. Don't worry about anything. Don't worry."

– 8 –

He studied his sutured face in the mirror, a square of scratched chrome bolted to a cement block wall that was painted ivory or white, depending on how sunlight slanted through the 6 by 24-inch plexiglass slits that were called windows at the Southwest Nevada Heritage Correctional Facility.

The old and crumbling prison, known as Silverheel and named for the mountain that dominated the view from its front gate, was a former territorial jail. A place where old west stagecoach robbers and gunslingers had once been locked up. The holding area at the facility was a transition blockhouse where new inmates were processed before being assigned a permanent cell. Given his notoriety and the publicity generated by the trial, the State of Nevada didn't yet know what to do with William Parker Jardine.

The swollen red welt that curved across Jardine's cheek was shaped like a scythe, the knotted ends of black stitches buried deeply into where the puffy skin had infected during his stay in the Clark County Detention Center. They had to re-suture his suppurating cheek twice to drain and clean the inflamed wound, a process complicated by the extraction of two cracked molars and a three-inch sliver of bamboo wood that had to be pulled from Jardine's damaged sinus.

The physician's assistant at the understaffed, undersupplied Silverheel infirmary told Jardine he should not be surprised if he spoke with a severe lisp for a while, thanks to the severed cranial nerve below his chin. And he also should expect a lingering headache, at least until they could do followup surgery to properly repair the torn sinus. But that would have to wait for the new clinic to be fully staffed in the nearby town of Four Palms, where out-patient treatment was temporarily being performed.

The ringing in Boyce's ear might or might not go away, the PA said. Or it could result in tinnitus and a lifetime of listening to phantom waterfalls and shrieking police sirens. The healed scar, he joked, might one day look like a fleshy version of that long farmer's blade on the flag of the former Soviet Union.

Jardine stretched his chin and stepped closer to the mirror, but a tingling pain shot down his shoulder and his arm briefly went numb. The facial nerve damage had also caused his lower lip to bulge into a slack, exaggerated pout.

He lost his temper and slapped the mirror with his open hand, which only made his shoulder hurt more. He turned and kicked the immovable stainless steel, lidless toilet that was bolted to the cement floor next to his bunk, but that only sent a throbbing jolt up his back, thanks to the pinched nerve caused by being tackled by three sheriff's deputies during the courtroom melee with Felicia Mendez.

He had been handed an envelope that morning that explained the rules for Cell Block D. There was the usual bullshit about attorney visits and meal times and sleeping regulations. No hanging clothes, towels or laundry. Pictures must be taped to the wall at the top only, and the wall could not be defaced in any manner, and that meant no making marks with one of those weeny ass golf pencils Jardine knew they would soon give him. One allowed flag of his choice could measure no larger than 10x12 inches and pictures of nudes should be displayed so they could not be seen from outside the cell. No metal clothes hangers. Music could be listened to only through headphones, and those would be of a certain type and material to be determined at a later date. Beds should be made each day before leaving the cell. Rules, Jardine thought, for a kids' summer camp.

He tossed the papers in the toilet and flushed, hoping the sonofabitch would plug up. Prison shitters, he knew from experience, were indestructible these days and this rig looked like it had a sensor that controlled the flushing pressure and water volume.

He stood on the rim of the toilet and tried to look through the narrow window. He saw a hazy, white desert sky above a welded black perimeter fence topped with razor wire. An old brick guard house shaped like a farm silo, left over from when Silverheel was a territorial prison, stood at the far end of the fence like a tower at a castle. It was a familiar sight; older and outdated digs with a new geography, in this case a dry and endless desert that stretched like a moonscape beyond the cell window. A single dirt road led to the front gate of the prison. Off on a hillside, he could see the little specks that were the buildings of the old ghost town.

A corrections officer stepped up and tapped Jardine's cell bars with his wooden keychain fob.

"Show the hands."

Jardine knew the drill. He pressed his crossed wrists against the steel pocket door that was operated by an old fashion foot lever in the hallway. The officer pulled away a creaking bolt and yanked open the heavy hinged door and waited for Jardine's hands.

"Put some pants on and a shirt," the officer said.

"I was working out," Jardine said.

"You should have washed. You got a sink over there."

"They already had me on a cleaning crew. It's hot. I think that's illegal, using a chain gang. I'll be telling my lawyer."

"You do that," the officer said. "You work. I work. Everybody works. Everybody gets sweaty in this place. Your mamma ever teach you how to keep clean?"

"My mamma taught me shit," Jardine said. "And my daddy was never there."

The tight cuffs pinched his thick wrists and he took one required step to his right and turned so he would stay in sight of the guard, who now reached and fastened Jardine's cuffed hands to a belly chain. Jardine's shoulder ached when he tried to reach up and scratch his ear.

While Jardine was being led down the hallway, the officer said again: "Jesus, you stink."

In a few moments he was standing alone in another empty concrete cube with a single, scratched plexiglass window that looked like it hadn't been cleaned for a long time. His wrist chain was fastened to a waist-high shelf that ran in front of the glass. On another steel shelf behind him sat a row of padlocked metal boxes that contained recording equipment. A camera hung from the ceiling.

Assistant Warden Pat Olson appeared from the shadows on the other side of the window and flicked a light switch.

"Do you hear me okay, mister Jardine?"

"I want to see a doctor," Jardine said, his voice muffled and surprisingly soft inside the small room.

"You look fine to me," Olson said. "I understand you were already treated."

"It's infected, take a look." Jardine said and made a show of turning his face and stretching out his swollen jaw. "It's like a goddamn drunk sewed me up. I'm a fucking mess. My head hurts. They said I could see a dentist. Where's the dentist? I don't see no dentist."

"No profanity, mister Jardine," Olson said calmly. "Not when you're talking to me, understand? You'll learn that around here. Your face, that happened over at Clark County. The State of Nevada has you now. If the physician cleared you, then you're okay to be here as far as I'm concerned."

"I want a real doctor."

"I'll look into it," Olson said. "But I'm told your attorney already requested that you be treated at the clinic in Four Palms, so I suggest that you be patient. We do our best with what we have here."

"I know my rights," Jardine said.

Olson leaned forward and studied Jardine's face. He smirked. "Kind of an unusual look they gave you."

"My lawyer he said you have to fix it. My face. I can't chew. I get headaches. That bitch knocked out my back teeth. I got this noise in my ear that won't go away and..."

"We'll look into it," Olson said. "Like I just mentioned, there's a procedure we have to follow. As soon as we get the word, I'll arrange for you to be transported to the clinic. This facility is in transition, so quite a few things have been delayed and put on the back burner. On top of that, we're short on transport van drivers and have had to contract with a private company, so I assume that might be the reason for the delay. That's all I can promise for now."

"It hurts when I eat. I'm filing a complaint."

"You do that, Mr. Jardine," Olson said. "We have an excellent research library. Legal books. Magazines. All the newspapers you want. Why, our inmates can even use the internet, even though the WiFi out here in the desert is a little spotty. They haven't built the proper cell phone towers out there yet, and what we do have is not up to par. But that will improve once the renovation is underway. I'm sure you'll discover a whole world of people to complain to, Mr. Jardine. Our facility might be old, kind of an antique you might say, but like I said...we do our best with what we have."

Jardine yanked up on the chain. "Well, your best...it stinks." He started to say more, but Olson interrupted him.

"Actually, you're fortunate to be here, Mr. Jardine," he said. "We're part of a private partnership now. Big ideas are coming, an experiment, if you will. That means, in some cases, more freedom in the long run for our inmates. I've begun policies to loosen the screening of inmate mail and other correspondence. There's also the renovation project I just mentioned. You'll have more time outdoors than you ever dreamed of after we expand the general population tiers. Once you feel better, expect to be assigned to one of our construction support crews. You'll receive a small stipend, of course."

"That's a chain gang," Jardine said.

"I disagree," Olson said, smiling. "That would be outdated and illegal. We like to think of it as physical therapy and rejuvenated personal career training. You'll earn a small wage for honest outdoor work that will be good for your body and your soul. There are no traditional isolation units here, but we do have resources for inmates who refuse to cooperate. Given your notoriety...well, you'll be treated somewhat differently. With your history and your sentence, you should embrace this. With the federal charges you have, they could have easily shipped you off to a maximum security hell hole where you'd be staring at those size sixteen shoes of yours twenty-three hours a day. Be grateful that you're with us."

Jardine lowered his head and rubbed his itching ear and stared up at the ceiling camera while Olson read from a list of other policies and procedures that had been drawn up especially for him.

"Given the nature of your crimes," Olson said. "You will not spend nights in the general population tier. You will not be allowed a cellmate. I'm sure you know how certain incarcerated individuals view people like you. Your crimes seem to be a distasteful concept for even the most hardened and violent individuals in a place such as this. We will keep your safety in mind at all times. Any questions?"

"I hope where you put me is cleaner than the shit bucket I'm in now."

Olson shook his head as he stood to walk away. "The language, mister Jardine...should I expect this to be an ongoing problem between the two of us?"

When they returned him to his cell, Jardine lifted the sheet from his bed and examined it carefully before he sat down. He folded the sheet into a neat square, smoothing the creases with his hand, and set is aside. He took his pillow, examined it closely, and propped it against the window so it would be exposed to the sunlight. Spiders liked the stuff inside of pillows. They hated sunshine. They liked to crawl into socks that you leave on the floor. And shoes; don't leave your shoes on the floor. He went to the sink and plugged the faucet with wet toilet paper and he did the same with the drain and the overflow hole.

Above his head he saw the small, finger-sized crack in the corner where the wall met the ceiling. Jardine took some of the wet paper that was still floating in the toilet and he kneeled on the small metal shelf next to the bunk and plugged the hole. You could never be too careful. They could come from anywhere. They liked pillows and blankets and dark holes. There were probably thousands of them living in the dark behind the wall right now, waiting to get in. Making thousands of babies. In an old place like this, they lived under the floor and in the ceiling, just whole bunches of them making babies and multiplying and just waiting to get inside. They could smell you. He had to be careful. The long skinny brown ones, especially. He hated the long skinny brown ones.

– 9 –

He followed the weedy gravel path behind the apartment complex where teenage boys in baggy shorts were skateboarding up the sides of a dry and abandoned swimming pool. Infants wailed and someone shouted gibberish from an open window and a shirtless man stood in a doorway fanning himself with a newspaper as he watched Colt walk up the outside stairs.

The woman's door was already open and when she asked Colt to step inside she immediately pressed the envelope into his hand. She wore the haggard look of someone who hadn't slept for a long time and didn't care if she ever would again.

"You're younger than you sound on the phone, and nice looking. I didn't expect that at all," she said and studied Colt's fitted black shirt and how it stretched across his powerfully muscled chest, the clean and polished shoes, the expensive leather folder held under his arm like somebody headed to a business meeting. She had not thought that such a man could be handsome.

"You must work out. I didn't expect that."

Colt handed back the envelope and when the woman refused to take it he dropped it on the sofa.

"I don't take money," he said.

The woman fanned away her hair with one hand. It was very hot in the small apartment living room and her face was flushed, but when she turned away he could see the wet sparkle on her cheek and the smudged eye makeup. She cleared her throat and wiped away the tear.

Colt looked at the floor. There was a feeling of sordid loneliness here, the air stale with the scent of bleach as if someone was trying the hide another, more disturbing odor.

The ceiling in the raftered third floor apartment seemed too low, as if the builders had run out of construction material. As if this was meant to be an attic. Traffic noise hissed through the screened windows and a broken air conditioner hung at a crazy angle from the wall. The apartment was unfurnished, except for the sofa and little kitchen table and two chairs that stood by themselves against a bare wall, perfectly aligned on each side of the living room doorway. The room was clean, vacuum streaks still on the worn rug. A pot bubbled on the kitchen gas stove beside a jar of instant coffee and the old round-cornered fridge was covered with a child's cartoon drawings fastened with alphabet magnets.

"Mister," the woman sighed. "I don't even know your name."

It seemed like she didn't know what to do with the envelope that she now picked up from the sofa, and so she clutched it against her chest.

"You say he's dead?"

"Quite," Colt said.

"So it's taken care of," she said.

"Yes, of course."

"Tell me what you did to him."

"That's not a good idea."

"Please. It's important to me. I'd like to know."

"I'm sorry," Colt said.

"I still hate him, you know," she said. "If he's gone like you say, I can still hate him all I want."

She looked at the envelope and turned toward the two chairs that seemed placed there in anticipation of house guests. Colt saw the outlines of vanished furniture on the wall: the dusty silhouette of another missing sofa, a former coffee table whose phantom leg marks were still impressed into the rug.

"I'm moving away from this place, you know," the woman said. "Minnesota, maybe. I want a winter. A nice cold winter with dead trees and dirty snow. I want to see a dark sky at noon and watch a rain storm. The desert is okay but it's the same kind of okay every single day. My Tanya never liked the heat. It was me who brought us here. I hate the desert now.

The desert is dead. I don't know why anybody lives here. You can't even sweat, it's so fucking dry all the time. I want to sweat again, do you know what I'm saying?"

The mothers sometimes acted crazy and Colt had resisted coming here, but she had asked. She said she would not believe him unless he came and told her the news in person.

"You won't tell me what you did to him?"

"I'm sorry."

"Couldn't you…"

"We shouldn't talk about it," Colt said. He was hoping the woman would not ask him to sit down. He didn't want to stay long.

"When you asked me to come here," he said. "I thought I was very clear about what I would discuss. To share these things wouldn't help you. I came here as a courtesy because I thought it might make this all easier for you."

"You've never said my name, you know that? It's Karen. Say it."

"Karen," Colt said.

"And my daughter's name. Say it."

"Tanya Ellinger," Colt said.

She stepped away as if she'd suddenly remembered something and carefully straightened the chairs that were already perfectly straight against the wall in the tiny living room, as if expecting someone who might at any moment step through the front door.

They were always so desperate to know the details, Colt thought. Some offered elaborate instructions beforehand, carefully printing everything out on a sheet of paper as if they'd fantasized their inventory of revenge for a long time. They would prepare lists with diagrams showing arrows and circles and precise instructions as to how Colt should proceed. It reminded him of how they must have daydreamed their schematic retribution. He would accept their list of bitter requests and nod patiently and later toss these murder blueprints away, feeling that he had betrayed their trust.

"Did you cut his privates?"

"No," Colt said, wondering if he should share just a few details.

"Tell me you didn't just shoot him. That would be so unfair, a bullet in the head? My lord, what a wasted chance that would be."

She sighed and shook her head as if she'd realized a new and sudden sadness. "I'd be so disappointed if you just shot him."

She kneaded the bulging envelope between her hands. The bills — fives, tens, folded fifties and many singles, bulged out. They were wrinkled and of varying condition and age, as if they'd been carefully set aside, placed faithfully in the envelope over time like someone saving for a gift in a piggybank.

"Funny," she said, holding up the money. "This feels filthy now. The whole thing feels dirty, not like when they gave me your name and it sounded so wonderful. The service you would provide, just like some avenging angel. I didn't expect it to be this way. I thought there would be some joy in it for me. I thought I would just fucking glow with happiness. I just feel heavy and sticky inside."

"But you didn't do anything, Karen," Colt said. "You have nothing to regret."

"You don't understand," she said. "I feel like I've caught a germ. Like he — that sonofabitch, had a cold and he sneezed and now I'm the one who's sick. Don't you get it?"

"Mr. Lee?"

"Oh, Jesus...don't call that asshole a *mister*," she said. "Please don't say his goddamn name in this house. Please. Oh, I wish you hadn't said his name. Now you spoiled it again."

Karen Ellinger, strangely invigorated, laughed madly and then seemed embarrassed by her giddy outburst.

You couldn't allow them to talk on and on, Colt thought. It would get out of control. For their own sake, you had to just report that he had given them what they wanted and then leave. Or better yet do it over the phone in a way that was cryptic and devoid of any emotion. If you showed emotion they would feed on this and their own mindless rage would emerge once more.

Colt explained how the police would soon pay her a visit.

"You already told me that," she said. "We talked on the phone when I first heard about you, and you explained it clearly. I'm not stupid."

"I just want you to understand how they'll ask you questions," Colt said. "Police officers are very skilled in how they ask questions. If you're not accustomed to speaking to law enforcement, they can be very tricky.

They're very devious and patient. If they suspect anything they'll have you sitting all day in a small room and they just won't give up."

"Get out," she said, pointing to the door. "I want you to leave now, mister good-looking, you with the buffed up big muscles. I can see you're trying to act cool and in control and make me feel stupid."

Colt nodded and turned away. He took one more look around the apartment: those chairs and how they were so perfectly placed against the wall, it troubled him. But he certainly knew what was going on.

He remembered to tell her that the man had wept.

She lifted both arms as if she wanted to shoo him away: "Get out!"

She dropped the envelope and picked it up and faced Colt defiantly. She was trembling, her shoulders hunched forward like she'd experienced a chill. She looked at the two chairs as if she was afraid someone might have moved them.

"What a cruel thing to tell me," she said. "I don't care if he apologized, do you understand? That's absolutely meaningless to me. Meaningless." She glanced away as if thinking of something else to say.

"I suppose I thought you would be comforted," Colt said.

"Well, I'm not." She held out the money again, stiff-armed, as if the bills were poison.

"Please, mister," she said. "It makes no sense that you don't take the money. I saved it up. I looked at every dollar I put in the envelope and I thought of what you were going to do. You must have had expenses."

"I never asked you for money."

"God, you keep saying the same things over and over. You're like a robot."

"Please," Colt said. "I have to go. Don't forget about the questions the police will ask you and what we discussed, understand? It's very important for you to do what we discussed. I don't want you to get into any trouble. I'm not concerned about myself."

The smothering heat in the apartment was unbearable. There were no curtains and the sun blazed mercilessly through the dirty window screens. You could see every mark on the walls, every nick and scrape. She'd tried to scrub things down; you could tell by the scratchy wipe marks. She wanted to rub away the history of this place. The dirty rectangles on the walls told where family photographs had once hung.

She kept touching her hair, brushing it back. She fiddled with the envelope, tearing tiny pieces of it away, exposing the thick wad of money inside. Maybe she had been drinking coffee all day long, waiting for him to come. Drinking coffee and not sleeping and waiting for Colt to visit this crazy, baking apartment to confirm the revenge she had dreamed about for so long.

The bathroom door was open, a toothbrush on the sink. She must have sold her furniture to pay him, he thought. The sofa, the living room table. There was no illuminated timer light on the kitchen oven. The electric wall clock had stopped at a certain hour on an unknown day and Colt knew her electricity had been turned off. She had sold everything and then lived in the dark in the place where her daughter had been killed. Colt expected that if he went into the child's bedroom there would still be the blood stains on the floor. He had seen the photos in the police report. She would not have been able to clean such a terrible mess. Even the bio crew hired by the police would not have been able to clean such a mess. Colt had seen in the forensics report that Karen Ellinger had refused to allow the police to enter the apartment once the investigation was completed.

How could she have remained in this place after so much had happened there? Had she tried to clean the bedroom rug? He guessed she had not touched a thing. The bed sat where it was on the night the killer climbed through the bedroom window. Where had Karen Ellinger slept? On the floor next to her daughter's bed, of course. So she could somehow be a mute communicant with that precise moment in time when she might have protected her child. When she might have stayed home that night instead of going to the store and leaving her teenage daughter alone and unprotected.

Colt knew exactly what that feeling was, to have left your family at the mercy of unthinkable evil.

Colt was surprised when she suddenly hugged him sweetly, her cheek pressed against his chest. Her thin, delicate shoulder pushed into him and Colt reluctantly put his arm around her waist. She smelled like hair spray.

"You can't do this kind of thing for long, you know that, don't you?" she said, looking him up and down. "You look like a nice man. The way you dress. That awfully fancy ring on your hand. A nice clean and handsome man. You do this for too long and you'll turn into something else. Something like them. You'll catch what they have, like it's a germ. This world is filled with monsters like them. Walking past you in the street every day, looking just like you and me, but they always want to see if there's a chance for them. If there is, they take it. Feeding on us like those wolves on TV nature shows, hiding in the grass and watching until they can chase us. We never see them until it's too late. Then the wolves just eat us alive."

She held her thumb and forefinger closely in front of Colt's face and pressed them together. She let out that crazy, explosive laugh, her lips spitty. Her eyes got big.

"Everybody, all of us, are this close to the wolves out there every day and we don't even know it."

She breathed deeply. "You won't ever be able to stop. "

She hugged him again. Her sudden familiarity was disarming and uncomfortable.

Paper scraps and food wrappers littered the balcony and when Colt passed an open door a strong monkey stink drifted out. A baby cried from inside the apartment. A man and woman were arguing, the drunken man's voice deep and slurred and the infant kept bawling, trying to catch its breath. An arm reached from the shadows and dropped a plastic sack of garbage outside, and the door slammed shut.

Karen Ellinger followed Colt to the top of the stairway, walking in short mincing steps, and she waved the envelope over her head like someone saying farewell to a loved one from a train station platform.

"Be careful, mister whoever you are," she said.

***

Later, at the Venetian Hotel on this Sunday there seemed to be a brief lull in tourist traffic, a truce between visitors and the visited.

Trying not to think of Karen Ellinger, Colt finished his weekend workout in the nearly empty downstairs gym, this time only arm strength exercises: barbell and heavy bicep curl, three sets, five reps; overhead triceps extensions, followed by a long four-set, ten-rep dumbbell curl that left him with a pleasant ache everywhere on his body. It felt good to hurt this way.

Back in his suite he showered and stood naked in front of the smoked glass window and looked out across the city, its neon casino banners and billboards the only color against the broken bare nothingness of rising dust against the brown hills beyond.

On a glowing billboard along the street below there stood an advertisement for some exotic animal circus act: white tigers leaping through fiery hoops, their smiling masters in jeweled jumpsuits carrying whips. Such happy fakery, Colt thought, remembering what Karen Ellinger had said about animals hunting their prey. The truth about nature, Colt knew, was that nothing about it was beautiful at all. Animals are not tender and kind. Animals eat other animals alive. Animals abandon their young. Nature is only confusion and chaos and one random accident after another, and we mistake this for balance and elegance when it is certainly not. Nature will kill you. You can be kind, but nature will not return the favor. Nature does not think. Nature is not beautiful and it is not polite and it does not listen or remember the past. These brown desert hills will still be brown when this city and its colored lights are gone and there will be no sentimentality for what came before.

He thought again how he should not have visited the woman's apartment. Too much thinking. He assumed he had trained himself not to ponder things too much.

He took his laptop into the lobby and looked up at the painting of the famous Venetian Lion of Saint Mark gazing distrustfully across the great plaza and its canal in miniature beneath the hotel's painted blue fake sky. A gondolier rowed past in a lacquered black boat and lifted his hand in a wave at a young couple who stood nuzzling on a cement bridge, yet another fake of something else.

He sat and carefully thought about things for a while. Karen Ellinger's unhinged soliloquy had bothered him, if only because others like her had seemed so accepting of Colt's vengeance on their behalf.

They did not know, of course. They did not understand.

He studied how the translucent glass statues of women on the lobby wall redirected the bright sunlight. He puzzled over the reproduction of an enormous armillary sphere that stood beneath a frescoed ceiling where cherubs and over-muscled, bearded men in robes squatted on painted clouds, themselves pondering Ptolemaic truths told by this skeleton version of the planet and its impostor polar circles and pretend longitudes and latitudes.

More masquerade landmarks lined the canal that was a mall that was Venice in counterfeit. Only the live shitting pigeons were missing.

There was a poor WiFi signal in the lobby so he went to an empty restaurant where waiters in white aprons stood loitering at the bar.

"I'll have coffee," he said.

"How would you like that?"

"In a cup. Black," Colt said, and pointed at the menu. "And that, please."

"Gaufres au Levain," the waiter said.

"Yes, the waffles."

He answered an email question from a former colleague at the Centers for Disease Control, a micro bacterial research specialist who worked in the Pathologic Evaluation Unit. He'd consulted with him years ago during a project on insect pheromones, in particular the bite necrosis rate of a certain spider species. The brown one, whose photo now appeared as a thumbnail at the corner of his computer screen.

This consultation had been for a murder case in which Colt needed to determine the timeline of a victim's death. The corpse in question, found surprisingly well-preserved and buried in the frozen soil of the suspect's own back yard, had been bitten by a spider whose venom usually causes tissue necrosis that can be measured and compared to the onset of rigor mortis following death.

Jasper:

Regarding your question about con-specific mate-searching attributes provided by certain fatty acids— namely palmitic, linoleic, cisvaccenic and stearic:

The short answer is, yes. Unmated females do indeed exhibit boosted amounts in order to attract a male partner. However, females who have already mated exhibit the same acids, but in less concentrated quantities.

My friend, I have to ask...is this for a project? I've not been keeping up and we've certainly lost touch, but why the sudden interest in these little fellows? You mention a case that you are working on. I thought you had stepped away from the game? If so, I'm happy that you're working again.

It would be good for you, considering. I never had the opportunity to speak to you since our last project, by the way, since I didn't know where to reach you. I hope you'll forgive me. Life takes over and I have had my own share of difficulties these past years. Still, you should know that I have thought of you many times.

Meanwhile, I have shipped your requested quantity of the synthesized 8-methyl, etc., pheromone. Let me know if I can be of further assistance. Please keep in touch. I miss the old days when we worked together while you were at Quantico. Are you consulting now? I've asked around and nobody seems to know where you are. It's like you stepped off the edge of the earth! Please let me know and let us not be strangers.

Best regards,

— Archie

P.S. I almost forgot. Remember when you were curious about the female strategy for attracting the best possible male? Females mostly "advertise" themselves, ground spiders especially, by secreting pheromone on their dragline — the tiny silk thread they trail behind them. The male senses this trail with its forelegs and then simply follows it to the female. If only our own love lives were that simple, heh? Sometimes the female will actually construct an impostor "chemical antenna" on her web, thereby accomplishing the same attractive stimuli. The best time for a male spider to approach the female is immediately after the female's final molt. The male spider, when he discovers the female, destroys the web so other males in the area will not find her. How devious these boys and girls are! The amount of pheromone doesn't need to be much. These fellows will travel thousands of meters to find their love –– the equivalent of you or I walking ten miles for a bit of love. It can, in fact, be a stampede of spiders if there is a concentrated population in the area...many thousands in fact, though the conditions would have to be precise for that to happen. I have never encountered such a case in any natural habitat.

When Colt finished with his polite reply, it took him only moments to access the Division of Human Resources home screen at the Clark County Sheriff's Department, which shared employment details with Las Vegas Metro Police as part of a cost-sharing protocol. He downloaded a few easily accessed files from the Detention Facility motor pool, including a list of deputized contract van drivers who regularly shuttled prisoners between Las Vegas and the prison at Silverheel. Their home addresses, along with work schedules and each driver's upcoming vacation dates, were easily located. A handful of supervising drivers -- deputized private transport techs, they were called, were allowed to take their vehicles home at the end of a shift, and two of those employees lived in the town of Four Palms, where he had already obtained the new clinic's patient appointment schedule.

A few key strokes later and Colt was ticking through a five-year span of case file synopsis reports that had been supervised by Detective Sergeant Francis Savic.

The detective had lately developed a bad habit of clicking on any enticing website or renegade phishing e-mail offering financial advice and/or pre-owned motorcycle parts and sales that caught his fancy. After a few page scrolls, Colt was roaming freely through Savic's linked Police Protective Association account, examining the details of his application for early retirement and the release of certain vested pension benefits. Savic's dues and subscription deduction account conveniently showed another dormant link to a canceled VISA credit card whose settings revealed a suspended monthly debit payable to the Wind Mountain Memory Care Center. After he downloaded those files Colt unlocked scans of Savic's personal police case notes, as well as an abbreviated confirmation of William Parker Jardine's processing paperwork at Silverheel that showed emails between the North Las Vegas Justice Center court clerk and the jail's assistant warden, Patrick Olson.

Colt, after confirming that he had the correct password for Olson's Nevada Corrections Association membership -- it was the same as his Amazon and Nevada Natural Resources Department fishing license accounts, he logged into the health services data account at the prison, specifically the Level 1 inventory procurement code used by Simon Johansen, PA., the prison's clinic supervisor. It took Colt a few moments to cancel a recent supply order, one that would certainly reflect badly on Johansen's competence — he was already on probation for some minor negligence, and this might possibly put the physician assistant's job in jeopardy as an employee of the State of Nevada. Johansen already had two complaints registered, and Colt assumed that a mistake of this nature might likely result in a mandatory action by prison officials. It might even get him fired from his job, something that would indeed put things at the Silverheel clinic in turmoil for a while.

Colt logged out, re-logged into the account with yet another pirated user name, and logged out once more. He connected his burner cell phone to a backup hard drive and was watching the documents transfer to a secure cloud account at his bank in Basel, Switzerland when the waiter came with his $18.00 waffle drizzled with a lumpy blood-red sauce that the menu had described as "...delightful, mouth watering macerated strawberries that will make your taste buds explode with pleasure."

– 10 –

Frank Savic stepped into the dim glow of a cheap table lamp that was stamped with the logo of the old Flamingo Hotel. He noticed a 60s ashtray filled with cigarette butts that was decorated with Elvis silhouettes. The table was sticky with spilled food and crumpled papers and a large black blotch of someone's dry blood.

Savic growled at the flustered rookie patrol officer who was stringing yellow crime scene tape outside the open doorway of room 8B at the Starbright Motor Lodge.

"I need more light, please," Savic said, trying to remain professionally un-grumpy while he tightened the surgical face mask that was already pinching the back of his ears. Everybody else had on a mask, too. He hated wearing a mask but the memo from Monaghan said everybody had to wear one for safety and cleanliness at any crime scene that had not yet been cleared by the lab's bio team. The placed smelled like shit, so Savic happily strapped on his blue paper face covering.

He barked at another young uniformed officer: "Can you open the shades? And sweet holy Jesus, get a fan in here!"

He'd rushed away early from his morning visit with Maria after getting a call from some preachy department IT dweeb who said he was going to rat on the detective unless he cleaned up his internet browsing habits. Monaghan had forced him to take a computer class that winter, thanks to Savic's sloppy adherence to an office policy about not opening email attachments or clicking on unfamiliar links. Savic didn't even know what a link was and when he complained that the new laptop they'd given him was acting strange, they said the thing had been infected with a virus that might have blown through the entire office network. Monaghan had given him a five minute speech about that...about these things called viruses. This time, he'd been trying to find newspaper coverage back east in Virginia about the home invasion and murder of a mother and her two children. William Parker Jardine had been vaguely linked to that crime and Savic was following up on a hunch, downloading some sketchy articles and conversation threads from amateur crime bloggers, when his computer suddenly froze and went dead. Crashed, is what they called it. They never spoke English, these people. Links that were sick with viruses and computers that crashed and people that tried to phish you, whatever the hell that meant. The IT guy, who spoke slowly to Savic like a kindergarten teacher talking to a toddler, that morning advised the detective who had helped solve nearly 300 murder cases in his career, to ask the procurement department to help him with in his on-line research.

Savic took out his new cell phone and snapped a few photos.

The hanging corpse drooped en crucifixus from the ceiling, limp arms hanging over a rope torso loop like some marble relief carving of a saint on a church wall. The man's garroted neck was pinched tight like a twisted sack, the head jerked sideways like he was studying the wall of the shabby hotel room. As if he was avoiding someone's gaze.

Thick slobber was crusted on the victim's chin, the dark dried blood covering his chest in a manner that told Savic the sonofabitch had been dangling there for a long time before he died. A long tangle of gray viscera, the tips of sprung rib bones revealing an exposed heart and lobes of dark and dried lung tissue, swung from the long straight incision on the man's belly and lay gathered on the rug like a hunter's gut pile. One of the man's arms seemed to point down awkwardly as if he was calling attention to the mess below his own suspended feet.

That is, if he had feet, which Savic immediately noticed he didn't.

The young patrol officer -- they all looked like they were sixteen years-old these days -- who was trying his best to avoid looking at the hanging body, came with a portable tri-pod light and a UV lamp and handed Savic an extension cord, remarking that the victim looked kind of like a scarecrow. Savic gave him a look and gruffly said to go get the hotel manager, who'd been told to wait in the hallway while the police did their work.

"And some baggies," he said. "Bring the baggies."

Savic tried to plug the extra light into the blackened plastic wall socket and saw that the fuse was probably blown. He tried another socket on the same wall and then used the standard outlet below the front window, the one next to the 220 plug above the disconnected air conditioner. He leaned and smelled the lingering fishy ozone odor of burned electrical wire and unscrewed the first socket and examined it and then lay it carefully upside down on the floor, assuming the techs would take it to the lab.

Outside on the motel walkway a crowd of gawkers had already gathered behind the caution tape, some of them covering their mouths with their hands as they tried to catch a look at the murder scene.

This was a place where people rented rooms by the hour or the month. The half-filled swimming pool outside, littered with leaves and floating plastic shopping bags, was painted bright pink and most of the nearby playground equipment was draped with drying laundry. Across the street two officers were trying unsuccessfully to enter a locked vehicle with a rubber air shim. They had already placed little plastic evidence flags in the street, where another squad car with lights flashing sat parked at an angle, redirecting traffic.

Thumping music blared from somebody's open car trunk. Shirtless boys clowned around in the parking lot, making amused hand gestures and shouting taunts at the policemen who came and went from the room.

The motel sat alone on a desolate street where empty gravel lots outnumbered the occupied buildings. Savic remembered when the gas station next door was a Texaco where a courteous attendant in a monogrammed shirt and cap changed your oil and handed out free highway vacation maps. Now it looked like a bomb had dropped on it.

Somebody switched on the portable tripod lamp and the room was flooded in a bright, peachy light, thanks to the weirdly colored shag rug and the pond of dried blood that lay beneath the hanging corpse.

While Savic and a crime scene technician were figuring out how to unsling the garroted dead guy from his wire noose, another detective was swabbing the bathroom toilet bowl with a long cotton-tipped stick. Somebody in the hallway was pushing a loud shop vac across the flooded floor.

The masked technician picked curly hair samples from the shower stall wall. He stepped out and held up a baggy containing a crumbled white substance and held it to the light.

"Could be boric acid in the drain. Some kind of hydrochloric, maybe. And fresh enough to still be white," he said. "Won't know for a while. Might just be Liquid Plumber that's been in there for a while"

Savic pointed at the toilet.

"Yeah, if somebody went potty something will show up," the tech said. "Might have to get a plumber to take out the wax seal."

Savic studied the drywall ceiling where a perfect rectangle had been cut in order to access a wooden rafter on which the thick wire and heavy rope had been anchored with three large hook screws.

"Somebody used a power saw for that," he said. "Those screws? Too big and deep to do it by hand. He had tools."

"The tech showed Savic the half empty beer bottle from the fridge before he dropped it into a large sealed baggie. "This should get us something," he said. "It smells like it's been scrubbed. We'll check it out, anyway."

Savic side-stepped past what looked like a partial bloody footprint and looked outside.

"Seems like two highly trained law enforcement professionals could figure out how to break into a damn car. What is it with those guys?"

"The lock was jimmied with a toothpick," the tech said. "And recently, from what I could see. I asked them not to break the window glass before we took prints. The plates are hot. Stolen four days ago from a middle school parking lot over in Henderson."

"How long before that toilet can talk to us?" Savic said and walked up behind the hanging naked corpse and took another picture of the ceiling with his phone. A thin trickle of dried blood wiggled down the victim's back from a puffy welt on his shoulder. There was a deep, circular bruise on his neck apart from the wound caused by the wire noose, as if something else had been tied there.

"This isn't the Marriott, Frank," the tech said. "I don't think anybody's cleaned the place for a while. Front desk shows they had twenty-five check-ins this week. Manager says the last guest for this room paid cash by the month. The door was sprung. Maybe a screwdriver. Not sure yet if this was the deceased's room."

Savic studied the battered chair which still held the puckered impression of the last person who had sat on it.

"According to the guest ledger," the tech said, "...the rooms on both sides were rented by another individual. They're checking it out."

Savic pointed at the print on the rug. "He wore booties to cover his shoes, look."

The man's swollen blue tongue looked like a gorged snail was trying to crawl from his gaping mouth. Savic took another disposable paper mask from the tech's kit bag and held it to his nose. Another uniformed officer walked in and began reciting dryly from a notepad: "Manager said somebody came by early this week and paid in advance for three days for the two other rooms but never actually checked in until last night. Said there was a Do Not Disturb card on the door handles of both rooms. Oh, and they wanted me to tell you there's blood on the street over by that vehicle."

Savic mumbled from behind the mask and stepped away from the hanging body. "That head is about to come off," he said. "Better figure out how to get him down before we get a bigger mess."

There was a bright camera flash that projected a brief, elongated silhouette of the corpse against the mustard-yellow wallpaper.

Savic squatted and studied the rug. He pointed toward the door. "He started bleeding there and then got up on that chair. Somebody bothered to measure for the stud in the ceiling. There's a pencil mark up there. How much do you think he weighs?"

The patrol officer grinned at Savic. "Before or after his feet got cut off?"

"I'm in charge of tasteless jokes around here," Savic said.

"I guess one-sixty or so, maybe more," the officer said.

Savic took another photo. "That wire had to be connected to the ceiling before the man got up on that chair, which means it was already around his neck when he was on the floor. Where he was already bleeding. Whoever lifted him was pretty damn strong. I doubt if this guy hopped up there voluntarily."

The technician, who had been using a tweezer to pick up pieces of bone matter from the thickly napped rug, tugged off his mask.

"The body's been here so long it might take a while to process. Rigo starts at the feet, but with this kind of torso trauma and the fact that he's totally bled out, and I mean totally, like a dressed deer...It'll have to wait for the lab profiles. And, of course, there are no feet."

"Somebody also made sure the sink overflowed," Savic said, wagging his hand toward the bathroom and looking at where the victim's two severed feet, the white tube socks still on, now stood side-by-side on a bloody rubber mat near the door like they were a pair of shoes.

The two men stepped into the bathroom and looked at the wet towel on the floor.

"I thought the same thing," the tech said. "Both faucets on full throttle, the towel shoved into the overflow. Whoever did this wanted somebody to come into the room, but not too quickly."

Another detective, after shooing away the growing crowd of spectators outside, stepped into the room and handed Savic a labeled Kraft paper evidence bag.

"Our vic is no Boy Scout," he said. "Name is Earl Lee. Joey Anders from Admin recognized him right away when I called it in. Has a history as long as a roll of potty paper. Walked free after a trial technicality back when that sloppy work at the DA's office made us all look like shit. What a nightmare year that was. Our boy here was up for murder one in a juvenile homicide, a no-doubt case, but the charges didn't stick. They arrested him two months later for petty retail theft and he drew a month in county jail. Anders worked the case before he got transferred upstairs and he tells me the verdict got overturned because the trial got compromised when they found out an assistant DA was engaged to somebody on the jury. While he was in county custody some alert judge managed to place him on a temporary hold because there was a chance of a re-trial on the original murder charge."

"Like Cavilleri over in Four Palms?" Savic said.

"Yeah, it was a banner year," the tech said. "Lee was on his way to a hearing when the Corrections Department transport van got in a traffic accident over on Decatur and Sahara, and our friend here escaped with four other inmates. That's when they started contracting out the transport service and doing that goofy deputizing thing with the drivers. From what I hear, that's not working out much better."

"Cops with badges used to do the driving," Savic said. "The union brass didn't like the change."

In the evidence bag was an eight-by-ten portrait photo of a smiling girl dressed in knee socks, white blouse and a plaid skirt. She was posed sitting on a straight-backed chair positioned against a wall hung with family portraits. A tidy little apartment, it seemed. A sofa with doilies on the arm rests. She was holding a plaque wrapped in a blue award ribbon that said, *St. Barnabas High School Volleyball.*

"Found it just laying on the sofa."

"Is it dusted?"

"Nothing there," the detective said. "You could tell it was wiped. There's brand new scratches on the emulsion. It wasn't laser printed."

Savic lifted the victim's wallet from the bag with his gloved hand.

"Hundred-fifty bucks. Twenties and tens. A paycheck stub," the other detective said. "Three condoms that have been in there long enough to dry up. Two bogus social security cards. A sloppy Utah driver's license printed on an ink jet. The laminate was trimmed with scissors. Looks like he worked construction on the new I-15 highway spur. A temp help day crew out of Vegas, according to the pay stub. We're checking it all out."

"This guy had a warrant out on him and he stayed in town and parked a car with hot tags in plain sight on the street? Then he somehow gets hired by a temp service." Savic said. "There must be an epidemic of stupid germs around here."

"I thought you were cutting back your hours, Frank?" the detective said. "Heard you were catching the retirement bus. Congrats on the Jardine case, by the way. The world's a better place with that ass wipe off the street."

Savic peeled off his glove and tossed it into the white hazmat bag that sat in the middle of the floor. He crumpled the mask and banked a shot off the ceiling, missing the bag. Two men came with a ladder and snipped the ceiling wire and lowered the body onto a wheeled gurney and covered it with a tarp.

"This was supposed to be an easy month for me after that trial," Savic said. "Some union paperwork, a few long lunches. Get to work at ten, leave at three and maybe have a beer with somebody. Plenty of time to take care of a few personal things that were on the back burner. Afraid those plans are on hold for a while. Cap wants me to finish up a couple of loose ends."

"Speaking of loose ends, what do you make of that?" the detective said, watching as the tech picked up Earl Lee's feet with a pair of tongs and placed them inside a Styrofoam box. He sealed the box and signed his name across the strip of red tamper warning tape with a Sharpie.

"Some fastidious psycho who wants to play games," Savic said. "Somebody who knows his way around a hardware store. Somebody who plugged something into that wall socket over there and blew it up. I doubt if this dump is up on its electrical code. You see where those feet were?"

"Like slippers waiting for daddy to come home," the detective said.

"Listen," Savic said. "Check with the examiner and get the notes on what was used to cut this guy open. Lee was hung and strung like a butcher did it. There's some skill involved."

"Like that thing with whatshisname in the desert?"

"Sounds too simple, doesn't it? This guy leaves a lot of dirty evidence behind, but he takes the time to wipe prints off that picture, and we still don't know why it was left here in the first place. I bet the window was open when he killed our boy. Even this dump has air conditioning. It was over ninety degrees last night. I bet if you plugged that AC back in it would work just swell. But he leaves the window open and that chair was dragged on that seedy-ass shag rug from the damn window. You can see the marks. He was watching for something. And then he bothers to put a half-empty beer bottle into the fridge, but first he scrubs it."

The technician came out of the bathroom holding a tiny sheet of wet paper with his tongs. He put it in another baggy and gave this to Savic, who held it up against the light.

"Hard to see anybody in this neighborhood with an admission ticket to a fancy art show."

"From behind the toilet," the tech said. "I lost a wallet like that once."

"Get the manager in here," Savic said.

Savic studied the ceiling. "Took a while to cut that so nice and careful, drill those holes and then clean out the bathtub drain. He didn't leave the picture of the girl by accident. He plugs the sink, but we know why he did that. But then he doesn't take the victim's wallet with the I.D. I'm getting way too old for this job."

He kneeled and looked at the gouts of blood on the rug. The tech had circled the stains with chalk, a long splatter that trailed from the door to the sofa. There were more drag marks on the rug. The tech had placed a numbered white sticker on the largest blotch and propped up directional arrows next to the skidding track on the rug.

Savic saw a pair of Nike track shoes march into the room. They were attached to a pair of spindly, extremely hairy legs.

The motel manager, dressed in cargo shorts and a Los Angeles Dodgers tee shirt, extended his hand and introduced himself. He was smelly. Garlic, sweat and tangy aftershave, the trio of odors distinct, as if coming from separate body orifices.

"I am Harold," the man said with a thick, slavic accent.

Savic put the bagged art gallery ticket in his pocket, something that the tech people might give him grief about, since they should be the first to process the evidence. He stepped to look at where the ceiling paint and drywall gypsum powder had pulled away when they removed the body.

"Harry," Savic began, still studying the screws that had been so sturdily fastened to the ceiling joist.

"You don't mind if I call you Harry, do you? Okay, let's begin. I want to know why an astute lodging and hospitality industry professional such as yourself, who is in his office not more than twenty meters away — three rooms down to be exact, doesn't hear it when one of his guests gets strung from the ceiling like a butcher shop pig. You have to think there was just a little bit of screaming, don't you agree? Maybe he said ouch once or twice?"

"Officer..." The man tried to avoid looking at the mess on the carpet.

"Sergeant," Savic said. "You got a last name or are you a famous rock star?"

"Sahkno," the manager said. "Harold Sahkno."

Harry Sahkno was short and thick. Chest wool sprouted from behind his shirt collar. His werewolf beard line went up to his eyes. He was sweating wet moons under both arms. He kept rubbing his hands like they were cold, though it was bacon-frying hot outside. His shaved head made it look like the top of his noggin was dirty. He wore gold jewelry, though Savic figured it wasn't real gold, like the story he now expected to hear.

"I am certain I have music on and it was very busy," Harry said.

Something in Harry's pants pocket played a tune, a few bars of a familiar nursery rhyme. Harry pulled out the flip style cell phone with a flourish. He spoke sharply in another language and returned the phone to his pocket.

Savic thumbed through the guest ledger handed to him by one of the uniformed officers.

"Okay, looks like not too many people checked into this world-famous resort last week. Not exactly the AMA convention."

He read the names until he came to the room number.

"So, a Mr. Johnson checks in for a week and wants both adjacent rooms. He has the Do Not Disturb sign up the whole time, is that right?"

The cell phone rang again. Harry Sahkno shrugged apologetically and spoke in a hushed voice. Ukrainian, some other Balkan language? Slightly Bulgarian. Probably Russian, Savic decided. Harry the hairiest person who ever lived slipped the phone back into his pocket and smiled sheepishly. Harry's round head sat in a ruff of black fur that encircled his double chin like a bird's nest.

"Some peoples want they are alone," Harry continued. "This is correct, what you say. He gave the instructions not to disturb. He himself put sign on door."

"How much was his privacy worth, Harry? You didn't think it was unusual that he wanted to get private in both rooms at the same time?"

Harry looked offended. "I am a naturalized citizen, you know."

"Never mind that," Savic said, wagging his finger. "Don't start that crap. My parents were immigrants, so I'm not interested in your status or where you came from. Don't pull that shit on me. I love and cherish all of humanity in each of its wonderful flavors, you know what I'm saying?"

The cell phone rang again. This time Savic grabbed it from Harry's hand and spoke into the phone.

"Pogrešan broj," he said and slapped the phone down on the peeling kitchenette counter top next to the fridge.

"You are not being nice," Harry said. "You speak another language?"

"You're observant," Savic said.

"I am a citizen of the U.S.A."

"Congratulations. I'll salute in a minute and we can both recite the names of the first ten presidents. Let me ask you again, how much did this mister Johnson pay you to stay in this bacteria-riddled urinal?"

"Four hundred."

"On top of the room rate?"

"This is correct. For both rooms."

"So he rented two rooms and gave you some juice on top of that. That's not what you wrote down on the guest register," Savic said.

"Well, let me explain..."

"No need to explain, Harry," Savic said, grinning. "You're not the first innkeeper in this town to play games with the hotel occupancy tax. I get it. I'm actually not too concerned with that right now."

Harry gazed longingly at his phone. It rang again. He shrugged. Sweat beaded up on his big round head, little droplets, one of which suddenly raced down the side of his jowly face.

"You didn't think that was strange, him paying that much?"

Savic stared over at the ringing cell phone, its throbbing green screen light reflecting against the scratched, laminated kitchen counter.

"Mister sergeant," Harry said. "You are noticing that our customers they are not traditional. Many transient peoples. Peoples from the road, as you say. Mens who have been kicked away from their house by their wifes and business girls, too..."

"Excuse me?" Savic said.

"Business girls," Harry said with practiced enunciation, the kind you picked up at the English night school over on Coronado Avenue. He made a circle with his thumb and forefinger and pushed another finger through it and gave a lewd grin.

"Hookers?"

"Yes, the hookers, of course. The business girls," Harry said.

He smiled through widely spaced teeth, Chicklet chewing gum teeth. Big front bunny rabbit teeth. Savic imagined what would happen if he took a match to this guy's jungle of chest hair. Poof, like campfire tinder.

Harry continued: "It is not my custom to ask why a man he wants the privacy. Maybe it will be sex. Maybe he is making the porno. I am a businessman, too. I hear the screams and I think it is part of why he needs the privacy. You know, screaming for the film. Maybe it is a sexuality party with homosensuals, you know. It is not my business who he has in the rooms. In America the privacy is important, no? I learn this in the citizen school. I am not the village priest, you understand? This is not my job to sit on them."

"Excuse me?"

"To sit on them."

"Babysit?"

"Yes, to be babysitter. Yes, of course."

"Well," Savic said.

With those big front teeth and the slight lisp it sounded like he just said *babyshitter*.

"Business has not been very good lately," Harry Sahkno said, sadly. "Four hundred dollars cash is very important to me."

"Tell me what this Johnson looked like."

"I am not remembering," Harry said, looking up in solemn amazement at where Earl Lee's body had once hung. There were speckles of blood fanned out on the dirty ceiling like somebody had flicked a wet paintbrush. The same on the wall, where a foot-wide swath of rust-red went from the floor to the ceiling, like the start to some abstract expressionist work of art. Jackson Pollack using blood in a squirt gun.

Savic, annoyed, spoke louder. "Was he short and dumpy like you or tall and extremely handsome like me?"

"This I am not remembering," Harry Sahkno said, not quite certain if he should smile.

"You just blushed, Harry," Savic said. "In my experience, that's not a good sign."

Savic had been observing the man closely. After all these years it just came as a habit, studying what people did when they talked. It was "perception management," sorting out the unconscious ways people sent their signals. The self-soothing way they crossed their hands after they answered a question; the interlaced fingers showing that something was troubling them. It was a poker game of back and forth body communication: you do this, and I'll do that. Shift over your chair in the interrogation room. Caging a hand of cards at a casino table wasn't much different from dragging your palm across your own cheek when confronted with an uncomfortable question. Babies are expert face readers, but most adults have forgotten the skill.

The cell phone rang again.

Savic took the phone and opened the refrigerator door. A cold, beery stink drifted out. The inside was an archaeological wonderland of ketchup spills and bits of mummified food. He saw a moldy yogurt cup wrapped in cellophane. The cell phone was still playing its kiddie tune. Savic tossed the thing into the fridge and slammed the door.

"Harry," he said. "I remember when this dump was a decent place. Now, because of what I do for a living, I've come to know everybody at the department of health, the secretary of state's office...you name it. Why, the head engineer at Sanitation is a gambling buddy and our wives used to go see Tom Jones together at the Flamingo. I guess he wouldn't mind doing a favor for me, like you having trouble with your trash pick-up or your water pressure. Or maybe I should drop a note telling people that you've got a few code violations here. Bad wiring, a little short on properly certified fire extinguishers, shit like that. How about an audit by the state revenue folks? I see a lot of cash transactions here and I bet, as you've just demonstrated, you haven't been too tidy with keeping the books on the two percent hotel occupancy tax they passed a few years back. Shall I continue?"

He retrieved the cell phone from the fridge. It was cold in his hand.

"Should I call now? On this bogus throw-away phone? Just so they have a record of where it pings on whatever tower this thing has pinged on in the last week? I'm told they can do that. Don't ask me how. After that, it gets too weird for me and I get a technology headache. Sorry."

Harry sighed. "I am understanding you, mister sergeant," he said. "The Johnson man, he was not tall as you. He had the very big muscles. A very handsome man. A younger man. The big strong neck. Like peoples have in the gym."

Harry held his open hands apart in front of his face, like somebody measuring a fish.

"He had a big neck, like this. And he was dressing too nice for here. Shoes shined. I think maybe here is a lawyer, a businessman. I do not see a car and he does not write his license number. He is saying nothing. Only signs the book. No smile. He says he wants the privacy and he puts the money in my hand. This is all Harold knows."

"You still have the cash?"

"I am taking it fast to the bank. I have a backwards real estate taxes payment due from last year. They take automatically every month from my account and I am short and so I rush in a hurry downtown very fast. And it is not good idea to have so much cash here, you understand. There are the robberies. The peoples in this neighborhood make many robberies."

"Harry in a hurry, huh?" Savic said.

"The lights are off each night," Harry said. "Believe me when I say he gives me no trouble. I have much troubles with people, but this quiet clean man he pays cash and he gives me no trouble and he dresses nice, so why should I worry or ask the questions?"

"Did he rent a movie? Get ice? I noticed you have the last telephone booth in the United States of America hanging on the wall just down the hall. Did he use that?"

"Everyone has the cell phone today. He did not use the telephone in the hall. They want to charge me fifty dollars too take away to junk store, so I leave it there."

"Of course," Savic said, suddenly feeling as if was being a little rough on this guy. "How about a movie?"

"No. But we have good movies," Harry said.

"I bet you do," Savic said. He handed back the chilled cell phone.

"Harry, please fix that thermostat and get somebody to look at your fuse box. You also got a loose wire hanging from the fire exit light. Wouldn't want to have this place be unsafe, would you?"

On the way out Savic was hailed by one of the other detectives, who walked up still holding his phone to his ear.

"That picture we found?" he said. "It's the kid Lee killed two years ago over in that apartment on Charleston Street. The one with the lady who said she wanted to clean up the place herself. Wouldn't let the hazmat people inside. Had to get a court order for the bio crew to go and finally scrub things down, and even then she yelled at them and wouldn't leave."

– 11 –

A tennis match was underway on the lobby waiting room TV where a row of Wind Mountain residents in wheel chairs sat entranced, their heads twitching from side to side as they followed the ball across the 72-inch screen. Two men in slippers and sweat pants struggled with a stuck puck at the Foosball table while a quartet of serious women sat playing cards off their laps on a corner sofa cluttered with magazines and newspapers.

Somebody scored in the TV tennis game and a few people mumbled softly and the two men at the Foosball table started arguing, one of them shouting, "And you can just shove it up your ass!" which quickly brought Nurse Fahey running over from the reception desk, her hands held high like an officiating referee attending to a sports dispute.

Frank Savic sat waiting in the lobby while Maria was getting checked by her doctor, so he fiddled with the new department cell phone they'd issued him, practicing his left-to-right swiping technique. He'd never swiped much before, except on the iPad somebody in IT had given him, but this was different. The old flip phone didn't need swiping. He hated to swipe. He felt like an ignorant candy ass and the keyboard buttons were too small for his big fingers. When he tried to dial Maria's name under "M" he always got Mario's Pizza & Pasta Palace over on Paloverdi Avenue by mistake. Even with the very tip of his giant sausage finger it always came up Mario instead of Maria and this small annoyance inexplicably crushed down on him like a great weight. Such a toy, he thought. Every chance they got they made your life more complicated, those evil plotting people in IT. He felt stupid and hopelessly inept.

From the cafeteria at the end of the long hallway came the echoing sound of someone singing a Woody Guthrie folk song. It was a woman's voice and she was hollering like Ethel Merman to the accompaniment of the home's out-of-tune upright piano. Breakfast plates clattered in the kitchen and Savic knew this must be Dog Visit Day because a man came walking down the hall with a leashed Golden Retriever wearing a speckled bandanna around its neck.

Up at the front counter Savic watched and listened as a tall woman, maybe in her thirties, with high shiny boots and a short dress and sweeping eyelash makeup that gave her a Hollywood Cleopatra go-go girl look, signed her name into the visitor register. She was 58.7 percent dressed, maybe a 60, tops. She chatted for a while, her pleasant young laugh mixing with the sound of the tennis match on TV and the garbled bickering of the two old Foosball farts who were still arguing over god-knows-what; maybe the score, maybe politics, maybe whoever won the World Series in 1947. The troublesome puck was still stuck in the hole behind the plastic Foosball goal tender and now Nurse Fahey was there trying to mediate things, like she always does. She's the Henry Kissinger of the compression stocking crowd, always drawing up peace treaties between residents at the Wind Mountain Memory Care Center.

The visiting Golden Retriever barked and the lady in the cafeteria now started singing a Bob Dylan tune.

The young lady at the front counter, who had long Rockettes at Radio City Music Hall dancing legs, she's smiling and nodding while one of the Foosball men, obviously the one in the wrong in this altercation, folds his arms indignantly and shakes his head and says: "I hate this fucking place. I'm calling the attorney general or the mayor or whoever runs this stuff and I'm lodging an official complaint! You'll be hearing from my lawyer!"

And off he marches -- actually marches in his nappy fuzzy slippers with the back heels smashed down, like he's a drum major in a Sousa band, and high-steps down the hallway, his sweat pants sagging south below his butt crack, way past the Tropic of Cancer, half way down through South America and thus exposing way too much white chicken skin and atrophied ass cheeks, continuing past the mouth of the Amazon River, until Marco the orderly runs up from behind laughing and helps him organize his faltering wardrobe. Helps him hike up his flannel sweatpants.

Even ties the little string at the front into a convenient bow and then taps the old man gently on the shoulder and guides him to his room, where he starts shouting more oaths with detailed references to the United States Constitution.

Chief Wind Mountain Peace Negotiator Nurse Fahey shakes her head and greets Savic with a patient smile and both of them roll their eyes while watching Cleopatra charm the staff up at the front desk.

"Who's that?" Savic said.

"Marvin Albright over in 119. She's with the family," Nurse Fahey said.

"The family you say. Like a relative?"

"Why yes, she visits twice a week at exactly this time on the same days. Doesn't stay very long, but at least she visits. Very nice girl."

"Isn't Marvin the one who got caught picking the lock on the cafeteria supply room?"

"Well, yes," Nurse Fahey said. "But that's been straightened out now. He was a locksmith, you know. Owned a shop for many years on El Tejon. He said he wanted a snack. I reminded him that there was no cooked food in the rooms after ten o'clock. But everything is okay now. He's eighty-three years old. Just wanted a little adventure, I suppose."

Cleopatra took lipstick and a mirror from her glittery purse.

"So, she's with the family, you say?" Savic said.

"Oh, yes. Nice girl," Nurse Fahey said.

They watched the young woman wave and turn down the hallway toward Marvin Albright's room. Marco the orderly was mopping up something next to the snack machine and he stopped what he was doing and turned and took a long look as the woman walked past, her high boot heels clacking on the linoleum floor.

Savic turned to Nurse Fahey. "While we're here, I wanted to ask you something about Mrs. Blasky. She's next door to Maria."

Somebody came up to Nurse Fahey with a clipboard and she signed papers for the new piano player they were hiring for Sing-a-long Tuesday, which was also Spaghetti and Meatballs Tuesday, which was one of everybody's favorite days at the home. Savic had taken Maria to lunch the week before when Gloria from 210 sang a pretty good non-Ethel rendition of *There's No Business Like Show Business*. They did an Irving Berlin medley, too, and then the whole place exploded with everybody singing

Simon and Garfunkle's *Bridge Over Troubled Waters* at the top of their lungs like it was the very last tune any of them would ever sing again.

"She's one of our quiet ones, Mrs. Blasky," Nurse Fahey said. "What did you want to ask? I have a meeting in a few minutes and..."

"Well, it's about her pajamas," Savic said. "The green pajamas with the buttons."

"The buttons."

"Yeah, the buttons," Savic said. "I remember, because you said my wife shouldn't have zippers on her clothes because they get snagged. So I brought the green pajamas and two other sets. With the buttons, like you said."

"Are we talking about Mrs. Blasky or your wife, Mr. Savic?"

"Both, actually," Savic said. "Mrs. Blasky is wearing my wife's pajamas today. It's not the first time. I thought maybe Maria gave them to her, but I don't think she did because it happened before and they don't really get along, the two of them. But Mrs. Blasky keeps wearing Maria's pajamas – – the green ones, the blue ones. Do you understand what I'm saying?"

"Well, sometimes things get mixed up in the laundry room."

"I do her laundry," Savic said. "I clean her clothes every Sunday and bring her fresh things on Monday. So, it's no mix-up in the laundry room."

"Sometimes there's an accident and we have to clean somebody's clothes, Mr. Savic. Maybe that's what happened. Your wife had an accident and we had to clean her pajamas and things got mixed up."

"Maybe, but I've brought her six new pajamas this month and I've never seen her wear any of them, not once, but I see Mrs. Blasky and guess what? And that's not all. The old Spanish lady, Esmeralda, who always talks to herself outside by the garden...she's been wearing them. And the two Norwegian sisters, Olma and Gretchen, well, the other day they were wearing the two sets of yellow pajamas I brought the week before. And Maria? She doesn't have accidents. She hasn't had an accident since she got here. My wife does not have accidents."

"We do our best, Mr. Savic," Nurse Fahey said. "With what we have, we do our best. I'll look into it, I promise."

Savic glanced at his watch. He stood and followed Nurse Fahey down the hall. He was ready to turn into Maria's room when he saw Carlo leaning on his push broom with a big grin on his face, smiling broadly at

Nurse Fahey like he couldn't contain himself. He waved both her and Savic over.

The three of them stood in front of Room 119 and listened.

It sounded like somebody was practicing bird calls. Or the chittering of a wounded small animal, and as Nurse Fahey leaned closer there came a breathless staccato grunting and the creaking of bedsprings followed by a yammering woman's voice that answered Marvin Albright's stern exclamation with, "...oh...right there!"

A few other very specific directional requests went suddenly silent when Nurse Fahey knocked loudly on the door, but after a pause they resumed with new urgency and with her hand on the door knob Nurse Fahey said aloud that she could feel the tiny percussions of Mr. Albright's bed knocking against the wall.

"Mister Albright? Please, mister Albright, is everything okay in there?"

After a time, in a breathless voice, he answered. "Yeah, I'm fine."

There was the sound of rustling and quick footsteps and furniture being moved around and then a woman giggling, followed by a loud whisper.

"I'll be right out," Marvin said.

"Does he do this a lot?" Savic whispered to Marco, who smiled and moved to the side and watched as Nurse Fahey pressed her ear against the door.

"And she really doesn't know what's going on?"

"None of them do," Carlo said.

"He's eighty-three?" Savic said.

"Oh, it's more than that," Carlo said. "Him and Jamal and another guy here have something going. Jamal's girlfriend works for a Urologist and those two have a nice little side gig selling boner pills. Fifty bucks a pop, I think. He does good business, mister Albright. His little friend there —her name is Misty, she visits all the time."

"And Fahey, she doesn't know..."

Carlo picked his tooth and looked at his finger and smiled: "That he's got a hooker who makes house calls? Who drives here in a new Mercedes? No, none of them know crap about what really happens around here."

Misty Cleopatra stepped from the room smoothing her blouse and swiping back her hair with one hand. She gave a sheepish grin and walked quickly toward the back emergency exit.

"Hey, you can't go out that door!" Nurse Fahey said, and the woman turned and quickly trotted as best as she could in those heeled boots through the lobby and out the front door.

Nurse Fahey shrugged and spread apart her hands and looked at Savic.

"And you're just letting her leave, just like that? I think I know what's going on here. Shouldn't you question her or something?"

Savic shook his head. "I'm in the homicide division and nobody died here today as far as I can tell. And I already know what the answers are if I talked to her. It's a waste of time. You know how many hookers there are in this town?"

"I certainly do not," Nurse Fahey said.

"Well, more than I want to spend time hauling back to the station for an interview. But I think you have a much bigger problem here and unless that gets straightened out it's something I absolutely will report. I should really call my office right now, but so far it's only a lonely old man who's looking for a little company."

"What's that?" Nurse Fahey watched while Marvin Albright poked his head into the hallway, looked both ways, and then retreated back into his room.

"Doctor Bony, MD over there may be engaged in the illegal peddling of prescription medication. I suggest you give him a talk and tell him somebody could get sick if he sells it to the wrong person."

Nurse Fahey gave Marco a stern look, and the orderly nodded.

"And you knew about this?" she said.

"Pretty much everybody does, ma'am," Marco said. "Everybody knows about Marvin and his pills. They call him and his pal the Blues Brothers."

– 12 –

It began for Colt with Mr. and Mrs. Foster.

The very wealthy Fosters, the Mayflower blue blood New England Fosters with their grand summer home situated like an impenetrable stone fortress on a private and lushly landscaped peninsula jutting into Lake Squamaqua, New Hampshire. The Fosters who once felt safe and protected by their money.

Spencer and Cleora Foster had not returned to their vacation family paradise since the night their son was murdered.

Years after his death, most of the furniture in the home had remained draped in white sheets, the locked and empty boat house abandoned to the swallows that now nested beneath its shingled shake roof. Where the Fosters' classic thirty-six foot mahogany speedboat once rested on its dockside power lift, there now sat a small fishing skiff tied to a rusting cleat that belonged to the property's year-round caretaker. There were simply too many memories here for them ever to return.

Everything was abandoned, all that once seemed so important now put aside and neglected. It was a home filled with ghosts that nobody in the family wanted to live in again.

Mr. and Mrs. Foster –– he of new Wall Street money and she an heiress to a pedigreed clan that could to trace its blood to the age of Miles Standish and Pocahontas. The kind of Plymouth Rock genealogy whose progeny enjoy a leg-up when it came to achieving a life of pleasant comfort and safety.

But the Fosters had hardly been safe or untouchable.

Colt had hunted the killer of their 16 year-old boy to a waterfront warehouse in Portland, Maine. This time he used a nine-inch fillet knife. He removed the murderer's hands with a fish oil press, wrapped them in chipped ice, and put the limbs in a rubber freezer pouch labeled Kennibunk-Neptune Export, Ltd., Purveyors of Fine Seafood, and he placed everything in a zippered vinyl gym bag.

He walked into the kitchen of the Fosters' abandoned lakeside home and opened the bag without ceremony. The father, in a somber voice, told his wife: "Those are what killed our boy."

A yellow house cat walked up on stiff legs, arched its back and rubbed against Colt's legs, lured by the smell of fish.

"I never thought this day would come," Mrs. Foster managed to whisper before she began to cry.

"How did you find him?" the husband said.

"It's a knack," Colt said, immediately realizing that he sounded too glib for what should have been a quiet and somber occasion.

Spencer Foster bent to stroke the cat. "That's a queer way to say it," he said.

"Oh, Spencer," his wife said, wiping her eyes with a tissue as she looked at the bag that sat on the kitchen table.

"It doesn't really matter how he says it, does it? All these years and the police found absolutely nothing, and this man only did the job the authorities were supposed to do. He gave us justice, isn't that right?"

Colt avoided her gaze and said, "I understood when we first met what you were feeling. I think I explained why I wanted to help. I had a very good reason, so you must know that I take this moment very seriously."

" Yes, you did," she said. "And we are grateful. We are. My husband and I are just very tired. To come back to this house is quite difficult. Our boy's things are still upstairs. We never removed any of his belongings."

Mrs. Foster turned away and gulped back another sob. Spencer Foster came from behind and put his arms around his wife's shoulders and gently kissed the top of her head.

"I'm sorry," he said. "We certainly are grateful. Forgive me. It's just the way you said it. We're not accustomed to these things," he said and nodded toward the bag.

Foster spoke with a plummy and measured aristocratic accent, his deep voice thick and yolky, each word pronounced with a practiced cadence that Colt thought might make anyone who spoke to this man feel immediately inferior and uninformed. But tonight he seemed diminished by his genuine sorrow. He looked defeated.

Spencer Foster wore neatly pressed pants and a monogrammed sports jacket, one hand in his pocket as he led the way from the kitchen down a long paneled hallway into the living room. He took his wife's hand and motioned for Colt to take a seat on a sofa whose white protective covering had been tossed aside. Foster excused himself and returned carrying a small leather suitcase, the kind someone would take on an overnight hotel stay. Colt assumed they would not remain here for the night. Perhaps they had flown on their plane. He knew they had an aircraft, the same one that had once picked him up at the private airport near Alexandria the year before and flown him to Boston. They had already told him long ago that they would never again spend another night in the lake house, yet they would also never sell it while they were alive.

Foster put the briefcase on the floor and looked up at the high, vaulted ceiling that was crossed with heavy wood beams like the inside of a English manor. Colt felt a slight draft coming through the empty stone fireplace. Through the large living room window he could see the shoreline darkening behind the trees, the last glow of the sun settling into the hills beyond the lake.

Spencer Foster sighed and looked around. "We have so many memories here," he said. "I can't bear to think about the pleasant life we once lived. Every inch of this house reminds us both of Richard. He spent every summer of his life here, you know. And the last day, as well. You know that, of course. We've certainly told you everything, so forgive me for being so chatty and sentimental."

Foster sat up straight and cleared his throat, reaching again to touch his wife's arm as she sat staring at the far corner of the room where a Little League baseball bat stood leaning into the corner.

Colt said firmly: "Now, you remember my instructions on how you should dispose of the remains?"

They both nodded.

"It's very important to get them to law enforcement in the exact manner that I said. They'll easily make the identification and I've arranged for some other details to be delivered to them to ensure that your case is finally considered closed. They won't suspect you of anything, I've made sure of that. When they visit you, and I'm certain they will, please make sure you are at your home in Boston. Is that clear? It's best if the police in Boston question you and not the local authorities here. I can't go into details, but the Boston authorities have been a bit diminished in their ability to share digital records with the FBI or the Portland police. But that won't last long, do you understand?"

"Why can't you just give that...those things in the bag to the local police?" Spencer Foster asked.

"Time," Colt said. "We need time to pass before, as they say...someone puts two and two together. In any case, you both will be beyond suspicion if you follow my instructions. There's nothing to worry about. I promise. I know it's an uncomfortable duty on top of all you've been through, but there was no other way for me to bring the remains here for you to see and arrange delivery to the authorities. Trust me."

"We do," Cleora Foster said. "You're the only person who has told us the truth about any of this. You've never held anything back. We are the only ones...you and myself and my husband who can possibly understand any of this. There's nothing we three could suffer that would be worse than what we've gone through these past years. Nothing. Nothing can be worse than losing a child."

Spencer Foster took the suitcase and placed it on the coffee table between them. The money was inside, neatly wrapped stacks of bills, each of the four layers encased in a zippered plastic sleeve stamped with rows of numbers and the logo of a bank in Basel, Switzerland.

"Random serial numbers, of course," Foster said. The cat walked on stiff legs back into the kitchen, where Colt watched it jump onto the table and start circling the gym bag, touching it tentatively with its nose.

"Money can't insulate you from everything, but this will certainly help," Foster said.

"I never asked you for such an amount," Colt said, shaking his head. "You paid for my expenses, and I appreciated that, but this is unnecessary.

I've told you what my motives were and helping you and your wife did offer me some satisfaction. That's enough."

"We insist," Foster said. "You're a young man. You have a future ahead of you and we want to help. The things you've involved yourself with must be expensive and you deserve more than just expenses. We have our reasons for doing this."

Foster informed Colt of additional sums that had already been deposited in the Swiss account, and he pointed to the envelope in the suitcase that explained certain financial technicalities involved in claiming the funds in his own name.

"Our banker, Franz Kreutzer, whose name is shown on the documents, has been instructed to assist you," Foster said. "Franz is an old friend of the family with impeccable credentials. He can be trusted and confidentiality is second nature for him. This may be the age of computers, but actual human beings working on your behalf are often the most secure way to keep things private."

The cash on the table, Foster said, was a sweetener. He called it road money for a job well done. It was the only time Colt saw him smile, an almost imperceptible wrinkling of the side of his mouth as if he was about to chew something. They shook hands curtly, like two businessmen sealing a deal.

"I understand why you want to pay me," Colt said. "But it's just not necessary. In fact, were I to take the money it would rather spoil things for me. I'd have the wrong feeling about it. Can you understand that? If I poison this…what I've done to help you, it has absolutely no meaning for me."

"And what meaning would you deprive me of?" Foster immediately said. "Take it."

The last thing Colt saw was the wife sitting on the sofa, her knees pressed demurely together as she stared at the cat as it sniffed at something on the plastic sheet that covered her expensive carpet.

It was late autumn, the tourists gone, boats on the lake tarped for the season and bobbing at their moorings, and the summer homes empty and shuttered except for the big house where the Foster's once lived, a single light glowing behind the massive living room window.

He stopped the rental car on the far side of the lake, and looked back at the house. He opened the bag filled with the money, the unfamiliar odor of freshly printed bills filling the vehicle.

Three months later the Fosters were discovered dead in their Boston penthouse. The two were found with Cleora slouched oddly against her husband's shoulder, a family album filled with photos of their son lying on the floor between them.

But before they died the Fosters had recommended Jasper Colt's unusual services to someone else.

– 13 –

Her stage name had been Sparkle Montana and she was 87 years old. She sat in her wheelchair outside the day room, greeting her fellow Wind River residents like a theater ticket taker. She was dressed in a floral smock, her drooping breasts resting in her lap, white stockings rolled to her ankles. She wore glittery owl eyeglasses on a rhinestone chain and her red lipstick and mascara and dark brows gave her a look of regal authority as she directed people toward the rows of chairs lined up for today's classic TV movie showing of *An American in Paris.*

Next to her on an art easel stood a poster showing Gene Kelly and Leslie Caron dancing around a light pole, and she greeted each of the men at the door as hey *goodlookin'* or *handsome* or *dearie* and nothing else. Her real name was Mrs. Morganson and she'd worked as a stripper of some fame at The Sands Hotel and Casino in the 1960s and was a friend of Dorothy McGuire, who once gave her a ride home in a chauffeured Lincoln Continental with a flower vase filled with roses that had been put there by her Chicago mobster boyfriend. Mrs. Morganson knew Joey Bishop and Peter Lawford and once performed her act in private at a party at Sinatra's house in Palm Springs, where she met her third and favorite husband, who was a body guard for Jackie Gleason.

"Hey, handsome," she said to Savic as he made his way to Maria's room. "How's my favorite constable today? Keeping the world safe for us damsels, I suppose. You and your honey in the mood for a movie today?"

"I think you can pretty much take care of yourself, Mrs. Morganson," Savic said. "You're no damsel."

"But I have been, dearie," she said. "Many times."

"What's playing today?"

"The best, Kelly and Caron. Nobody had better Hollywood legs than Caron."

"Nobody," Savic said and he touched Mrs. Morganson's shoulder, who batted her beautiful big dark eyes and smiled as she turned the wheelchair and pushed herself into the crowded day room.

Today he walked Maria outside to the small garden pond, where they sat and she studied the birds who came each day at the same time in small flocks that filled the palm trees that encircled the home. She said she was too tired to walk much more today.

"You need some exercise, honey," he said.

"Tomorrow," she said and pointed at the shaded courtyard bench next to the pond.

Savic kissed his wife's cheek and took a sack of seeds from his pocket. You weren't supposed to feed the birds but Maria enjoyed it and that was all that mattered.

Maria said something. With the AC condenser fan blowing loudly from the roof, Savic leaned closer and she repeated: "Twenty-seven," lifting her hand to carefully count the birds on one branch as if she'd been assigned to take some official avian census. They did this together on most days when he visited: watched the birds and counted them. She knew the fastest fliers and the fastest eaters and when one seemed to be missing it made her sad. She folded her hands into her lap as if she'd suddenly surrendered to something she'd long known was coming.

They did this for the usual time and Maria said exactly what she said each day when they finished. "I think I'll lay down for a while. Is that okay?"

"Of course, honey."

"Grazie di questo."

"For what?" Savic said. "We always come and look at the little birds, you know that. I like to watch them, too. But next time we walk longer. You need to walk more so you get your strength back. You won't be here forever."

***

The admission ticket receipt from the art gallery at the Venetian Hotel had no discernible prints and the bar code that might have shown a time stamp was too smeared to scan. The barely readable sequential number, Savic thought, might lead him to the clerk who had sold the ticket and so might identify the person who had bought it. The ticket could have belonged to anyone, but as Savic knew, anyone sometimes turns into somebody. Right now he had absolutely nobody.

Maria had once dragged him to an exhibition by a long-dead painter who, Savic told her at the time, seemed to specialize in triangle faces and weirdly colored nudes with chubby ankles that looked like they'd been sketched with crayons by a preschooler. He remembered one giant portrait of a group of women with nightmarish, horsey jaws and pointy blue breasts with nipples that looked like appliance dials. They all had one too many cheekbones, and no matter from what direction Savic studied the painting, the women seemed to be leering at him. These ladies with boneless legs were sitting somewhere on a riverbank, though you could not recognize anything familiar about the river or its bank or the trees that grew there. Their naked, foreshortened shapes were hopelessly entangled with colored foliage lit by an angry neon red sun. He just didn't understand what he was looking at.

Maria, who was scouting a field trip for one of her book club groups, explained patiently what the artist was trying to do, but he still couldn't understand. She always knew about these things; about the old Italian masters whose names she could recite. She could talk all day about a naked headless Greek stone statue riding a chariot and how the whole thing was really about some pagan god and the battle between good and evil, but Savic still couldn't get it.

"I guess it's like police work," he told her. "Except without the blue boobs and weird butts. I'll just have to try to figure it out my own way, so don't mind me."

"Just don't make fun of it, okay?" Maria said, annoyed. "I don't mock your motorcycle friends so don't laugh at this."

And now this woman who could once name all of Rembrandt's paintings no longer remembered the address to the small ranch house where she had lived on Summerlin Avenue for the past 25 years.

The garage at the Venetian Hotel was filled so Savic stuck his police department business card to the windshield of the Harley and parked in a construction zone on the Boulevard a block away. It was another toasty hot day with heat shimmer rising from the sidewalk and though he'd lived in the desert now for many years he sometimes wished for a nice, freezing winter. He never thought he'd miss scraping rock-hard ice off a car windshield. The desert was nice, but it was annoyingly predictable.

The pleasant freckled kid at the gallery regarded the receipt with disinterest and then carefully studied the police badge and I.D. Savic casually showed, looking up and back again as she tried to match his face with the younger image that lay on the counter. She brightened up.

"I'd just like some information," Savic said. "It's no big deal. All very routine, I promise."

He didn't feel like smiling but he smiled anyway. The girl looked sweet and a little nervous and Savic knew he sometimes came across as a scary grouch, so he smiled again just for insurance.

The girl called over another clerk to handle the line of customers that stretched out into the hotel lobby. The special exhibit at the gallery today had something to do with Italian angel sculptures, and Savic saw a wall poster showing a pair of ancient looking vases. They resembled big garden planters, the handles shaped like smiling cherubs gazing in rapture at the sky. The exhibit was called *The Angels of Venice: Renaissance Sculpture and the Age of Sansovino*, whoever that was. By the look of the crowd that was willing to pay $25 a head to get in, Savic figured this must be an important show. He stepped aside and looked past the red velour rope that marked the gallery entrance where a sculpture of the archangel Gabriel stood guard in a cape and holding out his hand like he was actually the guy who might be checking everybody's admission tickets.

The ticket girl tapped a few computer keys and without looking up, said: "Wednesday. One adult. Came in at 10:05 p.m. That's all I can make out."

"Kind of late for an art exhibit, isn't it?"

"No such thing as late in this town," the girl said. "You should have seen the show we had last year. We had to turn people away later than that. Do you like Matisse? That's the next exhibit we have scheduled."

"Never met him," Savic said.

She giggled. "That's funny."

"I'm actually not in a funny business, so try your best to remember," Savic said. "Was this a cash sale?"

"Yeah." She perked up and smiled as she waved a group of customers toward Gabriel.

"That red line here," Savic said, pointing to the ticket receipt. "Isn't that what happens when the roll is almost at the end? Kind of a heads-up so you can change the paper."

"Probably," the girl said. "I haven't changed the paper yet, so I don't really know."

"It's old school thermal, so the line means it needed to be changed. Like what you get at a gas station pump. There's about a foot left before the thing runs out. I'm surprised you folks still use one of those old machines."

"Our WiFi might have been weird that day. It's a backup, I guess. We usually just scan somebody's phone, but sometimes they print out the receipts."

"It might make you remember," Savic said. "Whoever got this paid when your machine was ready to run out of paper. You also let him in after closing time. Any of that ring a bell?"

She was corn-fed pretty, a wholesome Midwest type who Savic could easily imagine jumping up and down in a high school letter sweater at the sidelines of a Friday night football game with her cheerleader squad. If he and Maria had kids they'd be around this girl's age.

"A lot of people come here, most of them at night when the casino is busy," she said. "I mostly just see their hands, you know? Somebody gives me cash or a credit card and I don't always look up. There's no time to be friendly. I wish I could help more, sorry."

He pointed to the ticket again. "The white original, what happens to that?"

She reached into a drawer and took out a zippered cash bag, the kind used for bank deposits. She noodled around, closed the bag and put it back in the drawer. She stooped and reached into another box. After a time she found the proper day that matched the ticket date.

"This we keep," she said. "Look. Here it is."

"Make a copy, please. I'd like the original, if that's not a problem." Savic asked the girl for an envelope.

"Now that I think of it, there were two older ladies who thought I was taking too long that night. What happened is the printer jammed. They got super mad. So this ticket must be from around the same time."

"Any men you remember?"

"Sorry, no. It's mostly women who come, so I'm sure I'd remember."

Savic handed her his business card. The department had gone on a community public relations jag recently and ordered fancy cards with raised metallic gold lettering and an embossed badge logo. Savic quickly scribbled his new cell phone number on the back of the card.

"If you remember anything, call me."

He took a walk around the hotel. He'd been thinking that he should rescue Maria from the claustrophobic routine of the nursing home one of these mornings and take her here. He'd have to fill out paperwork, of course. Nurse Fahey wouldn't just let him waltz out the door with one of her charges.

Maria liked anything Italian. Maybe she'd like the angel sculpture show. The hotel, with its fake canals where pretend gondoliers rowed fake boats under the fake cement bridge that crossed beneath the parking garage ramp, might be amusing for her. Better than watching the same flock of little birds fly past her bedroom window all day long. He wondered if she'd remember that they spent a weekend at the hotel when it first opened; a two-night anniversary package during which, as expected, he quickly lost a half week's paycheck at the blackjack table.

Savic sat in the lobby for a while; it looked more like a giant mall with those faux clouds on the painted ceiling sky. He watched a herd of senior citizens dressed in Hawaiian shirts bounce their two-wheel luggage carts down the escalator to where a row of giant tour buses were lined up on the street.

He took out his phone and was looking for Monaghan's number when he saw that he had six more voicemails waiting from Felicia Mendez.

– 14 –

Fifteen floors up from where Savic began to tap the ridiculously small numbers on his new phone, Jasper Colt scrolled through a list of encrypted passwords and lines of code on his computer and plugged in his earbuds as the image of a man dressed in a white shirt and tie appeared in the corner of his laptop screen.

"Hi, Doc. It's been months since we texted. Actually, conversations are much better, don't you agree? Even if we have to do it this way. These days people don't hear each other's voices anymore," the man said as he reached forward and adjusted his own camera, the blurry image wobbling.

"I have the name you asked for," he said.

The man held a sheet of paper close to the screen so Colt could read it. "Here, I just sent it to the phone number you gave me. It's a Europe prefix. Where are you, Jasper?"

"I owe you," Colt said, ignoring the question. "And he's the assistant warden, correct?"

"Used to be supervising tier boss. Just got promoted. It sounds like he's in charge of a new expansion program over there," the man said.

"And, by the way, you'll never owe me, Jasper. It's the other way around. I'll send you his relevant personal pass codes and the GPS coordinates for the cell towers you requested. There are only two between Four Palms and the prison itself, which has its own dish. You'll be able to daisy chain the location pings very easily. The phone carrier could give it to you, of course, but it's a royal pain in the ass to get that. And it's not in real time, anyway. Once you let me know at my end I'll activate the Bureau's screen downstairs and clone it. You'll be able to see everything at whatever speed I manage to send you the screen shots. Just make sure you use the laptop you're on now. There's a problem with the root codes if we change computers and mess with the VPNs. It's a bitch to re-do it."

Colt listened to keys clicking, the man breathing heavily into the tiny mic clipped to his shirt collar. He knew the man had probably rigged the computer as a phantom, non-recordable terminal receiver and so needed an independent audio source that would keep their conversation out of any government archive. Colt imagined his friend sitting two floors underground at the FBI's Behavioral Science Unit at Quantico, Virginia. He visualized the familiar rows of ugly metal desks and the heavy steel door that led to the records vault. His own office and lab was once located on that same floor.

"Stand by," the man said.

More keys clicked. "Okay. I have it. Your individual has been transferred to the sentencing facility. It's confirmed. Had some medical issues treated by the county, and then he was gone."

"Please, and the other dates we talked about?" Colt said.

The man began to read: "Okay...let me see. I'm stepping away from the screen now. To Colorado from Ohio in 2018. To Nevada from there. The thing with the tattoo on his hand did it. Simple things like that always seem to do the trick. That's how they found him in Illinois...blah, blah, blah. He did his six previous years for a burglary at Joliet. Then out on parole two years ago before the Las Vegas police finally nailed him after he broke into a house there. Classic home invasion with another fellow that had been set up as a sting by local law enforcement."

Colt heard a whirring noise, the sound of tumblers rattling on the enormous archive vault.

"Illinois was one of the first places to database inmate tattoos, body piercings, that kind of thing. The numerals on his hand were recorded as a continuous sequence, so that's why nobody noticed what it actually stood for. You told me it had to do with..."

"Chapter and verse, yes. Biblical," Colt said and suddenly found himself growing anxious.

"And so, you know, I was looking for dashes. Like you see when somebody quotes the Bible. But I thought it was a gang reference, which is what they do."

"Excellent," Colt told the man.

"How did you know he had it on his hand?"

"A hunch," Colt lied.

He did not tell the man what else he knew about the numbers and that he had seen them before during an event at a place he did not now want to think about.

"So you're getting him?"

"I'll certainly try," Colt said.

"That facility is in the middle of nowhere, Jasper. He's untouchable. Maybe this is all you can hope for, my friend. Perhaps it's the next best thing, his conviction. You've done all you can. The next best thing to rotting in hell is rotting in that relic of a prison. I know that this is very personal, but you should let it go for your own sake. You've been doing this for too long and it's not healthy. I'm sure the others would say the same thing."

"I don't believe in the next best thing," Colt said.

He gave the man another e-mail guest login address, the one he changed every twenty-four hours along with a second party ISP that would be used to confirm the login attempt.

"Did you get the GPS coordinates I sent you?"

"Yes, I did," Colt said. "How's your family? Are they well?"

There was a long pause during which Colt could see the man look down as if he were embarrassed and nervous about something. As if Colt had caught him off guard.

There was a catch in his voice. "Very well, sir. Thanks for asking. We haven't spoken this long since the Fosters died, did you know that? Seems like yesterday. What you did for them was wonderful. I hope you know what you did for us was also the right thing, Jasper. Our family appreciates it even though I'm the only one that actually knows the details. I wish we still worked together, you and I. We could have done important things."

"I'm glad your family is well," Jasper Colt said. "I always like to ask."

– 15 –

Fat pink angels kneeling on clouds and flying in squadrons across a blue sky gazed down at Colt from the brightly painted ceiling.

The hotel security man tapped him on the shoulder. "You okay, sir?"

"I'm sorry, am I in the way?" Colt said, still looking up.

"People bumping into to you and all, I thought you might be lost. You've been standing here for a long time."

"It's lovely," Colt said.

"I saw you on the monitor."

"Excuse me?"

"The monitor," the security man said. "There's cameras up there."

"Of course."

"Nothing is private in Las Vegas, sir," the guard said. "There's cameras everywhere. I just wanted to see if everything was okay."

Colt studied the shapes of muscular saints floating among the cherubs, who seemed same-faced, like brothers and sisters. Colt was sure the holy gathering cavorted mostly unseen by the tourists who now wheeled their luggage buggies towards the busy lobby counter. He heard bells and buzzers from the hotel casino at the far end of the hall.

"Not authentic, of course," the security guard said, pointing at a group of statues in a small garden overflowing with potted flowers and shrubs that hung from the false facade of a Venetian palace. "But an exact replica of someplace in Venice, I don't know which."

"I've seen the original," Colt said.

"In Venice? Oh, that must be something."

"It must have looked this way four hundred years ago when it was brand new. The colors are so bright. The real Venice is a rather shabby place. But in a good way."

"I never thought of that," the security guard said. "Sorry about the interruption."

"You're very thoughtful," Colt said. "Hundreds of people moving around and you bothered to ask if I was okay. It's good to know the cameras are working. I suppose you also might have thought I was up to no good."

"Not at all, sir," the guard said. "We just have to be careful. Staying long?"

"It depends."

"You're here for a trade show, I suppose," the guard said, glancing at Colt's briefcase.

Colt looked up again. "Up there, do you see it? That's very accurate."

"So they tell me, but I've never seen the real one."

Colt continued to look at the lavishly painted ceiling. "They were rugged people, the Venetians," he said. "They built a powerful empire out of a swamp. Not even the hairy barbarians from the north could find them in those lagoons."

"Those Italians. Tough bunch."

"Like the mob?" Colt said.

The guard smiled. "Yes, sir. Just like the mob did with this city. Lansky's boys and that bunch from out east. They stayed out of reach, too, you might say. Built something out of absolutely nothing, just like those old Venice fellas. Except in the desert instead of a swamp."

"Made something out of nothing."

"Yes, sir. Out of nothing."

Colt walked outside into the bright night and stood for a time on the replica of the sixteenth century bridge that spanned the entrance to the hotel parking garage.

The entire city was a neon apparition rising from the dark desert. He could see the Eiffel Tower, Caesar's Palace. The Manhattan skyline was a block away, compressed, oddly foreshortened and seemingly off-kilter as if drawn by a cartoonist. The broad boulevard, packed with inching traffic, was a landscape pierced by the landmarks of dead and dying empires.

Colt heard the thump of cannon firing, the cheer of a crowd: the evening pirate ship performance at Treasure Island. He could see the swaying mast of a brigantine, a buccaneer in knee britches swinging on a rope past artificially aged and torn canvas sails.

He walked down a side street past a gaudy wedding chapel squeezed against a windowless office building, and from beneath another neon sign Colt watched a laughing bride and groom emerge, stooped and stumbling as they raised their arms and fended off a shower of rice from a handful of cheering wedding guests. The groom held open the door to a comically stretched white limo and the newlyweds were soon speeding away like celebrities rescued from their admirers. From within the chapel came the recorded voice of Elvis singing and from out of nowhere another couple appeared as if they'd jumped on cue from a parked car — he in a tux, she with the train of her dress gathered like white laundry under one arm. They both stumbled away, the bride's high white heels clattering on the sidewalk as they vanished into the chapel.

The diner next door had red vinyl chairs mounted on chrome pedestals. It smelled of bacon and eggs and Colt sat in a booth and ordered black coffee and pie that came on a thick white plate.

The man arrived wearing a business suit and he stood nervously at the cashier counter and when Colt nodded at him he looked left and to his right as if crossing a street. Colt motioned with his fork for the man to have a seat in the booth.

Colt cut his pie with the fork. "Mr. Berger."

Berger spoke hurriedly. "I had a stopover from Dallas. Thank you for seeing me."

"A coincidence. Your wife and I, we spoke," Colt said. "She wasn't able to come?"

Berger raised his empty cup for the waitress. "She..."

"It's uncomfortable, I know," Colt said.

"She didn't think she could handle it."

The waitress came. The coffee cup, stenciled with treble clefts and stair-stepped musical notes, was heavy and thick like sink porcelain. An old time roadside diner cup and saucer. She put the cup down too hard and it spilled and Colt winked a never mind and blotted the table with his napkin.

114

"You're not what I expected," Berger said, looking at Colt's muscular forearm as he reached for a sugar packet.

There was a clumsy silence while Berger took his coffee and ripped open a packet of creamer and stirred noisily, his hand trembling.

"What you do," he finally said over the cup rim. "...is take care of everything?"

Colt nodded and took a bite of his cherry pie.

"My business went bad after the trial and there's all the legal fees and my wife has bad nerves now. The expenses and the counseling, I don't know how we can pay..."

Colt chewed and smiled.

"I could give you a few thousand dollars."

"Mister Berger, I mentioned to your wife that no money at all would be involved. I made that very clear."

"But I..."

"So now you know." Colt finished his coffee. He set down the fork, aligning it next to the cup. He folded the empty sugar packet in half and creased it with the side of his finger and put the packet into the empty cup.

"I already obtained the trial transcripts and the examiner's report," Colt said. "Do you have the photo?"

Berger pushed the envelope across the table. Colt opened it.

"A beautiful child, I'm very sorry."

"The name is Henry Meffisti. I'm not sure if he calls himself something else now," Berger said. "In and out of jail for most of his life. Managed to time out his parole and stay out of trouble for two months before he...."

"Yes, I have all the documents. I already know most of that, Mr. Berger. And he still goes by that name."

Berger wiped his mouth with the back of his hand. He was wearing cuff links. He was sweating. He hooked his shirt collar with one finger and loosened his necktie. Colt reached across the table.

Berger pulled his hand away and leaned over the table and said: "I don't know how to thank you. I wish I knew your name. I wish I could tell you how I feel about this. It's so damn strange. I'm not really sure now who told us about you. It all happened so fast."

Colt had learned to meet them for the first time at a public place. Going to the Ellinger apartment had been a mistake. If you met them at home it would be a long meeting filled with speeches and explanations and they would bring out their family photos and show videos of their children. He thought he'd learned that from the Fosters; not to go to the personal space where their memories lived. He'd taken it too personally himself with the Fosters, making friends with them until they began to share their deepest feelings, which was the worst thing that could happen. Two sets of grieving parents in the same place turned everything into a therapy session. He had his own problems, after all.

The Fosters had been dead now for years. Spencer shot his wife first, then put the pistol barrel in his mouth, an antique collector's weapon the police said was worth thousands of dollars. The couple had gathered all the photos of their child and surrounded themselves in the living room of the house on the lake as if they were themselves part of an elaborate and theatrical shrine. Stuffed toys. Children's clothing pulled from the upstairs closet. A bicycle. School books. Their son's shirts and jackets and trousers, emptied onto the living room floor, still on their hangers. The dead boy's little league baseball uniform draped carefully over the back of a chair. They'd lit the fireplace, though by the time the police arrived the wood had burned into coals.

Colt had seen the headline in a national magazine. "Grieving Hedge Fund Millionaire and Wife in Double Suicide." There had been a note, a long and elaborate written chronicle of their unbearable grief, in which they willed what they had not given to Colt to an obscure victim's rights activist group.

"Afterwards," Colt now explained to Berger. "I'll inform you when my service is completed. The police will receive proof. You really don't have to worry about anything."

Berger swallowed and looked off toward where a guitar was mounted on the wall above a jukebox.

"Mister Berger," Colt said, hesitating. "I want to explain to you that revenge in itself may be a disappointment and that it certainly will not be a retribution. Revenge and justice are two very different things. You need to understand that. I explained this to your wife at great length, and that's why I was hoping she would be here so I could say it again to both of you."

Berger stared directly at Colt for a long time. "We know that you understand exactly how we feel."

"Which is why the information we both had about Meffisti has made all this possible," Colt said. "He couldn't have been found without what you and your wife shared with me. I just filled in the spaces."

That night Colt stood on the impostor Rialto Bridge at the hotel. In another life he had been married at that same spot 6,000 miles away in the authentic Venice, where he had talked to his bride about the long life they hoped would come. The children they would have. They had scratched their initials with a hotel room key into the ancient white limestone hand rail because they thought it would give them luck and let them both live forever.

– 16 –

There were no surprises in the autopsy report for Earl Lee that Savic now sorted into untidy stacks on his desk: the routine diagrams, undecipherable bar charts and hardly readable, smudged margin notes jotted by an overworked technician somewhere deep in the bowels of the police department's forensics lab.

Much of the report was in a common data base by now and he and Monaghan would likely have their routine sit-down soon to discuss if there were any similarities between Lee's death and that of Carlo Cavilleri, the headless printing press operator from Four Palms. One photo, its detail nearly obliterated by a crooked inked date stamp, showed an arrow pointing to the bruise on Lee's shoulder and some obscure chromatography math that Savic decided he didn't need to understand.

Sometimes it's not smart to know everything. He had discovered long ago that when the gathered evidence data of a case began to overwhelm him, it was best to find only a few small facts to believe in. And that is what he did now.

As Savic suspected, it had been a needle injection. Cavilleri had a similar mark, only he had an additional darker, puckered wound beneath the left armpit from what the report said was likely a drug with a tongue-torturing name, some exotic pain inhibitor delivered rather sloppily through a whopper syringe, possibly the kind used for a lumbar injection. That made sense. Cavilleri would hardly have stood still while someone injected him with such a pig sticking jab. The examiner said the 20+ gauge needle, something normally used for withdrawing enough blood for a multi-panel test, would be highly unusual for injection use unless you were a vet and your patient was a horse.

Savic studied the 8x10 of the corpse, the entrails hanging like ropes, the ends gathered in a pile below the stubs of Lee's suspended severed ankles. The gut pile on the rug seemed to have formed symmetrically, as if what had caused the strange spillage had been swift and orderly with hardly any lateral motion by the suspended victim that might have disturbed the viscera's trajectory. Lee, if he had indeed been alive at the time — alive to actually witness the long gullet-to-belly incision and possibly the saw cut through the sternum, he had not struggled at all. It was the examiner's conclusion that Lee was likely fully conscious when all this happened.

The lab said Lee had probably taken about an hour to expire while he hung from that ceiling hook, watching his own feet being sawed off. What a way to experience the second most important event in your life, Savic thought. The disemboweling, this carefully orchestrated evisceration, something Savic had never seen in his years of police work, had happened in quick succession: the garroting, the final swift belly incision, the sawing of the sternum and feet.

Among the drugs found in the victim were relaxation meds and a mix of opiates that would have left Lee in a state of unsustainable tranquility. He might have experienced little initial pain but quite a lot of frantic fear while he visually observed his own butchering. Normally, he would have bled out much sooner, but the tourniquet marks just below his knees and evidence of at least five internal arterial forceps clamps, showed why he did not. There was something startlingly playfully about the purposeful postponement of death and the care the killer had taken to make it possible for his victim to experience every last suffering moment of his lingering demise. This was not some strange and sensual murder mashup, yet there was something violently coital about how the killer perceived the passive passage of time and death. This was oblivion with foreplay.

This guy, someone strong enough to vertically hoist a grown man four feet off the ground and quickly fasten him to a ceiling hook, Savic thought...was settling a score. Rage had nothing to do with delivering such calculated justice.

Harry Sahkno the motel manager said the guest who called himself Mr. Johnson had insisted on using his own pen to sign the register with his left hand, though the department's handwriting expert said whoever had made the notation on the art show payment receipt at the Venetian Hotel had been right handed. Writing with the wrong hand was truly amateur, Savic thought. A contrivance that could easily be revealed and would accomplish nothing, though it certainly was another playful touch that might waste a police investigator's time. This killer trifled with time like he toyed with his victims.

The junker car that was parked outside the Starlight Motor Lodge was missing its ignition plate and had to be started by two wires rigged to a metal ballpoint pen cartridge that was found still dangling beneath the steering column when the police finally entered the vehicle. You clicked the pen to complete the circuit and the vehicle fired up. The car keys they found on the street only worked on the driver's door and Savic was still waiting for the DNA report on the sliver of toothpick wood that had been jammed into the door lock. They found an eight-inch skinning knife under the car seat, something a butcher or hunter would use, with Lee's prints on the smooth bone antler handle. Next to it, jammed between the seat springs, packed inside a mint tin that showed a row of Las Vegas feather dancers at the old Stardust Hotel, were a dozen unbroken two-inch cocaine wafers, which was probably why Lee bothered to lock a car that had no proper ignition. There were two .38 Smith & Wessons in the trunk hidden beneath the spare tire, both with the serial numbers shaved off with a hardware store circular grinder and the stocks wrapped in electrical tape. Nothing shocking there. Also a Remington 12-gauge pump shotgun. Inside the coveralls that lay beneath the pool of guts that had tumbled from Lee's tummy was a small sheathed knife that he'd never had time to grab. They found something else: several kids' costume necklaces hidden in another empty mint tin tucked into the windshield sun visor.

Lee, like Cavilleri, may have been a collector.

Savic's interviews in the neighborhood produced the usual array of people in bathrobes blinking out from half opened doorways and shirtless men with bad teeth who looked like they'd just slept off a drinking binge. Predictably, nobody had officially heard or seen anything suspicious at or near the motel all that week. Harry the hairiest man in the world hired a lawyer who wouldn't let Savic talk to his client without an attorney present. Savic hardly gave a shit now if somebody filed a complaint against him with Internal Affairs. By the time the independent monitor at the union found out, he'd already be gone and retired. They had too much to do, anyway. The DA, already overloaded with more cases than he could pay personal attention to, would hardly pursue anything, since Sahkno had not actually been charged with a crime.

Savic decided to pay another visit to the hotelier.

He parked the Harley near the front door of the motel where he could keep an eye on it. There was a For Sale sign taped to the rear fender. Along with the house, the bike was the next item on Savic's cash flow recovery list.

Monaghan had received complaints from a goodie-two-shoes at the department about Savic's use of the motorcycle during duty hours. The clerk in the gangs and vice bureau claimed since Savic was not working undercover, it was technically improper for him to wear civilian clothes while on duty. Monaghan, who called Savic's work wardrobe his "Easy Rider costume," knew it allowed his sergeant to move more freely through neighborhoods. Savic hated driving the department cruiser, an unmarked white SUV bristling with antennas and a ramming front bumper that stood out like a sore thumb wherever he parked it.

Harry Sahkno didn't look surprised to see him. The motel lobby had a fake fireplace filled with plastic daisies standing in a galvanized tin pail. The brown rug was rippled and worn, a big blotch in the corner showing where some plumbing mishap had occurred. Ozzie and Harriet must have purchased the lobby furniture: a laminated blonde wood coffee table, molded plastic web lawn chairs, and a naugahyde platform sofa with built-in ashtrays in the arm rests. Savic looked for the expected velour painting of Elvis on the wall, but instead found an enormous print of an English hunting scene in which eighteenth century gents on horses were surrounded by their little hounds on the grounds of a grand estate. An AC unit in the window blew air from the Klondike full blast into the tiny lobby.

"Did he read any of those?" Savic said, nodding at a magazine rack next to the front counter. "Or rent a movie?"

Harry raised one wormy, thick eyebrow. "I told you already, no movie. I see him only one time. When he pay. My lawyer, he said not to talk to you. I am sorry. I must obey my lawyer."

"Apology accepted," Savic said. "But I think it would be in your interest to listen to me today. If you want, you can just nod or shake your head. That way you can tell your lawyer you didn't actually speak to me."

It was 102 degrees outside, the glaring sky hazy white, and Harry was wearing a brown herringbone sweater. He was perspiring terrifically, sweat glistening from the dark hollow of his furry throat.

Savic observed the man carefully. He could read a face, even one with the explosive follicle forest of Harry Sahkno. He could read hands and elbows and the way someone crossed their legs or arched their brows while sitting at a small square interrogation table. He could count the times someone blinked, or cleared their throat and he did this without taking notes. When he happened to get an answer to a question that satisfied him, Savic would offer the suspect coffee or a soda pop and leave the room just so he could stand outside watching the TV monitor, observing how the person reacted when alone in the room. Savic could do this effortlessly for hours and he could sense when they would start to wear down. He could ask the same question a hundred times in ten different ways and no matter what they said it didn't matter because what they actually did was important. Frank Savic did not trust words. He only trusted their faces and at what point that little vertical funnel of flesh above their upper lip began to perspire. He trusted the way they crossed their legs and feet and how many times they scratched the side of their face, and Harry Sahkno was now scratching his face quite a lot.

"He stay alone to himself, this man," Harry said. "I tell you this already. No videos. No magazines. No ice. Not even coffee from the machine."

"By the way, your ice machine is busted. I checked," Savic said.

"I must fix it then."

"For the sake of public safety and civilization as we know it," Savic said. "...you really need to burn this place down, that's what you must do. Has your memory refreshed about what he looked like? The man who signed the register?"

"He short."

"How about the hair?"

"Like me up here," Harry said. He tapped the top of his closely shaved head and grinned stupidly. And I remember he have glasses. Professor glasses, you know, the black ones. He was a very nice looking man. Clean and nice.

"Luggage? Perhaps your concierge might have noticed if he had luggage when he checked in."

Savic took a breath and didn't smile as he looked over at the big weird fox hunting scene above the fireplace. In the print, a servant in a white whig was handing a tray filled with little brandy glasses up to one of the riders.

"Only the black small bag. Only the bag," Harry said.

"You never told me about any bag. What about the bag? How could you forget about something like that? He carried this bag into the room?"

"Yes, he carried the doctor bag. I just remember now. I recognize this because in my country they still use this bag. The doctors they sometimes use this old fashion bag when I was a boy to come to your house."

Harry's cell phone rang; that same tune again. Savic was in a sour mood. The credit card people had been leaving him messages all day. And there was Felicia to worry about. He was sure that if he avoided her any longer that she would show up at the office and Monaghan would have a fit. He wanted to grab Harry's phone and toss it into the parking lot. A few years ago he might have done just that, but these days such a move would surely result in bad publicity and he at least owed it to Monaghan to behave himself. And this guy had already lawyered up. Perhaps it was best that way. He'd been in the business long enough to know that a cop's worst enemy is often his own hot temper, something his superiors had been urging him to control for many years.

Savic turned and walked away while Harry was still yapping on his phone and walked down the hallway to where the room was still sealed with red evidence barrier tape that had been placed randomly across the door. He peeled enough of the tape away and squeezed inside, where the smell of cleaning solvent was still strong. In the dim light he went to the wall outlet and with his pocket knife removed the plastic plate. He was surprised they hadn't taken it to the lab. Holding it carefully at the edges, he wrapped the plate with toilet paper from the bathroom and dropped it in his shirt pocket.

He called the office and drove to a corner convenience store where steel mesh covered every window. He grabbed the biggest coffee he could find and nodded to the clerk to keep the change and then dialed the pathology lab as he walked to the parked Harley.

Forensics Technician George Dooley was in the middle of a coughing jag when he answered the call

"George. You okay?" Savic said.

"Sorry," Dooley said. "There's some industrial strength flu bug going around and I've had this thing for days. I can't catch my breath."

"Remind me not to kiss you on the lips," Savic said. "Why don't you just stay home?"

"Too much work," George said. "The wife has it, too. Worse than me. We can't stand each other when we're both sick."

Savic waited for Dooley to cycle through another hacking attack and said: "Did you get anything on that bottle from the Lee case?"

"Prints on the cap, yes. Somebody tried to wipe it, but the victim's prints were what showed. The saliva profile on the glass takes an extra day. We have to send it to the state boys at the NBI. Maybe tomorrow morning, if you're nice."

"Like he pressed it down with his thumb?"

"Actually, yes, thumb prints. Left hand."

"If I just killed somebody I wouldn't be saving my beer for a tug later on, would you?"

"What makes you think it was the killer? Maybe the victim capped it."

"Beer foam doesn't last that long," Savic said. "That thing still bubbled up when I looked at it. If it was a stout then the foam might last longer. This was a light grain brew, a lager, and the bottle was three-quarters empty. Good German import. Not everybody carries it. The store down the street is strictly Papst and Bud. He brought it with him from the outside, I'm sure. No way Lee was drinking that stuff."

"Congratulations, Frank. You know your beer. So what?"

"How much spit do you need to make a match?"

"How many angels on the head of a needle? Not much."

"You get it from the inside of the bottle?"

"Alcohol breaks it down, and we might not even be able to get a readable sample," Dooley said. He erupted into another coughing fit and

Savic could tell he was putting his hand over the phone to muffle the sound.

"We get it from the outside rim of the bottle neck where it would have had a chance to dry," Dooley said, gasping.

"So the guy, a southpaw, puts on the cap because he knows where you'll get his saliva. He wants to preserve it," Savic said. "I'm thinking he's protecting it, just like he made sure we found that photo on the sofa. I bet when you look at that toothpick they found in the car lock you'll find a world of gooey spit for your chemistry kit, or whatever the hell you guys use in that Frankenstein lab you work in."

Dooley said something like spectrafibriloscope. Or oscilliograph.

Savic said. "Yeah, your spit-o-meter."

There came another loud, wet wheeze. He remembered when Dooley was inhaling three packs of unfiltered Chesterfields a day. That's when people could smoke anywhere in the office. Now you had to stand in the alley like a dope fiend, though Savic had himself had kicked the habit decades ago. Dooley had more service time than Savic, yet he wanted to hold on for another five years to take advantage of some union health insurance loophole that would allow him to get gold standard retirement coverage for him and his wife. From the sound of his lungs, Savic guessed that Dooley might need it very soon.

"George?" Savic said. "This guy knows that the saliva can't come in contact with the beer if you want to trace it. He was smart enough to wear booties at the scene, so he's not stupid enough to overlook the saliva. How do you pronounce that drug they found in Lee? The stuff that had time to go into his feet?"

Dooley managed to say the word, timing it perfectly between two long coughs.

"So you need a prescription to get this ketowhatchamacallit?"

"You could steal it, I suppose," Dooley said. "It's actually on the street these days. But it's common in a surgical setting; something that has to be monitored closely by an anesthesiologist. The military used it back in Vietnam during combat trauma treatment. It's not something that would be prescribed, not at all. You're telling me this guy wants to get caught?"

"I'm telling you somebody who kills like this doesn't do anything without a specific reason. Nobody goes to this much trouble. And I just found out he was carrying some kind of black valise, like a medical bag. Does that make any sense in this day and age? What doctor carries a medical bag anymore?"

"You think he wants to get arrested?"

"I don't know. I think he doesn't want to be stopped, but that's a different thing."

"You're supposed to know, right?" Dooley said. "I'm glad I play with machines and little test tubes all day, Frank. I wouldn't want to think about how human beings operate, no sir."

He was whispering now so as not to trigger another cough. "I don't really like people at all."

"That's the pisser," Savic said, trying to continue his thought. "This guy played with his victims just like he's messing with us. Like he's warming things up before he kicks things into high gear."

Savic drove the long way to the nursing home so he could have time to think. Sitting in rush hour traffic allowed his mind to wander. He drove down Twain until it turned onto the old Sands Drive that morphed into Las Vegas Boulevard. The Venetian Casino's lights were lit, glowing in the foreground of the city's brightly illuminated fantasy backdrop. He remembered working a late shift in the 90s as a uniformed officer when they blew the Sands into pulverized cement and rebar. They had to keep the tourists away, though some had already crawled under the barricades to lift souvenirs from the old Copa Room, where Sinatra and the Rat Pack had once horsed around on stage like frat boys in tuxedos.

At the Wind Mountain Memory Care Center he signed in at the front desk where Jackie Bastiano from 212 grinned up at him from his wheelchair. He was wearing his pajamas bottoms and a sleeveless white tee shirt, a tiny Italian horn pendant hanging from the gold chain at his neck. He grinned up from the crossword puzzle book that sat on top of the plastic oxygenator tubing coiled in his lap. Bastiano spoke with an emphysemic wheeze and with a twinkle in his dark eyes he said: "No cops allowed in here."

Savic held out his flattened palm waist-high. "I'm looking for a little guy about this tall. Short little prick. I think he's from Calabria, someplace. Immigration has a deportation hold out on him. I'm supposed to take him in and put him back on the boat. You seen anybody like that around here?"

126

"No, sir," Jackie said, making a big show of looking over his shoulder. "I ain't seen anybody like that. I'm from Calabria, did you know that? Place called Cantanzaro. My people been there a thousand years, yes sir. What makes you think I'd tell a cop anything anyway, huh? Much less squeal on a brother calabrese."

The two men shook hands and Savic wheeled Jackie to the cafeteria, where the old man grabbed a donut by the coffee machine, took a bite and started talking through the crumbs in his mouth.

"How's that wife of you's doing?" he said.

"You know how it is," Savic said. "Depends on the day. They're washing her up right now. I think she'll have a good day. I always hope she'll have a good day. Thanks for asking."

"I look in on her once in a while, you know," Jackie said, grabbing Savic's hand with a double grip. "Don't worry. Nothing disrespectful, my friend. I'm thirty years older than she is. You got nothing to worry about with me. Just being neighborly, just so you know."

"Why would I worry about somebody as ugly as you?"

"I was married four times, Frank," Jackie said. "The first two were for practice and the third was just a mistake. I let my guard down. But the fourth — mio Dio, my Teresa she was an angel. Just an angel. When she passed on I went to pieces. Your Maria, now I got a feeling she's a good woman, too. I can tell, you know. I seen you two sitting outside by the pond out back over under those orange trees. I can tell."

They small talked about baseball and the heat and how cheap things used to be in the old days and how they didn't give tourists free brunch anymore over on the Strip. Savic mentioned how he'd been thinking about the old Sands Hotel that day.

"My favorite back in the day, the Sands. I don't care how fancy that new place is they built on top of it — that fake Venice amusement park, everything changed when they tore the old place down."

Savic handed Jackie a plastic food tray and followed him to the small salad bar where the old man loaded his plate with cold pasta and hunks of Italian bread.

" I shook Joey Bishop's hand once, didn't I ever tell you that? I used to work the tables pretty good in my day. Met Sam Giancana when he came by. Had that dame Dorothy McGuire with him, you know, with the singing sisters? You met Sparkle yet?"

Savic said he had indeed met Mrs. Morganson.

"Good. Lovely lady. She's got some stories, I tell you," Jackie said, his eyes getting big.

"Boy, that girl was something in her day. A beauty, and could she dance. Anyway, Sam gave me a big tip and asked what my name was and the next time he came to my table, and this was a week later, he remembered who I was. Isn't that something? Big shot like him knows a thousand people and he remembers Jackie Bastiano. I'll never forget that."

A sad, lonesome look came across Jackie's face and he glanced over at one of the four tropical fish tanks that were scattered around the building. One of the residents stood there tossing pieces of her Zwieback toast into the tank.

"Hey, Barbara," Jackie said. "Don't do that. You'll kill those fish."

Savic gave a sly grin: "Why, Jackie. I didn't know you were in the mob?"

"Oh, I did errands for a few people. But it wasn't anything like that. In those days you couldn't help but bump into that crowd. They ran everything, right down to the janitors and cleaning ladies at all the hotels. In fact, the second time Giancana came to my table I said I grew up in Berwyn, just outside of Chicago. I told him I had friends in Oak Park and he seemed to like that a lot. Asked me where my family came from. He was Sicilian, but he was born here, and he seemed to like that I came to this country on a boat. An immigrant boat through Ellis Island."

Jackie suddenly wore a frown, like he wasn't that excited anymore about reminiscing.

"Of course, I never let on that I knew who he was. That would have been bad manners. You didn't do that with those fellas. But I knew where Giancana lived over on Wenonah Avenue in Oak Park. Big old brick bungalow right there on the corner. My sister married a doctor and they lived two blocks down the street from him. Later on in the seventies, after they shot Sam in his basement, she said she missed seeing the FBI guys hanging around the neighborhood. Sometimes it's good to have a mob boss as a neighbor. There's always cops around, day and night, and it's probably the safest place in the world. Yes, sir. She missed it when the FBI goons were gone. People started locking their doors again."

Barbara was still feeding the fish, so Jackie wheeled over and started lecturing her. "Excuse me, Frank. I gotta 'take care of this," he said. "That straw boss Fahey is gonna 'go through the roof if this woman kills those fish."

The place smelled like soup again; onion soup, though by the time Savic made his way to Maria's room the cafeteria had already stopped serving. Somebody was scooping popcorn from the little wheeled circus wagon in the day room and the TV was turned on extra loud.

A man's crumpled white underpants lay on the hallway floor, and when Marco the orderly came carrying his pill tray with the little white drink cups, he carefully stepped over the tightie whities and disappeared into somebody's room. A guest wearing a UNLV tee shirt and his boxer shorts stood shaking his fist at the wall and then turned to Savic and said there was a snowstorm on the way and why didn't they put salt on the sidewalk outside so people wouldn't keep slipping. When Savic said he wouldn't be able to help, the man repeated the same phrase exactly, word for word...like a memorized line he'd be practicing for just this moment.

Another TV blared loudly from the room next to Maria, outside of which sat Mrs. Algreen from 156, carefully counting the fluorescent hallway ceiling lights. From the cafeteria, which they were now setting up with game tables, came the clacking sound of a bouncing ping pong ball. Savic realized that no matter where he looked, he was the only person who owned legs that still worked.

Maria's room had a bathroom warmth to it and he knew they'd washed her early so she could take her tests after the doctor came and examined her. Maria was dozing in her chair when Savic walked in and picked up the treatment chart to see what meds they'd given her today. She'd been running a temperature again. He rolled away her food tray, the half-eaten jello already dry in its cup. He took her hand. It felt cold and he tucked it under the small blue quilt that lay across her lap. He put the back of his hand against her forehead. Still warm. Next to Maria's chair was a small table with a basket filled with sewing tools and a scratched wooden darning egg she'd asked him to bring from the house, though he knew she would never use it.

She stirred and rubbed her eyes and blinked at him.

"Dove sei stato?"

"I didn't leave, honey," Savic said. "You just fell asleep and I've been here the whole time. I was outside in the hallway, talking to our friend Jackie."

The scent of lavender aerosol spray drifted into the room from the hallway and Savic knew somebody must have had an accident on the floor. Maybe it was the underwear. He was used to it by now. He recognized Mrs. McKinzie's voice arguing with Carlo about something and then Jamal the shuttle driver joined in and pretty soon three people were half shouting about something Savic couldn't understand, except he heard the words "elder pants" a few times and then Mrs. McKinzie would shout "liar!" and the whole discussion then seemed to start all over again.

"Oh, she has such a big mouth," Maria said, suddenly animated. She leaned forward and looked toward the open door and smiled. Her loose pajama top dropped away from her bare shoulder and Savic saw the top half of what looked like the figure of a giant rising phoenix bird, one outstretched wing reaching almost to her neck.

Savic tugged at the fabric and Maria quickly shrugged away her husband's hand and then broke out in a broad, mischievous grin.

Savic chuckled: "What have we here?"

"Oh, it's nothing at all," Maria said. "Last night they gave us all tattoos. None carino? I just love the colors. Adoro i colori."

And she reached out and for the first time in weeks she touched and briefly held his hand and looked at him with her big, pretty brown eyes.

Savic felt his throat choke up and he tried to hold onto her hand but she pulled it away.

"Okay, honey. So tell me all about how you got that thing on your arm."

– 17 –

From the bathroom Colt took the aerosol spray off a glass shelf crowded with bars of wrapped hotel soap and folded white towels and he dropped the tiny plastic bottle in his shirt pocket.

The room safe was hidden behind a heavy mirror that rolled away against the wall, and though it mostly had bracelet and necklace hooks for jewelry, the large bottom compartment was just big enough for the box.

He lifted out the heavy polished steel container and placed it open on the bed, studying the remains if they might reveal some great sepulchral answer to a riddle he had never posed. They looked like soft piles of dust now, reduced to a sterile gray and lumpy gravel that seemed more like dirt than the beauty they contained. He had emptied the urns and mixed their remains together because the thought of them being separated any longer was impossible to consider. They should not be apart ever again, his lovely angels.

There were messages waiting on the laptop, the first from Franz Kreutzer at the Raiffeisen Contonale de Basel, his banker in Switzerland. Franz was technically a trust administrator for the bank, but he did many other things and he also took care of the account the Fosters had created for Colt. In the years since he'd been introduce by Spencer Foster, Kreutzer had worked for just about every top tier Swiss bank — Credit Suisse, Vontobel, Baer, even stints with Rothschild and the Pictet Group, and Colt's substantial account had grown considerably.

My friend:

The information you requested was rather difficult to come by, so hence the tardy response. Some effort was involved, I'm afraid, but you'll have to follow up directly yourself if you require further details. This is as far as I can take this. I don't really understand these scientific things, but am of course happy to be your intermediary if necessary.

The particular arachnid pheromone is quite rare, I'm told —and very expensive, I might add. It's also part of an ongoing clinical trial and so will not be easy to obtain in the concentration you require, since it has yet to be approved by the EU's food and safety administrator.

In any case, the contact I suggest, a German gentleman, is indeed involved in a related research project at the University of Ulm. Something to do with the World Health Organization, I believe. I was party to a funding group for one of his pharma trial studies licensed by the WHO several years ago, and he has agreed to a confidential arrangement due to his university's close ties to our bank. His contact information is shown below, along with the experimental antibody description. He speaks fluent English. What he gave me looks like perfect gibberish, but I assume you know what he's talking about. He made me promise to tell you to study his extensive notes. In fact, before he would even consider this he insisted that I provide him with your credentials, including those from your former employer at the FBI. Are you taking up a new hobby, my friend? This is quite unusual, indeed. There are more responsive and attractive pets than spiders, I'm sure. ·

Contact me if I can provide further help.
Best regards and wishes... adieu, Franz.

Another e-mail gave the encryption handshake code used by the Nevada Department of Motor Vehicles that would allow an interface with the Las Vegas Metropolitan Police maintenance and transportation department. The same account gave Colt access to the Frank Savic's North Metro Sub-station assignment schedule, which provided another doorway into the detective's personnel file.

The message was preceded with a bright red alert that warned the code would be deleted after 30 seconds once it appeared on Colt's screen.

Frank Savic's work files were rather reckless and disorganized, his personal documents mingled with police case paperwork along with sensitive household financial references related to the Wind Mountain Memory Care Center. It seemed like the sergeant used his work computer as a catch-all file cabinet for everything from his weekend softball team schedule to the daily cafeteria menu at the rather expensive old people's home where his wife now lived.

Colt erased Kreutzer's note and wiped clean the main laptop's partitioned drive, which had been daisy chained to a backup and a burner phone from which he now downloaded another set of remote files, a series of architectural drawings from the construction contractor in charge of the expansion project at the Silverheel prison. These files, which included photos of the old mining operation that would soon be dismantled and hauled away, were labeled with the name of a design firm in Reno. The records included detailed drone footage of the area around the prison grounds, including the old unused Bureau of Land Management road that led from the interstate highway to the prison itself. Colt printed the map and folded it and put it in his pocket. He made sure his downloads were progressing, including the disorganized mess of detective Savic's files, and then turned his attention back to the laptop.

He typed the name into the search field and waited for the link to appear: *http//:bigloverboy@nevadacorrections.org.*

'Harmless and doing time: Sensitive, caring inmate wants a pen pal with an open mind. Photos welcomed. Send USPS only to address shown here."

William Parker Jardine's on-line classified ad on a website called *DarkerThanNight.com* was bordered in animated red cupid hearts that danced across the screen.

Colt stood and walked over to the bed and sat down. He touched the box of ashes, stroking it. He spoke their names softly, and as the sun sank beyond the desert horizon outside his window the room fell into shadows until the glowing laptop screen was the only light in the room. In the dark, as if he'd conjured some self-made, gloomy religious rite, he rocked back and forth with the box in his lap.

Before he returned the box to the wall safe he unscrewed the amulet that hung from his neck chain and reverently filled the tiny container with their ashes. When he rolled the mirror shut he saw his own silhouetted shape reflected against the half-dark glass and wondered about what he had now become and what he might be when this was over. The encounter with Mrs. Ellinger at the apartment had rattled him. He was feeling unsure of himself and he fought the urge to sentimentalize his actions during the past few weeks.

He went back and finished his letter and addressed the envelope. He printed the letter and took out the lavender scented spray from his shirt pocket and soaked the edges of the paper and the envelope. The strong aroma filled the room. He ended the letter with a flourishing signature with his wrong left hand, making sure it looked like a woman might have written it.

I like a big strong man. Send a pic that shows me all of you.
— Angel

– 18 –

Savic saw his own gloomy reflection in the bookcase glass behind Captain Paul Monaghan's tidy desk.

This guy read stuff that belonged in a college lit class. He didn't really know why his friend and boss ever decided to be a cop. It seemed like he'd be more comfortable as a tweedy, bearded professor somewhere at a leafy Midwest liberal arts college. Monaghan rarely cussed or raised his voice, but policewise he usually got results with his meticulous habits and love of analytical data and fancy flow charts; the very things that made Frank Savic fall asleep.

For Savic, police work was following A to B and on to C, and that was how cases ultimately got solved. Luck and instinct also contributed, along with the serendipity of improbable odds that often lead to an arrest. The thing was to plod ahead slowly, like someone moving carefully from rock to rock across a flowing stream. Never look at the fast-moving water.

During their days together as young patrol officers cruising the streets of the city it was always Monaghan who negotiated with unruly suspects. He was temper-free, nearly always cool and calm, and when faced with a potentially violent situation that was about to go south, it was professor Monaghan who was the man to call to do the talking.

Savic ran his hand over his balding head and looked at the stray hair strands in his palm where he had scribbled with a pen the amounts he owed his top three creditors. The smeared blue numbers ended just north of his wristwatch with an imposing five-digit figure.

Monaghan stood and hooked his thumbs into his suspenders and walked to the window. The view on this side of town wasn't impressive, so

Savic had no idea what his boss was staring at. The laundromat outside? The parking garage and the pizza shop at the corner? You could barely see the mountains from here, yet every time they had one of these serious conversations about a case Monaghan would do the same thing: hook his thumbs in those suspenders, and then get up and step to the window. Maybe he'd seen it in a cop movie once, or read it in a police procedural novel, but Savic thought it was long past annoying.

"You figured out what you're going to do?" Monaghan said.

"Union guy gave me my papers and it's all squared away, that thing you and I talked about. Haven't signed anything yet, but I guess I will."

Monaghan pulled a tissue from a box on his desk and cleaned something off the window glass; fly shit, maybe. Only Monaghan seemed capable of spotting fly shit on glass. He lowered the two shades a few inches, made sure the bottoms were perfectly horizontal, and stepped back as if the view of one of the city's least attractive vistas might have suddenly improved.

"How much?"

Savic consulted his palm and said a number.

Monaghan whistled. "Maybe I can help..."

Savic quickly wagged his hand. "Don't even think about it. If the house sells, I'll catch up. I have other options. The Feds can't take the house if Medicaid kicks in, but I haven't decided yet. I don't need to be in that big place, anyway. The 401k should help and I have vacation days I can swap for cash. They told me how I can withdraw some money without getting dinged on my taxes. I don't understand most of that stuff, but it looks like it's the way to go. The union guy explained about the early payout program, so that's another thing. Add all those together and stuff might just fall into place. I appreciate the offer, but please, that's the last thing I want to do. I got myself into this mess and I'll pull myself out. I might just take her back home with me."

"You know that would be wrong," Monaghan said.

"You haven't seen how that place operates, Paul," Savic quickly said.

There were neatly labeled in and out boxes on Monaghan's uncluttered desk. The city's three-volume municipal code was aligned on its own wall shelf, oddly positioned between southwest art bookends and surrounded by carefully arranged novels and non-fiction history books.

Below that, a barrister bookcase with leaded glass panels was packed with alphabetically marked government binders, apparently a precise history of every case Monaghan had ever worked during his decades as a police officer. There was a painting on the wall showing Spanish conquistadors glowering at Aztec Indians with bird plumes in their hair who were offering up baskets of food.

Savic's chair seemed too squarely aligned and centered in front of Monaghan's desk, so he angled it slightly to the side and watched to see if this might annoy his captain. It did not, and this rather annoyed Savic, who then pushed aside a few things on Monaghan's desk to make room for his notepad. This actually did seem to bother Monaghan. Equilibrium had been achieved.

"The computer fellas said somebody hacked my files again, whatever that means," Savic said.

"Is this a lecture, Frank? You about to make your speech about an all-analog world with dial-up princess telephones and paper file folders and the heroic return of the fax machine? Is that what I'm going to hear?"

"Sure. If you'd like to get educated. At least back in the day I had a key to my file cabinet so nobody could steal my shit. Now some asshole sitting in his underpants at a kitchen table in the Ukraine can push a button and empty my whole fucking bank account."

"If it's any consolation, Frank, at least a dozen people here had their files compromised recently," Monaghan said. "IT thinks it's a prank. Strictly amateurs. They were on it immediately, and it's been fixed. But you really have to be careful these days."

Monaghan took off his suit jacket and draped it over the back of his desk chair. He was wearing long sleeves and cuff links.

Savic studied him and grinned.

"You ever sweat, Paul?"

"It's Nevada, Frank. Nobody sweats in the desert."

"I do. Maybe I work harder than most fellas."

"Maybe you just sweat a lot," Monaghan said. "Maybe that's it."

"It's not normal. Not sweating when you're wearing a suit and it's over a hundred degrees outside."

"Are we finished with this conversation about the ability of the human epidermis to cool itself?"

"There you go, talking fancy," Savic said, hoping to get another rise out of his good friend.

"I'm not sweating like a horse inside an air conditioned room. Ever think about that, Frank?"

Monaghan shook his head and picked up Earl Lee's file.

They'd found what was left of one of his victims in a trash bag at a palm tree farm. Lee's court defense was heavy on his previous childhood abuse and the public defender claimed poor little Earl, raised fatherless by an alcoholic mother, was incapable of knowing right from wrong. A shrink testified that Earl Lee suffered from a personality disorder that manifested itself into extreme antisocial attitudes and behavior and a lack of conscience or empathy. It was claimed that he was so hopelessly alienated from society and its norms that he didn't know what he was doing on the day he killed the child in her bedroom while her mother stepped out on a routine grocery errand. Just climbed through an open window and stabbed the girl while she was watching TV. The jury went weak at the knees for the killer. The DA's sloppy prosecution and a few unlucky evidence-gathering errors took care of the rest.

Savic couldn't help but celebrate Lee's demise as well as that of Carlo Cavilleri, whose well-traveled severed paws had revealed the same nonsense numerical tattoo that Savic remembered was also on William Parker Jardine's hands. Surprise, surprise: Earl Lee shared the very same tat. Finally, Savic thought, such men —Lee and Cavilleri, had ironically met a death more ugly than the ones they'd inflicted on their innocent victims.

"How's the new kid?" Monaghan said, referring to the green detective they'd assigned to help Savic with the investigation. He handed back the Lee file and reminded Savic that the scanned version would be much easier to read on his computer.

"There's no reason to have a secretary print the thing out just so you can put pieces of paper in a paper folder. It's a waste of time. I just don't get it," Monaghan said.

Savic shrugged. "The new guy is pretty bright, actually. He's taking night law courses over at the Boyd School, I hear. UNLV just like you, professor. The works. It's like having my very own Rhodes scholar. Like a

Mini Monaghan, except he's looking down at his cell phone all day. Makes me feel like a GED graduate. But he's okay, yeah. I like him. Smart kid."

Savic absently consulted the smudged ink scribbles on his palm: $87,000 to various creditors, give or take, that was due in the next few weeks. Or else.

"I heard you interviewed the mother," Savic said.

"The Ellinger lady?" Monaghan said. "She just showed up here, yes. She seemed, let me say, very happy."

"Sure. She's happy the guy who killed her daughter is in a drawer at the morgue. Why wouldn't she be cheery?"

"Not like you think," Monaghan said. "She was joking like a standup comic when I talked to her. Remember how depressed she used to be? Missed court because she was in therapy. Wouldn't talk when we questioned her? A zombie. This time I couldn't get her to stop yakking. Would not shut up. I remember she wouldn't let them clean up her kid's room. Wanted everything left alone, even the blood. This time she actually asked if she needed to see the DA and talk to him but I said it wasn't necessary."

"She just showed up?"

"Said she read it in the paper," Monaghan said. "She was standing out in the lobby in the morning before my coffee got cold. Looked too perky. The word glowing comes to mind."

"She was glowing?"

"Like a lantern," Monaghan said. "Her hair all done up and she was glowing. Wearing perfume, the whole bit. Like she got dressed up for the visit. Gave me the creeps. I swear she was flirting with me."

"Flirting. I don't think she was flirting," Savic said.

"You know how a good lawyer doesn't ask a question in court unless he already knows the answer?" Monaghan said.

"So?" Savic said.

"She wanted to know how Lee died," Monaghan said. "I have to tell you she had no way of knowing any of the details, but she was smiling when she asked the question. The papers just said Lee was found dead in a hotel room. Nothing beyond that. We've kept a lid on everything."

"That's natural. To be happy like that."

"She asked if he'd been cut," Monaghan said. "The papers didn't give any details about how Lee was killed, because we haven't told anybody yet."

"That's when she started glowing?" Savic was smiling now.

"Like a hundred watts," Monaghan said. "Just to give her something, I told her about his feet. Figured she deserved knowing that. Well, she couldn't catch her breath, she started laughing so hard. Laughed all the way out the door."

"You told her about the feet?"

"It was a mistake. Could not help it. Unprofessional, I know, but at this point even if she tells the papers, it won't matter," Monaghan said. "The DA's office is releasing its own statement tomorrow."

"You're a guy who can always help it," Savic said. "Sounds like something I would have done, telling her about the feet. I'm proud of you, Paul."

"Yeah, well. I'm entitled to slip sometimes. I couldn't resist."

"God save us," Savic said. "You're human."

Monaghan pushed a few pink telephone message slips across his desk.

"On her way out the door she turned around and looked at me and gave me a little hyena laugh," Monaghan said. "You know what she said? She said 'the doctor knows best.' What do you make of that, Frank? What's your gut say about that?"

"I got gas, that's what it says right now. I had one of those four-pound breakfast burritos over at the home this morning, and now I got gas. That's what I got, captain. I don't know how they can serve burritos to old people."

Monaghan started lining up the things on his desk. He touched the sharpened pencils that were already standing at attention in a stainless steel cup. He pushed the stapler to the side so that it was aligned perfectly with the edge of his desk. Savic knew something was up.

"Frank, I'm getting questions from the commissioner's office. They want to know if we're close to something. Are we close?"

"So just tell them we're getting close," Savic said. "You know the drill."

"Is that true?"

"Of course not. We don't have shit."

Monaghan walked to the window again and looked at where somebody was power washing the roof of the neighboring building. He turned and reached to his desk.

"The computers have been wacky," he said somberly, like he was ready to apologize for something. "I haven't used paper phone message slips for a while, but these calls came to the front desk. I guess you haven't put your cell phone number on your business card yet. Temp help was at lunch so I took the calls."

He handed Savic the two telephone message slips.

"You got something going over at the Venetian?" he said. "She sounded pretty young. She asked if Frank was there. Not detective Savic...she said Frank. Said you'd know what it was about and that you should call her right away. A show girl, really? Frank, she sounded very young. The other message is from the Mendez lady. Said you won't return her calls. Said to tell you she needed to talk to you about something very important. You're a busy man, Frank."

Savic wasn't listening. He was reading the numbers on his palm again.

– 19 –

A siren wailed, faded and shrieked louder as the police cruiser turned the corner onto Pecos Street and raced past the Starbright Lodge, where Harold Sahkno stood in flip flops watering a patch of dead grass with a garden hose.

Felicia Mendez pulled to the side of the street as the vehicle ran a red light and sped down Alamogordo. Two blocks down from where Harry was still flooding his hopeless front lawn with the gushing hose, Felicia found a parking space between two disassembled cars that sat on cement blocks, their wheels and hoods missing as a man laying on a creeper dolly worked to cut away a bumper with a sparking grinder tool.

She sat for a while in the car and combed her hair and touched up her makeup in the visor mirror. She had grown up in this neighborhood and could still see the small playground, now empty and weedy, at the far end of the block. The alley she once explored as a girl with her brothers was now a maze of tipped trash dumpsters and discarded sofas and bed mattresses. An abandoned bicycle lay with a tree sapling growing between its spokes.

She'd had strange and fleeting thoughts since the trial about her Jimmy that came suddenly and without warning at the oddest moments of the day. Now, blinking into the visor mirror, she thought of her son again: his infant pink feet so tiny they did not seem real, the skin nearly transparent and as thin as tissue paper. This flash of aching reminiscence came and went so swiftly she hardly knew what she was thinking at all, but was left with a heavy, unexplainable sadness that sometimes stayed with her afterwards for the entire day. In the distance, in the abandoned playground down the street, she noticed the slightest bit of bright color and she wondered if it might be some child's toy near the swing set, and this sent her thoughts about Jimmy racing once more.

Two sniffing dogs raised their heads from where they were scratching at something in the bushes and they watched as Felicia stepped from her car and walked up the steps of one of the worn-out adobe styled houses that seemed to illustrate the neighborhood's prevailing architectural theme.

A shirtless man answered the door, a cigarette dangling from his lip. From the house came loud music and fruity oven baking smells that drifted out into the hot afternoon air. Through an open kitchen doorway on which hung a torn screen she saw somebody standing at a stove, pushing a pan back and forth.

The young man at the door was tall and lean with raised scars on his bare shoulder, the old knife wounds never sutured properly so that they now formed bumpy red welts that Felicia was certain served as a type of manly memento. Some street badge of courage.

"Usted tiene negocio aqui?"

"Bernardo knows me," Felicia said, making sure she sounded dismissive and casual so that the boy — and he really was a boy, wouldn't get the wrong idea.

Another pequenos muchacho with — literally, a chip on his shoulder, Felicia thought. 3D Lobos, one tattoo on his forearm proclaimed in gothic dark lettering set beneath the silhouette of a howling wolf. Blue and green jailhouse ink.

Felicia's brother, who was now serving twelve-to-twenty at Leavenworth for possession with the intent to sell on federal property, once told her how prison tattoos were made. You burned plastic from a ballpoint pen and wiped off the soot and mixed that with toothpaste and soap. Or hair cream and soot. You took a pencil with two needles tied to the point with string. You soaked the string in the ink and then poked away just like people did a thousand years ago. The results were always in the same colors: blue and that dirty green she now saw on the young man's arm.

The man saw Felicia studying the tattoo and he took a deep, dramatic tug on his cigarette and purposely flexed his arm muscles. Felicia looked at him sternly. Perizosa punk, you don't scare me, she thought. I survived an entire childhood of people like you.

"Where's Bernardo?" she said flatly. The boy flicked the cigarette past Felicia's shoulder.

She had always feared her Jimmy would one day end up with motherless gangbangers like this. Loose and feral on the streets like the dogs she had just seen and packing his pistol in his ridiculous sagging pants, barrel-down against the crack of his ass like it was some show of manly defiance to carry it so. She'd done her best to stay away from the old neighborhood, fearing any contact with those who remained behind would infect her son like a germ.

"Estancia eia aqui," the boy said, unexpectedly polite as he watched Felicia take out a tiny mirror from her purse and hold it to her face. She gave a slow shrug.

"Should I tell Bernardo you kept me waiting?"

Felicia smelled the monkey stink of dope, enough to blue the hazy air inside the house. There was the tinny clatter of Tejano trumpets, the norteño lyrics joyously celebrating some fugitive cartel leader down in Zacatecas, Mexico. A man was sitting on a brightly colored sofa with his arm around a woman and the two of them stared at Felicia as she passed, the man grinning, one gold tooth sparkling in the yellow lamplight. The woman with her Chiquita banana sleeveless white blouse and black heels and black hair frowned. She wore no bra and her breasts hung heavily beneath the loose fabric, the man nudging one nipple absently with his thumb like he was fiddling with an appliance dial. He nodded at Felicia and the woman feigned jealously and jabbed him with her elbow, and then they both laughed.

"Buenos," the two of them said together.

"Good evening," Felicia said in English, not smiling.

Another man appeared. He was short and compact, angular, his handsome face chiseled around a neatly trimmed black mustache and long chin beard that reminded Felicia of some breed of dark latin Viking. He tugged his shirt over the lump of a weapon handle at his belt. The pistol, thought Felicia, worn like jewelry. Bernardo Santoya seemed pleased to see her. He stepped off the porch with his arms extended, his feline smile independent of those familiar cold and immobile eyes. He moved slowly with a coiled and withheld strength.

"Usted esta para ciendo, bueno hoy!"

Felicia tried her best to look cheery. "You're looking good, too, hermano. It's been too long, Nardo."

For some reason Felicia didn't want to speak Spanish today. This bunch gave her people a bad name with their manners and the clownish way they moved with those crippled, palsy-finger gang gestures and their baggy pants. Oh, the baggy pants really made her angry. Her people had such a noble history and all these ignorant hoodlums could do in this miserable place was to make a mockery of it. They were lost, Felicia thought. Lost and drifting like the dead tumbleweeds that now bounced rootless through her old Pecos Street childhood neighborhood.

Bernardo bent forward for a kiss. He smelled of cigarettes and whatever he'd just eaten. Felicia, with her fake smile, offered her cheek and hoped he would smell her perfume.

"How long now?"

"Since my husband died," Felicia said. "It's been a while."

Bernardo stepped back and gave a long, admiring whistle. He flapped his fingers like he'd touched something hot.

"Bueno. You lookin 'so good. You sure looking good, my goodness."

"Can we talk someplace?" Felicia said.

He tried to hug her again, but she teasingly squirmed away with just the hint of a giggle and followed him down a hallway. She preened her hair as she walked, coiling a few strands around her fingertip.

Someone wearing an empty shoulder weapon holster gave her a worried look. There were more women in the house than she expected. She heard a beer tab pop and then laughter. Food sizzled somewhere and she again saw the man in the kitchen pushing his mysterious pan, a shelf lined with glass beakers and coiled copper tubes on the wall above his head like some hastily assembled school chemistry set.

Bernardo led her through small, unfurnished rooms. Everyone in the house seemed busy and on the way to somewhere else, carrying sacks and clutching bundles and boxes as if this were some grand delivery depot that was about to change shifts.

They stepped outside onto a screened porch where it smelled much better, yet there sat two more abandoned cars in the yard. A bright work light glowed from the ruins of an old garage. Mariachi music now blared from the house and Felicia noticed the small fenced garden in the corner of the yard with its cracked bird bath on which sat a pair of small cherub statues that were also streaked with dirt and neglected. This house had once belonged to Bernardo's parents and Felicia now remembered playing in the yard as a child, the whole neighborhood full of life and children running through the streets as if this were a small village. The little stone angels were streaked with rust water, the dry bird bath packed with dirt and dead leaves and from the garage came the sound of a whining drill and the clatter of metal dropping to the floor.

"I couldn't talk on the phone," Felicia said. "I need your help with something personal."

"You say the word, sister," Bernardo said, patting his chest with the flat of his hand. "Your husband Tony was a good man. He gave me a job after I got out. I guess I let him down. But his kindness was from his heart. I don't forget stuff like that, you understand?"

Tony touched his chest again. "Del corazon."

"The man who killed my Jimmy?"

Bernardo laughed. "El es un mono grande. I saw that fat motherfucker's picture in the paper. Oh, sister, you did some number on him didn't you? Everybody here talked about that thing. Right now, if I told everybody here who you were, they'd come out and want to shake your hand. Oh, you be some tough lady. You are. Yes, yes..."

"Jardine," Felicia said. "That's what I came to talk to you about, Nardo."

She sat and Bernardo eased into a broken white wicker chair with cigarette burns on the arm rest. There were sheets of newspaper on the sofa and when Felicia leaned back against the cushions the sour smell of former meals drifted out.

"You still have friends in the jailhouse?"

"Damn straight. More than I got out here," Bernardo said and smiled. "Everybody does their time. It's like the stinking army, you know that. You do a few years, do your hitch and you come home with stripes on your arm."

You stupid child, Felicia thought. Wasting your life with putas and dope and waiting for the day when you go back in jail where you really belong.

She tried to speak in her most pleasant voice: "Jardine is getting moved to the prison. The old place out in the desert."

Bernardo made no attempt to hide that he was studying Felicia's legs. She'd purposely worn the tight top today. Her bare waist showed. She wasn't bad for her age. Not an ounce overweight, her long legs darkly tanned. Muscled calves, her ankles crossed with thin black sandal straps and her hips small above an ass that could fill a man's cupped hands. Bernardo's appreciating eyes lingered on her as he took a long swig of his beer.

"Not a bad place, the old state prison," he said. "They got good food, clean beds, even though it's old and fucked up. I hear they're fixing things up over there."

"In two weeks he has to go somewhere for surgery."

"His face?" Bernardo smiled. "And you know this how?"

"Somebody in the police department, a friend. They don't have a proper clinic at the prison, but they have a doctor at some small town close by. That's where he's going. After they fix him up he'll be in isolation. Right now he's in the general population during the day."

Felicia crossed her legs suggestively. Bernardo swallowed, his tongue lifting beer foam away from the edge of the can.

"You need a drink, honey?" he said.

"I know you have friends," Felicia said, shaking her head.

"The lobos," Bernardo said.

"That's what I heard," Felicia said. "The lobos have power over there. At Silverheel."

"Hermana, you sure got that straight. We make the calls. Tenemas potencia."

Felicia, forgetting herself for a moment, said: "Quanto tiempo entregar un mensoje?

"No, I guess it don't take time to make arrangements," Bernardo said. "Those boys like it when they got a mission. Keeps their skills sharp. But that piss bag Jardine, he's not somebody who will be easy to reach. Even if he's in the population they still got to keep an eye on him. He's a celebrity.

Might go out for exercise, but that's all. That's a small window, honey. Not much room to work with."

He reached and touched her bare knee. "Everybody needs a mission. What did you have in mind, sister?"

"I have a little money. Insurance money, you know. And I've been saving up." Felicia said. "There's been no justice. Deseo la justica."

"I ain't seen justice my whole damn life," Bernardo said. "You come to the wrong place for justice, sweetheart."

"I want him hurt, Nardo."

"Looks like you already did that," Bernardo said and he let out another chuckle. "But you need a bigger knife, mi amor. That little puppy sticker you brought to court don't make the grade."

"I'm not good at that kind of thing," she said. "I thought I was, but I'm not. That's why I need your help."

She uncrossed her legs and smoothed one hand suggestively past her knee, down along her calf and she breathed deeply. She leaned forward and let Bernardo enjoy the view.

"I only want justice."

"You want revenge," Bernardo said. "There's a difference."

"They both feel the same," Felicia said.

She shook away her hair and tugged at the top of her blouse. She fanned herself with her hand.

"It's hot out here."

"I'll see what I can do." Bernardo edged closer. "But we have to wait and see what the situation is over there, understand? I can't just make a phone call and it happens. If he's outside and taking his walk, maybe it's possible. If they got him in the exercise cage all alone, that's different. Lots of details to consider."

Felicia opened her purse. "I told you I have a little money. He needs to be hurt before he goes to the clinic."

Bernardo squeezed her arm. His fingers were wet and cool from the cold beer can.

"Your money's no good," he said. "Those boys don't like the kind that hurts a kid. This shouldn't be a problem. He's the kind of fucker we don't like at all. None of us like that kind of animal. Maybe something can be done."

"Thank you," Felicia said.

"I'll make it my gift. No promises."

"I don't need gifts, Nardo."

"A beautiful woman like you needs gifts," he said. "You know, when you went over to Tony and married him I was jealous. I always liked you. Liked you very much since we was kids."

Bernardo pulled the chair closer. Felicia edged away, teasing him. He didn't follow. They both stared out across the tangled and overgrown yard, the dusky late day sun now making the downtown buildings appear stark like pencil drawings. The tops of the city's casinos glimmered in the distance like they were on the edge of some foreign, unreachable world.

He didn't try to kiss her. She'd been prepared for that. She'd been prepared to take it as far as was necessary. Nothing mattered now except hurting Jardine once and for all.

"That boy won't be happy once the wolves get him," Bernardo said. "Don't matter how mean and big he thinks he is. Won't make no difference at all."

He now reached across the sofa and stroked Felicia's neck, trailing one finger lightly across her bare shoulder. His lips tasted like the beer and when she reached and put her arms around the small of his muscular back she felt the heavy bulk of the pistol tucked behind his belt.

But now she didn't care at all as Bernardo stood and took her hand and led her back into the house.

– 20 –

Henry Meffisti was not one to waste an opportunity for careful self-grooming.

He preened and stretched his face into the rear view mirror of the moving car as if gazing at himself for the very first time. Impressed, he continued to study his dimly lit profile as he drifted into the adjacent traffic lane and nearly clipped a passing vehicle whose driver honked and lifted his middle finger out the window.

Meffisti reached under the seat and took the lightweight Ruger .38 and wagged it back and forth, pointing out the window, laughing as the other car suddenly fish-tailed and wobbled out of its lane and came to a sliding stop on the gravel shoulder of the highway. Meffisti considered turning around and having more fun, but he expected the police to be on alert by now because of the thing he'd just done at the store over on Mojave Road. There was no use pressing his luck tonight.

Though Henry Meffisti usually favored immediate pleasure instead of considering a future danger, he needed to take things easy for a while. He had months left on his parole and the pistol he now slid into the springs beneath the front seat of the car would be a hard thing to explain if he got stopped for a speeding ticket or a bad tail light. Still, it would have been fun to mess with the driver of that car for a while. He was in the middle of nowhere in the desert. He'd done this kind of thing many times before.

There was a game he played. Driving down some lonely road at night, Meffisti would flash his brights at the oncoming traffic. Flash and flash, until some bonehead would take the bait and highbeam back at him. Meffisti would immediately make a U-turn and get right up on their tail as he turned on the single flashing red police light that hung from a magnet on his mirror. The stupid ones would immediately pull over. Some he had to follow for a while, but they would eventually pull over. Meffisti would then swagger toward the driver's side window like a cop issuing a ticket, stopping just behind the door handle in case they did something stupid. They'd roll down their window and he'd make a show of bending forward with the .38 holstered onto his belt, speaking a polite hello while he quickly flashed the shiny Clark County toy Sheriff's badge that he'd bought at a flea market over at the county fairgrounds in Logandale.

There would be a short, practiced lecture about the hazards of erratic driving and Meffisti would make a show of examining their driver's license and walking it back to his vehicle, where he'd copy the information down before handing back the I.D. Then he'd say thank you ma'am or thank you sir and quickly drive away with his lights off in the opposite direction so they couldn't get a good look at his plates.

It was almost as much fun as killing them, but with less trouble or mess.

Meffisti now made sure he was driving below the posted speed limit as he passed beneath a familiar bridge where he knew the state troopers would often lurk at this time of night. He turned on the radio to see if there was any news of the robbery.

He'd taken the checkout girl at the convenience store into the men's room, where she peed on herself and started blubbering and almost ruined everything. Meffisti slapped her around and wrapped her mouth with cellophane packing tape that he'd snatched off the store shelf moments before. She seemed upset that he put the sticky tape on her hair, so he wrapped more of it around the top of her head and under her chin, making sure all of her nice long hair was covered, even strapping it across her eyebrows. She had thick, dark eyebrows and when he wrapped the tape he noticed it had caught the top of her lashes and she started screaming more, unable to blink as he violently ripped away the front of her buttoned blouse with one hand.

After it was finished his first job was to get rid of the car he was driving. He found a nice neighborhood with a big home that had bicycles and a toddler's plastic trike in the driveway. Swing sets. Porch lights on, shapes walking back and forth past the lit windows of the house. Meffisti saw the

Toyota two-door parked at the end of the driveway that was partly blocked on one side with hedges high enough to provide him with some cover. Clunkers were easier to spark up than newer cars, so Meffisti lay on his back on the seat, careful for his bent knees not to show above the door. He took his knife and bent open the steering shaft boot, which on this model split apart cleanly in two pieces, the four colored wires pulling out easily from the seam. The car fired up on the fourth try and Meffisti drove it slowly down the street to where he'd parked his own vehicle behind an all-night liquor store. He emptied out the glove compartment, making sure he removed his registration card and he stuffed his things and the cash from the robbery into his backpack. He took the pistol from under the seat and the small flashlight from where it lay on the dashboard. Something rattled inside the flashlight and he thought it had something to do with the batteries or the bulb but he didn't have time now to check.

The stolen car smelled like burgers. It was probably some teenager's used junker, but that was okay. Old cars were something the cops took more time to find. He tried the turn signal but the driver's side stuck and wouldn't blink. That would be a problem. Police just loved bad lights on a car.

Meffisti stopped at a gas station, filled up the tank half-way, and went inside and bought a replacement bulb for the turn signal, batteries for the small flashlight and a few candy bars and then phoned his house.

Willy answered in his slow, stupid numbnuts voice. He always talked like he was a little drunk, except he never drank anything but those kids' juice pouches that came with the straw in it.

"Where you been, Henry?" Willy said, sounding predictably excited. Willy was always excited about things. Everything seemed to be an urgent emergency.

"I'm coming back from Henderson, you retard. I told you where I was going. Picked up the cash. You ready?"

"Aw, don't call me that, Henry."

"Don't get smart," Meffisti said. "I told you I had things to do today. Did you pack up the stuff we talked about?"

"Don't say retard, Henry." Willy fell silent. "You know how that bothers me. How come you talk like that?"

"Okay, dickhead. Is that better? I won't call you retard," Meffisti said. "Do you remember what I told you yesterday?"

"Yeah, Henry. Are we doing the plan? Tell it to me, Henry. Mexico, right?"

"Not tonight."

"You said when you was finished we'd head to old Mexico."

"I'm not driving all that way tonight, you idiot," Meffisti said. "I got business to take care of. And I had to get some money first."

"Encinada, Henry They got pretty girls in Encinada."

"You retard, they got girls all over," Meffisti said.

"Come on, Henry. Aw, stop saying that."

"Okay, dumbshit. Is that better? Shit-for-brains. Dickwad. Lollyfuck. Turdbetween the ears. That make you feel better?"

Henry Meffisti actually had no plan at all. He just didn't like it when Willy knew what was going to happen next. You had to talk to him like a kid, always promising something and hoping he'd forget what you promised, which he almost always did. You'd tell him a story and he'd just sit there looking dumb, smiling and sipping on that juice drink of his, and then he'd ask you to say it all over again. Just like a toddler.

"Tell me about Mexico."

"Hold on," Meffisti said.

A woman and a man now walked out from the gas station. She was eating an ice cream, her tongue curling up the side of the wrapped sugar cone in long, lingering licks. The melted ice cream lay milky on her lips and chin and she took a napkin and dabbed her mouth. The woman saw Meffisti staring at her and she quickly wiped her cheek with the back of her hand and turned away.

"You still there?" Meffisti said.

On the phone, Willy was breathing hard, like he'd just shoved the phone down his throat.

"Meet me at the place," Meffisti finally said, still watching the woman as she said something to the man, who now glared at Henry as he lifted his hand in a lazy wave and drove away. That might have been worth it, Meffisti thought, but there were other cars in the parking lot and the man would have been a problem. It was exciting to think about, though.

Willy finally said, "The Red Rose?"

"Yeah, the Red Rose, retard," Henry said. "I told you that a hundred times. It's where we always meet. Where else do we usually go?"

"Henry. Aw, Henry. Why do you keep talking to me like that? Did I do something wrong? I thought I did everything right today, Henry. How do I get there? I don't have a car."

"Get where?"

"The place. The Rose," Willy said.

"It's only a fucking mile away," Meffisti said. "You walk. That's how you get there."

Sixty miles away in Las Vegas, at his desk in the $450 per night suite at the Venetian Hotel and Casino, Jasper Colt adjusted the volume on his ear buds as he listened to the pinging sound on the audio GPS location device he had placed inside the flashlight that now lay on the car seat next to Henry Meffisti. The blinking red light on Colt's laptop turned to green and began to move slowly across the screen.

– 21 –

Bob Anderson, hospitality industry field salesman for Let There Be Light, Inc., a decorative electronics distributor specializing in keeping Las Vegas casinos supplied with, as his business card proclaimed, "...every conceivable illumination need," sipped his coffee and glanced casually at the small man sitting in the booth at the Red Rose Cantina.

He hadn't been staring at anyone in particular; it was just a quick sideways glance like you'd do when you were sitting in a restaurant. Just checking things out, and since there were hardly any other people in the cafe, there were few other options. In this case, the only thing Anderson noticed about the man was that his overly large head was shaved and he wore a thin pencil mustache and a tee shirt showing the famous Hollywood hills sign in bright neon colors. He was very small, kind of bird-boned, and after he glanced over at Bob Anderson he made quick, darting movements like he was nervous about something. He kept studying his cell phone as if he was expecting a call, and then looked up and smiled. He had a pie tin face and an elfish nose crushed flat like he'd run into a wall. He couldn't have been more than five feet tall. His teeth were arranged in his mouth like crooked corn pellets.

Anderson had just completed his last sales appointment of the day, peddling 175 cases of frosted 60-watt fluorescent tube lights to the maintenance department at the Cactus Queen Casino and Supper Club on Boulder Highway. It was a very nice commission that would take him past his quota for that month.

So, before heading back home, he'd phoned his wife and told her was making a pit stop and gassing up the car at a roadhouse cafe just off the interstate. He asked about their five-year-old son and his wife explained that week's daycare and camp schedule, something they would need to talk about when he got home. She congratulated him on his big sale and smacked him an audible kiss through the phone, making a joke about how she'd looked in the basement and noticed that they had themselves run out of light bulbs.

"Physician heal thyself," she said and they both laughed.

"I'll be home in about two hours," Anderson said. "Love you."

While he was studying the restaurant menu the little fidgety bald elf was joined by someone else, a larger stocky fellow with a ponytail who wore a backwards baseball cap and carried a canvas rucksack that he tossed angrily on the floor. He said something sharply to the little man and then called out for the waitress to bring him what he usually drank. She nodded knowingly and disappeared into the kitchen.

Anderson tried to look away, but the man had already noticed him. He pointed his forefinger at himself in a theatrical and exaggerated way and made a big show of shrugging his shoulders.

"Mister, you looking at me?" he said loudly enough so that the few other people in the cafe all turned.

The man again turned up his palms.

"I said, you lookin 'at me?"

His little partner with the formless nose started snickering approvingly as Henry Meffisti stood and swaggered over to Anderson's table.

Meffisti sat down next to Anderson and picked up the coffee the waitress had just brought and put it to the side. He picked up a sugar packet and absently started tearing the little envelope in half, spilling the contents on the menu Anderson had been reading. Anderson reached and took a nervous sip of his coffee and then tried to scoot to the side with his chair.

The remaining cafe customers paid their tab and walked out and then it was only Meffisti and his goofy looking pal with the bald spaceman head, who walked over and also sat down next to Anderson, who now wished he'd simply driven straight home after his big quota-busting light bulb sale.

Meffisti reached down and patted Anderson's leg and let his hand linger there for too long, his fingers crab-walking a little too close to his crotch.

"Was that the best DeNiro you ever heard, or what?"

"I guess it was, sure," Anderson said. "Whatever you say." He had no idea what the man was referring to.

"Must not be a movie fan. You a movie fan?"

"Sir, I don't want any trouble," Anderson said.

"No trouble, meeester? You don't want no steeeenking trouble!"

Meffisti winked over at his little buddy. "Willy, he doesn't get it. He don't need no steeeenking trouble."

"Treasure of Sierra Madre!" The sidekick said and bounced up and down in his seat like an excited child.

Meffisti slowly took a sip of Anderson's coffee and nodded at Willy. "Over there. Now that's a man who knows his movies. Don't you agree?"

"I suppose he does," Anderson said. "But I still don't understand. What's this about, sir?" He tried to stand but Henry Meffisti reached down and gripped Anderson's leg and sighed.

"You're pretty rude, mister. You know that? I'm just being friendly here. You from around these parts, are you? I don't think you are. You got no manners, did you know that? You from the city?"

The waitress came with Anderson's order and Meffisti snatched a few fries from the plate and started chewing. He took a pickle and dropped it on the floor. Willy, mimicking his boss, reached over and did the same with one of the fries, snorting with laughter as he also took a bite out of Anderson's burger and looked over at Meffisti for approval.

Anderson tried to stand up and Meffisti grabbed his arm.

"Where you going?" Meffisti said. "You didn't finish your coffee. Relax."

"Go ahead, take it. You can have it," Anderson said and pushed away the half empty coffee cup and pointed at his dinner. "I better get headed home, anyway. Go ahead and eat this. It's okay. I don't want trouble, really I don't. If you thought I was staring at you and being impolite, then I'm very sorry."

Meffisti looked sadly at Willy, who frowned in fake sympathy as if he shared his partner's sudden disappointment.

Anderson stood and pushed past Meffisti and walked quickly to the men's room. He looked in the mirror. He was flushed, his forehead sweaty. God, he didn't need this. Jesus, not today when everything had been going so well. He just wanted to celebrate his big sale with a quiet dinner and go home and see his wife and then get up and do it all over again. He liked the predictability. He liked his job and his life and his family. He always tried to avoid trouble. He didn't need this at all. Oh, God.

He waited for a while in the men's room, splashing his face again with cold water, hoping the two men might tire of their little game and be gone when he came out. He washed his hands and looked at his face in the mirror and wondered if he should have stood up for himself more firmly. Nothing violent, just maybe said something that might have convinced those men not to bother him. But he didn't know how to do that.

Anderson took a deep breath and tried to march purposefully back into the restaurant, hoping he appeared confident as he made straight for the cashier counter. He was relieved to see that the two men were gone. He went to pay his bill. The waitress gave him a cautious look as she leaned over and spoke in a half whisper.

"That boy and his spazzy little pet are about as bad a pair as you'll see," she said, smirking. "Henry does that with people all the time. Just tries to go as far as he can. He'll get dangerous on me if I tell him to leave, so I just wait and hope he gets bored and goes away on his own. Sometimes people tell him to go away, and he usually backs down. I've called the cops but Henry just keeps coming back. Gives everybody a hard time. Seems that's just what he does. I've never seen him actually hurt anybody, but he's got a way about him that just gives me the creeps, I'll tell you that. You seem like a nice fella. I'm very sorry. This is usually a nice place, but around this time at night we get a few strange ones that wander in off the highway and Henry is the strangest of them all. You just had the bad luck to meet up with him."

She gave Anderson his change and winked. "I hope you'll come back. He never comes around here in the daytime. Probably sleeps 'till noon at that dirty trailer down the road where him and that little freak live."

Anderson pushed back the coins and added five dollars to the tip. He walked outside and got into his car and buckled his seat belt.

He felt a hand on his shoulder.

Meffisti popped up in the back seat. "Heeeere's...Johnny!"

Henry Meffisti was holding a beer and he emptied the bottle with a loud bubbling gulp and tossed it out the open window.

"Drive out slow," he said. "And don't try to get yourself a ticket. Saw that old trick on a Kojak re-run, so it won't work with me."

Willy pulled up next to Anderson with Meffisti's stolen car and rolled down the window.

"Where to, Henry?"

"Shut up, Willy."

Meffisti took out his flashlight and shined it down onto the front seat. The light flickered a little like the batteries were running low and Meffisti smacked it with his hand and the beam came on again.

"What's in the briefcase?"

"Just papers. Business things. I'm a salesman. I don't have much cash on me, but you're welcome to take it. Credit cards. I've got credit cards, of course. I just don't want trouble, mister. Please, I have to get home to my family. I don't know why you're doing this."

"Show me the money," Henry said.

"Jerry McGuire!" Willy squealed. That's from..."

"Keep your voice down, numbnuts," Henry said as he pressed the .38 against the back of Anderson's head.

"Say hello to my little friend," he said.

With Willy following in the other car, Meffisti directed Anderson down a side road to an empty field where a few trailers sat at odd angles behind a brightly lit storage warehouse. Willy got out first and opened the unlocked door of one of the skirted trailers that sat on cement blocks and had a large satellite TV dish fastened to a roof tripod. Meffisti walked Anderson up the stairs and when he was inside he pushed him down onto the sofa. Willy came and slipped the pillowcase over Anderson's head and wrapped it with tape.

Henry spoke gravely, reaching into Anderson's back pocket and taking out his wallet. "We're gonna' go out for a while, and you're going to stay here. Understand?"

Anderson couldn't breath inside the pillowcase. He heard the two men walking around, opening drawers and clattering silverware. One of them went to the bathroom and flushed the toilet and after a time the entire trailer began to stink. The microwave began to hum and he smelled something cooking. He could hear a window slide open and was grateful for the cooler evening air that drifted into the smelly trailer.

"I need to do some shopping," Henry said. "When we come back I'll be asking you to do some more driving."

Willy put a rope around Anderson's shoulders and slipped it down over his arms. There was the sound of more tape coming off a roll and then Willy wrapped Anderson's wrists behind his back and pushed him to the floor. He felt more tape wrapping around his ankles. Meffisti tapped Anderson's head with the barrel of the pistol.

"Be a good boy, okay?"

"I need to use the bathroom."

"Too late," Meffisti said. "And if I come back and you pissed on my furniture you'll be sorry, understand?"

The lights went off and Anderson heard the door slam shut. The toilet water in the bathroom kept running.

In the car Willy started laughing. "You see his face, Henry?"

"He had a bag on his head," Meffisti said. "How could I see his fucking face?"

"Before the bag. He look scared, didn't he? Oh, boy he sure looked scared, Henry! You scared the shit out of him, Henry."

"Shut up."

"Just wanted to talk about how he looked, Henry," Willy said.

"Shut up."

"I'd sure like some corn chips," Willy said. "We didn't finish supper back at that place. I didn't even start my meal. We eating something soon, Henry?"

Meffisti drove away and Willy stopped talking.

They went to the Cash & Carry store, where Meffisti told Willy to stay in the car.

"Give me some money," Henry said.

Willy took out his wallet and handed over a few bills and then showed Henry the receipt from the cafe.

"What's this?"

"I paid the bill back there for what we ordered," Willy said. "Here's the receipt."

"A receipt. I don't need no stinking receipt, numbnuts."

"Treasure of Sierra Madre!" Willy said, almost shouting.

"Yeah, yeah...keep it down, okay? What are you keeping a receipt for anyway, and what do I want with it?" He took the piece of paper and crumpled it and tossed it into the parking lot.

"I thought maybe you'd pay me back, Henry. I've been paying for everything lately and I'm kind of short myself."

Henry ignored Willy and instead turned and watched a woman walking across the parking lot. He was just in that kind of mood tonight and every woman seemed to catch his eye.

"Oh, boy. My woody just moved," Meffisti said.

"She's just a tourist," Willy said. "So, can you pay me back, Henry? You took that guy's wallet, so you got the money. I don't think it's fair. Not fair at all."

"I feel like some fun," Meffisti said, staring at the woman.

"Aw, Henry," Willy said. "We got time for that down in Encinada. All those girls waiting for us. She'll be trouble, Henry. I know how you get. Let's just eat something and get our stuff and go to Mexico like you promised."

"Got that guy's new car back at the house. We got cash. What's the hurry? That sucker back there isn't going anywhere, and I've got plans for him."

"You said the police might be looking for you. That's why we're going to Mexico, isn't that what you said? To make a new start?"

"I told you. Shut up."

Meffisti buttoned his shirt and looked in the rear view mirror and smoothed his hair behind his ears and turned around his cap.

He walked up to the woman, who was loading groceries in the trunk of her car. He offered his best boy scout smile.

"Ma'am, I wonder if you could tell me where the interstate highway is?"

"Oh," she said, startled. She looked around. The parking lot was empty at this time of night. "I'm a visitor. I'm afraid I just don't know. Sorry. But I'm sure somebody in the store can help you."

Willy pulled up the car so that it blocked the view to the store and he reached over the seat and pushed open the back door. Meffisti pulled the woman down by the back of her head and dragged her into the car. He slammed her down on the seat. His hand was immediately on her mouth and when she struggled he slipped it up over her nose and held it there until she stopped moving. She lay whimpering and trembling.

Willy drove the car across the street to where a shallow little desert creek turned into an aqueduct that ran behind a grove of cottonwoods that grew thickly next to the road.

Henry stayed in the back seat with the woman, pushing her head down. She was chubby around the hips and she smelled nice and sweet, a wholesome soapy cleanliness to her that aroused Meffisti. When Willy parked behind the trees he turned off the headlights and Meffisti pulled up the woman's skirt for a look. He told Willy to get out. Willy walked away from the car and stood looking toward the creek that rushed loudly through the cement viaduct and he noticed a semi truck parked not far away with its lights off and the windows dark. He walked back to the car to tell Henry.

"Get lost!" Meffisti said.

"Aw, Henry," Willy said. "We probably shouldn't..."

Meffisti pushed himself up with both hands from the back seat. Willy could see the woman's feet sticking up and her one arm was pressed behind her head against the window and she was sobbing.

Meffisti screamed at Willy. "It ain't we that's doing anything, so shut your hole. And go see what she has in her purse."

Willy took the purse from the front seat of the woman's car. He tried not to listen to what was going on. When Henry got this way you couldn't talk him out of anything, and if you tried it only made things much worse.

Willy put the purse onto the hood of the car. He used Henry's flashlight and as he searched for her wallet the purse fell and spilled everything. He tried to gather things up, but he was so nervous he kept dropping the purse and then hoped Henry wouldn't finish before he could clean things up.

He put the money into his pocket and when he tried to take out his wallet he dropped that and spilled his own money. He crouched with the flashlight and when the wind started blowing things around Willy panicked and stuffed everything he held in his hands into his jacket and his pockets. He heard Henry calling for him and that's when he accidentally kicked the woman's purse and the wallet under the car.

Henry heard the woman screaming now and he walked away toward the river and hoped the noise of the rushing water would make it so he couldn't hear the sounds he'd already heard so many times before. When Henry got like this, you couldn't stop him. He tried to think about Mexico and the pretty girls that were waiting for him but then Henry started yelling louder than before that Willy should get his bony ass over there and quick.

– 22 –

It had not always been a hipster brew pub serving cream stout infused with helium or thoughtfully glassed beers with names like Smooth Hoperator or Arrogant Bastard Ale.

The same owner, who now wore a white bushy Santa beard and a man bun, had run the place as just another neighborhood saloon since the 90s, but times changed and he upgraded things. There was now a row of three one thousand-gallon stainless steel brew kettles standing along one whole wall of the establishment, and the young wait staff served a clientele that included mostly Vegas tech workers and entrepreneurs who rented space at the loft-like buildings that now lined the street. But in the older section of the building, the part that had housed the former neighborhood tavern, it was still pleasantly dark and gloomy and where the management continued to cover the floor with peanut shells. The papered walls still had old posters of classic muscle cars and 80s head banger bands and trophies from Savic's softball team that the saloon sponsored each summer.

There was a bank of vintage single crank slot machines lined up against the wall, across from another row of Foosball tables. The owner was originally from Wisconsin, so here they still served Pabst Blue Ribbon and Hamms beer. Packers games were shown on Sundays during the season and Monaghan and Savic had been loyal patrons of the place for years, usually sitting at a back table near a pair of swinging rubber kitchen doors. You had to speak above the clatter of noise from the kitchen, but it was a place where it was impossible for anyone to eavesdrop on a conversation. Which was why they liked to come here to talk shop.

Monaghan loosened his necktie.

"Spent the morning at the chief's office," he said. "God, how I hate the chief's office."

"You were made for the chief's office," Savic said.

"I don't like the new brass over at the admin building."

"You are the brass, in case you haven't looked. You're the most senior captain in the department and you know what that means."

"I don't really want a promotion, Frank," Monaghan said. "I've seen what it does to those people up there. I used to want it. I don't anymore. I never felt like this before. I've been hanging around you too much."

They ordered beers.

"I read in the paper about the guy over on Pecos," the waiter said.

"I can't say everybody's not happy," Savic said. He looked at Monaghan. "I'm pretty sure we both feel the same way."

"You got that, brother," the waiter said. "Good riddance to bad garbage."

He wiped the table with a part of his stained white apron and both men kept talking.

"Saved you some work, whoever did that to Lee," Monaghan said.

"That's one way to look at it," Savic said. "But I think we have some kind of vigilante here."

"That's the only way to think about it for now," Monaghan said. "Maybe everybody gets lucky and these scumbags start murdering each other off. Wouldn't that be a freakin' treat? Efficient, too."

"I don't think the killer is that kind of person. A Robin Hood, I mean," Savic said. "There's something else, but I can't put my finger on it right now. You know, I went back to that room the other day and turned off the lights and just sat there in the dark."

"I never understood why you liked to do that," Monaghan said. "Sit in a place in the dark where somebody just got murdered."

"Sometimes things come to me," Savic said. "Maybe it's the smell. There's always that smell. I think I see things clear when I sit in the dark. I can't explain it."

"Just don't tell anybody but me that you do that at a crime scene, okay?" Monaghan said. "They'll lock you up."

There was a large single window opposite the booth and both men looked outside at where a film crew was shooting a movie or a TV commercial.

Actors and extras stood in line waiting to get food from a catering truck and a cameraman sat in a boom chair high above the street intersection where traffic had been blocked off.

"I wouldn't want to do that," Savic said. "Looks boring."

"I don't get acting," Monaghan said. "But I suppose it's not easy to do."

"We're all actors," Savic said. "Everybody acts. The only time we don't act is when we're asleep."

"Still, you have to memorize things."

"And you don't memorize what you're going to say before you meet with the chief?" Savic said. "I've seen you in action, Paul. You should get an Oscar."

"Even so," Monaghan said. "It can't be easy pretending you're somebody else."

Savic picked up the menu that had not changed its graphics in a decade. "I'm pretending right now that I don't know what I'm ordering for lunch today."

The menu was a greasy sheet of laminated yellow paper that featured three entrees, no dessert and four kinds of beer —Bud, Grain Belt, Hamms and the Pabst. If you wanted something more specialized you headed to the far end of the building where they served two dozen fancy home brews.

"I'll have the Lamb Ass," Savic said.

"Excellent choice," the waiter said, and with a flourish draped his wet terry cloth towel over his forearm and bowed every so slightly. "May I suggest the peppercorn sauce? And perhaps a Chateau Puillie eight-six?"

"Of course," Savic said. "Excellent suggestion."

"And you, sir?"

"The same," Monaghan said.

"Two meatloaf plates coming up," the waiter said. "And a pair of PBRs."

Monaghan pulled off his tie completely and massaged the back of his neck. Somebody in the noisy kitchen was singing in Spanish.

"I heard Jardine is already getting settled in over at Silverheel," he said.

The dishwashers in the kitchen started laughing about something and banging spoons in time to the music. Monaghan took a long pull on his beer.

"Can you believe that busted old dump is getting a hundred-million-dollar face lift? Governor's pet project. There's some stink about using the inmates for demolition work. Some prisoners are suing him. The ACLU hired new staff here just to work on the case."

Savic chuckled. "Jardine won't like that, working on a crew."

"You can't go wrong with a fifty-cent an hour labor force."

"That's not what I mean," Savic said. "He hates bugs. If they make him work where there's bugs — outside or in those old buildings, he'll go through the roof. I'm sure it says that in his prison file, so they ought to know. Whenever he's been in jail he makes a big deal about it. They have to know he hates bugs."

The waiter came with two steaming plates of meatloaf and mashed potatoes with fried okra and a bowl of coleslaw. He gave another expressionless, mocking bow and turned gracefully on his heels and walked away.

They were about halfway through their meal, eating in silence, when Monaghan pulled his ringing cell phone off his belt. He nodded and handed the phone to Savic.

"How about you let me do some honest work for a change?" Monaghan said. "They found a Jane by the viaduct and the old Sloan rest stop off the interstate. It's the Sheriff's jurisdiction, but they think we might want to take a look. I just don't want to go back to the office today."

"You already took your tie off," Savic said and smiled. "No way you can go back now."

He and Monaghan hadn't teamed up on a crime scene for longer than Savic could remember. They'd worked for years as young detective partners, and when Vegas transformed itself into an adult amusement park, both had been assigned to a special gaming task force charged with investigating the downtown casino district.

A trooper met them at the exit off I-15 and they followed the dirt road where they had already rerouted traffic past the old dry reservoir. The woman lay next to the viaduct in the bushes behind a stand of trees and reeds with her blouse pulled over the back of her head, her arms stretched out like she was getting ready to jump off a diving board. You could see she'd struggled by the way the clothing had been yanked up, her severely bruised face wrapped in tape that had begun to come undone. Her bare knees were scraped and from the marks in the gravel Savic could see she'd managed to crawl some distance before being stabbed in the throat.

Her bra hung off one shoulder on a broken strap, the back of her neck wedged at a severe and fatal angle against a tree. There was blood, but by the look of the sandy dirt and the direction of the earlier drag marks from what must have been a parked vehicle, the woman had put up quite a fight.

"Twenty-eight years old. Wedding ring," the state trooper at the scene recited from his notepad. "Lives near the Air Force base in officer housing. Out of state vehicle registration, according to what we found in a purse out in the parking lot. There was a cell phone in the purse. Husband is out on a training exercise in Barstow, way out in the desert. We haven't been able to reach him. She's been dead about ten hours, give or take. Trash truck driver was loading the dumpster from that service station and getting ready to start the compactor when he saw somebody's underwear and a pair of lady's shorts laying on the ground. He said he saw the blood in his headlights and when he got out to take a look he called 911."

The trooper pointed at a semi truck parked in the gravel lot across the road. "Guy in the Peterbilt rig says he heard something last night when he pulled over to get some sleep at the rest stop. Truckers and RVs use it mostly. But last night nobody was there except this guy. When he heard a noise he figured somebody was checking into the campground. There was arguing, but he didn't think anything of it. It's the honor system: you pay with a credit card and you get a sticker, and the manager of the service station comes by and checks. Very casual. No electrical hookups. City viaduct runs heavy this time of year so it's hard to hear anything. But he said he definitely heard a man's voice. That's all we got right now."

"You said there was a vehicle?" Savic said.

"Vehicle tracks, but we're confirming those now."

The medical examiner was snapping down the wheels of a rolling gurney that he pulled from the back of an unmarked black van. He carried a folded rubber bag under his arm.

Savic carefully pulled the woman's stiff and bloody blouse away from her face. She'd been gagged after she was taped, which seemed unusual and told him that the killer might have changed his mind about something. A long length of the tape was wrapped tightly several times around her forehead. She'd bitten her bottom lip and the blood had dried on her chin.

Savic squatted and ran his hand over the sandy ground.

"This place doesn't get much traffic. If somebody pulled in late you should be able to make the tire tread easy."

"We did," the trooper said. "A small sedan. Two men. No prints from the woman. She was probably carried part of the way. One pair of shoe marks took her straight to the bushes. Dropped her by the viaduct. It's officially a river, but they cemented this thing years ago. Comes out of Lake Mead in a round-about way. Anyway, these guys did what they did and then left. Didn't bother to hide her very well, almost like they were in a hurry about something. They didn't care or they were just stupid."

The trooper handed Savic a plastic baggie containing the wrinkled piece of paper.

"We found this next to where it looked like they parked the vehicle. It's from the old roadhouse a few miles from here. A sheriff's deputy went there and questioned the waitress and she definitely identified two men. They're regulars. Gave us names and everything and she verified the receipt. Said they were involved in a ruckus with one of her customers and the check got paid and they left. There's a time stamp, so it's from about an hour before the truck driver said he thought he heard the noises. You should be able to verify the prints. I guess that's why the sheriff figured you'd want to be involved in this. We ran a check on one of the names the waitress gave us and he's got a long record with Vegas Metro.

"Jesus, these people are getting stupider every year," Savic said.

– 23 –

Felicia Mendez lived in a drab gray apartment building that looked like a cement high-rise in a depressing black and white movie where a 1950s East German spy in a trench coat and fedora walks down a rainy street in Berlin.

The structure's fifteen concrete stories and ninety identical wrought iron balconies provided a good evening vista of the glittering Las Vegas skyline. Her corner unit, decorated with hanging potted plants and a giant cactus, gave Felicia an even better view of the casino where she worked.

She answered the door wearing her employee badge on a standard-issue cocktail waitress outfit: mile-high heels, black mesh stockings, Egyptian silhouette glyphs of Queen Nefertiti on the hem of the short black dress and her hair piled high like a cage dancer at King Tut's birthday party.

Tonight she spoke in her cooing, obvious husky seductress voice, the one that made Savic's advance bullshit detector buzz in his head like an oven alarm.

Variously sized and shaped candles flickered from every available shelf and tabletop in the apartment like some witchy waiting room where aromatherapy was just another ploy to steal your soul. Savic, who had been thinking about this necessary visit for days, immediately felt that maybe he should just turn and walk away. Or better yet, run.

She batted her big dark eyes: "You've avoided me, Frank," she said, almost sternly. "Come in."

Cigarette butts spilled from the tray on the coffee table, where two empty glasses stood next to a bottle of wine leaning in a brass ice bucket. The glowing candles gave the darkened room a blurry, brothel look, and though he'd been here once before Savic noticed for the first time the photos on the bookshelf: her wedding portrait, her late husband, the larger picture of her son draped with a rosary and lit by a Spanish veladora candle of its own like a shrine to a church saint. There was a touching spookiness to the scene that Savic could not explain, and it made him uncomfortable. How he'd gotten himself into this situation, he didn't really know, but it had to be fixed tonight.

She'd moved to this place after her boy was killed. It made her feel safe, she said, to live in a big ugly box with identical, anonymously numbered steel apartment doors where you needed a key fob to use the elevator, and where a sleepy lobby guard made at least a cursory check of visitors.

Where nobody could crawl through your window.

She gave him a cool, lingering kiss on the cheek. The tight dress rustled against her legs. The spiked shoe heels made her four inches taller so that she now came nearly eye-to-chin, and as Felicia briefly stroked and patted his shoulder and stepped aside, the pendant at her throat sparkled brightly and Savic recognized it as the one she had worn in the courtroom.

"I kept calling, Frank," she said. "I left all those messages but you ignored me."

"I know. I counted," Savic said, feeling like he'd just stepped into one of his own interrogation rooms back at the police station.

She sat on the sofa in an unfamiliar, demure manner, like a pianist preparing to play, and handed him a glass.

She flashed him a beckoning look: "Is something wrong, Frank? I just wanted to talk to you, that's all."

"So they told me," Savic said, explaining that he had spent the week on two new murder cases, not to mention the pile of union paperwork he was sorting through for his pending retirement. He left out the part about his dwindling checkbook. Then there were the daily visits with Maria at the home, but he didn't want to start that conversation. It wasn't any of her business, anyway.

He hadn't planned to sound hesitant and sheepish, but now he did just that. He found himself apologizing for something, though he didn't really know what that was. He started to get angry at himself for being such a wussy pushover when all he wanted to do was to tell this woman that he had no intention of ever seeing her again and that he was sorry for being such a dumb and naive sonofabitch.

She stood and stepped to the door and latched the two heavy deadbolt locks and came back and poured their wine. A soft warm breeze came through the open balcony sliding door and the candles in the room flickered briefly, all at once, as if calling attention to some announcement that was about to be made. As if some drama was about to take place.

"I know you feel guilty about her, Frank. Your wife. And that's understandable. I don't want to make trouble for you."

"Guilt has nothing to do with it," Savic said. "That little thing that happened back at the DA's office, it meant nothing. I was just consoling a friend, is all. Just that. If you feel it was something beyond friendship, then you've got it all wrong. That's why I came here tonight. To set things straight so there's no confusion. I made a mistake –– a professional error, getting personally involved in your case, and I never did that before. It wasn't fair to you. I was stupid."

"Straight? Set things straight?" Felicia almost whispered and studied her glass of red wine as she flashed Savic a full frontal view of the lower-than-low cocktail dress.

Savic glanced at the balcony view of the city as if the words he was trying to say might conveniently appear imprinted against the evening sky.

"It was a lapse in professional judgment," he said. "Let me just put it that way."

"I didn't think of it as a lapse," Felicia said. "That's not fair, Frank. You're saying I was a lapse, is that what you're trying to tell me? That I'm not attractive? Is that all I'm worth?"

Again, she gave him that sultry gaze with the droopy dark eyes; a slight tip of the head, one hand coming up to brush a strand of her hair from her cheek, where now in the candlelight glow of the room her makeup seemed overdone and theatrical.

Savic repeated again: "I gave the wrong signals."

"I liked the signals very much," she said. "I know a signal when I see one. Men give me those signals all the time. Your signal didn't seem wrong at all."

"Then you misunderstood."

"Now what we had was a misunderstanding? First a lapse, and now a misunderstanding. Are we teenagers, Frank? Can't we tell each other the truth?"

She lit her cigarette like she'd practiced just such a move many times, took two quick puffs and twisted the butt into the crowded ashtray. She took another drink.

"Just because she's sick shouldn't change anything between us."

"Are you listening to me? There's nothing between us. This between us thing doesn't exist. I don't know where you got that idea."

She gave a hard, mocking laugh. "And you came all the way here to tell me that? I thought we might have an actual adult discussion about things."

"Yeah, and I just did. I'll repeat myself if that's what it takes. There are no things to discuss," Savic said. "But there's something else, Felicia. Something actually more important," he said, raising his voice. "Probably more important than this romance you think exists. What's this bullshit with Jardine? I was told that you're trying to get information about him over at the prison."

Felicia stood and folded her arms and looked out where her potted cactus was swaying in the wind on the balcony.

"The clerk at the court said you've been trying to get his file," Savic said. "You can't just walk into the courthouse and start talking to people about police matters."

"It's public record."

"Not the part you want," Savic said. "That's still sealed and with the DA. Let it go. We've talked about this before. You have to move on. Jardine has been sentenced and he'll be in jail for the rest of his life. That's what you wanted, isn't it?"

"I wanted the death penalty, you knew that. Can't blame a lady for trying."

"You knew that was impossible from the beginning," Savic said. "It's politics. I told you it was politics with the death penalty."

He thought about taking a drink of the wine but decided against it.

"And another thing," Savic said. "You were recently seen on Pecos Street. Twenty cruisers drive through that neighborhood every day, and most of the time they're on the look for hot tags and stolen cars. Did you really think your license plate wouldn't show up and that somebody wouldn't tell me about it? Everybody at the office knows who you are. Your little red Honda is hard to miss in that neighborhood. That's not a place for you to be seen."

"I was visiting friends. Frank, I grew up on that street. Now you're following me? I thought you didn't care about me?"

"You should get new friends. You should forget about the ones you have in that neighborhood. And you should get it out of your head that there's anything else you can do about Jardine. Jesus, you sliced his face up and he's doing life in the worst lockup in the state. Be satisfied with that."

"There's nothing wrong with being curious about what the man who killed your son is doing. You know my husband grew up in that neighborhood. I still know people. They're not all bad over there."

"Most are, and you know it. That whole block is filled with car boosters and drug peddlers."

"I just want to know what he's doing."

"He's rotting in a cement jail cell and taking dumps on a steel toilet. That's what he's doing."

Felicia sat, her elbows in her hands. She smiled and spoke softly.

"Really, I'm trying to hurt a guy who weighs three hundred pounds. Is that what you're saying?"

Felicia wiped something from her eyelash with her pinky finger and Savic saw the badly fitted ring on her hand, her dead husband's wedding band.

"I need to know exactly where he is, Frank. If I don't, then he's standing next to my bed when I'm asleep. Or he's in the back seat of my car when I'm driving home at night. I look over my shoulder all the time. Do you know what that's like? It's why I have to know; I can't explain it any other way. I asked the lobos to tell me, if you must know. They run that prison. Nobody does anything in there without their permission, and I just need to know what he's doing so he doesn't haunt me."

"Those boys are the wrong people to ask for a favor," Savic said. "Don't take on a debt you can't repay. That's all I'm saying."

"I owe them nothing."

"You will," Savic said. "I've been locking up a whole generation of that gang for a long time and I know how they operate. You're out of your league, Felicia."

She reached and took his hand and stroked it.

"How is your wife, Frank?" Her tone seemed surprisingly genuine, respectful.

"You're changing the subject," Savic said and pulled his hand away.

"You're right," Felicia said. "I won't be going back to the neighborhood, I promise."

"If the DA finds out you're trying to have contact with them about Jardine, I guarantee he'll rescind the order to drop the charges for your stunt with the knife at the courthouse. The only reason he didn't lock you up is because of the bad press he'd get. It's an election year and the last thing he needs is to be the bad guy who came down on a grieving mother."

"I'd like to cut out his heart, Frank," Felicia said. "That little scratch I gave him is nothing. I want to pull out his heart and drop it on the floor and step on it. You can't understand what I'm feeling."

"If the lobos get involved for you against Jardine in that jail I guarantee they'll brag about it. Those people don't know how to shut up, and unless the other gangs know what they did then it serves no purpose for them. This isn't a complicated PR game for them. They'll need to get credit and it won't take long for the trail to lead right back to you. You mean nothing to them. By that time you're expendable, you know what I'm saying?"

"I don't have the money to hire a hit on Jardine."

She gave him a flirty school girl's kiss, this time a quick, darting peck that caught the edge of his lip as he tried to clumsily squirm away. He smelled the fabric softener on her freshly laundered sleeve.

"You worry too much, Frank. It's actually touching, the way you worry about people. It's not good for you, but it's very sweet. For a cop, you've got a heart. It's why I was attracted to you. It's why I think it could work for us."

She said something quickly in Spanish and reached for him again. Her hand slid over his shoulder down the front of his shirt and Savic hesitated before he gently pushed her away and stood to leave.

"Let me say it again. Stay away from the lobos," he said, trying to keep the conversation on track. "They're poison."

"We could be good for each other, Frank. Two adults, no strings," she said, ignoring him. "Nothing complicated, I promise. Just you and me. I don't do so good when I'm alone. I don't think you do, either."

"I know," he said. "That's a problem. But this thing isn't going to happen."

He stood and turned to walk away and as he fiddled clumsily with the complicated two-lock deadbolt system Felicia had installed on the apartment door he felt the glass bounce off his back, the wine splashing across the wall. He turned and caught her two windmilling fists as she leaped at him, screaming "Maldito hijo de puta! Get out of here you sonofabitch!"

She exploded into a ball of flying elbows and kicking legs. The glass coffee table tipped over, sending the open bottle of red wine onto the white rug. When Savic tried to step away Felicia came at him with the corkscrew in her hand. Wobbling on her high heels, she tripped and stumbled forward at his feet like some dazed supplicant suddenly felled by religious fervor. Savic seemed stunned and stood staring down at her as she got to her feet and looked at where her tight dress had torn halfway up her thigh, and she began to cry.

She lurched up at him. He took her shoulders and twisted her around, and her legs came up kicking the air again, both high heeled shoes flying off her feet as he struggled with her across the room and lifted her onto the sofa. He held her down as she screamed louder, spinning and twisting until her bare foot struck the ice bucket and it too sailed across the room and rolled to the wall. And then they both fell to the floor, she hollering her garbled Spanish cursing nonsense and trying to twist herself around, both fists now pounding his chest as he wrapped his arms around her and said, "Jesus, stop it. Just stop, will you?"

"Get out!" she said.

He held her down and she was breathing heavily, jerking back and forth and her feet scrabbling against the rug with her dark, fallen mound of hair tangled across her face as Savic said again: "Jesus. Just calm down."

They both lay on the floor, their arms and legs hooked together, Savic pressing her down with his weight and every few seconds Felicia trying to jerk away until she finally went limp and began crying again. A deep, throaty sob mixed with gibberish sentences and more mumbled oaths aimed at Savic and the inexplicable cruelties of the world in general.

He stood quickly and said he was sorry and wished her the best of whatever luck was possible. When he walked through the unlatched steel apartment door and into the hallway he turned and saw her standing there wearing a forlorn, abandoned puppy expression with her dark hair a mat of hanging curls and the braided gold necklace twisted across her bare shoulder, the black dress and the black satin slip beneath it torn and hanging ripped and wine-stained. Felicia Mendez just stood there, small and defeated.

Savic shook his head and wished he'd done this some other way with better forethought, since he'd known perfectly well how she would react. How this evening would end. He understood how she must have felt and yet it only made it worse to pretend that this could have gone any other way than it had.

That didn't work out well...did it, he whispered to himself as he walked quickly down the hallway and wondered if he should just take the stairway downstairs instead of waiting for the elevator while she stared at him.

– 24 –

While he was on hold with his call to Basel the recording played a soft Mozart minuet. He looked out the window of his rented van at the fake Venetian canal with its blue painted bottom that was partly visible next to the hotel's parking garage entrance and he thought absently about the trip he'd taken recently to Italy.

Although he had other business to settle, this was a visit to meet with a former colleague who now worked for the World Health Organization's European office in Rome. Siddhartha Raspatikan's primary field was entomology, but he'd also spent years as a private contractor consulting with the FBI in Quantico, Virginia. Raspatikan and Colt had worked together on several forensic entomology reports for the FBI that needed to establish an estimated postmortem index, including a corpse's length of dormant position following death. Larval stage observation was one of Raspatikan's specialties, and Colt had been corresponding for some months now about his friend's thoughts on arthropods. As a hobby, Raspatikan had been experimenting with pheromones and their affect on the sexual habits of a certain spider that, under some conditions, could live in the desert climate of the American southwest.

But Colt also had a sentimental reason for his visit to Rome, where the brief meeting with his friend Siddhartha had lasted only a few hours and a short lunch at a cafe near the Pantheon. They'd made their arrangement easily and Colt had tactfully avoided his friend's insistent questioning about what project he was currently working on. Colt only told him that he no longer worked for the government and was now in a specialized practice.

While he waited on the phone, he remembered how the familiar train from Milan had slowed teasingly to a crawl some miles before arriving at the Santa Lucia station in Venice, the gray water of the Grand Canal impressively calm and empty at the end of tourist season. He never got tired of how the city looked when you first stepped from the station: like an abandoned theatrical set, the colors at the time muted in the sunless October dusk.

Colt had taken a Vaporetto to his small hotel, the water taxi pleasantly roomy and absent the usual crush of summer visitors. The tiny penzione was tucked into a cobblestone alley on a canal with a bridge decorated with late season flowers growing from the arms of marble angel sculptures. A construction crew was digging in the canal, the excavation blocked from foot traffic by government signs, one side barricaded by a barge loaded with wooden pilings. Workers in yellow hard hats were pulling buckets of mud from the canal while a few gawkers watched and took pictures.

The ancient building had filigreed balconies and an enormous iron doorway and the owner, Nicolo Braga, took him to a dormered room that overlooked the canal, from which he could see the full lagoon and the tiled roof of the Metropole Hotel, where he and Adriana had stayed so long ago. Where he and his wife had once made plans for a long life together.

The two men retired to a flowery courtyard where Braga's wife brought coffee and grappa and creamed finger cakes that she said were a specialty of their home village near Lake Como.

Braga lifted his little shot glass and gestured slowly over his shoulder.

"Lord Byron the English poet lived not far from here above a clothing shop on the Calle Valleresso."

Braga studied Colt's hand as he held his drink high in a toast.

"The medical profession," he said. "The ring. The sign of the snake."

Braga immediately wondered if the question had been too forward. He had learned not to pry into the lives of people referred to him by the Swiss banker Kreutzer, whose clients tended to be wealthy and secretive and not as outwardly friendly as this unusual American seemed to be. Still, he had to be careful. To annoy or disappoint Kreutzer would not be wise, especially during times when such a source of reliable income was invaluable.

"I never attended to patients," Colt said. "My job was on the technology side, pathology and things like that. *Forense*, I believe you would say. I really don't know why I still wear it. It's very clumsy and looks like sports jewelry, don't you think?"

"Like one of your American football rings," Braga said.

"I'm too sentimental," Colt said, deciding not to mention that the ring had been given to him by his former section chief at the FBI. It might confuse the careful conversation he was about to have with Mr. Braga, a complete stranger.

"I admire sentimentality," Braga said. "I believe even a man of cold science can be sensitive. Just think of our DaVinci."

Colt smiled. "Darwin, you know, studied human emotion. He tried to apply science to grief and tears. To what was invisible to science. You wouldn't think someone like him, a clinical and methodical man, would have done that. But he had more than a few emotional difficulties and maybe that gave him some insight that most scientists would not have."

He could see Braga wasn't interested in taking the subject any further, so Colt said he admired the number of flowers that were planted in pots around the courtyard.

"It helps with the smell from the canals," Braga said. "A misfortune of living in a city that is twelve hundred years old, is that it's quite stinky at times. We've never solved our sewage problem. Especially during the aqua alta, the yearly high tides that begin in October. This time of year the entire lagoon seems to gather up its odors and deposit them on our humble doorstep."

The innkeeper explained that he had once been a civil engineer until his company went bankrupt during the most recent recession.

"We purchased the house here in a most decrepit state," he said. "Fortunately, my background made it possible to renovate. Now, the Germans seem to be our best customers. And the Swiss; we see the same people, entire families, each year. Those Frankfurters are very habitual. Always the same dates, the same tours, the same requests for food. I believe they enjoy the reliability of our history. Even Napoleon could not change Venice, though he tried. Sometimes the English come. The Brits are more casual. They will strip themselves half naked at the first hint of sunlight, the result of living in a land where it rains so often, I suppose. The

Americans seem to prefer the larger modern hotels along the lagoon, the ones with television and room service and porters to carry their luggage to the Vaporetto."

Colt pointed at the large stone tile fastened to the front of the inn, above the doorway, like a seal with scrolled edges.

"The angel?" Braga said. "A legend. We have hundreds of legends in this city. In fact, I'm not sure if this one is true."

Braga finished his coffee with a loud vacuuming sip, took the last of the cake and wiped his chin with a cloth red napkin that had been twisted and folded into the shape of a rose. He chewed as he spoke.

"They say in the fifteenth century there was an esorcismo here. The bishop himself performed it. It's told that when the demon was finally chased from the home he escaped through a hole that was later covered by the image of the angel you now see up there. They say that while that angel remains over the hole the demon can never return."

"Has he tried?" Colt said, smiling.

Braga laughed. "I always look to see if the angel statue is still there, if that's what you mean. Out of habit now, I look every day. So, I suppose he has not yet succeeded. I'm sure he has tried. Satan is very persistent. He can't be destroyed, only delayed. They say if you cut out the devil's heart that it will continue to beat."

Colt asked about the canal they were digging up.

Braga shrugged sadly and poured grappa into his empty cup and poured more coffee and stirred it with a tiny spoon.

"The water rises each year, the tides grow stronger. The pilings below the buildings — God knows when they were put in place, are rotting. They find furniture and antiquities in the mud when they empty a canal so they can fix a wall. Some of it very valuable. They find this all the time, of course. It is of no rarity in Venice."

Colt, informed by Kreutzer the banker, already knew the answer to his next question: "Who pays for such a thing? This expensive excavation."

Braga tapped his chest. "At least partly, we do. It is a government requirement. They decide what must be preserved and if it happens to be on my property, or if my building in any way touches the area of repair, I have no choice."

Braga rolled his eyes. "Our government has many requirements."

"All governments have requirements."

"None as many as here," Braga said.

"In my country they would be more practical," Colt said. "Pour cement and quickly brace your hotel with steel beams and a supporting structure that nobody would see, and then be done with it."

"We have lasted ages with our curious methods," Braga said. "Our sixty-foot-long wood pilings are the best example. The special cement that we still use for the floors of our buildings. You can't bring back what is dead; you can only keep it alive as long as possible as a fantasy, no matter how difficult it is. A fantasy always lasts longer than reality, do you understand? Memories and legends are nearly impossible to destroy. They only grow stronger with age."

After a clumsy silence, during which Braga poured grappa into his coffee and looked absently over his shoulder as if waiting for someone to bring more finger cakes, the innkeeper explained that he and his wife were struggling to pay the taxes on the penzione, which seemed always on the edge of crumbling again into ruin. The cost of the required government canal restoration would further complicate matters.

"Frankly, Dr. Colt, I don't know how much time we have left here. We are always grateful for the visitors we have."

Colt told Braga the next day, quickly and with a familiarity that surprised the innkeeper, that he wished to help with the restoration.

"Certainly you don't want to go into the hotel business!" Braga said. "There are many requirements, as I said. You're a physician. Why would this interest you? And besides, I am not interested in selling."

"It's more selfish than that," Colt said. "And I don't wish to buy your hotel."

"Then what would you gain?"

"I would gain a friend," Colt said. "Who I would then ask for a favor."

"I would have to consult my wife, of course."

"You're not offended?"

"I'm quite amused that a stranger who I have known for such a short time wants to give me money. Out of the blue, as you Americans would say. Perhaps I should first ask about the favor before I agree. Favors often have undesired consequences."

Colt said he had noticed one particular sculpture by the canal. It showed three lovely cherubs, stone carvings, their arms wrapped around a large urn as if ready to fly away with it. The workers had already carefully removed the relic from its pedestal and were resurfacing the cobblestones that lay at its base. Braga said the sculpture technically was on property which he leased from the city, though any repairs of a historical nature remained his responsibility.

"It will be completely restored and cleaned. We are on the Calle del Angelo, you know. You would say Street of the Angels. "

Braga pointed up at the facade of the inn. "At one time, when this very courtyard was part of a larger palace that included the home of the Doge's daughter, it was actually called the Garden of the Ashes, since it was part of a cemetery. But they changed the name many years ago. In any case, this is a unique location, garden or not, in a city with 75 lion statues on the Porta della Carta alone."

"I'd like to pay for that," Colt said suddenly. "The restoration of the urns and the pedestal, I mean."

"But you still have not told me the favor you wish to ask. Nessen passo senza recompensa — no footsteps without reward, as we say."

"I want to place something inside the urn when it's finished." Colt said somberly. "When the restoration is complete and they've put the angels back in their proper place. An urn usually holds something and I presume this one is empty?"

Braga nodded. "Ah, you wish to hide something? Now I am beginning to understand. Doctor, I do not wish to be involved in something illegal even if it is with a polite and intelligent man such as yourself. I hope you understand."

"Nicolo, this is a very sentimental and personal request. Perhaps foolish, yes. It is not illegal, I assure you. It is of great importance to me."

"Ah, that sentimentality again," Braga said. "And if I tell anyone of this?"

"You have nothing to gain. So, why would you? As you said just now: no footstep without reward."

He told Braga the amount of money he wished to donate. The innkeeper slumped back in his chair and he let out a slow whistle and quickly wiped his face with one hand. He finished his drink and filled the cup once more and brought it to his lips and smiled.

With these Americans you could never be sure, Braga thought. Drugs, perhaps. Americans were often very relaxed and disarming about even the most sensitive and dangerous subjects. No Italian would make such a request, yet the man's bold proposition had an element of simple honesty to it. The amount the American offered was more than what it would take to make the repairs on the sculpture. It would also soften Braga's government tax bill considerably. Nicolo Braga had much more to lose by refusing the American's surprising request.

"Your angels and whatever you put inside the urn, of course, will be perfectly safe. That is, if you do what you say," Braga said. "Our laws forbid any tampering with artifacts on this property, even if I sell the penzione or die."

"What will you tell your wife?"

"That you are a man who I've known for a few hours and that you want to give us a gift of fifty-thousand American dollars. My wife knows when I'm trying to tell her a false story. We have been married a very long time, you understand."

"And what will she say to that?"

Braga now laughed. "My dear wife is from Lombardy. Her ancestors were barbarians from the north. Very practical people, the barbarians. She will not refuse good luck, in whatever form it comes. She will insist, however, that you tell her the reason. It will be a requirement. I'm not curious at all. But she will want to know everything in order to give her blessing."

"Of course," Colt said. "More requirements."

"I warned you," Braga said, smiling.

Colt lifted his cup of grappa with its small dose of coffee and offered a toast.

"You will tell us both," Braga said. "Tell my wife and I together. It's the very least that we deserve if we are to be partners. We will talk at breakfast here tomorrow. Then you can tell us everything."

From his room that night he watched pigeons lift from the plaza and swarm above the dome of the ancient cathedral. He leaned from the window, the salty sea scent announcing the ebbing tide. The canal trembled with dark varnished light as the current twisted against itself back toward the sea. There was a shop across from the inn on a corner where another canal converged with the street. A sign on a wall said Calle Mallapierno, the street where Casanova was born. It was a carnival costume shop and in the window stood a dimly lit mannequin wearing a black cloak and a white mask that had a long nose that looked like the beak of a bird.

Death disguised as something alive, he thought. Death always visits us disguised as something other than what is expected.

Now, all these months later, as he sat in the van at the Venetian Hotel in Las Vegas, he remembered the promise he'd made to his wife beneath the balcony in Verona where Juliet had swooned over Romeo. They would one day take a grand Italian tour, weeks of museums and Roman ruins and galleries and perhaps a cruise down the Adriatic coast to Dubrovnik. She'd joined him on a business trip to the WHO office and they'd stayed at the Metropole Hotel, taking the vaporetto each evening to the casino and then walking hand in hand through the city's twisted streets to St. Mark's, where there was always a concert on the plaza outside the Florian Cafe. They listened to Mozart beneath an umbrella, the two of them, the drizzle making the ancient city smell fresh and new. His wife had told him that Venice was an old woman wearing heavy makeup who still tried to dress her very best, and they'd both laughed at the joke and said wasn't it wonderful to think about their family and the promises of the future.

– 25 –

Colt was still on hold as he took the interstate exit and parked along the shoulder with his lights blinking and imagined Kreutzer's secretary sitting in the reception room in the bank office in Basel. There would be the Black Forest cuckoo clock on the wall behind her Euro chrome desk with its shiny metal top and the uncomfortable looking brushed steel chair. There would be the expansive window view of the Rhine River, busy this time of year with barges and tourist boats cruising upstream past the serious looking buildings of this city of serious money lenders.

On hearing Colt's name and his request for "Herr Kreutzer," the secretary changed from her rough brogue Swiss German to clipped and proper British English.

"I will inform him directly. I'm very sorry for the long wait."

Some recorded chamber music clicked on, a lovely minuet.

The cell connection was fading so Colt stepped from the vehicle with the phone pressed to his cheek to block out the highway traffic noise.

"I'm so sorry to keep you waiting, Jasper," Franz Kreutzer said. He seemed out of breath. "Amalie took a while to find me downstairs."

"Franz, you didn't need to run," Colt said. "I have time."

"Then you are the exception from my other clients. You are always so understanding. How can I help you today?"

Kreutzer now had a considerable sum of Colt's understanding hidden from scrutiny in three separate accounts, though he knew he might be one of the banker's smaller customers.

"I need a courier, Franz. I assume some of your clients often have need of such a service?"

"Oh, yes. Quite often," Kreutzer said. "This is for a package not suitable for FedEx or one of the other carriers, am I correct?"

"Yes. Not suitable at all. Unfortunately, I can't do this myself right now. I would prefer a service that's discrete and very safe. I have other commitments."

"Certainly. I can recommend a highly professional firm. A German company I have trusted many times with sensitive matters. This is for funds, I assume?"

"More important than funds."

"Of course," Kreutzer said. "If you'll give me a few moments? Let me inform Amalie to see who is available."

"I have time."

The minuet returned, Brahms competing with the noise of semi trucks barreling down the interstate.

It was hot again. In the distance, the Las Vegas skyline —the miniature Manhattan, the Eiffel Tower and the top of the Mirage resort decorated with a blazing lit mural of a Cirque du Soleil show — pierced a thin veil of smoky haze hanging over the city. The sky was cloudless, the mountains dusty brown behind a shimmer of rising heat. One hundred fifteen degrees today.

Colt wiped his forehead. There was nothing to wipe, the air was so dry. He was dressed in a tee shirt, khakis and track shoes. He'd worked out that morning: heavy lifts only, his legs and shoulders now feeling thick and pleasantly sore and so he walked back and forth, trying to stretch things out.

The laptop computer was on the seat, connected to a booster antenna on the roof of the van. The passenger window was open and a message bar blinked on and off on the screen, and while Colt waited for Kreutzer he leaned through the window and touched the keyboard and watched a GPS icon dissolve into a flashing green light on a map of Clark County.

Henry Meffisti was still at home.

"Mein Herr?"

"Franz."

"I'm sorry again for the delay but we contacted the courier and they will be expecting your call so you can give them instructions directly."

Kreutzer gave the phone number of the bonded courier from a firm in Shaffhausen, Switzerland with a name that sounded like a charity relief outfit that fed starving refugees: The International Assistance League of Samaritans.

The laptop's message bar now changed colors and a pair of updated coordinates appeared on the screen.

Henry Meffisti was on the move.

"They will have to meet me at McCarren Field in Las Vegas," Colt said. "I'll send you a signed fax authorizing the costs to be deducted from the usual account, as well as customs paperwork for the couriers. I prefer they travel seated together in first class, of course. The additional arrangements I expect will be handled by you once they transit through New York. I'll have all the original and verified paperwork available for the courier."

"You don't have to drive to the airport," Kreutzer said. "They could easily come to your hotel."

"I prefer the way I suggested," Colt abruptly said.

"Of course," Kreutzer said. "I must mention that for security purposes this courier insists upon two people. A backup, as you say. They are highly professional. But very expensive."

Kreutzer seemed excited by the implied intrigue.

"Are they armed?" Colt said.

"Of course, and there could be a diplomatic waiver through one of the embassies if that's required. If I may ask, where is the parcel to go? I will call ahead and inform them you will be telephoning soon. The firm only works for the banking community. But they will require the instructions from you personally, for technical reasons. A matter of Swiss law, you see. Perhaps a verification of some sort, which you can do on-line. I'm afraid you shouldn't expect this to come together in anything less than one week, if that's acceptable. What's the destination?"

"One week is fine. It's going to Venice," Colt said. "The parcel is going to Venice, Italy to a private residence."

"A wonderful city," Kreutzer said. "I adore Venice."

"I'm fond of it as well," Colt said. He said goodbye and hung up as he watched Henry Meffisti's location quickly change on the laptop screen.

Colt entered a number and clicked up an additional screen. He drove quickly onto the interstate ramp, scanning the car radio until he found a station that played pleasant classical music.

Lush violin strings filled the van's cool interior. It was Mozart's *Eine Kleine Nachtmusik.*

A ...little night music, Colt thought.

How suitable.

– 26 –

It had taken him a very long time to clearly sort out what had happened that night, and his conclusion was that it was Adriana who had been the first to die.

The children, agonized by the terrible sounds they could likely hear, had been killed much later.

Colt knew the police autopsy report by heart, every word and scientific notation. The photographed faces of his angels were pasted onto a sleeved yellow card at the back of a looseleaf binder, arranged crookedly and without much regard to the neatness that Colt would have preferred, as if someone who was very tired had hurriedly assembled vacation snapshots into a scrapbook.

Adriana. Rebecca. Tasha.

Each time he saw their names he experienced the same depthless emptiness in his stomach: not my family, not my family. *Please. Not them.*

It had been a very cold autumn that year. It was raining, an ice storm blowing in from the east when he finally arrived home late from work that night, the fireplace mantel clock ticking loudly as he opened the door leading from the garage into the hallway off the living room.

Adriana usually had music playing in the kitchen at this time of the evening, the *Three Tenors* or some favorite collection of romantic Italian arias that he was expecting to hear when he stepped out of his shoes and began to hang his coat in the mud room closet.

Instead, it was dark, the big kitchen wall clock also ticking faintly in the soundless gloom of the house. He could hear sleet pelting loudly against the roof and gusting against the windows. In the unexpected, foreboding silence the basement furnace fan was rattling loudly and there seemed to be a chilly breeze circulating throughout the house, as if someone had left a door or window open. In this weather, he thought.

The girls should have been asleep upstairs by now: Rebecca, he thought, would be in her pink monkey pajamas and clutching her doll and perhaps pretending to read to it from a book; Tasha, the eldest and the one with her father's calm and sometimes maddeningly detached temperament, would likely be reading past the time when her mother had sent both children to bed.

Entering the unlit living room through the hallway in the dark, Colt's foot bumped into the family's pet dog where it lay on the rug in front of the ajar front door, where the blowing rain had already formed a puddle on the floor. The dog lay open-eyed with its head on its paws and it was not sleeping.

A saucepan was bubbling softly on the kitchen stove when Colt, his heart racing, turned on the light. The pan's rim was black and charred, as if something had been cooking there unattended for a very long time. Another pot -- he could smell the distinct peppery aroma of Adriana's pasta sauce recipe -- had boiled over and doused the flame on the neighboring stove burner, the gas so strong now that Colt covered his mouth and opened a window above the sink. He dropped his old fashioned leather physician's bag to the floor. He had begun carrying the bag as a sentimental quirk, a comical nod to the old days of physician house calls and something he now used only as a briefcase. He ran into the living room, stepping over the dead dog as he bounded upstairs where all the lights were on and where he could hear more rain blowing through the window drapes of the master bedroom. He shouted Adriana's name. Downstairs, the mantel clock chimed loudly and began to clang its repertoire of musical 10 p.m. church bells.

He had called home two hours earlier, apologizing and explaining once more why he would be home late. A big case at the lab, he said, for which he needed to make a late evening conference call to his Interpol counterpart in Europe. His boss at Quantico had insisted that he participate.

He had made similar calls to his wife three times that week and he could hear the obvious anger in Adriana's whispery voice as she promised to warm up dinner for him when he finally managed to get home. Tonight, there had been an important school teacher's conference which Colt had promised to attend and Adriana was always one for taking such formalities very seriously. Colt knew that she would have her notes from the meeting ready when he got home and he had promised they would discuss Tasha's troublesome grades. Tasha, the precocious and creative child who was always the rebel, the one who got into arguments with her teachers, the aspiring and temperamental little artist who associated with the wrong kids at school.

"I'm really upset that you weren't there. Very disappointed," she said on the phone in her icy inquisitor's voice. They had a discussion only a few days ago about Colt's increasing work hours and his time spent on weekends at the lab, and he had agreed to take part in more of his children's school activities. Instead of being there for his family tonight, however, he had only delivered another broken promise.

"I had to work. You don't understand, it was unavoidable. I'll explain when I get home," he said impatiently as he looked at his wristwatch to make sure he wouldn't miss his conference video call. "I have to go now. We'll talk."

"The teachers asked about you again," Adriana had told him. "Jasper, it's like they aren't quite sure that I'm married to anybody. Sometimes I feel like a widow. I'm very embarrassed by it. And I think the girls are, too, when they never see their father at any of their events. This is getting ridiculous, Jasper. We have to settle this and you have to decide which is more important, your office or your home."

She hardly ever called him *Jasper*. They had always made jokes about his first name, and Adriana said it made him sound like an Edwardian butler.

"We can talk about it when I get home," Colt said.

"Yes, we should. We should talk about quite a few other things as well, Jasper. Quite a few things that really need to be figured out between us. This isn't normal, the way you work and travel. Do you know how many days you were out of town last month, do you? Twenty, that's how much. And almost the same the month before. The girls don't even ask anymore if you're going to be home at night. They assume you'll be off somewhere on one of your big shot FBI cases. I can't remember when you've read a bedtime book to your daughters. I caught Rebecca dressing up one of her dolls and calling it daddy and asking it to read her a Peter Rabbit story. It broke my heart."

"We'll talk. I love you," Colt said, cutting her short. But she had already hung up.

He now felt his chest tightening as he ran downstairs again to see if maybe they were all in the big basement playroom where everyone sometimes watched TV on the weekends. It was Friday night, so it would be reasonable that Adriana might have allowed the girls to stay up past their bedtimes. He hoped it was so.

As he passed the kitchen he noticed that a drawer had been pulled open on the island cabinet. Knives were missing from the butcher block holder, a few of the blades scattered on the counter and others lying on the floor. Adriana was always meticulous about her kitchen, never a spoon or cooking gadget out of place. Not a pot unhung or a knife not in its proper home. He shouted out her name again. He called out the names of his children.

Colt now ran upstairs, trembling, every inch of his body chilled as if his blood had stopped flowing. Every bedroom door was open, the beds inside untouched, the warm glow of a Disney Princess night light shining from the wall socket next to Tasha's nightstand. The children had never gone to bed.

Schoolbooks were scattered in the hallway, his youngest child's pink unicorn backpack still zipped and laying as if tossed against a wall with a colorful water bottle tucked inside its mesh pouch. A single sheet of wet notepaper, Tasha's homework assignment for the week, lay at the top of the steps as if it had been blown there by the wind that now sprayed rain through the open window in her room. In the brief instant that it took him to run down the hallway and glance down at the paper Colt recognized the child's doodlings: clown faces and lightning streaks and her own name drawn large and boastfully in dramatic serif swirls. Always the show-off, always wanting to be the center of attention. Drawn boldly on another sheet of paper, the headline: The Amazing Tasha Colt, it said above a pasted photo of herself and the dog that was not at all sleeping downstairs on the bloody rug by the broken front door.

The upstairs bathroom door was open. The floor was soaked and a muddy footprint showed on the white tiles, smeared sideways as if its owner had slipped. On the window sill he saw the outline of a palm, as if whoever had entered the house through the second story had lingered there first, bracing himself cautiously with both hands before he stepped to the floor. Without thinking, Colt immediately registered the fact that the prints had already begun to dry and that whoever had made them had done so after climbing first onto the yard shed that stood conveniently next to the house. He thought about the broken front door. He thought about the unusually large shoe print downstairs by that door.

There had been two of them.

Adriana lay with her cheek pressed oddly up against the hallway wall, her arms tucked to her stomach, crossed at the wrists, and her hips twisted as if she'd physically been tossed there like a rag doll. Colt shrieked, a guttural and throaty howl that seemed absolutely unfamiliar to his own ears. He fell to his knees and tried to lift her, one hand sliding by trained habit quickly to the side of her throat to feel for a pulse. The front of her dress was torn away, her lacerated and dislocated bare shoulder twisted backwards. Colt held her by the waist, immediately feeling the lumpy edges of a broken rib, and when he tried to smooth back her long hair so he could examine her eyes his palm came away gummy with blood.

He ran to the girls' rooms. The sisters lay on the floor in the small alcove coat room off the hallway, holding each other, their thin little arms entangled as if they were dancing in some desperate, grotesque prone position that told Colt that they might have still been alive when the killer left the house. Alive and frightened as they held on to each other. Rebecca's dark curly hair seemed carefully arranged, fanned out on the rug behind her bleeding head. One of Tasha's hands lay on Rebecca's shoulder, her fingers smeared with blood that had dried so that her hand now clung glued to her sister's blouse. He'd never seen them this way. So peaceful. Comforting each other, their tiny delicate mouths closed.

Tasha's dilated eyes were open, the corneas with a bluish pallor, her gaze lowered as if she wanted to be careful not to step on her sister's feet during their strange horizontal dance there on the floor. They were still wearing school clothes, Rebecca's Minnie Mouse barrette hanging loosely from a few strands of hair. Had she herself pulled it away? If they still wore their school clothes it meant that they had not changed before sitting down for dinner. Adriana would have insisted that they put on their play pants before dinner. Later, Colt would realize that the killer upstairs had likely been waiting for them in the house when they returned from the evening PTA meeting, perhaps patiently lurking as Adriana began cooking dinner in the kitchen while the children went upstairs. Had the girls seen the killer before the second man came crashing through the front door?

He held each of them in his arms. The crusted, bloodless wound on Rebecca's throat opened and Colt removed his suit jacket and covered them both carefully as if he were tucking his daughters into bed.

He went into Tasha's room. Her drawing easel was tipped over, boxes of colored markers and crayons spilled across the floor. On the large drawing pad she had begun a watercolor, tiny bottles of paints knocked down by someone who had bumped into the easel while coming through the door. She would not have done that. There were marks on the rug from a muddy child's shoe; Tasha had come from the school meeting with her mother without taking off her shoes in the garage. She would have known the easel was standing so close to the door and she would not have knocked it down. She had been chased by whoever belonged to the upstairs shoe print. Chased by someone who had been waiting in the hallway.

And then he noticed the scrawl across the watercolor in Tasha's distinctive script: the numbers 14911, scratched above the imprint of the heel of her bloody palm. And then across the room there were other smeary marks, as if she'd stumbled into the wall with both hands outstretched.

The rain blew the wet room curtains and Colt's impulse was to close the window but then he realized that he must not. Next to the window stood Tasha's chalkboard easel and he noticed the drawing of a giant figure standing with its feet apart. It was a hastily drawn stick cartoon, the eyes extraordinarily large, exaggerated black circles that had been drawn so aggressively that the crayon had broken and left scrawl marks on the chalkboard. Next to the man's outstretched hands, written in a slant as if the numerals were falling off the hand, were those numbers again—14911. He knew his daughter would not have written on her chalkboard with crayons unless there was something important about those numbers.

He felt sick and went to the bathroom and dropped his head under the sink faucet. Sleet blew through the window and pattered against the dripping wall and gathered into a pool next to the larger shoe print that Jasper Colt had not yet seen.

– 27 –

Maria, casually and as if such an observation was obvious and would only be overlooked by fools, had told him about the numbers.

It was nearly six months before they caught up with Jardine, whose crimes had grown sloppier to the point where it was agreed the killer might be a candidate for a trap that could take advantage of his carelessness. Maybe use his favorite bait: women and children in a vulnerable and preferably unlocked house at night.

After he'd caught Earl Lee for his last offense, Savic brought the case file to the house one evening and had the photos laying on the small corner desk that he used for his home office when Maria walked into the living room while he was watching TV. He'd just cranked back his old recliner chair and was about to dig into a bowl of ice cream when she held up the paper clipped stack of poorly exposed Polaroid prints that showed an inventory of prison tattoos.

"Quite the art gallery," she said, looking at the crude prison tats, profane slogans and variously rendered fire-breathing serpents and winged dragons.

"These guys like their dragons, don't they," she said.

"And snakes. And dog faces. And guns and knives. Tigers, wolves and Dracula teeth."

Savic aimed the remote and clicked through the TV stations, the bowl of ice cream balanced on his horizontal stomach.

"It's like they try to outdo each other. I never figured out why, but that's for the psych team to explain."

"Well, this one here," Maria said and lifted a close-up shot of Henry Meffisti's hand. "It's in the Bible, you know. Him and that Jardine guy, they both have the same thing on their fingers. But I'm sure you knew that."

Savic turned. He was watching a *Gunsmoke* re-run. He already had his feet up, the spoon aimed at his mouth.

" What?"

Maria waved at him with the Polaroid. "I just saw this," she said. "You've been saying how this case might be tied to that Jardine thing and so I thought I'd throw in my two cents. You said if I ever had any police ideas I should just talk. So, I'm talking now. It's from the Bible, those numbers. I think without the dashes it might be hard to figure out. I just watched a movie and the man had the same thing. That mark of the beast thing."

Savic paused Matt Dillon in mid-smile just as he was starting to flirt with Miss Kitty, who was leaning provocatively across a bartop at the Long Branch Saloon. He took the photo.

"See how the numbers are each separated by one finger? Fourteen-nine-eleven. It's in the Bible. I don't remember what the verse says, but I bet if you looked it up it might make sense. Ever think of that?"

"No, Sherlock, I never did," Savic said and put on his reading glasses. Maria bent down and took the melting bowl of ice cream back into the kitchen.

Savic stepped to his little desk with the photo. "We all thought it was somebody's birthday. Those people tattoo just about anything on their hands and it's mostly just garbage and gang codes. But maybe you're right."

"I am," she said from the kitchen.

She was.

⁂

Savic was still looking up at the image of the left hand thumb print they had found on the charred underside of the plastic wall socket plate at the Starbright Lodge when Miriam Holter, the department's senior forensic digital investigator, pushed up her glasses and handed him a list of names from the class of '02.

"Too bad those prints got degraded. The plate must have still been hot when it was taken off, but I think we have enough with the partials. Just maybe, if the plastic didn't melt too much," she said. "What made you think of that? Looking behind the wall plate?"

"A hunch."

"Well, detective. That was lucky."

"Hunches aren't accidents," Savic said.

He had returned the phone call from the girl at the art gallery at the Venetian Hotel and she'd told him in an excited voice that she remembered something about the customer who had bought the ticket that night for the Age of Sansovino sculpture exhibit. The show with the little angels and marble cherubs and all those vases in Italy

"Like, I just remembered it yesterday," she said. "There's this jock, and he's really a pain and always wants to come by and talk, and he works here and he's got a big football ring from school and he was going on and on about some stupid game that he played in –– like I really care, you know? And then I remembered it. The guy who bought the ticket. I never saw his face but I saw his hand and he was wearing a giant ring."

"He was wearing a sports ring?" Savic said. "Like a team ring?"

"It had a snake on it. I never saw a team ring with a snake on it like that, all twisty and climbing up a pole. So that's why I called. It's probably nothing, but you said to call, didn't you? I kept your card and you said to call. So, I like...did. I couldn't read your writing on the back, so I called the other number and they put me on hold, like, forever."

"Our best candidates don't seem to match any timeline," Miriam Holter said. "Too bad your girl didn't see the date on the ring. Not all medical schools give graduate rings."

She continued: "The top three are deceased. Number four, Edgar Barkley, is at Presbyterian St. Luke in Chicago, head of pathology. Been there forever. He's on the verge of retiring and is in his late seventies, so that probably rules him out. Jeffrey Lieber never practiced. He teaches at a small dental school in San Diego. Strictly an academic who never got out of the classroom, and he hardly fits the description we got from the motel owner."

Miriam brought out the hard copies of all the available prints gathered at the crime scene, including the degraded partial from the back of the wall plate at the motel room.

"The others were inconclusive with the national retrieval data bank, except for the thumb on that wall plate, and that one doesn't tell us much. We know it was fresh because it imprinted perfectly onto the carbon residue caused by the short circuit spark. Somebody took off the plate and then screwed it back in, probably immediately after the short circuit. I have some matching partials from the federal association of State Medical Boards, but it's mostly dead ends. I'm guessing saliva and DNA, once we finally get it, might stand up. But if you're correct, Frank...that he's playing games, he may have contaminated those samples on purpose just to continue with the tease.

"We know there was training involved, just from the examination of the body at the hotel," Miriam said. "The way the incisions were made. There might have been a surgical skill, I'd say, or a level of knowledge that implies surgical experience that would rule out even a general practice physician. Still, we're faced with more options than answers. More potential dead ends than actual paths of conclusion. Frank, this could take a lot of time."

"Take me back to the thumb print," Savic said.

Miriam stared up at the screen and smiled. "Actually, I'm glad you finally asked. I wanted to make sure you knew we'd pursued the other leads, but wait 'till you see this."

Savic found a chair and sat and looked up at the array of wall monitors in Miriam's office. One of them blinked to life and started displaying a row of document thumbnails images.

"If this is actually our suspect, then the FBI field office in Alexandria, Virginia used him on contract work before he got recruited for a full-time position. He spent most of his career in the D.C. area. Taught classes for the profiling team at Quantico, and then got assigned to a pathology task force that made good use of his actual specialty. Had a solid, relatively short career. A few citations. He was brilliant and considered valuable to his employer. He left the Bureau ten years ago. As far as the paperwork shows, he hasn't worked for anybody since then, at least on anything that required the renewal of a medical license or a board certification. The IRS only gives us so much without the DA getting involved, but I can tell you he hasn't filed a federal tax return since he left the Bureau, which is a major red flag. Physicians generally leave a trail a mile wide, but not with this fellow. His banking records go dry about a year after he left the bureau. His last license number was with the Virginia Department of Health. I'm not sure how anybody could wipe out their past like this without some professional outside help. This guy was very good with computer data, but not this good. "

"And he never worked for anybody for a decade?"

"No, and he could have worked anywhere for anyone, at least in the medical profession. In school he was an academic star. Came out near the top of his class. The Bureau put him on some heavy hitter cases, some very high profile international deals where he needed an upper tier security clearance to work with several people on a congressional intelligence committee. That's when he got assigned to the profiling team. Taught classes with the behavioral unit at Quantico. Went to Europe six times in one year with the assistant deputy director, that's how much they thought of him. But Frank, there's only so much we can retrieve from the Bureau. We tried to get more personal family information but they started stonewalling. They flat out said they didn't want to talk about his personal life at home or give details about his work. Even a public on-line search only gives little snippets. It's like somebody scrubbed him from the internet."

"Because he's one of them? The FBI brotherhood thing?"

"Maybe because he was involved in those high stakes cases, I don't know. He gave a testimony at The Hague when they sent somebody from the World Health Organization to jail for skimming money from an Ebola research fund in Africa," Miriam said. "There's no jurisdiction regarding the murders, of course. But the feds don't like former employees to go renegade on them. To leave the Bureau and just disappear, which is what this guy did. Just up and quit. They're sensitive to anything these days since that Timothy McVeigh screw-up and their own people selling secrets to the Russians. Nothing makes them more nervous than a former employee who they can't keep tabs on. I think that's what we have here: politics. If the FBI gets wind that we know something they don't, I'm sure you'll get a visit, and it won't be a friendly one."

"If they thought we were sniffing up their shorts they'd have an agent visit this office in twenty-four hours, I guarantee it," Savic said. "But I'll let Monaghan decide. I don't know if I want to be tripping over a bunch of goons in suits and neckties right now. Those people get on my nerves, always did."

"Your call," Miriam said. "I did a records retrieval out of the Quantico co-op data base. You can bet they log that sort of thing and it will get noticed. A police department asks about one of their former forensics stars and they already know something's up. They might call you before you call them."

"Why would somebody, a doctor with everything going for him, quit at the peak of his career?"

"I was saving the best for last," Miriam said.

She pointed for Savic to roll his chair next to her computer. Miriam smelled like cigarettes. She started to play the keys.

"Physician's Family Found Dead," said the newspaper headline. The photo showed a large suburban home encircled with police tape. Two officers were rolling three gurneys out the front door, followed by men in FBI windbreakers carrying large paper evidence bags and document boxes.

Miriam advanced the screen. "Wife, two children," she said. "Never solved. An apparent home invasion with multiple suspects. The Bureau had a trail on somebody but it went cold after a few months, if you want to believe them. They thought someone might have been looking for FBI material at his house--case files brought home, maybe, but that was never clarified. Local cops didn't get off first base. The Bureau immediately froze them out of the investigation. Not long after that our boy resigned and vanished. Far as we can tell he hasn't been employed since then. He just vaporized. He was listed on the county assessor's list as the owner of the Alexandria home for three years afterwards, and then paid the mortgage off in a single installment."

Savic said: "No job, but he still hangs on to the home and manages to pay a mortgage? A Washington, D.C. suburb can get pretty pricey. And then, after not being employed he suddenly pays the note on the house with cash and sells it. Why didn't he just sell it first, and where does he get all that money?"

"We're working on a transaction in what may have been one of his bank accounts, a federal credit union withdrawal and transfer that happened after he sold the house," Miriam said. "By the way, was Earl Lee involved in this thing in Alexandria?"

Savic shrugged: "If he was, then why kill Cavilleri, too? It's been all those years since his family gets murdered, then these two get snuffed within a few days of each other. And all here in Nevada. There's nothing to tie the two together except they had the same tattoo and they probably crossed paths in jail at some point. They were both in and out of the lock-up all their lives. I bet a thousand convicts have those same numbers on their knuckles."

"How does our doctor find these people as easy as if he's looking up old army buddies in the phone book?" Savic said.

"People don't really look up anything in the phone book anymore, Frank."

"So shoot me," Savic said.

"I suppose the doc didn't all of a sudden get dumb the day he left the FBI," Savic said. "He probably still has contacts at the Bureau. Knows his way around a computer. And he knows exactly how the feds and local police work. Knows the whole game inside and out, every investigative protocol."

Miriam took off her glasses, rubbed her eyes and pushed herself backwards on the wheeled desk stool.

She said. "Then, if he's all that smart, how come he leaves such a big trail for us?"

"He knows about procedure, about how law enforcement does things," Savic said. "He knows how clues are assembled. He's not so worried about being caught, he just doesn't want to be stopped—not yet, at least. I think when he shipped those hands with UPS he wanted us to notice Cavilleri's tattoo. He wants us to know that Lee had the same thing on his hand. I also think he knows about what's on Jardine's hand."

– 28 –

They brought him to see Olson the next morning. He was wearing his orange transit jumpsuit from Clark County. Olson had tried to find a shirt that would fit the most famous inmate at Silverheel prison, but Jardine still made a fuss about his pants being too short and his shirt being too tight. There was also the problem of size 16 shoes. The prisoner wore a bandage on his cheek and Olson was asked again about when he would get the surgery to fix his sinus problem.

"I blow my nose and air comes out from next to my eye," Jardine said. "Like there's a hole there."

According to his file his IQ wasn't low enough to qualify as an imbecile, but he wouldn't be giving lectures on quantum physics anytime soon. He had the largest, bluest eyes Olson had ever seen on a man. They were feminine and luminous with long exaggerated lashes, like something you'd see on a child's doll.

Jardine squinted at Olson. The wrinkles of skin on the back of his thick neck bunched as he lifted his bound wrists and furiously scratched the skin deformity that hung from the lobe of his ear. He seemed to pay a great deal of attention to that thing on his ear. William Parker Jardine didn't seem pleased at all with his new surroundings and he stared at Olson with those saucer eyes and then looked him up and down before signing the papers he'd been handed as the warden motioned for the two guards to step away.

"Mr. Jardine, I run a clean facility. I don't tolerate fighting among inmates. No talking after lights out. If you do, then it's isolation, or what I call the adjustment cells. Those particular housing quarters were built in 1888 and they are not pretty, believe me. Repairs at this old place are not a top priority with the state right now because of the planned renovation, so we've managed to bend some rules a little. If I catch you lighting up anything, then you get my personal smoking cessation cure — six weeks of adjustment downstairs. In your case that means you'll also be severely restricted for your personal exercise hour for the foreseeable future. Because of the nature of your crimes your interaction with the general population will be limited for reasons I'm sure you understand. If it were up to me you would be in twenty-three hour confinement, but for some reason the State of Nevada has decided that our isolation facilities are not suitable."

The warden nodded toward the far end of the tier. "You'll be only fifty yards from the tier officer. My job is to keep you locked up and safe and healthy, nothing more than that. Any questions?"

Jardine lifted his hand and scratched his ear.

"Suit yourself," Olson said. "Lunch is at 11:30. Dinner at six. TV goes off at 10. We have cable. TVs are old time analog. Same reason as before — the budget. The last time they let us purchase TVs around here was 2002, and the ones you see here we procured from the auction of a hotel chain in New Mexico. Inmates vote among themselves and decide which programs to watch on their tier, and in my experience they seem to be very loyal to the principals of democracy. We don't interfere with minor disputes. Inmates who don't agree with the vote usually don't enjoy a successful stay here. I see from your record that you've done this many times before. We'll have to see how you're able to do things our way now."

Olson took a moment to read from an email he'd received that morning. "I've been informed that you'll be going to the new clinic just down the road from here to take care of that wound on your jaw and for an appointment with the ENT specialist. It's an out-patient procedure, those sutures, and nothing that won't take too long. I understand it's preliminary to the reconstructive surgery that your attorney requested. I still need to get approval from the department for that."

Jardine glanced at the row of narrow skylights that ran across the ceiling of the ancient brick building. It looked like a relic greenhouse roof, the heavy wire-reinforced glass streaked and darkened with decades of soot. Jardine had been in prison much of his life, but he'd never seen a place like this. From the outside it looked like an old castle, all red sandstone bricks with a heavily arched front entrance that reminded him of a museum.

Warden Olson instructed the guards to take the new inmate to his permanent cell.

Jardine had to stoop through the low doorway. The steel door slammed shut behind him and he turned and pushed his wrists through the small opening so the guard could remove his cuffs.

There was a single light bulb, bare and shielded in wire mesh, and it poked from the wall up near the eight foot ceiling. Raising his arm, Jardine could easily touch it. He did and cement dust snowed down and he quickly stepped away and slapped the gritty flakes from his bald head.

He rubbed his arms and went over to the stainless steel toilet and flushed it. He stooped and turned the faucet and splashed his face, the water with a faint sulfur smell to it. There was no towel so he sat and pulled away a corner of the bed blanket and wiped his face, arching up his neck so he could violently rub his itching ear with the coarse fabric.

And then he saw the spider crawl from the air vent on the wall.

It walked across the ceiling and then dropped, hanging and swaying on its barely visible thread. The spider lowered itself quickly and smoothly to the cement floor with a dull audible sound, it was that heavy. It was a fat one. It was fat and brown, a red blotch on its back and when it raced away its perfectly round rear end tilted up and stayed that way as it scurried toward the wall

Jardine pulled his legs up and stood on the bed, his bent head pressed up against the ceiling, and watched the spider disappear under the bed. He flinched and fell back against the cement wall, breathing heavily as he slid back down onto the bed, where he pulled his legs under him and folded his arms and started shaking. He stayed that way for the next half hour and remembered what Olson had said about the downstairs isolation rooms. In a place like this the old punishment cells were bound to be dark and dirty and probably wet, which is the way they liked it. The way the spiders liked it. He thought about the big spider that was in the wall right now. He wondered where exactly behind the wall it was at this very second and where it would be at night when he went to sleep.

He did not want to go to an isolation cell. Not with the spiders.

– 29 –

Felicia Mendez waited on the back porch. There was a garage on the opposite side of the tiny yard filled with tools and air compressors and orderly shelves stacked with rows of new car tires. Two men stood stooped under an open hood, loud music playing, while someone in a welder's mask kneeled beside a shower of flying sparks as he repaired a metal bumper on a foreign car with out-of-state plates.

Bernardo was dressed like a nightclub dandy in tight black pants and he strutted out from the house smoking a cigarette, a thick gold chain glinting from behind his unbuttoned matching shirt.

He dropped the cigarette and stepped on it with one boot and held out his arms. Felicia allowed Bernardo's hug and when his hand lingered on her hip she twisted into him teasingly as if this had now become their standard greeting ritual. He nuzzled her neck and she returned his kiss, nodding at the garage:

"Quite the operation you have here," she said.

Bernardo winked. "We have an investment in the automotive repair and re-purpose industry."

An overhead porch fan pushed around the hot air and Bernardo sighed deeply and wiped his forehead with the heel of his hand as if he'd just performed something strenuous.

"They need some sugar," he said. "Something to show that you're serious about this Jardine thing."

"The lobos?"

"For their trouble, yes. Look at it like it's a fee," Bernardo said. "They already know about your man at Silverheel, but the trouble is I don't know nobody over there anymore. At the county jail, maybe a favor could have been done because of our local contacts. But Silverheel is different. Those boys want favors from us in return. It's a matter of trust. It's the best I can do right now. They need to know that you're serious. That's all I can say."

"It would be a favor, you said?"

"A matter of pride," Bernardo said. "They got their pride and favors come second. First is their pride. Once that's taken care of everybody is open to favors. If the other inmates hear that something is done for free for somebody on the outside then the lobos in that place lose respect. There's two things you got in prison, and they're more important than food and sex. Power and..."

He said the Spanish word.

"Status," Felicia said.

Bernardo nodded solemnly. "They do something for free and word gets around and they lose respect and so they lose status. You understand? There's no negotiating that, I'm sorry. It's a simple fact."

Felicia had not worn the black skirt today. It was her day off. She had on denim shorts and the tight floral blouse and her sunglasses were pushed back on her head. Some loose hair strands hung down her cheek. Bernardo took out a thick envelope.

Felicia flapped her hand, dismissing him. "No mule work. I can't do that. I won't get involved in your business. I'm not carrying drugs for anybody, Nardo. You know how I feel about that. It's what killed my Tony, that shit."

"They do it all the time, hermana," he said. "Simple as going to the store." He held up the two condoms.

"You never said I'd have to do that." She turned away. His hand was on her leg immediately as if he were about to console her. He stared at her intently.

"You do this one thing, just one visit to Silverheel and you give this to somebody who knows what they're doing and then you wait and we get Jardine for you. Nothing could be so simple, heh?"

"If I get caught then I'm in jail. That's pretty simple, too," Felicia said.

Bernardo tossed back his head and laughed. "Listen, you ain't going to jail. You ain't getting caught. Half those guards in the visitor room know what's going on. They get taken care of, too. It's beautiful sometimes how this business works. Like a dance. Just like a beautiful dance."

"I have my life straightened out, Nardo. I can't risk it. I've already lost too much."

"Of course, and it stays that way after you do this single favor. Your life stays straight and you make justice for what happened to your boy. You owe him that, don't you think?"

He stroked her arm, reaching up to touch her long hair.

"These people, the lobos, they only want something for their pride," he said softly. "A little dope that you give somebody and you walk out and everything gets taken care of. Nothing is for free in this world, Felicia. Nothing. It's ten minutes work and your little favor gets done. Jardine is a dead man. That's guaranteed."

The nearly translucent condoms were flesh colored, twisted at both ends and tied off with non-soluble surgical thread, the egg-shaped bulge revealing a lump of irregular chips that had been packed into a capsule that floated in a small amount of liquid.

"I'll get caught," Felicia said. "I'll get nervous and I'll do something wrong and I'll get caught."

"You just put it inside you," Bernardo said with a dismissive wave of his hand. He looked at the floor. "You walk in and you take it out from where you got it hid and you give it to him. He'll tell you how to do it. This isn't the first time they've done this."

Bernardo clarified in great detail where and how Felicia would have to carry the drugs.

"A little petroleum jelly. It's easy."

"Fuck you, Bernardo. Easy for you to say. I'm not doing that."

Bernardo pushed another cigarette out of his shirt pocket. He bent over and lit a match by scraping it on the floor and then he stepped on the match, the floorboards already scarred with other burn marks. He drew deeply as if he needed time to think.

"After you take it out you put it in your mouth and you kiss our man and he takes it from you. His name is Arturo and he used to work for me on the outside. They'll be watching you when you kiss him, so make it look real. Make it a long kiss, like you mean it. Give him a little tongue so it looks good. Two months he's been in, so Arturo he's got no reputation yet.

The guards in the room, they know it's his first visit from his girl. That girl is you. There won't be any suspicions. They'll warn you not to touch him, but that's for show. Nothing will happen, I promise. You just do what I tell you, understand?"

Felicia started speaking rapidly in Spanish and she looked away and said, "This is shit."

Bernardo ignored her. "You wear a short loose dress that day. You walk in and you take the balloons out and when you say hello you put your hand over your mouth like you're excited about seeing your man after so long. That's when you put it in your mouth. Give it to him with your tongue, you know? Wear your hair long and loose that day so you can use it to hide the sides of your face. There's cameras in there. When you say good-by you take the second bag out and use your mouth the same way and put it in his mouth. Simple as that. Do I have to keep repeating myself, sister?"

"Where will he hide it?"

Cigarette smoke flowed sideways across Bernardo's face as he made a great show of swallowing.

Felicia said: "They'll get Jardine? You promise?"

Bernardo tipped his head and let a white smoke ring float to where the ceiling fan pushed it away.

"You can do this, sister," he said. "You're going to do this for your son, remember?"

"One of the girls here can show you how to hide it," Bernardo said. "They won't do it for free, those boys. Nothing's for free. They need this favor before they do anything. There's no other way, corazon."

Bernardo took Felicia's hand and he squeezed it. He moved close and he kissed her, his tongue touching her half-closed, reluctant lips.

"It's your last chance to do something for Jimmy. You better take it."

210

– 30 –

Nobody puts a half bottle of beer back into a fridge, thought Savic. Soda pop drinkers do that. Not apparent aficionados of a relatively scarce German import that sells for twenty bucks a six-pack. He'd checked the liquor stores and the nearest one that carried the killer's brand was miles away, on the boulevard in a casino gift shop that sold Cuban ripoff cigars and expensive brandy. A tourist place that also carried wine and champagne and the kind of beer with a name nobody knows how to spell. Only two other stores in the whole city stocked it. Savic figured this guy was some incurable creature of habit, a detail freak with peculiar tastes. Always drank the same beer. Had a thing for art shows. A meticulous care for repetitive procedure that a surgeon would have. Perhaps some other habits would reveal themselves soon.

Savic believed this man killed not in a quest for power or for the pure joy of manipulation and witnessed suffering. There was certainly no rage involved. The killings were slow and methodical, scripted beforehand. To prowl the streets and indiscriminately decide another human being's fate can become as heady as any drug for some of these monsters, but that wasn't the case here. Savic could sense it wasn't that way. Like a rape that has nothing to do with sex, these were murders that had nothing to do with death. Even vigilantes act out their final fantasy with blind and unconstrained rage. With this guy, fury and anger were not part of the equation at all.

Savic called Miriam at the lab.

"I'm about set to go home, Frank. It's six-thirty, for godsake," she said. "I've been here since seven this morning. Mostly working on your stuff, of course. You checking up on me?"

"I have to connect a few dots," Savic said.

Miriam gave a long sigh. "I can only connect so many dots at a time."

"Remember that job a few years ago when we were trying to lock that school teacher away?"

"Sure," Miriam said. "The pervert algebra tutor. Guy should have been on file as a felon. Six abuse cases in five years. Had three teaching jobs. Nobody ever suspected him, nobody checked. He fell through the cracks."

"That was before Megan's Law," Savic said. "Now somebody gets out on a kiddie charge and he's on a shit list that follows him everywhere."

"In theory, it's the law. But it doesn't always work. So what are you asking me, Frank?"

"He had that tattoo on his back, and that's how we connected him with the other assaults. By building a timeline. We do the same thing with Lee and that tattoo on his hand. I'm trying to see who he served time with in jail and when. I think there's a connection to Jardine that goes beyond what we know. And I bet if you took another look at the photos of Cavilleri's UPS hands things might become clear."

"Frank?" Miriam said after a long silence during which Savic heard her typing something. "The prints on that beer bottle? I just saw that they belonged to Cavilleri. But the DNA on the glass belonged to Earl Lee. What do you make of that?"

"Impossible," Savic said. "The autopsy estimated Cavilleri's time of death at 48 hours before we found Lee at the motel."

"And that spit test came back from the toothpick that got jammed in the car door at the Starbright Lodge?" Miriam said. "I'm looking at it now. It came back as Lee's saliva. Why would he stick a toothpick into his own car door?"

– 31 –

Jardine could not sleep. It was the lights. He kept his eye on the air vent on the wall. He'd covered the metal grate with wet toilet paper and now he wondered if the moisture would attract the spiders even more. He'd have to think of something else.

He carefully touched the side of his face where his cheek had begun to swell again and with his tongue he felt where they had extracted his broken teeth. That was starting to hurt, too, like something was getting infected. His cheek was hard and hot and he felt like he was running a fever. He decided he would not tell anyone about the fever.

It was 1 a.m. Somebody was coughing in the cell next to him and he heard a guard's footsteps in the hallway. The fat guy a few cells down was taking a dump, farting and grunting so loud that another inmate shouted for him to shut up.

Jardine stepped to his steel sink and leaned over to spit, his face close to the steel rim where he steadied himself with one hand. The spider raced out from behind the leaking faucet and crawled quickly onto his hand and then scooted up his arm. He could feel each ticklish, feathery step of the tiny legs. His breath caught mid-scream like a startled child and he stumbled backwards into the cell bars, where he began slapping away at his sore face and head with both hands like he was putting out a fire. And then he went crazy.

At this hour, the six person prison suppression team took twenty minutes to get suited up in their body armor. The detention officers shuffled down the cell block in lock-step, one behind the other. The drowsy inmates on the tier, now awake and chattering, stood like agitated zoo creatures in their cages along the long hallway, arms dangling through the cell bars as they shouted at the team gathered in front of Jardine's cell.

When they unlatched the cell door the prisoner was holding a broken faucet handle and banging away at the metal sink where water was now spraying up at the ceiling. He'd taken off all his clothes and had wet himself down and soaped up his head and body, so the cement floor was slippery with suds when the team finally rushed in.

The first two officers held up their plexiglass shields and they pushed Jardine against the wall. He windmilled his arms and one guard chopped down with his billy stick, which he then held horizontal and brought up under the prisoner's chin. Jardine started spitting and kicking as the team fell forward in a heap and pinned the prisoner down, each man assigned beforehand as to which particular limb or body part to grab with his gloved hand.

Outside on the noisy tier, fully awake and entertained, the inmates were chanting and laughing, singing in a taunting and off-key falsetto the same phrase over and over again.

"...itsy bitsy spider crawling down the wall. Itsy bitsy spider crawling down the wall..."

After they dragged Jardine away, one of the officers walked into the cell and saw where the prisoner had sealed up every hole on the wall with tape he'd stolen from the infirmary. He'd found the taped spots before and always opened them up but knew Jardine would just get more tape. The prisoner would have to get used to bugs and spiders, he decided. The place was loaded with spiders. It was old and crumbling and god knows what lived behind those old walls and the guard knew that where Jardine was going next it would be worse.

The cell was a mess. A steel bookshelf was torn from its bolts. You could see where Jardine had tried to lift the steel sink, its bent anchors now jerked loose. The steel pipe beneath the sink was ripped away and water was flowing out across the soapy floor and out into the hallway, where two other inmates with squeegees had been recruited for clean-up duty. The metal grate that housed the two recessed ceiling fixtures had also been knocked off. Jardine had tried to peel the chrome mirror from the wall. The other inmates were having a grand time cheering Jardine as the intervention team tried to lift and carry the kicking naked prisoner along the narrow catwalk that led to the exit stairway.

In the infirmary Jardine lay on his back strapped to a bed, the blurry shape of a white lab coat hovering above him. He felt somebody tugging at the loosened stitches on his cheek and then his face went cold as if they'd put ice on it. Something stung his arm that felt like the spiders were biting him again and he tumbled into a hovering half-sleep in which more people pricked his face again and again. Maybe now they were nibbling at him, he thought. Bite by bite, they were eating him and soon they would slowly wrap him up in their white thread ball and he would hang for eternity in a web behind the dirty wall in his cell in the dark.

In the infirmary Jardine dreamed he was crouching at night outside the window of a house, the first floor, the easy kind to climb into, and he was watching a spider crawl across the glass, its button shape distinct in the dark against the glow of the street lights outside. It was a soft, warm night and he was sweating and the insects were screeching in the bushes beside him outside the window of the bedroom into which he wanted to crawl. He looked up and saw the enormous spider web above his head, swaying and puffing in and out like a white blanket, speckled with captured bugs. In the corner of the web sat the fat spider with its legs folded against itself, ready to jump at something. Jardine ducked his head as he reached and slid the window open. Inside the house he heard a woman say good-night and someone laughed and then it was quiet.

He slid his hand beneath the window sash and lifted it quietly. There was a small motionless shape in the bed and a cat mewed somewhere in the dark where the light glowed faintly from the hallway. He saw the cat's shadow, its tail raised stiffly as it walked through the partly opened bedroom door.

While he waited, he watched the spider move across the web above his head, its little crooked legs skittering. Jardine's heart was pounding. A black cricket hung wrapped in a pouch on the web, its long bent legs grinding back and forth and Jardine shivered and finally pulled himself through the open window and into the room.

The cat came back and sat in a pool of hallway light and looked at Jardine and lifted one paw and licked itself. Jardine took out his knife and crept toward the bed and when he reached for the shape the cat jumped on the bed and a whistling alarm sounded. He heard footsteps and voices in the hallway and more lights suddenly came on in the house and Jardine heard a woman shouting into a telephone just as he began to crawl back outside through the window.

The spiders were waiting for him.

The web that looked like a sheet of spun white frosted sugar fell on his head. He felt them crawling on his face as he stumbled backwards into the bushes, where the giant web dropped loose and covered him. Jardine started screaming. He screamed so loud that he didn't notice that the lights inside the room had come on and somebody was shouting at him, too. Outside, the back yard of the house was lit up like a baseball field, the security lights flashing down on him from the eaves of the roof as he wildly flapped his arms and twisted around in the dark bushes and then began to scream again.

He was almost grateful when the police came.

When they pulled him from the bushes, detective Frank Savic stared down at him, expressionless as he pressed the barrel of the pistol against the top of Jardine head. Jardine remained on his knees. When he tried to reach up and swat something that was crawling on his face Savic smacked him hard with the pistol.

"Thanks for making this so easy, asshole," the policeman said.

– 32 –

Meffisti flashed his headlights and drove into the oncoming traffic.

"Watch this," he told Willy.

The approaching vehicle wobbled across the center line and continued to drive past in the opposite highway lane without a response so Meffisti flashed his brights again, taunting each oncoming car until someone finally answered with a responding beam and a long honk.

"Bingo," Meffisti said, skidding onto the shoulder and turning the car around.

He followed for a few miles, staying close enough so the driver of the vehicle would know he was being tailed. After a while the car turned into a darkened gas station, where Meffisti pulled alongside and rolled down his window.

"Mister, this place has been closed for years," he said to the driver, trying to sound friendly. He tipped back his cap and smiled.

The driver blinked at Meffisti like he'd just woken up.

"Were you following me back there?"

"I don't know what you're talking about, sir," Meffisti said. "I just saw you drive in here and thought I'd do you a favor."

"Okay," the man said. "Looked like it was you. Know where a fella could get some gas?"

He was old and sat slouched in his seat and wore a buttoned cardigan sweater and one of those floppy geezer fishing hats. The man grinned nervously and looked around until he spotted Willy, who nodded to him from the passenger seat. He scratched his head and looked over at the boarded up gas station, still confused like he didn't quite know where he was.

Willy started snickering. "Henry, he looks like Norman from Golden Pond," he said.

"Shut up," Meffisti said.

"What's he talking about?" the old man said.

"Oh, don't mind him," Meffisti said.

"I saw the pumps," the old man said. "I thought it might just be open. I think I'm lost. Are you from around here?"

Meffisti spoke politely and pointed at the highway: "About twenty miles up would probably work for you. A Conoco, I think. But it closes in about fifteen minutes. When you get this far from the interstate they don't stay open much past ten."

Meffisti kept staring intently at the old man, who now appeared more worried and looked nervously at the darkened gas station. He squinted at his wristwatch. He turned his radio off and looked over at the passenger seat and seemed to be searching for something.

"Oh my," the old man said. "I can't find my telephone."

Telephone. Nobody calls it a telephone anymore.

"I think I got lost somewhere back at the crossroad."

Meffisti stepped out and looked into the old man's car: scraps and wrappers on the seat, the smell of fast food and a newspaper lying on the floor, a box of tissues on the dashboard and something religious -- a tiny crystal angel and crucifix, dangling from the mirror.

"Tell you what," Meffisti said. "Park your wheels here and come with us and we'll drive you to a station. I'll loan you a fuel can. It's no trouble. We got time. Hate to see somebody in a pickle this late at night. You sure don't have enough juice to make it that far, from the look of your gauge. I'd sure want somebody to do me a favor if I was you. You don't want to break down out here at night."

The old man glanced at Meffisti's car, where Willy nodded again and gave him a goofy open-mouthed grin.

"I guess I don't have much of a choice," the old man said. "You're a gentleman for offering to do that. I'm not from here, you know." He waved his hand toward the phone booth that sat next to the station.

"Maybe I'll just call for a tow," he said. "I don't want to bother you. I've got road service from the insurance. They'll send somebody out."

"Oh, that phone hasn't worked for years," Meffisti said as he got out of the car.

The old man rooted through a pile of papers on his front seat. "I sure wish I knew what I did with that little telephone."

The old man opened his door. Meffisti quickly shot Willy a cold, familiar stare and came up from behind and hooked his forearm under the man's jaw. The old man staggered as if he'd suddenly gone drunk and then went limp and dropped to his knees. Meffisti cocked him on the head with the pistol.

"Pick him up," Meffisti said to Willy. "Old fucker hardly weighs anything."

He scooped out the old man's glove compartment and loaded his pockets with whatever papers he could find. He popped the trunk and found a small suitcase and took that without opening it. He rolled the old man over and jerked out his wallet.

"Four hundred," Meffisti said and whistled.

He peeled off the cash slowly and shook the wad of bills back and forth like he was fanning himself.

"Not a bad night's work, what do you think? All because I had a hunch back there and tried my luck. Yes, sir. That's the way to roll sometimes. Just lay it all on the line."

Illuminated by the headlight beams of the two parked vehicles, Willy hopped up and down and twisted himself into a clowning ballet dance, twirling one arm over his head in celebration as he performed his jig in the parking lot.

" Oh, boy. We got lucky again, didn't we Henry? "

While Meffisti continued to search the car trunk. Willy stooped and touched the old man's chest.

"He's not breathing, Henry."

Meffisti shoved the wad of money in his pocket.

"Shit."

"Yeah, Shit," Willy said, and he started nervously pacing back and forth.

"Put him in the trunk," Meffisti said, and Willy took the body by the feet and started to drag it away.

"Not my trunk, you idiot. His trunk. Jesus fucking almighty Christ. Are you stupid?"

The old man's mouth was open, his glasses hanging from one ear. Willy stood and stared down at him.

"Oh, shit, Henry. He's sure dead. I know he's dead."

Meffisti took the old man's car registration papers and his license from his pocket and tore everything up into small pieces and he flipped the scraps over his shoulder like somebody who had just been disappointed by a losing lottery ticket.

"Lift him up. And put him in the trunk — his trunk, got it?"

"Henry, I think..."

"Shut your hole and put him in the trunk," Meffisti said. "And then take his car and drive it around behind the station and leave it there. Nobody comes here anymore and the troopers hardly drive down this road. Wipe the steering wheel. Do I have to do that myself, or are you going to remember to wipe the damn steering wheel? I don't want your prints on it. Can you handle that, fucknuts?"

They drove back to the trailer.

Anderson the light bulb salesman was leaning through the kitchen window, stuck halfway outside with his pinched arms still taped behind his back. Meffisti walked up and slapped his face.

"I should just go ahead and do you right now," Meffisti said. "But you're driving us to Mexico. I don't have my license and my insurance is expired, so you're about to do us a favor by using your credit cards and your car and taking us to Mexico. Got it? If you weren't useful, I'd shoot your ass and bury you under the trailer."

"I don't know why you had to mess with that old man back there," Willy said. "He wasn't worth anything."

"He was worth four hundred bucks, retard." Meffisti shouted while he was yanking Anderson back into the kitchen by his feet.

"I'm mixed up, Henry. I'm real confused," Willy said. "There's too many cars. How come we have so many cars?"

"We're leaving the other cars where they are. We'll be in Mexico soon," Meffisti said. "This genius is driving us to Mexico."

Willy brightened up. "Yeah, Mexico!"

"Go park the car someplace where nobody can see it from the road. Do the same with mine, understand?"

"Yeah, Henry," Willy said. "You mean the car you stole, that one?"

"No, nitwit. My Mercedes," Henry said.

There was a long silence from Willy, and then: "You bet."

"Yeah, the car I jacked! Now do it!"

"Whose car do I hide, Henry? Your car or the lady's car?"

"Both," Meffisti said.

Meffisti pushed Anderson back onto the sofa and started to re-wrap his mouth with tape when the salesman quietly and shyly said:

"Just so you know, I can't drive that car to Mexico."

"Say what?"

"The rental form," Anderson said. "It's in the glove compartment. It says you can't take the car across the border. That's standard, you know. Rental companies don't let you take a car over the border unless you pay something extra. I thought you'd know that."

Willy turned around at the door. "What's he talking about, Henry?"

"I'm saying they'll check the papers at the border," Anderson said.

"Henry, why can't we go to Mexico! What did he say?"

"Shut up," Meffisti said.

"But he said we can't..."

"Shut up, dipshit," Meffisti said.

Meffisti went to Anderson's car and clawed through the glove compartment until he found the folder from the car rental agency. He slammed the compartment shut and when it fell back open he kicked it with his foot. He ran back into the trailer and tossed the folder on the sofa.

"Where's it say that? Show me."

Meffisti took Anderson by the collar and started shaking him. "You prick, how come you didn't say anything! You don't own this fucking car? Are you telling me you don't own this goddamn car?"

"Henry, are we still going to Mexico?"

"Shut up."

"Henry?"

"Shut up, retard."

– 33 –

The Rio Seco Aero Center looked like it might blow away at any moment just like the scraps of dry creosote that bounced across the gravel road that led to the small private airstrip south of Highway 160. A man dressed in a greasy jumpsuit with cut-off sleeves was leaning into the engine cowl of a single-prop crop duster with oil streaks on the fuselage when Jasper Colt parked his van and walked over with his hand extended.

"I'm looking for Duane McCord," Colt said and offered his best smile.

The man wiped his hands on his chest. He spit and pushed up the bill of his cap with one end of a crescent wrench.

"You're early."

"I gave myself time to get lost," Colt said. "I don't think I saw two cars the whole way here."

"Hard to get lost out here. I'm at the end of the only road out. You find the road, you find me."

McCord had square hands and a square, raw face and the greasy imprint of a thumb marked his forehead like a hurried Ash Wednesday anointment. He pulled a Red Man tin from his pocket and peeled off some chew and pushed the black plug deep into his cheek. He worked his tongue and gave Colt another cockeyed gaze as if sand had suddenly stung his eye. He spit again.

"They rent planes in Vegas, you know," he said. "Seems a long way for you to drive."

"I was referred."

"Yellow pages?"

"A business associate."

"I mostly do work for the state these days. You must have got it from them."

"Of course, I must have," Colt said.

As far as he could see McCord's fleet consisted of the Red Baron relic he was working on and a fairly new Bell helicopter with a gaudy blue tail that sat tarped behind it on a concrete pad. There was a small corrugated hut that looked like it had been hijacked from a Korean M.A.S.H. unit. Some crookedly planted palms surrounded the hut, their dusty leaves torn and drooping and a dog napped in the shade of a Pepsi vending machine in front of the airport's only hangar.

"Follow me," McCord said and wiped his hands on his pants.

In the quonset hut there were faded photos of World War II fighter planes pinned on a wall corkboard, each uniformly askew. Music played dimly from an unseen radio on a shelf stacked with parts catalogs and a large jar filled with machine screws and metal washers.

McCord handed over some papers he took from a tray next to an unrecognizable computer monitor.

" Standard liability form," he said. "Sign at the bottom. I don't take charge cards. I don't get good WiFi out here and the bank won't take the old credit card slips anymore, so I told them to shove it up their ass with the cards. Like we talked on the phone, payment is in advance."

Colt signed the sheet. He handed over five one hundred dollar bills.

"It's only three for the hour you wanted."

"That's in case we go a little longer," Colt said. "If not, then it's a tip."

Colt had told McCord that he was a contractor for the U.S. Geological Survey field office out of Grand Junction, Colorado. He said he was completing a watershed analysis project. He knew enough fake rock science lingo to tell McCord he wanted to take a look at some uplift formations along the base of the Lorrell Mountains. He made up something about an ancient river watershed that needed a future survey for the new prison rehab project at Silverheel.

The helicopter was a bubble top Bell. Colt clamped on the headset and McCord nodded and they lifted, the rotor wash spraying sand against the quonset hut and tearing off leaves from the doomed palm trees. The dog woke up and shuffled out of sight around the corner of the building.

"You know -- and don't get me wrong, but I'm not somebody who turns down money. I could have sent up a drone and saved you some dough. Probably more efficient and you'd have a video for the record. You seemed set on my chopper, so I didn't bring it up."

"I may ask you to land so I can make a personal inspection. Can't do that with a drone," Colt said. He held up the camera he had with him. He'd brought a topo map and spread it out on his lap. He had no intention of reading it.

McCord shrugged. "I have to charge if we go past the hour."

Now annoyed, Colt said: "I gave you the extra two hundred."

They flew low over a small trailer park, where Colt saw laundry flapping from sagging clotheslines. A painted school bus sat on cinder blocks, a satellite TV dish on its roof.

"Hippies," McCord said through the headset. "They've been out here forever, way before I bought this place. There's a freshwater seep spring down there and those folks pretty much stay to themselves. Don't even lock their doors at night and they must own fifty dogs, so nothing's going to bother them. I can't say I've ever talked to any of them. They make their living digging up gemstones and old shit over at the ghost town near the prison. Odd jobs, too. Feds caught them trying to tap into the old gold mine and put a stop to it. They were hauling out ore with the old rail wagons."

The chopper dropped altitude and banked toward the ghost town.

"Those bigger double-wides you see, that's where some of the prison guards live. The younger ones who don't make the drive home every night to the city. Once they build up the employee housing at Four Palms I supposed they'll leave and then it's just me and the Woodstock generation down there. Those hippies aren't going anywhere. They'll do anything for a buck, and I suppose what they do isn't all that legal, if you know what I mean."

"What's it called? The ghost town."

"Goodspring," McCord said, pointing toward where a thin blue ridge of low hills stretched across the horizon.

"Jail's over there," McCord said. "That's gonna' double my business soon. Got a contract to ferry in the engineers and tradesmen for the new expansion. Until they build a new access road, they won't let those guys drive in on their own for security reasons. The one road is the only way in and only state vehicles get to use it. Visitors come in with a bus. I can only fly so close with this thing." McCord said. "It's restricted air space."

The prison appeared like a wagon wheel painted onto the featureless desert. It sat between two barren cliffs that stretched into the distance like a fortified medieval stone wall. Colt could see the round silo shapes of the cell tiers. The central building was a domed pentagon, each side extending into a separate arm that ended in a guard tower. Colt could clearly see the guard posts and the bright shiny coils of perimeter wire that sat on top of each wall. The parking lot was a mile from the prison walls, connected by a wobbly gravel service road. He saw only one tower guarding the entrance to the road.

Colt pointed toward the scattered remains of the old ghost town that sat a half mile away from the prison.

"Take a spin around that, will you?"

"Thought you were looking at rocks?"

"I'd like to take a picture. Just to show the office, you know. We were talking about it the other day. I hear it was a famous place in the old days."

"Desperados, gunslingers," McCord said. "The prison used to be like Alcatraz in the old days. Nobody ever escaped. Now it's a dump. They're building a whole new complex right on top of the ghost town."

McCord pointed as he banked the aircraft and began to circle back toward the road, the small chopper shuddering in a sudden updraft.

"Can't really go any closer to the prison," he said. "Not unless they know I'm coming. You can understand why. I guarantee somebody's watching us now. They made me paint the tail to this thing blue and put bigger numbers on it so I wouldn't surprise anybody."

"They think somebody might try to help a prisoner escape?"

"Twelve did last summer," McCord said. "That's when they decided to go ahead with the modernization. Governor got a lot of heat for it."

The road that led to the prison pierced a deep road cut, and on the far side of that Colt saw old mining sluice chutes that pointed to where some stream beds had dried up long ago.

"Is that the mine?" Colt asked.

"A few thousand folks lived down there in the old days. Had a hotel and a dance hall. In the fifties somebody tried to run a whorehouse for the folks in Vegas. I sure wouldn't drive all this way just to get laid. Nobody else did either. Then they wanted to make it a wild west tourist town with cowboys and shoot-em-ups. That plan went down the toilet pretty fast. The buildings the whores used still have the door locks on the outside."

Colt asked the pilot to fly closer to the ghost town.

"Okay, but I have to be careful," McCord said. "The ghost town is on BLM land, so we can't stray too far beyond that."

"What's that tower over there?" Colt said, pointing to what looked like a tall wooden stool that sat above a hole.

"The main mine shaft," the pilot said. "Nobody's been down that thing for years. I wouldn't go near it. Hardly anybody ever does, except for those hippies before they got caught doing their illegal mining stunt."

Colt pointed at the shaft tower and asked McCord to land.

"The deal was a flyover," McCord said. "You didn't say anything about landing anywhere."

"Actually, I did," Colt said.

He looked at his watch. "We have two hours left. I gave you five hundred. Land down there and give me a few minutes to look around and we'll call it a day and you'll still be ahead of the game. Think of the fuel you'll save. A deal?"

McCord nodded and brought the chopper down directly in front of the mine shaft opening. Colt took his camera and stepped out of the small helicopter, stooping low under the spinning rotors and as he headed for the cavern opening. He took his camera. Colt walked past the rusty rail cars that sat hooked together on their tracks and walked into the mine.

When they lifted off twenty minutes later and flew above the empty road that led to the prison Colt looked down and wondered what William Parker Jardine was doing today.

– 34 –

Savic peeled away the heavy canvas tarp and squeezed through the door. He slid his hand along the wall in the dark until he found the RV's light switch and sat down on the floor in the little kitchen so he could think things over.

The narrow closet next to the shower was filled with hanging clothes he'd had no time to take into the house after their last trip north to escape the Nevada heat. The fridge gave off a faint, stale smell and he took out the half empty ketchup and mustard bottles and a lone shriveled apple. He turned on the other flickering lights and began to box up cooking pots and pans and what was left of the silverware in the drawer next to the sink.

As he removed the bedsheets he felt crushed by memories he'd promised himself not to have. He'd been dreading this day. He thought about their plans to travel and when he emptied the glove compartment he found a stack of brochures and road maps from the trip where Maria got sick. In a small zippered pink bag on the bedroom shelf he found her makeup and lipstick and a tiny, dusty mirror and he felt a sudden dreadful heaviness, like he'd just heard news of someone's death.

It seemed like such an awful waste. Time and its relentless passing seemed such a waste. Savic felt that the ground had been cruelly pulled from under his feet, the world altered and rendered unrecognizable with little promise of returning to what had been. None of this was expected, yet he knew he was expected to fix it. The motorhome, an escape for them both, now sat useless beneath the tarp that was already starting to rot in the desert sun.

He turned off all but one light and in the gloom, curtains drawn, it seemed like every conversation they had ever had was afloat in this dark space, ready to be remembered at the worst possible time. His regrets tortured him.

Outside, the old galvanized steel planter sat by the backyard house steps and was filled with daisies that he'd been trying to keep alive. He picked as many of the flowers as he could and filled a plastic vase with water from the garden hose and he took this to his police cruiser.

At the home nurse Fahey asked why Savic didn't drive his motorcycle today and he lied about it being in the shop. He saw Marco the orderly cleaning up an accident in the hallway and heard the story about Mrs. Petigrew in Room 96 who had escaped the night before and walked through four lanes of highway traffic to get more artwork for her arm at the tattoo shop across the street.

"Now they all want tats," Marco said. "The old lady started a trend. Isabella Sanchez in 40 -- what, she's ninety? She's got a little red tulip on her cheek."

"I thought they fixed that with Tattoo Night in the cafeteria," Savic said.

"I guess the washable kind don't do the trick," Marco said and started laughing. "You might want to check your wife's leg. I think she got a new one."

Marco pushed the wheeled yellow plastic pail with his foot and started wringing his mop.

"Bob Luzinski in 48, they caught him trying to do the same thing. Fahey called the cops and they went across the street and dragged the poor guy back. He was yelling this and that about how they owed him money for stopping the tattoo man before he finished the hula girl on his chest."

Marco swept a pile of black dirt into a dustpan that was already loaded with clumps of roots and gravel.

"What's that about?" Savic asked.

"Mrs. James," Marco said and shook his head. "From the end of the hall. She likes to pull plants from the garden and put them in her room. Dirt, too. She takes dirt from outside and hides it under her bed."

Maria was sitting by the window holding a cup of tea and a saucer in her lap. She'd spilled food on herself and her breakfast tray was still full,

228

the scrambled eggs and bowl of wrinkled fruit hardly touched. Her hair was tangled in knots like it had been left to dry without anybody combing it and her slippers were on the wrong feet. She looked at her husband and gave him the slightest smile and then went back to watching her birds through the window while Savic brushed her hair.

He took Maria's framed family pictures from the night stand and put them into the small suitcase Savic used each Sunday to carry home her laundry. He stepped over and looked into the hallway, where Sparkle Montana was flirting with Jamal while Carlo tightened the axle bolt on her wheelchair with a wrench.

Savic closed the door to the room. Her medicine, her pajamas, a pair of gym shoes and a sweater –– he took those from the closet and packed everything in the suitcase. Her couldn't find any of her other pajamas. She liked looking through her old magazines and he took those along with an envelope filled with her medical paperwork and her little bag of sewing supplies. She liked to hold the spools of thread and the wooden bobbins and her boxes of needles and old buttons, though she had never used any of it during her time at Wind Mountain.

He carried her suitcase to the squad car and on the way back stopped at the accounting office. He put the envelope with the check from the sale of his motorcycle in Mrs. Gardener's in-box and walked out quickly before anybody saw him.

He went back to the room and tried to get Maria to drink her juice, but she made a sour face and said she wanted to keep watching the birds.

"How about we go outside for a while, okay? The garden, would you like that? You can watch them there."

"Forse voglioni mangiare?"

"Your pals are out there and you bet they're hungry," Savic said.

He snatched a handful of soup cracker packets from the cafeteria and walked Maria out the front door, where nurse Fahey stood next to a pile of boxes signing a computer tablet for a UPS delivery guy in brown shorts and sunglasses.

He'd parked the car near the back delivery entrance and after they sat for a while feeding the birds and looking at the quiet and shaded pond Maria started to get tired and she slumped back against the bench and sighed deeply. Savic took her arm and they walked slowly around the back of the building, where he'd positioned his police vehicle so it would be hidden by the parked shuttle bus. When they were seated in the car he gave her a kiss and Maria opened her eyes and looked around, confused.

"It's okay, honey," he said. "I'm taking you home. To your sister's house for a while. And then to our place. You shouldn't be here anymore."

When she was belted up he brought out the daisies and set the vase in her lap. He looked into her eyes and said, "I'm taking you home. It's okay. I'm just taking you home."

As he drove and watched her smell the flowers he thought about what remained in his checkbook. There was money to come from the union, and he wouldn't get the full IRA for a couple of years. There was no social security, of course. He was too old for most things, but too young for that. Maria got two hundred bucks a month from the nursing union association disability pension, though her health insurance coverage would lapse in a few months. He still owed more to the nursing home and he'd signed a note promising to clean up the amount in ninety days. He hadn't slept well all that week, thinking about the money he owed.

Mary was confused by the traffic and seemed frightened to turn her head and look out the window. She said she needed to use the ladies room. Savic pulled into a gas station and walked her inside, where she wouldn't let go of his arm when he opened the ladies room door.

"Look, let's try this," he said and took her hand and led her to the toilet stall, where he grinned lamely at another woman who was washing her hands at the sink. Someone else walked in and the two exchanged glances as Savic helped Maria pull down her blue pajama bottoms. When she was finished he led her to the sink where she stood and stared at the running faucet water as if it were the first time she'd seen such a thing.

"You're doing good, honey," he said. "Take your time. Don't worry about anything. I'm not going anywhere. We got all the time in the world. Things will get easier when we get home."

Maria turned, and with an embarrassed look she pointed down. "My buttons," she said, and Savic buttoned her up wondering how the other ladies at the nursing home were enjoying wearing his wife's pajamas.

– 35 –

Anderson listened to the head banger music blasting loudly from the trailer as he lay twisted in the back seat of his own car with his arms tied behind his back.

His mouth was taped shut, his feet bound with a laundry rope that was pulled tight under the front seat and knotted around the steering wheel. A door slammed shut and he heard voices laughing and managed to stretch himself high enough to see the two women dressed in tight furry jackets standing outside the trailer.

Shivering in the cold desert night, they stood wobbling on their high heels, smoking cigarettes as Anderson tried to kick the car door and get their attention. From inside the brightly lit trailer he could hear Henry Meffisti shouting something at Willy and he watched as their silhouette shapes passed back and forth behind the drawn window curtains. The trailer door then opened and Meffisti stepped outside and took out his wallet and handed each of the women cash money and then watched as they both walked away until all you could see was their two glowing cigarettes bobbing up and down in the dark.

When Meffisti opened the car door and saw Anderson struggling to loosen the rope from his feet he smacked the salesman with the back of his hand and pulled him halfway out through the door. He untied the rope from the wheel and yanked it loose like a dog leash and made Anderson hop back toward the trailer like someone in a sack race at a country fair.

"I guess I have to keep an eye on you," Meffisti said and pulled out the pistol that was tucked into his belt. "You do one more stupid fucking thing and I'll shoot your ass, understand?"

Crushed beer cans and Styrofoam fast food containers lay scattered on the floor of the trailer, some of the mess swept or kicked into the corner next to a bulging plastic trash bag. A pizza carton lay on the stove top next to a paper bag containing the flashlight batteries Meffisti had bought at the convenience store.

Meffisti shouted at Willy to clean the place up and Willy mumbled something and hunched himself up on the sofa where he'd been watching TV. Meffisti finished drinking from his beer and threw the empty can at Willy.

"You know how sick I am of you? You spaz. You're a dummy and a spaz, did you know that? You're just in my way, you useless numbnuts."

Willy stared down at his feet, looking like he was ready to cry, and then finally looked over at Anderson, who was sitting with his bound legs stretched out on the kitchen floor.

"What about him, Henry? What do we do now? I sure wanted to go to Mexico tonight, Henry. What do we do now?"

Meffisti pulled the tape from Anderson's mouth. "He's gonna 'drive us to his house and we're taking his real car and then he's driving us south. To Mexico. That's what we're doing. It's easier than stealing another car and he's got papers and insurance and..."

Meffisti grabbed Anderson by the hair and shouted: "...and if he doesn't cooperate I'm gonna' fucking make him watch while I kill his wife and if he's got kids, I'll kill them too. Got that, mister salesman? That's the plan. Are you listening? Am I being clear?"

Meffisti stepped to the sink and pointed at Willy and told him to stand up.

"Get over here, retard," he said. "I got something to show you."

Willy sheepishly got up from the sofa and shuffled past Anderson where he lay on the floor and then stood at attention before Meffisti like a soldier reporting for duty. Like a child being reprimanded.

Meffisti calmly turned and from the sink took the unwashed kitchen knife that he'd used on the pizza and he hefted it in his hand for an instant before swinging his arm and thrusting the long blade sideways into Willy's neck. Willy stood perfectly still and straight, his bony little shoulders lifting as if he was trying to shrug something away, and then his eyes fluttered as he tipped back on his heels and crashed down without a sound on the kitchen table. He rolled away and fell bleeding to the floor next to Anderson, who was now screaming and trying to scrabble away as Meffisti bent down, pulled out the knife and drew the blade quickly across Willy's throat.

"Okay," Meffisti said as he tossed aside the knife and looked down at Anderson. "Now I only got your sorry ass to worry about."

Anderson screamed again and started to flop around on the floor. Meffisti kicked him and took the loose rope and again tied him up and told the salesman to stay put while he loaded up the car.

Meffisti washed his hands and began gathering his things. He stepped over Willy, who lay dead with his eyes open, one bent arm folded around the back of his raw and bleeding neck as if he'd decided to take a nap on the floor.

Anderson sat staring from where he had managed to twist himself upright on the floor. He watched Meffisti come in and out of the trailer as he loaded Anderson's car with luggage and boxes and more rope. Meffisti took a handful of bulging plastic bags from a drawer that were filled with pills and packets of dope and from behind the large TV on the wall he pulled out two pistols wrapped in their leather holsters. He went to the bedroom and came back with a shotgun and a box of ammo that he stuffed into a backpack.

"If I was you," he told Anderson. "I'd keep my ass right there on the floor. We're getting out of here, you and me, in just a little bit. If I come back and you've moved an inch, I'll cut you."

Meffisti then took Willy by the feet and dragged the body outside.

It was on the third trip to the car that Anderson thought Meffisti may have just driven away and left him there. He didn't hear a sound from outside. He didn't dare move and try to look out the window, but then saw a vehicle's headlights begin to flash on and off, as if somebody was signaling.

Outside the trailer, Meffisti stopped loading the car trunk when he saw the flashing lights. The van began to move slowly toward him and when Meffisti took out his pistol the vehicle immediately stopped and he watched the driver's door open, the blinding bright lights now shining at him steadily so he could see nothing else but someone's vague shape stepping away from the van in the dark. He walked closer, pointing the pistol, shielding his eyes, and waited. Nothing. Something moved in the shadows. He walked closer, holding up his hand to block the bright light.

"What do you want?" Meffisti shouted. "This is private property. Who the fuck are you?"

He felt someone's thick, powerful arm grasp his neck from behind. He tried to point his weapon as he fell backwards but he was quickly stretched out on the ground with a knee pressing down hard on his back.

And then something stung the side of his neck like he'd been bitten and Henry Meffisti felt suddenly calm and heavy.

"Hush now," said the voice sweetly as Meffisti gratefully felt the weight of the knee lift away.

"Hush, or I'll hurt you more."

– 36 –

Felicia followed the stripe of red arrows painted on the floor of the prison Family Welcome Center to show where visitors were required to walk to meet the inmates.

A line of people snaked through an indoor checkpoint past two detention officers holding x-ray wands. She dropped her purse and cell phone into a labeled plastic bin and followed more taped arrows to the walk-through scanner where another female guard handed her a numbered plastic card.

"Did ya'all read that big sign in the hall? You know, the one that's about six feet tall?" the guard said and wagged her hand back and forth as if suggesting Felicia should twirl and perform a ballet pirouette.

"No clothing that accentuates the body," the officer said. "If you read it, that's what it says. You sure got on some tight clothes today, honey."

"I thought that meant, you know, spandex or tights. Something like that," Felicia said.

"No, it means no tight clothes. Like in none. You got on tight clothes. Your boobies, they about to pop out. I can see everything you own, honey."

"I'm sorry," Felicia pleaded. "It's two hours to drive out here, and I was really counting on this. Please let me see him today? Please, it's so important to me. I thought I was dressed okay, I really did."

Felicia began to choke up like she was starting to cry and the guard rolled her eyes.

"Somebody had to tell you about what you could wear, and then we got that big fat sign and still you people come in here dressed like hookers out for a walk at midnight."

The guard waved her arm. "Go on. You can go on. I ain't got time for this."

Felicia held the plastic card tightly in her hand and stepped into a large, barren room with unpainted cement walls that looked like an old military mess hall with its steel sinks and serving counters with rusted food tray rails that were now stacked with more numbered plastic bins that stored the visitors 'valuables. The polished metal picnic tables with their attached benches bolted to the floor were arranged in widely separated rows. Felicia sat down at the far end between a pair of low table dividers, and she waited.

There was a loud rattle and a heavy wheeled door panel slid open. The inmates dressed in their jumpsuits walked one by one past two standing guards, some prisoners waving happily while others stood looking glum as if hoping their own visitors might have thankfully not showed up. The identically dressed men scattered. One guard held up his arms and shouted that there was no running or embracing while standing and that no one could touch hands until they were seated with the table between them.

Arturo Gallegos was boyish and slender and he smiled confidently as he walked last into the room with a slight swagger and searched for the woman he was told would be wearing a bright yellow barrette in her black hair. He nodded to Felicia where she sat alone at the far end of the room. He was stopped by the guard, who ran his hands beneath Arturo's armpits and touched the top of his head. He then told Arturo to shake his long hair forward with his fingers and took out a small inspection wand and ran the tool between the prisoner's spread legs before nodding for him to walk on.

Arturo stepped up to where Felicia was sitting and surveyed the room before he smiled indignantly and sat and looked her over.

She thought she'd dressed properly but Arturo's leering gaze told her otherwise. She brushed back her hair nervously and reached out her hand.

"What are you doing?" Arturo said, shirking away as he glanced past Felicia to where one of officers was staring at him.

"Don't do that. You're supposed to be my girlfriend and you're shaking my hand? You crazy?"

"I'm sorry. I wasn't thinking. Can they hear us?" Felicia said.

"Act like we're happy to see each other," Arturo said and once again studied her.

"They let you in dressed like that?" he said. "Okay, lean across the table and kiss me. Just a little kiss. Keep your hands flat on the table. That's good. Now I'm gonna' hold your hand again and look at you like I miss you so much. You know what I'm saying? If you put your hands under the table they get real nervous, these people. So do it like I'm showing you to get them used to us moving around. La juda assholes are lazy and after a while they just stop watching. You listening?"

Felicia dropped one hand into her lap and nodded. She knew now that she shouldn't have worn such a tight dress. Arturo kept looking her up and down. It was a regular skirt, but it was too tight when she was sitting and now she realized this might be something to worry about. It might be a problem. How could she be so stupid. So stupid.

"That's good, what you're doing now," Arturo said. "Do you have it with you?"

Arturo had large, watery brown eyes and his thick dark hair fell across his forehead to cover them when he turned his head. He pushed back his hair and Felicia saw the half finished, uncolored tattoo of a pair of intertwined capital letters that snaked up the side of his neck past the jumpsuit collar. He reached and stroked Felicia's hand mechanically, without feeling, and leaned across the table. He kissed her.

"Yes, I have it," she whispered. "How long do we get?" Felicia said.

"I get only fifteen minutes because of the tier I'm in. I was a bad boy last week so they're giving me a little punishment," Arturo said, and then spoke quietly.

"When somebody starts to stand up and say goodbye you give me a few more last minute kisses, you hear? It gets noisy in here when they start to stand up and the juda are trying to watch everybody at once, so that's when you do it. Keep smiling when you're talking to me now. Don't look serious. They'll think we're up to something. The way your face looks now, it's too serious. You look too worried. Don't look so damn worried, understand? Big and sloppy kisses is what I want now, like you're missing the shit out of me."

"How do I give it to you?"

"When everybody's swapping spit and saying goodbye. That's when you do it. There's too many for them to watch, so they're only gonna look out for the trouble makers. I'm new here so they don't know what to expect. They watch out for the trouble makers. You take it out from where you got it. Maybe I could reach down and get it myself? How about that?"

He gave her a lewd grin. "Let me do that, okay? I haven't touched any of that down there for a long time."

"Shouldn't I take it out before I stand? How do I take it out when I'm already standing?"

"Yeah, you pull it out before you stand," Arturo said. He was hissing now. "Shit, Bernardo didn't tell you how to do it? "

"No," she said. "They said how to put it in but not how to take it out."

"Jesus. You don't know how to take it out?"

"Not really."

Felicia squirmed sideways in the too-tight skirt that had now slid halfway up her thighs, twisting herself against the metal bench while Arturo continued to pretend he was conversing with her, flashing fake smiles and kissing her other free hand again while Felicia tried to retrieve the balloons. The dress was much too tight. She was only able to take out one of them.

"Put it in your hand and wipe your eyes like you're crying. Then you blow your nose. That's why they got tissues on the table so you don't reach into a pocket and do stuff like that. Go ahead, take a few tissues from the box. Good. You go ahead and cough or something. Got that? You cough. You take the second bag out the same way and you put it in your mouth after you kiss me and give me the first one. You give me that sloppy kiss, you understand? You got that? Don't fucking swallow the bag, understand? What's wrong? How come you're looking stupid at me? What's wrong?"

"Should I put it in my mouth now? I'm so nervous."

"I thought they told you how to do this. Shit."

The guard in the far corner by the entrance door crossed his arms and was now watching them.

"I need to know if I push it with my tongue or do you do the work?"

"You push it. Shit," he said. "Jesus, I thought you did this before?"

"No, That's not true. They told you that?" Felicia said. She wiped her forehead with the tissue in her hand. Her heart was pounding now. She once more wiped the sweat from her forehead with the tissue.

"Ayee, Yali madre. Don't do that," Arturo said. "Don't wipe yourself like that. Girlfriends don't look nervous when they see their men, you understand? You look like you just saw a ghost."

"I've never done this."

"Don't do that again. Shit."

Arturo licked his lips nervously and looked over at the guard and smiled at him and shrugged his shoulders and spun his finger against the side of his head like he was saying his girlfriend was a little crazy. An inmate and another woman were arguing a few tables down and the guards started watching them.

Arturo made a big show of leaning across the table, hoping to look like he had nothing to hide and was just being an exuberant boyfriend. Felicia brought the first balloon up with the tissue and she put it in her mouth. She pretended to blow her nose.

Arturo's tongue ticklishly curled up behind her teeth. He tasted like cigarettes and his mouth was very dry. He sucked the balloon from her mouth and held his hand to the side of her face to hide what he was doing and she watched his throat tighten as he quickly gulped and swallowed.

"What's wrong?" he said.

Felicia sat back on the bench and squirmed and reached under her dress.

"The other one, I can't get it out."

"Pendejo," Arturo said and leaned back. "Look who they sent me. They sent me an idiot."

A buzzer rang and the room got loud with shuffling feet and the sounds of a few people sobbing, some visitors crying openly and the two angry ones from the other table exchanging their final shouts as the guards walked up and down along the table rows, pointing with their batons and instructing everyone to follow the painted lines on the floor.

"It's stuck," Felicia said again.

Arturo leaned across the table.

"You stupid bitch."

"I think I cut it with my fingernail," Felicia said. "When I took it out I cut the second one. Oh, God."

"Didn't they tell you to lose the long nails? You're not supposed to have long fingernails, puta."

Felicia sighed and closed her eyes. She stood up. "No, oh please."

A guard came and tapped the steel table with his baton. Arturo shrugged dismissively and shook his head at Felicia and walked away.

She felt something warm expand inside of her and then the liquid trickled down the inside of her thigh. She looked at her wet skirt. She tried to take a deep breath but there seemed not to be enough room inside her chest for her pounding heart.

She showed her plastic ticket and went to the bins where they had her purse and phone. She felt her insides get warmer, her head heavy. Her heart shouldn't beat this fast, she thought. She had a strong metallic taste in her mouth and she could not swallow. Her heart felt like it was swelling up as it pounded harder. Someone's hand touched her shoulder.

"You okay, honey?"

Felicia tried to smile; her lips felt rubbery and numb like she'd just come from the dentist.

"You okay?" the officer said.

"I don't feel good."

She just could not catch her breath and her heart was leaping and stuttering and the faster she tried to breath the more her heart pounded. She tried to aim her feet toward the door though she hardly knew what she would do once she got there. Her head was now thumping, too. The voices in the room were still, just a deep low murmur like listening to something distant that was underwater, not real at all. She felt the same two hands hold her from behind as she fell forward against another pair of arms and together the mysterious and detached hands lowered her gently and dreamily to the cold cement floor where she again tried to take a deep breath but could not.

In the ambulance, with its shearing bright ceiling lights and blowing icy air, there were white shapes stooped over her and voices saying hang on, hang on and then the pinching sting of something on her wrist and the same voices repeating what they had said over and over again, everything muffled and growing more silent as her heart pounded louder.

The burning heat in her stomach began to spread and roll back and forth as if something wanted desperately to get out and now she could not feel her legs and now she felt herself falling backwards, falling and tumbling as if pulled from behind while the ambulance voices continued to plead hang on, hang on. Somebody was running across a room toward her with his arms held out as she felt the poison thing that had wanted to escape finally burst inside her.

Mommy, mommy, said the sweet little voice.

– 37 –

It took no time at all to confirm the body of Daniella Clayton, age 26, of Dakota Creek, Kansas. All the necessary papers lay where Willy had dropped them.

Bob Anderson's wife had called the police when her husband failed to show up that night and the car rental agency, after charging a $76 late fee to her husband's credit card, provided the Nevada Highway Patrol with the GPS reading from the standard tracking device that was installed on its newest vehicles.

When they arrived at the trailer Henry Meffisti was on his back on the kitchen table as if sprawled across some cluttered altar stone, arms spread wide in supplication beneath the bright fluorescent ceiling light. He lay with his hiked up legs bent at the knees as if mocking the labor of giving birth. To Savic this strange horizontal kitchen crucifixion seemed like a purposeful gynecological parody, a grisly joke about the beginning and ending of life.

Every light was switched on, as if to make sure you could see the trailer easily through the trees from the highway. The TV was blaring loudly, a re-run of a M.A.S.H. episode in which Radar was asking Hawkeye to hurry to the surgical emergency tent. "We have bleeders," he announced calmly into the P.A. mic, the camera panning to wounded Korean War GIs being carried by medics from a military helicopter on green canvas stretchers.

Savic and Monaghan stood speechless. They watched a highway patrol officer take his photographs. The trooper seemed reluctant to get too close to the carefully posed and positioned body.

Bob Anderson squatted and rocked on his heels on the floor with his hands on his face, moaning. The trooper stepped over with his camera, took another picture, and tried to peel away the several layers of tape wrapped around Anderson's mouth.

When the tape was removed the light bulb salesman, who was spattered from head to toe with blood, started jabbering incoherently, trying to stand while the police officer held him down and advised that he needed to remain where he was until the ambulance arrived. But Anderson kept struggling, flapping his arms toward where Meffisti lay and chattering nonsense, apparently trying to describe in every detail what he had witnessed.

Henry Meffisti's chest had been sawed open, the ribs spread apart with a pair of broken barbecue tongs jammed vertically into the open position with two kitchen forks. A bloody wooden cook's spatula was jammed beneath Meffisti's protruding sternum like a supporting tent pole, the remaining exposed and sprung rib bones apparently clipped in half by the bolt snipper that lay on the table next to Meffisti's expressively twisted face. Clumps of shiny viscera hung spilled from the womb-like hole between his bent legs and they trailed for several feet across the kitchen floor.

Savic stood at the edge of the puddle of God-knows-what that covered the floor, trying to figure out if they should step closer to the body or wait for the technicians and their gear to arrive.

There was a scrap of paper fastened to Meffisti's excavated chest with a pushpin. It was folded around the strange piece of children's jewelry that hung around his neck, a smiling rhinestone pony on a chain that looked similar to the one the lab had found embedded in the neck of Carlo Cavilleri back in Four Palms.

Next to the note, connected by four wires attached with tiny alligator clips to a pair of AA flashlight batteries, lay Henry Meffisti's fully exposed and beating heart. The finger-thick veins leading from the heart into the chest cavity were throbbing imperceptibly in a way that made it seem like the organ might yet be struggling to keep its host alive.

"Is he dead or what?" Monaghan said.

"Not sure. Technically, I guess," Savic said. "Look."

He pointed to the sofa cushion on the kitchen table that had been wedged under Meffisti's head.

"It's like he was forced to watch, don't you think?"

"To watch his heart?"

"To watch everything," Savic said. "It took a long time, all that cutting. If it's beating now it was damn sure beating when he was alive."

"Never seen that before."

"I don't think anybody's seen that before."

The organ continued to jitter, and from within its pale epicardium sac there was a persistent prodding as if the heart contained some *thing* that wanted to escape. The clear plastic bag that lay next to the body contained the white powder that Monaghan said might have helped the heart continue to beat.

"I bet there's dope in that," he said.

The leathery unhealthy lungs, mottled with lumpy black striations from Meffisti's daily two-pack cigarette habit, remained still and deflated. Without oxygen, yet powered by the batteries, the faux heart continued to beat.

"Look at his face," Savic said. "Except for the eyes, he doesn't even look dead."

Both men looked at the smudged thumb print on Meffisti's forehead.

"Looks like dirt," Monaghan said.

"You're Catholic, Paul," Savic said. "That's not dirt."

Savic pointed to Anderson, who was being comforted by the trooper.

"If that poor fella' ever gets out of counseling, maybe he can tell us what happened. I can't wait for the lab to explain how this science fair exhibit got rigged up."

Savic stepped away and looked at the empty store bag with the battery wrapper set aside on the stove next to the flashlight. He put on his gloves and unscrewed the flashlight and held up the tiny tracking transceiver.

Meffisti's severed hand with the tattoo lay next to the sink on the kitchen counter, the clamped forceps still attached to the stumps of his wrist where they had been used as a hemostat to control the bleeding.

"He doesn't seem to care anymore about leaving his equipment behind," Savic said. "What's that note say?"

Monaghan took the paper from behind the little necklace chain and read the neatly printed verse:

Close your mouth
lest your tongue escape
the smell of your stinking heart

"Who the hell is Fritz Shakespeare?" Monaghan said.

Before Savic could answer, another trooper poked his head inside the trailer and asked both men to quickly step outside.

"You might want to see this," he said and pointed to where two powerful lamps on their tripods were aimed beneath the trailer. Another officer wearing gloves and a cloth mask squatted over a shallow hole, carefully troweling away dirt with a flat piece of wood. The trailer sat high on cement blocks, its underside a tangle of electrical wires and tossed trash, a few car tires stacked to the side next to rows of storage bins and boxes. Savic was handed a mask and when he stooped halfway under the trailer he abruptly shuffled back and sat down and stared up at Monaghan. He shook his head.

"God," he said and sighed loudly. "Oh...dear God"

"When we got here I called for the canine unit," the trooper said and pointed under the trailer.

" Figured the way the inside smelled there might be dope under there, too. The dog went nuts and dug up that instead. The bio crew is on its way."

Savic and Monaghan both crouched down and looked under the trailer. Willy's feet were sticking out from behind a pile of trash where someone had begun to dig a fresh hole.

And then, in the harsh beam of light they both saw the piles of bones gathered in a shallow trench, a dusty and heartbreaking ossuary of small and delicate broken limbs, little shoes on desiccated feet, the half dozen tiny skulls pressed hastily into the earth in a manner hinting that more of Henry Meffisti's terrible work might soon be found.

– 38 –

Jasper Colt needed to kill some time.

At the Liberace Museum the old woman explained as she handed him his admission ticket that the singer himself had supervised the placement of many of the exhibits. The tour ended in the singer's reconstructed bedroom where she spoke sadly about the day the performer died and how much money it took to maintain the museum's collection of rhinestone studded pianos. The pillows in one of the twin beds seemed used, the faint impression of a head print still there. He imagined the woman crawling into Liberace's bed after the place was locked up and closing her eyes and imaging her hero lying beneath the satin sheets beside her.

"He performed on each of them, you know," she said.

"The beds?"

"The pianos," she said, blushing. The pleasant and soft-spoken woman had a doughy dowager's hump at the base of her neck and her cone of white hair was teased into a stiff hive.

"Of course," Colt said, and on the way out of the museum he dropped a fifty dollar bill into a donation box that was decorated with hand drawn musical notes and crookedly pasted gemstones. The old woman's devoted work, of course. For her beloved piano man, whose shrine, said the sign next to the exit door, would soon be closing for good.

He took a taxi to the airport, where the somber couriers sent by Franz Kreutzer stood in their business suits among a crowd of tourists dressed in shorts and tee shirts.

He identified himself and they each shook his hand politely and Colt turned over the briefcase containing the box of ashes of his children and his wife. The bigger man snapped a handcuff to the handle and fastened the other end of the chain to a metal clip on his belt that looked like a mountaineer's climbing carabiner. The courier handed his partner one of the two keys and they nodded to each other and never said another word.

Colt imagined their flight to Washington, D.C. and then landing in Milan nine hours later. From there they had been instructed to take the train and not drive a car the remaining distance to Venice. The three hour high-speed trip aboard the Le Frecce Express from Milano Centrale was safe and discrete and the train would never have a flat tire. At Venice his angels would be placed on the Vaporetto and in five minutes the two men, now at home in their tailored Italian suits and polished leather shoes, would be at the Zacharia dock. One block further, a walk across two bridges and down a curving stone stairway, and they would arrive at the penzione on the Calle del Angelo, their shoes sounding hollow on the old cobblestones that led to Nicolo Braga's door, the carved image of the penzione's guardian staring down at them from above.

Colt returned to his hotel and lingered in the lobby, feeling as if he'd said goodbye to his angels again; as if they'd died once more.

He stared at the painted ceiling, studying the cavorting angels and he allowed himself to think about his children. He remembered their cool cheeks as he snuggled with his daughters on the tiny bedroom sofa, reading a tale about castles and fairies and knights on galloping white horses. They sometimes both fell asleep in his arms and he would carry them to bed with their feet swinging, smelling and kissing their fresh little faces. He would call down to Adriana and they would both sit on the floor beside the beds and hold each other and stare at their beautiful sleeping children, the room smelling of crayons and paint and the soft summer breeze blowing through the open window.

The torture of their memory somehow brought him strength and their deaths had given his violence a strange and balanced equilibrium, as if such opposites had formed a peaceful vacuum into which his unbearable rage could flee. This is why he had no feeling for these people, their killers. They were not worthy of their own dust or ashes. They were nothing.

Braga telephoned his room in the middle of the night. Colt had never gone to sleep. He'd been in the hotel gym. He needed to be as strong as possible.

"Your angels are safe," Braga said.

"Grazie."

"I assumed you would bring the parcel yourself."

"It wasn't possible," Colt said.

"I will take care of everything, my friend. Will you be visiting us again soon?" Braga asked, but Colt had already hung up. He needed to sleep. He had one more task to do.

– 39 –

Savic sat across from Monaghan's desk thumbing through the Jardine file as they both waited for warden Olson to have William Parker Jardine brought to one of the interview rooms so he could take their video call.

They could hear Jardine's shuffling footsteps and the clank of a steel door closing long before Monaghan switched on the video feed.

"I don't have to talk to you," Jardine immediately said.

"You could have refused," Savic said as Jardine casually looked away from the camera and scratched his ear.

"Maybe I just miss you," Jardine said. "What do you want?"

"We just need a minute," Savic said, noticing the prisoner's cheek, a dark blue bruise running across his chin where a row of new stitches made the corner of his mouth looked like the bunched fabric on a darned sock.

"When are they fixing your face?" Savic said.

"Tomorrow. A real doctor is doing it tomorrow. Thanks for your concern," Jardine said. "Now what's this about? They put chains on me and made me drag my ass downstairs so you could have a minute? I'm already bored with this conversation." Jarvis pointed at his face.

"Does it look like I'm in the mood to talk to you?"

Monaghan broke in: "I hope they're treating you okay. This is Captain Paul Monaghan of Las Vegas Metro. Sergeant Savic and I would like to ask a few questions. It won't take long. It's in your interest to cooperate with us."

"You worried about me? There's nothing you got that I'm interested in."

"We understand you're in the general population now."

"I don't socialize."

"You might be pretty low on the food chain in that place, anyway," Savic said.

"They don't mess with me," Jardine said.

"I hear those Mexican boys might disagree with that."

"I've been cut before, and I've been in fights," Jardine said. "What's this about?"

"One of your old roomies, Earl Lee. He's dead. And so is Carlo Cavilleri."

"Like I give a shit," Jardine said and smiled.

"You boys did time together a few years ago. Different jails, but I know you and Lee both got sentenced at the same time. They couldn't connect you three musketeers to the same murder, but we both probably know the truth about that, don't we?"

"Should I start crying now?" Jardine said. "I don't think I should say anything else. I think I should tell my lawyer about this conversation. I need medical attention and you're harassing me. Lawyers like to hear that kind of stuff."

Jardine ducked away from the camera and asked someone to take him back to his cell.

"How about Henry Meffisti?" Savic said. "He's somebody else you were tight with. If I recall, Meffisti got out on parole awhile back after doing eight years with you out east in Illinois. At Cook County and then at Joliet."

"You guys get him?" Jardine said. "Did Henry fuck up again and now he's back in the can? Ol' Henry, now there's somebody who could never control himself at all."

"No. He's dead, too," Savic said. "And we think it was the same individual who got to Lee and Cavilleri. Do you understand what I'm saying?"

Savic stood and stretched his legs and walked once around Monaghan's office.

"Don't worry about me, detective. I'm safer than you are," Jardine said.

"Look, Bill," Savic said. "We know now that you and your three sidekicks were part of the same strange, weird-ass club. That screwball thing with the Bible verse on your hand. Wearing kids 'necklaces and who knows how much other sick shit we haven't been told about yet. My bullshit detector says that you probably were in on the same crimes at one time or another, kind of a tag-team thing out in Virginia way back when. Somehow, nobody connected the dots. We finally caught up with you for something else you did after Virginia. My point is, somebody else out there knows this besides us. And he's trying to kill people one by one for reasons we can't tell you yet, and he's just about achieved his goal. You're the only sonofabitch left on his shit list. We both know how easy it is to get to somebody in prison, especially that place. There's a dozen ways you could die in there and it could happen right after you head back to your cell today. Right in that stinking little box that probably smells like the toilet two feet from your bed. You could take a shiv in your neck and nobody will shed a tear except the state of Nevada will probably save money by burying you instead of feeding your fat ass food every day."

"You know they record these conversations, don't you," Jardine said. "I'd hate for you to get in trouble, detective."

"Any idea who might want to kill your friends?"

"Don't have a clue," Jardine said, now reaching with both of his chained hands to furiously rub his ear. "And if I did I wouldn't say."

Just then Monaghan's secretary stepped unannounced into the conference room and anxiously handed the captain a note.

"Let me finish with him, Frank," Monaghan said, waving his hand toward the office door. "Something's come up. You better go take this call."

The secretary showed Savic to an empty office cubicle where a phone sat on a bare table, its hold button blinking.

Savic picked up the phone. It was Maria's sister. "She's gone, Frank. She walked away. Out of the house."

"What do you mean, walked away? She's not strong enough to walk away"

"I was getting ready to take her to the store. She got dressed up for it and everything." Suzanne said. "She seems to like it when I take her to the market and when I came back from locking the back door she was gone. She just walked out."

Monaghan finished up with Jardine and walked into the cubicle and took a seat. Savic turned on the phone speaker.

"She's been more alert lately, you know," Maria's sister said. "That's why I thought taking her out as much as possible would be a good idea. I called the neighbors. I thought she maybe wandered off to the wrong house. I left the goddamn door wide open. I'm so sorry, Frank."

"Suzie," Savic said coldly and shook his head at Monaghan.

" Maybe she's sitting on somebody's front steps in the neighborhood," he said. "I don't think she'd go very far."

Savic said he was heading to the house and Monaghan stepped away and came back holding up his car keys.

"Do you have her picture in your phone?" Monaghan said. "Text it to me and I'll send it to dispatch."

"I don't know how to do that, Paul."

"Frank, give me your cell."

Monaghan scrolled to a photo that showed Maria standing outside the RV, smiling and pointing to a road map.

" What's her medical?" Monaghan said.

"She takes heart pills twice a day. I saw her take one this morning. At dinner she needs another one, for blood pressure. Nothing serious, but if she gets upset about something I don't know if it turns into a problem. The damn front door. I told her sister to keep it latched with the deadbolt."

They were pulling out of the metro police garage with the cruiser lights flashing when Maria's sister phoned again.

"Frank, a neighbor said he saw her by the bus stop. I think it's the free shuttle that takes people downtown."

"The one that drops tourists off at the casinos, yeah," Savic said.

Monaghan was on his phone reciting from Maria Savic's personal stats that now appeared next to the missing person's alert on his dash-mounted screen.

"She hasn't been on a bus in thirty years," Savic said.

Savic now called the city public transit office and was told the last free shuttle from the corner stop near Suzanne's house had left twenty minutes ago.

Monaghan swiveled the dashboard computer tray so Savic could see it and pointed to the screen.

"The west-bound bus that she took makes sixteen stops, starting with Treasure Island. Last stop is at Caesar's. The eastbound route only goes to nine hotels, starting with Mandalay Bay. But they overlap. Eastbound bus is smaller, so they alternate pickups to cover everything in half-hour increments."

"Which one stops at the Venetian?" Savic said. "That's the only casino she's ever been to. She absolutely hates gambling. She only went there because I said it looked like Venice."

"The westbound. Fifth stop," Monaghan said.

They found the empty shuttle parked in the casino's bus lane, the driver helping somebody down the steps of the vehicle. Savic showed his badge and the driver pointed toward the lobby where the escalator was filled with people trailing wheeled suitcases and carrying shopping bags.

"What's this about?" the driver said.

Savic showed him the photo on his phone. "We have a woman here with a health condition. She may be lost. You picked her up at the Coronado Street stop about forty minutes ago. Does she look familiar? She's an older lady, about five-eight."

"They're all older ladies, officer," the driver said.

"Your first drop was at Treasure Island?"

"I think three got off, yeah."

"How about here?" Savic said, pointing at the escalator. "Are those the passengers you just unloaded?"

The driver nodded and while Monaghan remained in the parked police SUV making more phone calls, Savic headed into the hotel and hoped his hunch was correct. He also hoped she hadn't just started wandering down the street. He imagined Maria trying to cross Las Vegas Boulevard during the part of the day when traffic from the airport was at its busiest. She hadn't been around this many people and this much noise in months and the idea of her being frightened or falling down made him sick.

He heard the shuttle bus driver call after him.

"Hey, I only picked up one passenger from that corner today," he said. "I remember now. Some foreign lady. I remember because she didn't have a purse with her. Seemed strange, a lady her age not carrying a purse. They all carry purses, you know. She started talking to me in some other language."

Savic raised his hand and thanked the driver and then walked as fast as he could into the hotel lobby.

He dodged a cocktail waitress dressed in a white seventeenth century wig who was flirting with a gondolier in a striped red shirt and a straw hat. He shouldered his way up the escalator through a crowd of Japanese conventioneers, half of whom were using this an opportunity to pose for group selfies as they emerged into the grandly decorated lobby of the Venetian Hotel.

He hailed a uniformed security officer who was standing in the lobby with a walkie talkie pressed to his mouth. The man nodded to Savic, who held up the badge fastened to the lanyard around his neck.

The officer squinted at the gold sergeant's shield. "You with the sheriff? We already got two calls."

"Metro," Savic said. "I'd like to see your security camera footage from the last half hour."

He followed the officer to a basement elevator that opened directly into a room filled with rows of wall-mounted screens.

Savic watched her walking with her arms folded past the concierge desk, unsteadily at first and then faster as she turned into a hallway and was momentarily out of sight. On the next screen Savic watched Maria stop and gaze up at the decorated ceiling for a moment before she shuffled off again and vanished.

"That was eight minutes ago," the security officer said, pointing to the time stamp on the paused screen. "I'll call two other people in that zone and tell them to watch for her."

Savic was already headed out of the room by the time the man clicked off his walkie and was turning to say that Maria had just been spotted entering the casino foyer. The guard sat at the hotel's security console and toggled one of the cameras in time to watch a live feed showing Maria staring up at the casino's enormous chandelier.

He keeps watching the screen.

From there…she wanders away and walks up to a row of slot machines and sits at one that's decorated with blinking and animated images of Elvis Presley. A well-dressed man sits on the stool next to her and starts talking. She smiles and nods, as if he'd just asked her a question. The man, wearing a jacket and powder blue shirt, puts a token in Maria's machine and seems to urge her to pull down on the handle. She does, and the wildly flashing Elvis images suddenly explode into a huge digital spinning roulette wheel and Maria has apparently won something. The winnings window blinks brightly and displays a three-digit number.

She smiles shyly, and then they talk again. The man looks down at his phone and taps it a few times, turns around as if he's expecting to see someone, and then stands and bows his head slightly as if saying goodbye. He puts another token into the machine and walks away, turning to smile and wave. Maria lifts her hand and does the same.

A moment later Savic walks into the camera's field of vision and wraps his arms around Maria's shoulder and kisses her several times as she points up at the slot machine and begins to laugh.

On camera, Savic turns and looks in the direction where Maria claims a kind stranger has walked.

"What do you mean, honey?" he said. "Did he tell you what his name was? Maybe he was from the hotel, right? He probably worked for the hotel."

"Spoleto Italiano," she said.

"He talked Italian?"

She nodded. "Not very good. He was nice, though. He said I should sit and wait and not go anywhere until someone came to take me home. I said I was lost and he said no, I wasn't lost anymore."

She showed Savic the receipt that had printed from the Elvis Presley slot machine.

"Five hundred bucks. You won five hundred bucks?"

"I told the nice man thank you and he just walked away," Maria said. "He said you were coming. How did he know you were coming, Frank?"

It was the first time she had said his name in months.

The security officer from the camera surveillance room arrived on a golf cart and drove them both outside through the shipping and receiving dock, where Monaghan was waiting with his car.

Outside, Maria smiled up at the hotel's false facade of the Doge's Palace, the San Marco campanile and the Rialto Bridge, where a row of tour buses were lined up waiting for their next load of passengers.

"Bella," she said, pointing at the high campanile with its square clock tower.

Monaghan walked up with two paramedics carrying their emergency kit bags. "Let these boys check her out, Frank," he said. "They were in the building on another call that I heard on my radio. I asked them to come by."

Savic turned to his wife. "You sure you're okay, honey?"

"He showed me how to play the machine," she said. "He was a nice man. I said thank you, I did."

Monaghan took a phone call while Savic watched as one of the paramedics put a blood pressure cuff around Maria's arm.

"That was the lab," Monaghan said. "They're sending over the case report from those Alexandria murders. Miriam said she managed to shake the file loose from the feds. She told them the information we were after was related to Jardine and not our Doctor Colt and the FBI bought that story with some help from the DA. After I get you both home I'll go check it out."

When Maria was settled in the back seat of the police cruiser Monaghan asked Savic to step away from the vehicle.

"Frank, the office said the Department of Corrections called. Our friend Felicia Mendez?" he said quietly.

"She's still leaving messages for me?" Colt said.

"I don't believe they have phones where she's at now," Monaghan said. "She tried to mule dope into the prison. I'm not sure how she got her name on the visitor list or why she was even there, but I'd bet the lobos had something to do with that."

"She didn't do drugs," Savic said.

"She had twenty rocks inside of her in a balloon. Her heart stopped on the way to the hospital."

Nobody spoke as they drove back to the house, but when Monaghan saw that Maria was asleep in the back seat he turned the dashboard screen monitor toward Savic and told him to hit the return key and scroll down to that morning's condensed media alert report.

Savic read the newspaper headline aloud:

GOVERNOR ON HOT SEAT FOR
CHAIN GANG USE AT PRISON

"You didn't hear about Silverheel?" Monaghan said.

"Sure, the rumors," Savic said. "But I didn't think any of it would stick."

"They put the brakes on everything. Might be a few heads rolling over at the DOC," Monaghan said. "Especially the warden's staff. Seems like a few dollars ended up in the wrong pockets."

"Not good in an election year," Savic said, doing his best to use the computer's touch pad to scroll through the article.

"Says here that somebody sent a video to the TV station," Savic said. He turned to check on Maria, who was leaning against the passenger window, fast asleep.

"They keep a pretty close eye on that air space over the prison," Monaghan said. "I'm surprised somebody got close enough to film it."

"There's always a way," Savic said.

− 40 −

After they treated Jardine's infected sinus, cleaned his festering cheek wound and sutured his torn lip for the fourth time since Felicia Mendez cut him with her kitchen knife, the chained prisoner was taken under heavy security through the back door of the Four Palms Community Medical Center.

Police Chief Harry Nesmith stood watching from his parked cruiser across the street, where one of his officers stood guard with a rifle and redirected what little traffic there was around the town park. He watched the two privately contracted and armed transport employees lead Jardine to the waiting unmarked van and wondered why they didn't also have an escort cruiser following the vehicle for its trip back to the prison. Not his problem, he decided.

Nesmith drove behind the Department of Corrections van until it reached the town limits and then immediately headed back to his office, relieved that a man like William Parker Jardine was no longer in Four Palms. Jardine's all-day stay had made Nesmith nervous and he was relieved when the two-hour dental procedure and outpatient surgery were finally completed.

Before the van turned onto the highway for the trip to Silverheel, one of the detention officers decided he needed to visit the row of portable toilets that sat in the rest stop that was being used as a construction staging area for the new state highway expansion project. The lot was crowded with parked trucks, bull dozers and wheeled crew shacks, next to which sat another van that was identical to the unmarked state prison transport vehicle. A paving gang was noisily pouring asphalt nearby.

While the officer took care of business, his partner remained behind the wheel in the van to watch over Jardine, who sat chained to a bench in the back of the vehicle, still groggy from his surgery and snoring loudly through the thick gauze bandage wrapped around his face.

When the first officer unlatched and opened the wobbly plastic porta' potty door, an arm quickly reached out from the dark and stabbed him in the shoulder with a syringe. Jasper Colt, grasping the struggling man in a bear hug, closed the door and held the officer until he went slack and slumped down onto the toilet seat. Colt tied up the unconscious man and removed his pistol from its belt holster and quickly stepped back outside. He walked to the parked Department of Corrections van.

The van driver, who was staring at his cell phone, did not look up when he heard the passenger door open. He did not look up when Colt took his seat and dropped the heavy black physician's bag on the floor, or did he notice something was wrong until he felt the pistol barrel press firmly against the side of his head.

"What's your salary?" Colt said.

The driver sat motionless: "What?"

"How much do you make in a year? I'm asking this because I want you to think about what's important, your life or your paycheck. Now, listen. This is very simple," Colt said. "You do exactly what I say and you might be home for dinner with your family tonight. Toss that phone out the window and put both hands on the wheel."

The man flicked the phone past his shoulder and quickly nodded. Colt reached and pulled the officer's pistol from his shoulder holster.

"Now drive," Colt said, looking down at the two-way UHF Motorola radio fastened beneath the dashboard. He kicked the plugged handset from the device with his foot and pulled the power cord from the dash.

The driver kept staring ahead: "Where?"

"The prison, of course," Colt said.

"What is this? Where's Jack?"

"He's safe. He'll wake up later this evening. None of this concerns you right now. Where are the other cuffs?"

The man shook his head. "I...don't have..."

"Tell me where you keep your extra cuffs and the stun gun and the pepper spray."

The man nodded toward the canvas kit bag hanging from the steel mesh cubby window that blocked off the inmate seating area, where Jardine still sat sleeping on the bench with his mouth open and head tipped back.

"You know this has GPS on it," the driver said, looking down at the radio. "They track us. They know where we are all the time."

"You mean the cheap transceiver under your rear bumper?" Colt said. "I put it in your friend's shirt pocket back there in the toilet. They'll just think you were delayed in Four Palms for a while."

"What did you do with Jack?"

"He's taking a nap," Colt said.

"You left him in the toilet?"

"Don't worry," Colt said. "I tied him up nice so he wouldn't fall in. My beef isn't with you two fellas. Keep driving."

When they reached the Goodspring trailer park Colt pointed down a heavily rutted supply road he'd seen from the air during the helicopter flight. Up ahead he saw the broken rail car tracks leading to the mine's cave-like opening. There was yellow barrier tape strung across the flimsily gated entrance, where a sign proclaimed "BLM Restricted Area Do Not Enter."

"They might have a crew here today. I don't know what this is, but somebody is bound to see you," the driver said. "You can't get away with this."

"We both know they shut this thing down yesterday," Colt said. "The construction project. It was in the papers. Turn here and back the van up close to the entrance."

"There's nothing here," the driver said. "Where do you expect to go? "

"Do what I say," Colt said and pointed the pistol.

He found the handcuffs in the bag hanging behind the seat and ordered the driver to turn and cross his arms behind his back. He pushed open the passenger door with his foot and pointed with the pistol.

"Get out and keep looking at me."

The jagged opening to the mine had been scooped from bare rock and the small ore car sat parked on the narrow rail tracks.

He made the officer walk backwards into the mine and sat him down on a pile of broken beams stacked like cordwood next to heaps of rusted metal trash and empty ordnance crates. It was much colder inside the cave and the man began to shiver as he looked to where the sloping tunnel stopped at an open pit, above which hung a block and tackle with rope tied to the square box that had once delivered men to their jobs in the mine shaft several hundred feet below.

Colt held the pistol to the officer's head and reached and pulled away the ring of keys and another pair of handcuffs that were clipped to his utility belt. He pointed to the flashlight in the officer's pocket.

"I'll let you keep that in case they don't find you before tonight. I'll be on my way after I finish up here. Apologies for any discomfort."

Colt kept the pistol pointed as he walked back to the van and returned with his doctor's bag and a length of rope, which he looped through the cuffs on the officer's wrists and beneath his arms from behind. He tossed the rope over one of the low ceiling support beams and pulled everything tight so the officer had to sit stooped with his back against the stone wall of the mine.

"If you try to get up and pull on that rope the knot only gets tighter," Colt said. "I suggest you sit."

He walked ahead and studied the thick hemp cord that hung from the heavy wooden block and tackle above the dark mine shaft. The rope was stiff and dry and kinked in places but strong enough to support the open wooden box designed to hold four nineteenth century gold miners and their heavy gear. He kicked the box until it swung and came to rest on the ground next to the open pit.

When he opened the side door to the van Jardine was sleeping, his feet spread and leaning back against the wall with his chained hands folded in his lap. Another shackle on his legs was attached to a metal post on the floor, and that was what Colt unlocked first with the keys he'd taken from the driver.

He opened his physician's bag. The first injection ensured that Jardine would enjoy a longer nap. If he did manage to wake up, Colt had the Taser hanging on his belt.

He unlocked Jardine's wrist cuff from where it was secured by a chain to a ring on the bench and then pushed him down and began cutting off the prisoner's jumpsuit and his underwear. He took off the size 16 shoes. He felt Jardine's thickly muscled naked back with the tip of one finger until he located the first of the five lower vertebrae and then reached for the loaded lumbar syringe.

While he was injecting Jardine he looked at those enormous hands resting in the killer's lap, the hands and the tattoo his daughter Tasha had seen that night at the house. The crooked and hastily inked numerals now seemed insignificant and smaller than he had envisioned, faded in spots and smudged by the untalented artist who had made them.

He looked at his wristwatch. He had fifteen minutes. Colt unscrewed the little amulet that hung from his neck and shook the ashes onto his fingertip and then took his thumb and pressed it to Jardine's forehead.

"This is from them," he said and pulled away the bandages from Jardine's face.

It took all of Colt's considerable strength to pull Jardine from the van, whose sliding weight crashed loudly into the loose dust next to the vehicle. With the killer flat on his back he dragged him by the feet past the silent and horrified corrections officer, who squirmed away when Jardine's six-foot-seven naked bulk slid past him in the dirt.

When Colt reached the edge of the mine shaft he untied the rope from the box and fed it through Jardine's ankle chain. He stepped close to the deep hole, kicked out his foot and waited a few long seconds to hear the echo of rocks striking water far below in the shaft.

He looped the rope through the tackle block and winched Jardine slowly into the wooden box, which he attached again by its four heavy metal cleats. He took more rope and tied Jardine's cuffed hands to the pulley cord.

From his bag Colt took surgical suture tape and completely covered one of Jardine's ears. The one that always itched.

He again turned the winch with the geared stop latch that was fastened to the stone wall until he could kick the box away so it hung suspended beneath the swinging block and tackle. When the ropes tightened they lifted Jardine slightly so that he lay sprawled in the box with his arms stretched over his head and his legs spread apart against the ankle shackles.

He held the syringe in his teeth as he took the pheromonal fluid from his bag and returned the glass vial carefully to his shirt pocket so it would not cool too quickly.

The spiders moved and tumbled like clumps of feathery wool inside the plastic container, and when he unscrewed the jar there were so many of them they gave off an audible hissing sound as they began to rush toward the opening. He closed the lid and lifted the jar and saw one spider clinging to the underside of the lid, the delicate mark on its rump in the shape of a tiny violin.

He looked at his watch and once more injected Jardine's shoulder. He took the vial and began dripping the pheromone on the killer's arm, then each leg, then along the rope that led to his feet so the insects could have a trail to follow. He moistened the tip of his finger with the fluid and wiped Jardine's face and lips and eyelids. He put pheromone on the killer's single, uncovered ear and smeared the sticky fluid across his shaved head.

He took Jardine's blood pressure and listened to his heart and with his two fingers touched the killer's windpipe and felt the throbbing carotid artery. He did not want Jardine to die, although Colt knew he might soon wish for it.

He tipped the jar against the edge of the box and watched the agitated insects swarm frantically from the container, tumbling over each other and falling in dark boiling clots as they charged toward where the overpowering lure of the pheromone now teased them toward a mate. They skittered like orderly soldiers along the rope, hopping excitedly on their twiggy, filament legs and their speed increased into a frenzy once they touched the warmth of Jardine's bare feet, where they began to race up his naked legs.

William Parker Jardine was about to get fucked by 3,000 spiders.

When he woke and looked down at his immobile and anesthetized limbs he began to scream. He tugged wildly with his chained hands and watched as the spiders disappeared into the thick hair on his chest. The more he moved the more the spiders moved. He could feel the slight pinprick of their tiny bites on his arms and face and when they began to crawl into his ears he furiously shook his head and howled as he looked pleadingly at Jasper Colt, who only turned and walked away.

Colt brought the pepper spray from the van and tossed the can at the corrections officer.

"You might need this if the coyotes come around tonight," he said. "I'll make sure your boss knows where you are."

He looked back at Jardine, who was shrieking, his voice rising into an operatic howl as his tied feet thrashed against the sides of the box.

"Enjoy the show," Colt said.

When he got into the van he saw the police vehicles blocking the single-lane gravel road ahead, their blue and red lights flashing.

– 41 –

Assistant Warden Pat Olson decided to wear his departmental uniform today, the gray jacket with the black piping, although he knew that ass kissing and adherence to any dress code would not help his cause today.

The formal hearing room at the State of Nevada legislative liaison office on Saguro Avenue looked prefab, as if it had been assembled and installed from a FEMA disaster response kit.

Olson's union-appointed lawyer, a man in a baggy beige suit whose services came free of charge, smiled calmly at his client from where he sat chatting with a Las Vegas police officer whom Olson recognized. The detective nodded at the attorney and went back to his seat.

Someone seated in a high-backed chair at the long dais at the front of the room directed Olson to a table positioned directly in front of the empty public gallery. The lawyer joined Olson and together they waited for the proceedings to begin.

There were five members on the Department of Corrections Standards Review Commission and as they entered the room a security officer directed a pool of reporters to another row of chairs behind a velour rope strung between brass stanchions like an aisle divider at a movie theater.

The special session to investigate corruption charges at the Nevada Correctional Facility at Silverheel was officially called to order with the thump of a wooden gavel.

Pat Olson was prepared to watch his long career go down the toilet only 30 days before he would be fully vested for his retirement pension.

One of the commission members made a request to correct yesterday's hearing minutes before the chairman, a former Nevada state senator named Gottlieb, cleared his throat and adjusted his microphone.

"Please state your name and position," Gottlieb said. He shuffled a few papers. They always shuffled papers, Olson thought. It made them appear in control. He did the same thing when he interviewed inmates at a parole hearing.

"Patrick Olson. I'm a Corrections Officer and the Assistant Warden at the Silverheel prison facility."

"You people don't like to be called a guard do you, Warden Olson, even though that's really your job? To guard people."

"No sir," Olson said. "We prefer Corrections Officer. I think most of us would say that, yes."

Gottlieb peered over his reading lasses. He fiddled with his fountain pen and conferred briefly with one of the other commission members, one hand covering his microphone. He nodded.

"Mr. Olson?" Gottlieb looked over Olson's head, actually addressing the media people in the room. He shuffled his papers.

"We've heard extensive testimony this week about the operational procedures at your facility and we would like to ask you specifically about the incident with the inmate...William Jardine and the matter of the two injured transport vehicle drivers."

"Mister Jardine was a prisoner in secure transit," Olson said calmly. "If that's what you're asking."

Gottlieb's tone told Olson that his chances were between slim and skimpy that he would leave the room today still employed. They wanted to blame the Jardine embarrassment on somebody and he was the most convenient target. He was certain that the commissioner was asking questions as a warm-up to a political speech.

"Now, in your own words," Gottlieb began. "Please tell us the chronology of events last week, beginning with the inmate's visit to the medical treatment center in Four Palms."

Olson conferred with his lawyer, who took out a sheet of typed paper and handed it to his client.

"This is not a court proceeding, warden Olson," Gottlieb said. "We would prefer to have you use your own words. There is no jury here. I don't want to listen to a prepared statement."

Olson shrugged and his lawyer nodded.

"Well, according to the Las Vegas Police Department, someone with a connection to Mr. Jardine may have been responsible for overcoming our two transport vehicle drivers during the return trip from Four Palms to the facility. You probably have more details about it than I do. Both officers were found later that evening and treated but the perpetrator escaped."

"And Mr. Jardine?" Gottlieb said.

"Inmate Jardine was found in one of the mine shafts, sir. At the old ghost town."

"And you said whoever this person was who, for the lack of a better word – kidnapped Mr. Jardine...he, in fact, escaped?"

"It was getting dark and someone reported seeing lights at the mine and a team was sent to investigate," Olson said. "We spotted the transport van and gave chase for as long as we could."

"For as long as you could?"

"Those vehicles are four-wheel," Olson said. "The company we contract with uses four-wheel drive vans exclusively, which was a determining factor in hiring them. Our patrol units are two-wheel. We tried to chase, but that old dirt road is pretty rough, sir. One of our vehicles got stuck. We couldn't keep up."

"Mr. Olson, didn't you call ahead and alert other law enforcement? There's only one way out of that place, I'm told, and it would have been easy to contact the state troopers and have them handle it."

"We did try," Olson said. "Our telephone service is in the process of being converted to a digital protocol. The landlines had been temporarily disabled that day and we were relying entirely on communication with cell towers between here and Las Vegas. The computer people tell me those particular towers were also out of commission for a number of hours that day. The cell towers were dead, sir. For about three hours. Nobody knows why."

"How convenient," Gottlieb said. "And you don't have some sort of radio two-way system? A dispatch system, perhaps?"

"That's also being integrated with the 911 network, sir. It was down. The radio in the van itself was not responding, nor were our vehicle radios working properly"

"Seems unusual, doesn't it, Mr. Olson, for all those communication methods to be down at the same time?"

"I suppose," Olson aid.

"What condition was Mr. Jardine in when you found him?" Gottlieb said. He looked down at the photos that were being handed to each of the panel members.

"He was alive."

"Explain exactly what you saw."

Olson's lawyer handed him a notepad.

"Inmate Jardine was secured with a rope in a box hanging from a pulley of some sort. One of the old winches they used to lower the miners into where they did their digging."

Olson cleared his throat and looked at the ceiling. He felt woozy, thirsty. He'd already explained this countless times. The deputy department director had interviewed him personally.

"Mister Jardine was covered with insects, sir," Olson said. "Spiders, I'm told. I couldn't see his face. I got about five feet from him and then I saw he was hanging over a deep hole and so we couldn't get closer. The winch that controls the pulley was disabled. He was screaming. I suppose those bugs were biting him. I never saw so many spiders in one spot. Then I got called away."

"By whom?"

"They were outside yelling that they'd spotted the van, so I got into one of the patrol cars and that's when we chased him for as long as we could. Since our radios didn't work, we had to drive all the way back to the facility in order to dispatch our ambulance. It took some time to remove the inmate from the box. Had to use a fumigant. It wasn't healthy for Mr. Jardine, but that's all anybody could think of doing."

Gottlieb adjusted his microphone and turned a dial to crank up the volume. He cleared his throat and sat up stiffly in his chair.

Here it comes, thought Olson. This is where I get screwed.

"Isn't it true, warden Olson, that you were cooperating in the kidnapping of the inmate, William Parker Jardine?"

"That's absolutely not true."

"Isn't it true that the individual who assaulted Mr. Jardine paid you money to help in the kidnapping? Our investigation and that of the Federal Bureau of Prisons indicates that there have been irregularities with the contracting procedure at Silverheel and that you were intimately involved in the letting of construction bids?"

"No, sir. That's also not true," Olson said.

Gottlieb held up a sheet of paper. "Isn't it true, warden Olson, that there is an organized crime element at the prison that was actively seeking to harm Mr. Jardine and that you assisted with that? This document shows the recent deposit of a considerable sum of money into a small, out of state bank account registered to your name."

Olson said nothing and looked at his attorney.

"I've already told your people that I don't know anything about that bank account. Somebody is trying to play games here."

"Let me be more specific, Warden Olson," Gottlieb said, his face flushed. "Did you directly assist in the kidnapping and torture of Mr. Jardine in return for bribes furnished by the notorious organized crime element known as the Lobo gang at Silverheel prison?"

Savic woke up counting money he didn't have.

It was dark and Maria lay breathing next to him in bed, her leg tangled in the sheets in a pleasantly familiar way, the house air conditioning humming faintly. He got up and took the file from the kitchen counter, a thick numbered envelope stamped Metro Archive, and decided to see if reading about inconsolable mayhem and murder might help him go back to sleep.

He had tried these past days to forget Dr. Jasper Colt and Jardine so he could concentrate on his own looming mess, but like his finances, these things refused to leave his head.

Miriam Holter in IT, likely as a gesture of analog politeness and knowing Savic would probably ignore anything he was e-mailed, had snipped the newspaper article from the Las Vegas Sun and paperclipped it to the front of the envelope.

SUSPECT WHO STALKED MURDERERS
AT LARGE FOLLOWING PRISON KIDNAPPING

A man who police say is already a suspect in three homicides also tried to kill convicted serial murderer and prison inmate William Parker Jardine after he was kidnapped this week during a routine visit to the Four Palms Community Medical Center.

The incident took place following the announcement by the Nevada Department of Corrections that it was investigating contract irregularities at the territorial State Prison at Silverheel. The historic correctional facility, once slated for demolition and now undergoing a controversial expansion and renovation, is also the subject of a federal probe alleging fraud and corruption that may involve members of the Governor's staff.

Police have not released information about Jardine's medical condition, but report that two state prison correctional officers who were injured during the apparent vehicle hijacking have been hospitalized and remain in good condition.

Sources say Jardine, sentenced earlier this month to life without parole, is recovering and undergoing treatment for his injuries at a state mental hospital in Carson City. Police confirm that a nationwide search is underway for Jardine's unidentified kidnapper, who is considered armed and dangerous.

Savic spread the 8x10 lab photos from the Hiawatha Lane investigation in Alexandria, Virginia on the table. One poorly lit closeup shot, blurred by the camera flash halo, showed one of the victim's hand prints smeared across the bedroom wall. Had Colt seen the numbers his child had drawn on the chalkboard?

Another photo and its accompanying coroner's diagram showed the obvious bruise where the child's necklace had been torn away. Stapled to that was a photocopy of the inventory of items reported as missing from the residence, along with a short handwritten statement by Colt identifying the missing jewelry as something his daughter had received on her birthday: a tiny pair of angel charms, cherubs with their hands raised in prayer, similar to the larger versions Savic had seen at the Venetian Hotel art gallery exhibit.

Smaller Polaroids showed Tasha Colt's crayon stick drawing of a large man standing with his feet spread apart, the face rendered with large, exaggerated cartoon eyes. There was also a lab report, requested by Colt himself, that indicated the scraped samples of the crayon used to draw on the chalkboard contained traces of the girl's blood, something that had gone undetected by the crime scene investigators.

Colt certainly was aware of every detail of the report. He had to know about the muddy size 16 shoe print left near the downstairs doorway. According to a statement only released that week by the FBI, he had told police that his daughter never liked to draw pictures of monsters or ogres or anything scary. She liked watercolor unicorns and princesses and castles and dancing ballerinas. The picture of the big and scary man sketched that evening was out of the ordinary.

Miriam Holter had also included something else in the file: the FBI's brief transcript of Colt's most recent travels, partially redacted notes that showed the doctor's four short trips to Italy, none of which had been surveilled in time to confirm his actual whereabouts. The notes seemed like a bureaucratic afterthought, something done in haste, much of it obliterated with black stripes to show that the government might not want to divulge everything there was to know about their former employee.

Savic stepped outside with his phone, where the dawn sky had begun to lighten; the last few moments of relative coolness before the daily Vegas heat arrived.

Paul Monaghan wasn't happy when he got Savic's phone call.

"Frank." Monaghan said in a raspy whisper. "It's five o'clock."

" I know this might be a long shot, Paul," Savic said. "But I got a hunch."

"Can't you get your hunches at noon?" Monaghan said. "What's up?"

"Listen, I think our guy isn't in the country anymore."

"The doctor? Why are you still worrying about this?" Monaghan said. "The DA turned over everything to the feds. This mess with the Governor's office and the prison, now it's all Uncle Sam's problem. I would think you'd be happy about this, Frank. You wanted to retire, remember? As far as they're concerned, Colt is a federal fugitive because the crime took place on BLM land and the prison bribery investigation technically puts it in the hands of the U.S. Justice Department. The man was also a former FBI employee. If you ask me, good riddance. Let the spooks have him."

"I couldn't sleep," Savic said.

"It seems that way."

"I think he's in Europe," Savic said. "The thing with the necklace and the carvings and the angels. Even him staying at the Venetian here in town. It has to tie together, I just don't know how."

"Frank, you're retired in two weeks. If you want to tell all this to the Bureau, then go ahead. I have a feeling they'll just nod and tell you to have a nice day."

"I wanted to get it off my chest," Savic said.

"And now I know," Monaghan said and yawned. "How about a retirement lunch this week over at the beer place?"

"That would be nice."

"I'll bring your gold watch."

"Don't you dare," Savic said and hung up.

The administrative office at the nursing home usually opened early, so he gathered the loose case papers from the kitchen and wrote a thank you memo to Miriam on his old Royal manual typewriter, figuring she'd appreciate the irony of the reply not coming through an e-mail. He made coffee and got a cup of tea ready to be warmed up for Maria. He thawed frozen waffles and set them aside for when she woke up. He walked out front to the driveway and pulled away the tarp that covered the RV. A potential buyer was coming by for a look in a few hours, so he wiped off the windshield and the side windows and cleaned things up inside.

He went into the back yard with his phone and decided it was time to beg for mercy from Mrs. Gardener. He also had some explaining to do about why he'd decided to liberate Maria from the Wind River Memory Care Center.

His call was answered on the second ring and when Savic identified himself there was a long and pronounced silence, during which he could hear the faint gurgle of the tropical fish tank that sat against the wall behind Mrs. Gardener's desk.

"Mr. Savic," she said icily. "I believe nurse Fahey has been trying to reach you regarding..."

"Yes, of course," Savic said. "I'm sure she has. But that's not why I'm calling. I wanted to talk to you about my payment this month. I'm afraid I have to be late again. I expect to have some cash very soon, but I didn't want you to think I was avoiding the issue."

He heard Mrs. Gardener typing something on her computer and her voice suddenly turned chirpy as if she was now talking to her very best friend.

"Oh, but Mr. Savic," she said. "It appears that your account is up to date. Everything seems to be in order. Thank you for your payment."

"Excuse me?"

"The balance, I'm looking at the screen now. Paid in full. Yes, a direct bank wire transfer. Perhaps from one of your other accounts? You usually pay with a debit card from a local account, but this was definitely a transfer."

"Now I'm confused," Savic said. "I never transferred anything. I don't even know how to transfer something."

"Oh, yes. I have it here, Mr. Savic. We appreciate your settling this matter so promptly. I know you had difficulties and I'm glad we were able to resolve everything. We're disappointed that you decided to remove Mrs. Savic, of course. But that was your choice."

"What accounts?" Savic said. "I have one checking account and it's empty except for the hundred bucks to keep it active. I didn't make a payment. In fact, I'm two weeks late."

Savic listened while Mrs. Gardener typed.

"Sixty-six thousand... four hundred and seventy-five dollars. Yes, it was a transfer. A foreign bank. I can confirm the account number if you like. I can e-mail you a note and receipt today, but you don't seem to answer your e-mails. Shall I send it regular mail? I'm looking at the transaction on the screen. Yesterday at three-seventeen in the afternoon. Is there anything else? How is Mrs. Savic these days?"

"Very well, thank you," Savic gulped his coffee. "Who did you talk to at this foreign bank?"

"It was a direct ACH transfer." She tried to pronounce the German-sounding name of the bank, gave the phone number and thanked Savic profusely for being such a responsible customer.

He made a note: it was something called a SWIFT number and he looked at his watch. It would be the middle of the afternoon in Basel. Swiss banks were buttoned up tight and he doubted a call from an overseas stranger wanting to confirm a large transaction would get him anywhere fast. After a few button stabs during which he had to select from one of six languages, a young woman answered.

"It is not permissible."

"But I have this number here," Savic said.

"Precisely, sir. Not allowed," the woman said. "You understand, of course."

"I can find out, you know. You're a bank and I can find out. I'm a policeman."

The woman chuckled. "You understand that such information is quite privileged. The banking laws here are specific. If you are a policeman, as you say, then you must certainly be aware of this. I suggest you pursue a legal avenue, but we here, myself, I must not give you the information. It's impossible. Not on the telephone. Perhaps I can give you our e-mail with the names of the individuals you should contact?"

"First it's not permissible, and now it's impossible?"

"Yes, to both," the woman said. "Is there anything else I can help you with?"

Frank Savic hung up and finished his coffee and watched the sun begin to rise above the trees that surrounded his little suburban yard.

He then decided going crazy might just feel like this.

The bedroom light came on and he walked quickly into the house, where he found Maria sitting on the bed, smiling.

"What's so funny?" Savic said.

"I had a nice dream."

Savic put his arms around her. She didn't shirk away like she often did at Wind River. Maria relaxed her arms and snuggled slightly against him.

He had asked Human Services to juggle his unused vacation time so he could spend his remaining active duty days at home, where he had brought Maria after her short stay with her sister, who would still be pulling sibling duty at the house to help Savic whenever she could.

The change in Maria's appearance and attitude surprised him. She seemed more alert and had gotten accustomed to his amateur cooking, though he thought this week might be a good time to do a few restaurant experiments to see how she took to being outside in a crowd of people. She still asked why the doctor didn't come by to do his tests, but that had happened less frequently over the past few days. Savic had great hopes, and until he didn't...until he'd exhausted his optimism, this was life from now on.

He decided to call Monaghan later in the day and get his advice about this craziness with the bank transfer that he didn't think existed. Maybe it was just another nutty computer thing that he would never understand.

He made breakfast with the waffles and tea and as they sat by the window two hummingbirds darted past and hovered next to the red feeder, flitting in circles and doing their freeze-frame sipping.

"Bella," Maria said and watched a noisy flock of chickadees arrive in the yard and arrange themselves in a row on a power pole wire like tiny, well-behaved spectators to some anticipated outdoor event.

"They must be thirsty," Savic said and pointed to the hummingbirds.

He stepped away and came back with the thick photo album he'd been looking at the night before and opened it.

"Suzanne dropped this off yesterday when she came to visit," he said. Maria traced the images on one of the larger photos with her finger.

"She thought you might want to look at the family back in the old country. We haven't seen some of these for years."

The picture showed a dozen very Italian-looking Italians posed on crumbling stone steps in front of a house overgrown with vines. It was a garden and the house had orange clay roof tiles. Everyone was all teeth and wide grins, the men dressed in white shirts rolled up at the sleeves, the women in skirts and blouses and formal leather shoes. Something from the 60s, he thought. A bowlegged old woman wearing a babushka stood off to the side dressed in a black smock, stockings rolled halfway down her legs. She looked angry, her scrawny shoulders hunched over a walking cane like a fairytale forest crone. Maria's twice-removed cousin Desideria, dressed in flashy bright red, stood in the center of the portrait, grinning proudly like she was the ring leader of the whole gang. Her hand was raised in a wave and when Savic said her name Maria immediately nodded and smiled as if she'd suddenly discovered something long lost and now found.

Savic pulled another group shot from its plastic album sleeve. Maria's lips moved as he read their names from the scribbles on the back of the photo, reciting them as listed from left to right: Antonia, Giovanni, Pero, Mara. She pointed to her cousin's burly husband, a cigarette dangling from the side of his mouth.

"Georgio," Savic said. "He looks like a tough guy."

"Si," Maria said. She smoothed the photo with her hand and gave it back.

"I guess they're the only family you got, the ones in this book. Them and me and your sister, of course," Savic said. "Maybe we can look at it again later, the three of us."

"Si," Maria said.

She cocked her head and looked up into his eyes.

He kissed her. She smelled fresh and clean, and with his eyes closed he kissed her again and she turned and for the second time in only a few days said it plainly and clearly:

"Oh, Frank."

– 43 –

He lay each day blind and suspended between the rubber straps. The nurses came in pairs and turned him every two hours as if he were a large ham cooking on a rotisserie.

He wore pajama pants tied into knots below the stubs of each knee and his necrotic arm stumps were capped with gauze bandages that were changed twice each day. The stomach tube curled from his nose to a pneumatic metal cylinder on the wall while another opaque hose ran from a taped groin incision to where it emptied into a plastic bag that hung beside a catheter sack suspended from the unusual bed.

"He likes to have you scratch that thing on his ear," the physician's assistant said, handing over a clipboard to the new shift nurse that showed the daily treatment schedule for William Parker Jardine, who now slowly turned his milky blind eyes in the direction of the two women.

"The what?"

"The thing on his ear," the PA said. "It must itch a lot and he'll ask you to scratch it. He likes that."

"Can he hear?"

"He knows when you walk into the room," the PA said as she turned a knob on the wall and listened to Jardine's breathing through a stethoscope "But no, he really can't, unless you shout."

They stood and watched as the tube that came from beneath Jardine's pajama pants convulsed and filled with liquid.

"They transferred him here last month," the PA said. "With the infections, I don't know how he didn't die. The necrosis was terrible."

"Does he talk?"

"Not much. Unless he wants you to scratch that thing on his ear and then he gets chatty. He doesn't make much sense, though. They just took out his tracheal tube."

"So, the tissue damage was everywhere except for the ear?" the nurse said.

"Interesting, isn't it."

Jardine lay on his back, pressed between the rubber straps that crossed his limbless torso, a small shelf at each end to support his head and what was left of his legs.

" Why don't they just take that thing off his ear if it bothers him that much?" the nurse said.

"He's already had eight surgeries. I suppose there were more important things to worry about."

"I hear you," the nurse said and they both tried not to smile.

"Our job is just to keep him comfortable. He'll be here a long time."

"He came like this?"

"First, there was the necrosis on his feet at the other hospital and then things got out of hand," the PA said. "They took his legs and then the arms. I hear they had people from all over come and look at him. It's a very unusual case. They sent students from a medical school."

"He was a murderer, you know," the PA said.

She adjusted one of Jardine's straps and turned a respiratory dial on the wall.

"I think he'll be around for a long time," she said. "In this condition, I mean. His heart and lungs check out just fine. Once they get the infections under control he'll be pretty healthy."

"Too bad for him," the nurse said.

"Yeah, I can't imagine."

They walked out of the room and Jardine watched their blurry shadows move across the ceiling like shapes seen from beneath the water. His ear began to itch and he tried frantically to twist his head to rub it against one of the straps, but he could not.

He always had this thought each day: the little spiders had been thirsty, so they drank his eyes and that was why he could not see. He told the doctor about the spiders and his eyes but nobody believed him.

Another thought: the doctors didn't believe him when he explained that the man who had hung him by the rope had smeared him with something the spiders liked. The doctors said the spiders had killed his skin. He hardly had any real skin left, they said. We don't know how you made it, they said.

They'd crawled into his ears looking for a place to make babies. After a while, hanging there in the dark, they made a web on his face. The web felt sticky. And then they drank his eyes.

The nurse with the big feet came and touched him and shouted: "Here we go -- one, two, three," and she flipped the bed with the crank she pushed with her foot. Jardine felt the straps loosen and the nurse began rubbing him with the stuff that smelled like nothing and it made the burning go away for a while. He tried to ask her to scratch his ear but she wouldn't listen.

"Did you sleep, Billy?" she said. She rubbed Jardine's back with the towel and tightened the straps again.

After she flipped him, Jardine felt a pain in the empty space beyond his knees. Both the empty spaces hurt the same way and at the same time, though he knew nothing was there anymore to hurt. He tried to remember more about his legs and his arms but his brain just gave up.

That's the way it goes, he thought.

He shook his head. He didn't like to sleep because then he would dream about being in the dark in the box with the rope.

"Spiders fuck you and then they eat you," he told the nurse, but she just looked down at him and smiled.

He watched something drip from his mouth onto tile number fifty-three on the floor. Sixth from the left, one up from the bottom of the front leg on the bed frame. He knew all the tiles. They were all white but they were all different.

"You told me about that already," the nurse said. She smelled like Juicy Fruit gum. "But we don't have to use that language, do we Billy?"

"My skin's dead, you know," Jardine said. "Did I tell you about the eggs?"

" Yes, Billy, you did," the nurse said and examined the gauze bandages that covered the ends of what was left of Jardine's arms.

" There's a problem with your arms, Billy. The doctor wants to take a look in the morning. There could be another infection. My goodness, all those antibiotics they gave you and it didn't seem to work."

She turned him onto his back again and pulled down his pajama gown and pulled the tube from his dick and sprayed his dick with the stuff that made it tingly and numb and then wiped it off with the cold wet cotton. He didn't know why the spiders hadn't touched his dick. She slid the tube back in and like always, it burned and he immediately had to pee and when he did the tube swayed back and forth, like a snake dancing, the dark urine climbing and then quickly flowing until he could not longer see where it went in the tube. Sometimes, when he was flipped face down he could watch the pee flow through the tube and curl under the bed into the little plastic lunch bag. He looked forward to watching his pee flow through the tube from his dick. It was a nice game. Sometimes it changed colors. And then he would count the tiles again.

All his tattoos were gone, except the partial numbers that remained on the stump of his arm. The spiders had eaten everything except his dick and the thing on his ear and the skin beneath the number 911. He wondered why they didn't eat the itchy thing on his ear. He didn't remember anymore what the number meant. Maybe it was to keep track of you at the hospital, like a license plate. Maybe they had put the emergency number on his arm in case something bad happened.

In his dream the spiders always had little people faces.

He didn't like the nurse with the big feet. He had to ask her over and over to scratch his ear and she hardly ever did.

Jardine knew the eggs would hatch one day and boil out all at once. Maybe they'd swim up his dick tube and eat the rest of him from the inside, like the little river worms he'd seen on a TV show about the Amazon. Baby spiders doing upstream breast strokes. All the baby spiders with their baby people faces, shaped like M&M candies with legs.

The nurse came back and said, "...one, two, three."

"You just did that," Jardine said.

"That was two hours ago, Billy," she said.

"Did I tell you about the dream I had?"

"Is it about the spiders again, Billy?"

"Yeah."

"You've told me that dream. A thousand times. Now go to sleep."

He dozed, his head sagging through the rubber belts that held him by the chin and forehead. A spider with a little girl's face crawled up his cheek. She had the tiniest mouth and she opened it and closed it as she jittered on her silky legs and disappeared back through the hole in his throat.

Itsy bitsy spider, crawling down the wall...

Billy counted the tiles again, hoping he would not fall asleep because he knew the spider babies would soon be waking up inside of him again.

He remembered the man with the needle and his own legs feeling heavy, unable to move while he lay in the box in the dark. He screamed and begged the man and told him that the spiders would kill him.

"Oh, dear," the man said and took a long, deep breath as he came closer with another needle.

"I would never let that happen. If it were up to me, I'd make you live forever."

– 44 –

Casanova once trolled for women at the Florian Cafe on the Piazza San Marco where pigeons now wheeled above the old brick campanile that stood guard above the Venice lagoon like a watchtower.

Jasper Colt had sat nearly every day in the cafe in the same upholstered booth from which he could study the tourists who gathered in front of the cathedral on the ancient city square.

The sea wind blew sheets of rain across the lagoon, the tide higher than usual the night before, and there were pools of water on the plaza that reflected the lights of the cathedral. School children in white and blue uniforms stood and listened to their teacher explain how they'd smuggled the bones of the city's patron from pagan Alexandria in 829. The teacher pointed to the clock tower and at the gold statue of the archangel Gabriel, the messenger. The children's angel.

Colt, who had walked the same route around the plaza each day, now took a detour along a calle where bare honeysuckle vines trailed like hair in the canal, the strands moving in the ebbing tide above the stone steps of an old palace pier where empty gondolas bobbed in the water.

The white bridge balusters where he crossed were worn smooth where he stopped and watched one of the boats pass by, its single oar groaning, the gondolier's voice muffled as he chatted with his passengers, whose feet made hollow sounds against the bottom of the wooden boat.

Colorless and wet, the city was covered in a cold mist in which buildings hung detached, as if all were about to float away, yet this seemed the happiest of places in the rain. Venice was so green and slippery, Colt thought, and it looked best when wet, like a fresh painting. Even the rotten smell of the water seemed appealing, the ancient city somehow able to conjure beauty from its ruins.

Colt went to the cathedral and walked down the marble steps and stood before the enormous brass door that guarded the vault where the bones of St. Mark lay entombed. He lit three candles for Adriana and his daughters and he said a prayer, though he knew such a thing from an impostor like him might be ignored.

Two muscular stone angels stood guard on either side of the tomb door, their expressions sour, as if warning Colt that his kind was not welcome.

He walked outside across the plaza to where waiting tourists stood huddled at the entrance to the clock tower, their black umbrellas touching like flowertops in the rain. He climbed the long staircase to where a young woman working in the gift shop smiled as he stepped to one of the windows that overlooked the plaza 310-feet below.

From here he could see the entire city as a gray blur, cold drizzle gusting through the window's steel mesh cover and his coat blowing in the wind. In the lagoon far below the canal water was dark beneath the fog and he tried to see the distant penzione on the Calle de Angelo where his three angels now rested safely forever, but he saw nothing.

One of the windows was marked with a construction repair sign and Jasper Colt pushed aside the wooden barrier and climbed onto the ledge, in his dark wet clothes himself now crouched like a gargoyle gazing down from a church, voices shouting loudly from behind as he stood and spread his arms.

He fell forward with a slow avian grace, the long coat billowing and flapping from his back like a single wing as he vanished into the mist below, soundless, as if such a final flight might matter little to the world after all.

As if it had always been forbidden for certain angels to fly.

- THE END -

ABOUT THE AUTHOR

Gojan Nikolich is a former Chicago newspaper reporter, editor and public relations agency executive. He graduated with B.A. and M.A. degrees in English Literature from DePaul University, served as a U.S. Army sergeant with both the 2nd and 4th Infantry divisions and worked as a journalist in Korea and Japan. He lives with his family in Colorado, where he and his wife once owned a weekly newspaper. This is his second novel.

Note from the Author

Word-of-mouth is crucial for any author to succeed. If you enjoyed *Ashes in Venice*, please leave a review online—anywhere you are able. Even if it's just a sentence or two. It would make all the difference and would be very much appreciated.

Thanks!
Gojan Nikolich

We hope you enjoyed reading this title from:

BLACK❀ROSE
writing™

www.blackrosewriting.com

Subscribe to our mailing list – *The Rosevine* – and receive **FREE** books,
daily deals, and stay current with news about upcoming releases
and our hottest authors.
Scan the QR code below to sign up.

Already a subscriber? Please accept a sincere thank you for being a fan of
Black Rose Writing authors.

View other Black Rose Writing titles at
www.blackrosewriting.com/books and use promo code
PRINT to receive a **20% discount** when purchasing.